MASTER MIND

ANDY DANE NYE

ARTAVIA
PUBLISHING

First published in 2024 by Artavia Publishing

1 3 5 7 9 10 8 6 4 2

A CIP catalogue record for this book is available from the British Library.

ISBN 978 1 913351 06 9

Typeset in Crimson Text by Google Fonts

Printed and bound in Great Britain by Clays Ltd, Elcograf S.p.A.

Cover design © Artavia Publishing 2024

Cover background image: The Crab Nebula as observed by the
NASA/ESA Hubble Space Telescope, courtesy of:
NASA, ESA and Allison Loll/Jeff Hester (Arizona State University).
Acknowledgement: Davide De Martin (ESA/Hubble)

Previous books in the trilogy:

Master Piece

Master Plan

Acknowledgements

Apart from thanking the Universe for allowing me my brief glimpse of it, I would like to express heartfelt gratitude to those who assisted me in the writing of this trilogy… even if some of them didn't realise quite how much at the time.

A huge thank you to all six foot, six inches of Major Brian Rogers, MA of The Household Cavalry, for constantly insisting I get *Master Piece* published. His imposing, military physique and no-nonsense stare – along with the fact he'd forsaken his morning perusal of *The Times* in order to read my story whilst still a collection of unwieldy A4 sheets – made me work that little bit harder to ensure it eventually saw the light of day… and that I could finally look him in the eye without twitching.

An equal thank you to Justin Haynes for doing something similar. Although not as tall as Brian – few are – he's packed with just as much enthusiasm and encouragement. They are both perfect examples of how one should never underestimate the positive ripples kind words can generate.

My greatest thanks of all, of course, go to my beautiful-in-all-ways wife, Sarah Jane... for not only putting up with the countless hours it's taken to get what's in my head onto paper and never complaining, but who has been absolutely brilliant in making me look smarter than I really am by spotting those pesky grammatical and other such errors before they gave the game away... and just when I was convinced I'd successfully crossed my Is and dotted the Ts!

And, on this last point, a hand-on-heart thank you to the wonderfully talented Claire Stowe for assisting with her own ruthless dustpan and brush.

My final thanks are reserved for you, the reader. If it were possible, I would have your name printed here. Having taken the time to journey with me this far, you've made every keystroke worthwhile. Without you, these books would be as pointless as a universe devoid of observers. For entrusting me with some of your incredibly precious *ticks* and *tocks* (this will make sense later), I cannot thank you enough.

Andy

Dedicated to the unknown individual who broke his leg, resulting in my father stepping in as a replacement blind date for my mother at the last minute.

Tick... tock... tick... tock...

Destiny is a trick of hindsight.

We cannot know the future.

But it is within our power to determine it.

Reverend Galveston Humbold III struck the wooden lectern separating him from his congregation heavily with a fist, leaving both in no doubt as to the strength of his ire.

The atmosphere was charged... as had been those listening to him. Ministering to sinners didn't come cheap... apparently.

'The Devil has come amongst us!' he bellowed into a spittle-coated microphone, his voice booming around the packed auditorium. 'That foul and loathsome purveyor of darkness has firmly set his stinking, cloven feet upon this earth.' He paused and looked out at the besieged faces staring back at his. 'Except... those feet ain't cloven anymore!' He wasn't sure if they were still stinking, either... but that was beside the point.

Numerous mouths dropped... as hoped.

'That despicable creature has tried to fool us all by making his appearance in human form!' Gripping the much-abused lectern and shaking it violently, he tipped his head back... forcefully drawing in just enough divine strength through offended nostrils to continue. 'So devious and depraved is his sick and twisted mind that he's chosen to do so in a body designed to tempt every living man on this planet,' he warned ominously... before adding as an afterthought, '... along with any liberal-thinking ladies.'

His paying flock registered its outrage via anguished cries for immediate heavenly intervention before eagerly settling down for an explanation... especially about the last bit.

Reverend Humbold leant forward, his voice dropping to a tortured whisper in order to maintain the drama. 'Such is the evil-one's trickery, he has adopted this wicked incarnation in that sweet, innocent ol' country of London... home of the

Virgin Queen Elizabeth the Second of England, Saint Winston Churchill, Benny Hill, and bad teeth.'

There was a collective gasp.

'Oh, yeah,' he nodded dramatically. 'No doubt in the hope its occupants' preoccupation with drinking tea will allow his sick plan to go unheeded. But let me tell ya'll this...' He raised himself defiantly. 'He'll need to get up earlier than an insomnia-riddled rooster with an alarm clock to fool *this* proud disciple of God!' He bullishly pounded his chest... much to the relief of the lectern.

Empathetic shouts of *amen* from sofas across America endorsed the sentiment, as cable channel subscribers atoned for a Sunday spent lazing at home.

'Now... while most of you out there might be wondering why he needed a disguise when he could've easily moved around that green and pleasant land camouflaged against their red double-decker buses, I'm here to inform you this cynical incarnation he's chosen is a disguise *upon* a disguise and purposely designed to *get* him noticed!'

Crinkled brows crinkled further.

'Yes, indeed.' The reverend's eyes widened knowingly. 'For he is engaged in audacious subterfuge... duplicitously declaring himself on the side of the righteous by claiming to be the next saviour of mankind!'

The air was inhaled in disgust.

'And that's when God spoke to me and allowed me to see through Satan's perverted plan.' He shook his head smugly. 'He said to me... Galveston... do ya *really* think I would send a *woman* for such a task?'

The air was exhaled in shock.

'That's right, folks! I'm tellin' ya'll... Beelzebub has brazenly displayed himself for all to see in the guise of a well-endowed floozy whose morals are lower than the front spoiler on my nephew's pimped Ford Mustang.'

Loud cries of *'shame on him,'* and *'are there any pictures?'* permeated the auditorium.

Reverend Humbold nodded aggressively at a section of the hall. 'Hell, yeah, there are pictures,' he sneered, his wildly rocking head violently changing direction. 'Which I have been forced to endure in the service of the Lord.' He telegraphed his pain. 'For they show this wanton Jezebel *before* she displayed her hand... and it ain't just her hands I found myself lookin' at, I can tell ya'll that!'

Fifty percent of the auditorium leant forward.

The reverend bowed his head and rested his indignation on straightened arms, his stubby fingers fiercely gripping the lectern. 'These eyes have been forced to witness the abomination of her flesh,' he strained. 'For God commanded I examine *every* minute detail of it in order that I may know my enemy and prove myself above Lucifer's temptation.' He temporarily released his grip and dabbed the sweat from his brow with a sodden handkerchief. 'And let me tell ya'll... three *days* I examined it!' he winced. 'Three days in which my eyes were burned with Satan's depravity.'

His dedication to the task was met with mutterings of appreciation.

'I finally emerged from my study in a state of exhaustion,' he revealed.

A huge screen behind him broke into life, displaying a web address.

'Now... I do not believe I'm the only one here courageous enough to show his undying service to the Lord in such a selfless manner. You *too* can prove the strength of your faith by visiting our website and submitting yourselves to those vile, pornographic images for just nine dollars, ninety-nine cents an hour plus subscription fee.'

A large nine, ninety-nine flashed up behind him, confirming the fact.

'Such commitment to His cause has never been greater!' he wailed, lifting his eyes to the rafters. 'We are entering apocalyptic times. Global tales of desecration and unnatural happenings have been filling our news channels on a daily basis these past few weeks. Dark forces are amassing. I believe the time prophesied as Armageddon has come upon us and that we must rise up against those seeking to defile the name of the Lord!'

Cries of support bolstered the appeal.

'Satan has come to lead his troops in the form of a harlot. But don't just take *God's* word for it. The evil-one has spelt it out for all to see. It has adopted the name *Xanthia* for its work. And in that name lies incontrovertible proof!'

He turned and pointed accusatorily at the screen now displaying the name in block letters.

'See for yourselves! He's chosen the symbol of our Lord's cross disrespectfully tipped on its side to announce his perverse intentions!'

The X on the screen helpfully rocked backwards and forwards so as to prove his point.

Mouths fell agape.

'And if you take the friendly greeting out of the remaining letters...'

The graphic obliged by removing the H and I.

'...cunningly placed amongst them so as to lull those encountering that name into a false sense of security... and replace it with the far more apposite sign of a snake...'

An S dropped into place.

'...you get "antsa".'

You did indeed.

Those of a higher IQ saw the next bit coming. But for those not acquainted with word puzzles, the letters on the screen began swapping places until a more familiar name announced itself to the stunned congregation.

'SATAN in disguise!' yelled the reverend, slamming the lectern for the umpteenth time with one hand whilst fervently stabbing a finger at the irrefutable evidence with the other.

A number of children, watching through widened eyes, breathed a sigh of relief, having momentarily caught the name SANTA in the whirling graphics.

Adults were less comforted. Pandemonium ensued... thoughts of how many hours at nine, ninety-nine they could get away with temporarily suspended, as husbands put reassuring arms around their spouse's shoulders.

'You are right to be afraid,' sang the reverend above the commotion, stoking it further. 'Whilst this evil temptress has been comprehensively pilloried by her own country's media, her outrageous claims are being perniciously fanned around this planet by that other great force of evil... the internet. You can read about my thoughts on *that* particular subject via my website. But I'm here to tell ya'll now... it's our God-given duty to put a stop to it. The world needs to know the truth about this she-devil... and I intend shouting it for as long as the Lord gives me breath in my body!'

Cries of 'Hallelujah' accompanied his stepping back from the lectern to signal his sermon had reached its end.

He raised his shaking hands to the skies.

'So... while we contemplate the eternal torment unimaginably hideous plagues of hell will inflict upon us and our loved ones if we fail in that mission,' his voice quaked, 'let us join together in our next hymn... *All Things Bright and Beautiful.*'

A prissy-sounding organ teased out the opening melody as the words appeared on the screen behind him, a bright red ball sitting above the first line and preparing to bounce appropriately... though somewhat upstaged by the figure of nine, ninety-nine flashing away inside it.

*   *   *

Of all things taken for granted, the most astonishing is being *able* to take things for granted. Or to be more specific... marvelling at the fact we actually exist to do so in the first place.

Not in the *human race* sense... but in a far more individual *what shall I have on my toast this morning?* kind of way. After all... *Homo Sapiens* are no greater a miracle than the spreading bacteria on a petri dish. If the dinosaurs hadn't found themselves gatecrashed by a passing lump of rock all those years ago, we wouldn't be here to contemplate the fact we very nearly weren't... and they wouldn't be suffering the indignity of having bits of themselves on sale in coastal gift shops. The fact we *are* here as a species is simply down to the laws of gravity and a little bit of good fortune at the expense of somebody else's.

However, the good fortune required for us to be able to process that fact as unique, sentient beings is of a mind-numbingly greater magnitude altogether.

Consider the maths.

Biology decrees we have two parents... and logic, four grandparents. As unpalatable as it might be to think of the aforementioned indulging in anything other than trying to get to sleep at bedtime, your reading this is proof that a little nocturnal activity *did* occur once the light went out. Had mother conformed to the image you'd rather keep of her in your mind – or either of your nanas declined an early night and continued with their knitting – this page... as far as *you're* concerned... might just as well be blank.

Furthermore... those nights in question had to occur on the *exact* days they did – not a single day early or a single day late – for the relevant progeny to be conceived to enable you to read this. And [*brace yourself*]... given grandpa probably ejaculated at least seventy-five million spermatozoon per early night, it was *essential* that a particular one of his determined little wrigglers triumphed over all others. That's like the entire population of the British Isles taking part in a swimming race and there being only one winner. *You.* Three times in a row, as far as both grandpas and dear old dad were concerned.

Now, if *that* doesn't induce wonder and appreciation for actually being here in the first place, delving deeper into the mathematics surely must. For each nana and grandpa had nanas and grandpas of their own... meaning a further twenty-four grandparents of varying greatness that need to be brought into the equation. That's thirty individuals whose lives had to be lived *exactly* as transpired... partners met, dances danced, hearts won, commitments made, yawns yawned... before countless sets of knitting needles were put aside and gold medals won. A different corner turned... one *single* second place on the podium... a *solitary* missed event, out of trillions of interconnected and essential circumstances that would've negated the firing of a starting gun, and things would be like this for you:

But they're not. So, relax and take a breath... though make sure it's a deep one. For those statistics merely apply to the last four generations of your family tree. Double that... and, as the amount of direct ancestors with each subsequent branch you climb does the same, the numbers start to make you dizzy. With five hundred and ten grandparents required to turn up for a crucial bedtime appointment by successfully negotiating the perils, pitfalls and politics of the last two hundred years, that's a scary amount of critical seconds in which fate's pendulum *had* to swing for each one of them *exactly* as it did... not a single *tick* or *tock* out of place.

Tick... tock... tick... tock...

But why stop there?

Travel back a *thousand* years and you can be forgiven for giving up on the mathematics altogether. Proving death is no bad thing when it comes to buying birthday cards... statistically, you have over one *billion* ancestral nanas and grandpas to thank for being here.

Yes... you read that right. 10^9... as in one and nine noughts... or a thousand times one million, if it hasn't quite sunk in.

Impressed?

You should be. Put in perspective, the world's population when the oldest were alive was less than a third of that... a fact worth remembering the next time you insult someone by calling them an inbred.

Tick... tock... tick... tock...

Now... suck up an *extraordinarily* deep lungful of air.

We've only reached the eleventh century... a time when Julius Caesar seemed as distant to William the Conqueror as William the Conqueror seems to us today. And bear in mind that even Julius marvelled at how ancient the pyramids were. Because one thousand years in the life of life itself is but an infinitesimal speck on its staggering *curriculum vitae*... a record conveniently boasting your ever-expanding list of ancestors.

The interbreeding doesn't bear thinking about.

Tick... tock... tick... tock... not *one* single action allowed to fall out of sync with fate's script.

Tick... tock... tick... tock... not a second of history altered... even if for the good.

Tick... tock... tick... tock... each swing successfully avoiding the jeopardy of unrequited love, child mortality, sickness, famine, floods and pestilence... or finding yourself on the wrong end of a sword.

Tick... tock... tick... tock... and *never* a single yawn ignored.

Tick... tock... tick... tock...

You get the point.

Suffice to say, distant cousin... had just *one* of our greatest grandparents missed their footing when crawling out of the primordial slime, the rest, as they say, *wouldn't* be history.

But your wonder shouldn't end there.

While contemplating the chances of there being a *you* at all, perhaps you should take a moment to consider what actually defines the boundaries of that *you*.

One's physical perimeter is rarely open to debate... unless you're a pedantic student of philosophy wearing an extremely thick overcoat. The surface of a fingertip is just one of many points at which you cease to be and something else takes over. Having a body is convenient... a bit like a spacesuit for all those squidgy bits required to operate in an otherwise hostile environment. Life could get rather messy without one.

But you're unquestionably more than the sum of your parts... more than simply ten fingers with some other stuff attached... or twelve, if your ancestors didn't travel much.

What about the most important thing that makes you *you*?

The very fact you're able to contemplate that question gives you the answer.

Your thoughts.

Ever taken a moment to figure out where *their* boundaries start and end?

The truth is... it's impossible to tell.

Give it a try.

See.

But perhaps it's irrelevant, anyway. For, have you ever stopped to consider that the person you fondly like to think of as *you* might not be entirely *you* at all?

Every thought processed... decision arrived at... action taken... is coloured by a lifetime of influences. So at what point are we completely our own mind and not a subliminally indoctrinated, patchworked jumble of other people's?

Now... hold that borrowed thought... because it poses a far more intriguing one.

What if you knew *everything*?

Would this make you infinitely wiser and stronger of mind? Or... given you'd be subjected to every opinion ever conceived... even less able to be yourself?

Either way... you have to admit... it would certainly present a few problems.

*　　*　　*

484

Xanthia slapped the back of Norman's hand. 'I've told you before. Don't bite your nails!'

'If it helps my nerves, why not?' he mumbled through stubbornly bent fingers.

Xanthia paused her gum-chewing and stared at an imaginary point just above her brow. 'Well... apart from the fact it's incredibly unattractive... there's the risk of transferring harmful pathogenic bacteria to your mouth... developing paronychia around the corpus unguis itself... getting finger warts from human papillomavirus... and causing malocclusion of your anterior teeth.'

'You could've stopped at incredibly unattractive,' he winced.

'Oh, believe me, I wish I *could*,' she sighed. 'It's as frustrating my end as it is yours. When you've access to so much knowledge, it's painfully hard to condense everything you know into a simple thought... let alone a single sentence.'

'I know,' he groaned. 'I'm still reeling from your overly detailed discourse this morning on the origins and subsequent route of methane molecules inhaled from another individual's flatulence.'

'Well... you should've kept *yours* under the bed sheet, then,' she glared, resuming her chewing. 'Besides... it's *me* who should be nervous today.'

He nodded heavily. 'You're not wrong there. You certainly can't afford to mess *this* one up. With the way things have been going, I reckon it could be our last chance to convince people to take you seriously. It's finally time to show them what you're *really* made of!'

She smiled. 'I keep telling you... it's more a case of showing them what *they're* made of.'

Norman lowered his offending fingers and forced a smile of his own. Who was he to disagree? Arguing with her about anything had become futile since she'd acquired her extraordinary gift. But her insistence that it shouldn't be used to change people's thinking by creating negative ripples of fear and intimidation had left him not only frustrated but extremely concerned. Two weeks on from the incident at Stonehenge, her positive message of love and understanding had failed to make an impression.

Well… it had… but it wasn't the one they'd been hoping for.

Recuperating from his near-fatal injury, he'd been forced to watch helplessly from the sidelines as she'd set about informing the world she was in possession of powers that could save it from an impending disaster.

Its reaction had been predictable.

He'd witnessed the worst a savage tabloid press could inflict upon a single human being… their response all the more brutal, given she'd once been one of their own.

As far as the rest of the media was concerned, there wasn't even a story worth reporting. Despite Stonehenge providing the perfect platform from which to push her agenda – an eager press scrambling for an explanation as to what had occurred that solstice morning – Xanthia's honest answer merely induced open mouths. But it didn't take long before their corners curled and the vitriol began.

He'd begged her to silence her detractors by giving a potent demonstration of what she was capable of. But she'd insisted that such an action would void the reason for her being given such a gift in the first place. As she pointed out… you couldn't cure an alcoholic by forcing them not to drink. The change had to come from within. Her message, therefore, was simple. The world needed to learn to love itself again. Only then would it lose its addiction to all things destructive.

The trouble was… that message was being drowned out by the sound of laughter. Mercilessly promoted as the butt of a national joke, she'd been forced to retreat to the tiniest of flats, lent courtesy of a friend who *hadn't* deserted her. The tabloids were using her as a circulation *piñata*. The harder they hit, the more they were rewarded.

At least now she'd been offered a chance to hit back.

'You'd better get changed. The car they're sending will be here in fifteen minutes. You can't be late. It's a live broadcast.'

She stared at him blankly.

'Sorry,' he blinked. 'Did I inadvertently say that in Chinese?'

'Don't be facetious,' she scowled. 'Besides... I'd have understood even if you had... in any of over two hundred dialects, as it happens. I was simply wondering what you meant by *changed*.'

'That's a turn-up for the books, *you* asking *me!*' he exclaimed. '*You're* the walking dictionary these days!'

'Yes... and you're being pervicacious. So... would you care to explain?'

He squinted. 'Shall we start with the skirt?'

Wiggling her hips, she smoothed its red, leather sides provocatively. 'What's wrong with it? Are you saying it's inappropriate?'

'Does a bear defecate in the woods?'

She considered the question. 'That depends. *Ursus maritimus* would be mightily inconvenienced if having to... given it's a *polar bear*... and many arboreal species live in *forests*. So, technically... not always.'

'It's inappropriate,' he clarified.

'Then, what do you suggest?'

He wondered how best to couch the answer so as not to add to the torrent of ridicule she'd already endured. 'If you *genuinely* want my opinion, I'd say you should be looking to wear something...' He fished for the right word.

'Showing a little more cleavage?'

'No!' he cried, horrified. 'That's exactly what we *don't* want! I was going to say... that'll change the public's negativity towards you... not *enforce* it.'

'Well... I'm definitely not wearing trousers,' she huffed.

He looked at her exasperatedly. 'You don't have to, Xan. But with everything that's been thrown at you recently, it's crucial we get this right. You need the public to start taking you seriously... and to convince them you're the one who'll lead them to victory in the battle they're about to face.'

She playfully put a finger to her lips. 'Let me think... I'm not sure I've got a sword and scabbard in my wardrobe.'

481

'You can joke,' he glowered. 'But, apart from a pathetically small following on the internet... much of it *highly* dubious... you've not exactly got people camped outside this door falling over themselves to support you.'

She glanced across at the curtained window. 'That's not strictly accurate. It's not *all* baying press out there, you know.'

'True,' he nodded. 'But the exception you're thinking of hardly counts. He's only falling over himself because he's intoxicated... and I'm not sure he's so much camped as homeless.'

She brushed off the remark with a look of resignation. 'Look, Normy... we've gone over this a thousand times. My goal is to change mindsets. So, first, I have to gain people's trust. They need to believe I'm being honest with them... not suddenly pretending to be something I'm not. They've long carried an image of what I'm like in their heads... so it's a bit late for me to start putting clothes *on*. I intend to win that trust purely by what I say.'

Norman took a moment to reflect on the image she was referring to. 'I'm not sure words will be enough,' he said diplomatically.

She shook her head. 'No wonder you insisted on putting wings on Gabriel.'

'There you go!' he exclaimed, pointing at her enthusiastically. 'You've just proved my argument. I saw what I *expected* to see.'

'No one *expects* to see an archangel, Norman,' she scoffed.

'Case proven again. I certainly *didn't*. But envisaging him the way I did, I was prepared to listen to what he had to say.'

She narrowed her eyes.

'Most of the time,' he conceded. 'That's why it's important we carefully consider your look.'

Xanthia bowed her head. 'Okay, then... let's do that.' She exhaled wearily. 'So... for whom do you suggest I tailor my appearance... a Christian audience or a Muslim one?' She didn't wait for an answer. 'Or maybe I should be aiming to get the Jewish nod of approval. At least they're *expecting* someone to turn up and help them out of this mess.' She looked up and put a finger to her cheek theatrically. 'Hang on a second, though... where would *that* then leave the millions of Hindus I need to convince... and Sikhs... and Buddhists? And we'd better not complicate it further by considering the sensibilities of all those Taoists, Shintoists and Jains out there... or, in fact, the multitude of *other* religious groups who've set their minds on how they'll be expecting me to look.' She stared directly at him. 'You see, Norman... there's a whole spectrum of belief systems out there... from Atheists to Zoroastrians... all with their own individual expectations of what I should be wearing.'

'I think it's safe to say none of those expectations will include stilettos, though,' he ventured.

She blew a bubble with her gum until it burst. 'So what are you saying? You want me to pander to a general stereotype in order to manipulate the audience?'

'Yes,' he nodded firmly.

She blew another bubble and considered the possibility.

'You just need to give them something really obvious,' he pushed, sensing the tide might be turning his way.

'I know you,' she sighed. 'In your head, you're thinking *floaty*, aren't you?'

Norman scanned the image circling his thought process. '*Could* be.'

'No, Norman... it *couldn't*,' she returned assertively. 'And do you know why?' Her eyes widened sarcastically. 'Because I don't have a single thing in my wardrobe that shouts *VIRGIN!*'

*　　*　　*

Reverend Humbold removed the sweat-dampened jacket of his impeccably white suit and handed it to one of the fawning acolytes busying themselves around him. 'How are those collection plates looking?' he drawled.

'Still in the process of being counted, sir,' said one.

'But visibly up on last week,' offered another, handing him a fresh handkerchief.

Reverend Humbold wiped his brow and nodded appreciatively. 'That'll be the fear factor. Always good to remind folks of their mortality. Makes 'em keener to secure their place in Heaven.'

'There's been a sudden increase in demand for pledge forms too,' said the acolyte brushing what little hair the reverend had left and skilfully forcing it go where nature hadn't intended. 'I guess for the same reason.'

'You guessed right. The smart ones figure they ain't really losing out by donating a few extra dollars, given they won't be able to take it with 'em. They're prudently hedging their bets.'

Someone stepped forward with a large, gold watch, its fascia ostentatiously ringed with diamonds.

The reverend proffered his wrist. 'Talkin' 'bout dollars... how we doin' on the sales of those new prayer cushions we just got in?'

There was a noticeable silence.

'Well?'

'Sales are down compared to the old ones, sir,' braved the watch fastener.

Reverend Humbold stared over the man's head. 'Guess I oughta give 'em a mention during my next sermon. Make people take a little more concern over their knees when they're requesting of the Lord.'

'I don't think it's lack of awareness in the usefulness of the product that's the problem, sir.' The speaker coughed uncomfortably.

'Then what in hell's name *is* it?'

'Sales have dipped since you ordered a change in the picture that's normally embroidered on them,' came the answer timidly.

Reverend Humbold straightened his neck. 'But I think it's an *excellent* likeness of me.'

'It is, sir... only...'

He waved away the awkwardness. 'Okay. Point taken. Change it back to that other fella, then, if you must.'

'You mean... *Jesus?*'

The reverend nodded curtly. 'Guess I'm never gonna be able to compete with all that hair.'

The person rearranging *his* paused momentarily and allowed himself a private fantasy.

'The car's waiting for you, sir,' announced a sharply dressed individual, entering the room and dismissively waving the others away.

'Thank you, Steven. I can't afford to waste time here. The Devil's got me busier than a whore on payday.' He took a moment to inspect his white shoes that had just been buffed. 'We don't want him getting the upper hand, now do we?'

'Don't you mean *her*, sir?'

'We've moved on from the whore, Steven. I'm talking about Beelzebub!'

'So was I, sir.'

The reverend squinted his confusion.

'You said in your sermon that he'd come to Earth as a *she*.'

Reverend Humbold pursed his lips. 'Yeah, I did, didn't I… Well… that was figuratively speaking.'

'Figuratively?'

'It's quite a figure, though… I'll tell ya that!'

'So… this Xanthia's not the *actual* Devil, then?'

Reverend Humbold placed an arm around the young man and dropped his voice to a level of privacy. 'Let me tell you something about a sermon, Steven. It's a performance… and a little theatricality is sometimes what's required to keep our flock… *on message,* as they say. If you wanna climb higher in this organisation, you'll need to appreciate that. But the Devil seeks to do his work through others… and there's a good reason the Lord has drawn *this* particular acolyte of Satan to my attention. Now… she may not be the actual Devil herself, but you can take it from me… there's evil oozing out of every pore of that strumpet's body.'

'Figuratively speaking, sir?'

The reverend patted him on the shoulder. 'You're a quick learner, Steven.' He adjusted his collar. 'You'll go far.' He placed his arms behind him and allowed a fresh white jacket to be slipped over them. Shrugging it into place, he nodded his desire to leave.

As the two men strode purposefully along a wide corridor leading to the auditorium's loading bay, a number of curious heads popped out from busy corners, eager to catch a glimpse of the man in white. He obliged them all with quick, nodded blessings... his hurrying gait suggesting anything else was out of the question.

'Just so *I'm* on message, sir,' clarified his assistant. 'Will we be maintaining, as far as the public is concerned, that this Xanthia *is* actually Lucifer?'

The reverend gave a subtle smile. 'You saw for yourself the reaction that lil' ol' piece of allegory generated,' he answered. 'And as the Devil is clearly working *through* her, that's *exactly* what we'll be doing. We don't wanna lose any advantage on a simple technicality. What's more... that harlot – with her *duplicitous* claims – has stepped from the shadows at an apposite time. I built this church by rescuing people's souls when the world lost its way in that art-driven market crash, and the Lord saw fit to reward me handsomely for it. Well... it's teetering on the brink again, and now there's an even *greater* calling to be answered. I intend letting this planet know that I'm the *only* person who can save it. For that, I need publicity... and Satan has unwittingly handed me the means. She might be struggling to gain a following at the moment... but all the fuss and feathers created by those Stonehenge shenanigans has given this flesh and blood abomination of his a chance to promote herself and influence the minds of the gullible on a global scale. Not only do I intend stopping her... I intend taking advantage of her efforts and using them to my own ends. And being flesh and blood... trust me... when I cut, she'll bleed!'

As they reached the loading bay, a waiting chauffeur offered the interior of a white, stretch limousine.

'I guess our Lord must regret giving her that flesh and blood in the first place,' said the assistant, placing a protective hand over his charge's head as it prepared to enter the vehicle.

The reverend paused mid stoop and turned back to face his protégé. 'All I can tell you is this, young man.' He fixed him with a wistful look. 'It might be the Lord who fashioned a body for her soul... but I reckon the Devil *sure* gave her those titties!'

* * *

'Xanthia! Xanthia! Go on... give us a smile!'

Reality momentarily stuttered as strobing splatters of light danced to the click and whir of cameras.

'Any tips for the three fifteen at Cheltenham tomorrow?' shouted one wag from the melee of reporters.

'Can you use your powers to tell us the best way to combat this sudden plague of aphids attacking everyone's allotments?' hollered another.

Xanthia smiled politely, forcing her way through them and into the building they'd besieged.

'At least you still have their attention,' grimaced Norman, as they finally took refuge in its foyer.

She knew he was being kind.

'Xanthia!' A young man hurried towards them, a hand extended beyond his clipboard. 'I'm Simon. I'm with the production team for tonight's show.' He looked at them both mischievously. 'Though, I suppose Xanthia has already divined that!' A snort suggested he thought his remark demonstrated wit, even if his two guests clearly didn't. 'I'll take you to the green room,' he grinned. 'We've laid on something for you to eat.' His mouth quivered at its edges. 'We're only talking a few loaves and a couple of fishes... but I'm sure you'll make it stretch!'

'That's very kind... but we made sure we were fully sated before we *came*,' Xanthia replied graciously. 'Much like *you* do during your evenings alone with those special videos you love watching.' She looked at him sweetly and smiled.

The young man ran his tongue around a mouth that had suddenly dried. 'It's this way,' he said timidly.

'I know,' she winked.

The green room – as it turned out – was beige... the only green things being stacked in a fruit bowl on a coffee table filling the space between two large sofas.

'Someone will come and get you when it's time to go on,' Simon addressed the floor, trying to avoid eye contact with her. 'That'll be in about forty minutes. The other guests should be arriving shortly.' He flashed a quick look at Norman and beat a hasty retreat.

'Helpful man,' said Norman.

'*Troubled* man,' she muttered.

Norman rubbed his hands anxiously. 'I wonder who those other guests will be.' He playfully slapped his forehead. 'Duh... I forget... like you wouldn't know.'

'I don't,' she said. 'I'm not clairvoyant and I can't read minds. My knowledge of everything only extends up until the moment the sphere was created. Seeing as the guests for tonight's show were booked *after* that, I'm as in the dark as you.'

'Have you planned what you're going to say?'

'The truth,' she smiled.

Norman picked up an apple and bit into it with faked nonchalance. 'Perhaps the witnessing of a little miracle or two wouldn't go amiss... just in case.'

Xanthia looked at him the way a mother might a foolish child. It was something he was getting used to now the balance of intellect had seismically shifted. 'Norman... I'm not a *magician!*'

'No, no... of *course* not.' He stared at her awkwardly. 'I'm just saying... perhaps you could use your superior understanding of science to create something that *looked* miraculous. It'd certainly make everyone sit up and take you seriously.'

'I'd like to think that what I have to *say* will do that.'

'I know... I know. But... given the current climate of antipathy towards you...' He put his hands together as if in prayer.

She shook her head resignedly. 'Okay. You win. I'll perform just *one* trick tonight. But... like all good magicians... I'll need an assistant. So... I want you standing beside me in a low-cut,

474

sequinned dress and a peacock feather headdress. I'll leave the amount of encouraging hand gestures up to you… but don't forget to smile a lot. That'll *definitely* have everyone sitting up and paying attention. Shall *I* call wardrobe or will you?'

He was about to sulk when the green room door flew open and the first of those "other guests" staggered in.

'Stump!' she exclaimed. 'What on earth are *you* doing here?'

The object of her surprise looked unsteadily around the room and rested his gaze on a small fridge nestled in the corner. 'Same thing as you, I expect,' he slurred, making directly for it.

'You're being *interviewed?*'

'Well… I tried to persuade them to allow me to perform, but they said it was pre-watershed.' He yanked the fridge open, holding onto its door for support whilst trying to focus on its contents. 'Anyone fancy a beer?'

Xanthia flashed a look of alarm at Norman. 'I don't think that's a good idea, Stump,' she said. 'I've a feeling we'll need to have our wits about us tonight.'

'Don't I always?' he swaggered.

Impossible to answer without hurting his feelings, she didn't.

Grabbing a bottle, he looked around for an opener. 'So… are we having a threesome tonight, then?' he drawled.

Norman stepped forward protectively. 'I think that's uncalled for!'

Having found what he was looking for, Stump turned and faced him. 'The interview,' he announced with perfect diction. 'Is it the three of us on the couch? The *studio's*, that is… before your dishcloth of a mind has other thoughts. I assume we've been asked here because of Stonehenge.'

Norman winced at having walked into so easy a blow. 'They don't know about my involvement. Stonehenge's mystery benefactor is *still* a mystery.'

'Not for long!' sung Stump. 'You've opened a massive can of worms with that particular stunt. I've heard there are calls being made for a public enquiry!'

'It doesn't matter,' responded Norman. 'We produced the sphere of knowledge. That's all that *does* matter.'

'Not quite,' Stump countered. 'Some of us have reputations to maintain. This hasn't exactly been good for my image, you know.'

'You're kidding!' Norman scoffed. 'It's *ideal*. You're at the centre of the biggest scandal to hit this country in decades! Surely that's *right* up your street?'

'Yeah... but with Xanthia here claiming to be the next Mother Teresa... and me having helped her... I'm in danger of looking like the *good* guy if she ever persuades the public to buy her story.' He downed his beer in one. 'Anyway...' he belched, 'at the risk of appearing soft... I have to say it's a relief to see you standing there and drawing breath. The last time I set eyes on you, they were dragging you away from my chopper... a fate normally only reserved for groupies. I'll be honest, mate... I didn't think you were gonna make it.'

'I wouldn't have, if Xanthia hadn't provided such forensically detailed medical advice,' said Norman, ignoring the smut. 'It's what pulled me through and ensured such a speedy recovery. The doctors said they'd never seen anything like it.'

Stump squinted. 'So is it true, Xan? With this gift you say you've been given... are you really gonna save us sinners?'

'That depends on how big an audience I'll be allowed to reach,' she answered.

'*Allowed?*' frowned Norman uneasily.

She waved away his concern. 'Another time. At least the media's interest in Stonehenge has given me a starting platform.'

Stump raised an unsteady hand in support of Norman. 'Nah, nah... he's right to be worried. You wanna be careful that platform you've been given doesn't turn into a gallows. Most people think you're simply cashing in. They're venting their anger 'cos they believe you're taking them for mugs. You'll need to do an awful lot of convincing to turn that perception around.'

'That's precisely why I'm here,' she smiled. 'So... I take it I can count on *your* support tonight?'

Stump fixed his attention back on the fridge. 'Do you know what? I think I'll have another beer.'

* * *

Alien One stared out over the sterile landscape and at the coal-black sky rising above a numbingly flat horizon. Only the shimmering stars offered the eyes any relief from boredom. Nothing had been said for the best part of a day... which, given the planet took thirteen and half Earth ones to rotate, was quite a considerable time.

Breaking the silence, Alien One enquired of Alien Two – sat beside him – if he considered it *remotely* possible that some other being existed out there in the vast, twinkling void.

Alien Two took a while to consider the question... then replied that he'd be deliriously happy if some other *thing* existed *anywhere*.

Alien One gazed around at the flat, featureless, grey rock stretching into every imaginable distance and knew exactly what he meant.

Another day passed.

Alien Three – sat alongside them – broke the excruciating monotony with a sigh.

Alien One enquired what the matter was.

Taking the best part of another day to formulate an answer, Alien Three eventually replied that he'd forgotten.

Alien Two suggested Alien Three had succinctly highlighted the nub of their problem.

Alien Three looked surprised, given he didn't realise they had one... or at least couldn't remember what it was if they *did*.

According to Alien Two, it wasn't just the sheer tedium of existence... it was the fact they'd been enduring it for so long they'd completely lost track of how they'd got there in the first place.

Alien Three suggested that perhaps they'd *always* been there. After all... none of them could remember a time when they hadn't.

Alien Two agreed.

Alien One didn't. He suggested there had to have been a beginning at some point. Given the stars had been slowly spreading away from them in every direction over the millions of years they'd been sat there observing them, there must have been a time in the past when all those stars were at precisely the same place.

Alien Three asked him where he thought that place was.

Alien One replied that it had to be exactly where they were sat.

Aliens Two and Three stared at him in silent astonishment... until having mentally calculated he was right.

By which time, the stars had spread a little further.

Alien One then stated that... given it would've been impossible for them and the stars to have been in the same place at the same time without it seriously damaging their health... the three of them must have originated *after* the stars had set off on their journey. Therefore, their lives *had* to have had a beginning.

Aliens Two and Three were impressed... until realising it raised a disturbing question.

What *caused* them to be there?

The stars?

No... *them*.

Alien One made a strange gurgling noise and confessed he knew what they meant all along. He was just joking.

Aliens Two and Three looked at him blankly. Doing... *what*?

Alien One explained *joking* was an idea he'd come up with to make life less tedious... to momentarily subvert the logical thought process so as to provide a little entertainment.

Alien Two admonished him for being silly.

Alien Three concurred and demanded he answer their original question.

Disappointed by the lack of enthusiasm for his new concept, Alien One merely shrugged and mumbled 'God knows.'

Aliens Two and Three would've looked at him even more blankly than they had the first time, were it not for the fact such a thing was impossible.

Who?

Alien One explained it was another idea he'd come up with… like joking.

Another one?

Yes. It helped him pass the time. God was a name he'd chosen to give all those things that were unanswerable. By doing so, the unknown didn't seem so vast and scary. It was his coping mechanism.

Was this one of his… *jokes?*

No.

So God represented his ignorance?

Alien One preferred to think God represented his wonder.

Then… this hypothetical extra life he'd initially wondered about… would that also be called God?

Alien One supposed it would.

And if this particular *God* with a mind existed… would it be friendly?

Alien One had no reason to suppose otherwise. He couldn't see how minds that *weren't* friendly could exist for long, given they would invariably end up destroying each other.

Alien Three agreed with his logic… and said he was relieved Alien One hadn't tried to momentarily subvert it.

Alien Two wished he had… because what if this God was *alone?* It could survive even if filled with extreme hatred.

Alien One didn't see a problem. If they ever came into contact with it, there would be three of them and only one of God.

Alien Two respectfully pointed out that numbers would be an irrelevance. If this God had managed to survive all by itself for so long, it would probably mean it was far superior to them.

Alien Three's eyes widened sideways as a thought occurred to him. If it was superior, maybe it was that God who was responsible for creating them.

Aliens One and Two continued to stare at the twinkling stars in silence.

It was only after another four days had passed that Alien Three realised he hadn't said his thought aloud.

The mistake corrected, Alien Two voiced one of his own. If Alien One's God created them, surely it could *end* them. He suggested it might be an idea if they appeased this hypothetical God by openly acknowledging their inferiority to it... just in case it *did* exist and was watching.

And how might they do that?

Alien Two replied that they could destroy something valuable so as to demonstrate their allegiance to a higher being.

Alien One looked around the expansive, empty terrain and then back at Alien Two.

What, for instance?

Alien Two looked at Alien Three and then slowly back at Alien One.

Alien One gulped and said Alien Two couldn't be serious.

Alien Two held his stare for a few more days before emitting the same strange gurgling noise Alien One had made earlier.

It was only then that Alien One – contrary to an earlier assumption – realised Alien Two *had* grasped the concept of joking after all.

* * *

Davy Fury was as cool as it got. The kids loved him and the dads wanted to be him... while mums secretly wished their husbands *were* him. His dry sense of humour and quick wit made his chat show a must-watch if you happened to be at home on a Sunday night. But he didn't just go for laughs. He'd built his reputation on being able to mix the serious with the absurd... a delightful combination if you got it right.

He always did.

Xanthia was under no illusions as to which side of that equation she'd been booked to represent. Her assumption was confirmed as Davy introduced his final guests.

'Joining us tonight for the last part of the show are three people I'm hoping will shed some light on the bizarre happenings at Stonehenge recently. You'd have to be a visiting alien not to have heard about them, and a stupid one at that not to understand the controversy they've caused. If you think turning our most iconic Neolithic monument into something resembling a tawdry theme park was a great way to get the kids interested in pre-history, you'll be delighted to hear there are now plans to build a burger concession inside West Kennet Longbarrow and a waterslide down Silbury Hill.'

A cheeky grin guaranteed the laughs.

'First up is someone who's being rocking for so long he probably remembers the scaffolding going up at those sites... the incorrigible and ever-so-slightly-dangerous-to-have-on-a-live-show lead singer of *Trouzerbulge*... Stump.'

It had been a while since his first guest had been allowed anywhere near a TV studio, his last appearance sparking outrage when he'd advocated the use of amphetamines at school sports days to get children to run faster. Aware of ratings, Davy privately hoped for more of the same... unlike the show's more conservative producers, who'd only taken a risk because the story was too good to miss.

Stump acknowledged his reputation with a peace sign, the back of which predictably got shown to Davy.

The audience cheered affectionately.

Davy waited for the noise to subside. 'Next is expert psychologist and esteemed author on the subject of the human mind... and the only one of my guests *not* to have had sex with each other... Professor Hugo Wotaspanner.'

The professor acknowledged his more muted welcome with a nod of erudition... an exposed, check-patterned sock at the end of a crossed leg confirming his aforementioned academic credentials.

'And finally... well... where do I start?'

The audience giggled nervously.

'We've seen more of her than anyone – other than a particularly inventive contortionist – has ever seen of themselves... ex-glamour model, tabloid agony aunt and now self-proclaimed saviour of us all... Saint Xanthia of the Top Shelf!'

The audience erupted with howls of laughter, while Xanthia gracefully weathered their scorn.

Davy pointlessly tugged at an earlobe and turned to his first guest. 'Now, Stump... the question I've been dying to ask – before we get to the more fanciful aspects of this story – is how on *earth* did someone manage to get permission to mess with the monument in the first place and let you and your band play in front of it?'

'I believe it was a bribe,' slurred Stump, as matter-of-factly as his condition allowed. 'Quarter of a billion quid turns a lot of blind eyes... apparently.'

'That's the money paid out by this mysterious benefactor we've been hearing so much about,' clarified Davy. 'Which begs the obvious question... *why?*'

'Let's just say... he likes his music,' Stump replied.

Davy nodded his respect. 'That's *some* fan!'

'Yeah... and he *too* has had sex with one of your guests... though I should point out it wasn't with me.'

The audience fell about laughing... whilst the professor's sock twitched uncomfortably. Xanthia bowed her head.

'Wow!' beamed Davy, turning quickly to the camera. 'I think Stump might've inadvertently given us a massive scoop there!'

Just *compos mentis* enough to realise he might've let the cat out of the bag, Stump attempted to stuff it back in. 'I just hope her current boyfriend isn't watching the show and finds out,' he covered.

'You mean her secretive boyfriend who's reputedly an extremely wealthy and private individual?' countered Davy, with a knowing wink at the camera.

Stump looked across at Xanthia. 'Not any more,' he belched.

'No,' laughed Davy. 'You're right. He can certainly forget about his privacy now!'

A cry of despair – unheard by the studio audience – sounded in the green room.

'Suddenly things are beginning to make sense,' said Davy, leaning forward. 'Was this the loving action of a wealthy man looking to breathe fresh life into his partner's flagging career? Was it nothing more than a publicity stunt to put an international spotlight on Xanthia?'

'You'll have to ask her,' said Stump, looking to extricate himself from a deteriorating position. 'I was simply looking to fulfil a dream and play my music in front of those sacred stones.'

'Very loudly by all accounts,' nodded Davy. 'There's a rumour flying around that you were going for some sort of volume world record that night. Is that right?'

Stump cupped a hand around one ear. 'Pardon?'

The audience loved it… a fact not lost on Davy, who had no intention of being upstaged.

'But now I need to cut through the clowning and get a little serious with you.' He waved down the cheers. 'Where this all gets rather murky is not what people *heard* but what they claim to have *seen*.' His expression hardened. 'Was it *you* responsible for conning the public with that ball of light hoax… or was it just a PR stunt that simply got out of hand?'

'I don't know what you mean,' said Stump deadpan.

The audience sniggered.

'Come on!' joined in Davy. 'Thousands of people claim to see a miraculous ball of light at one of your gigs and you haven't put them up to it?'

'I didn't need to,' Stump fought back. 'Our light shows might've always been out of this world… but that was something else!'

'Well… it would've been had it actually happened,' said Davy, looking to the audience for support. 'But as we all know… that wasn't the case. Despite numerous claims that something other-worldly occurred, not *one* piece of evidence exists to back them up. Not *one* photo. Not *one* video. Which is rather odd… wouldn't you say?' He leant back in his chair having landed what he knew was a killer blow.

Stump slouched in his. 'My understanding is the light was of a frequency not conducive to being captured on film… that's all I'm gonna say.'

Davy seized the opportunity to attack again. 'Understanding from where?'

Stump shifted uncomfortably.

Davy waited for an answer.

Stump's eyes wandered.

'*Well?*'

'Xanthia,' mumbled Stump, awkwardly rubbing his nose.

Davy snorted theatrically. 'How *very* convenient!'

'*Everyone* who was there saw it,' she interjected calmly. 'Not one person has said otherwise. Policemen… doctors… the site's staff. They've all testified to the fact the phenomenon actually occurred.'

Davy already knew that, which is why he'd invited his other guest. 'So… Professor Wotaspanner.' He turned to the man and his sock. 'What do you have to say about *that?*'

The professor gave the sort of smug nod that suggested not only did he understand the conundrum, he also had the answer. 'Oh, I don't doubt in their minds they all saw what they thought they did,' he opined. 'But the mind is easily influenced, not least when emotions are heightened. We can cite numerous instances when one person claiming to see something out of the ordinary has produced a chain reaction in others around them. We call it hysterical contagion or mass hysteria. Whether it be a group sighting of a UFO or a weeping statue of Christ… those sharing the delusion firmly believe it to be real. One has to consider that in *this* example, there existed a particularly incendiary cocktail of circumstances. A revered and enigmatic site evoking wonder… a strobing light show enhancing a hypnotic rhythm being pounded out at a volume that caused everyone to feel nauseous… thus creating a shared panic. All fuelled by a night without sleep and everyone *expecting* the arrival of a special ball of light – namely, the solstice sun – I don't think it a coincidence the imagined sighting occurred at the exact same moment its rays struck the stones. Throw into the equation hallucinogenic substances undoubtedly partaken of by many of those in attendance and you have the perfect recipe for what occurred. I think it less a mystery and more a masterclass in how to produce the perfect communal delusion!'

Davy couldn't agree more. But he knew the viewers at home would be wondering about one important detail… as was he. 'Playing devil's advocate… surely not *everyone* could be affected by such a delusion? Yet not one single person who was there has claimed *not* to see it,' he pointed out.

'Or, interpreting it another way… not one person who *didn't* see it has wanted to admit the fact,' explained Dr Wotaspanner, his sock nodding in agreement. 'It's not uncommon for people to go along with the majority and accept the status quo for fear of appearing the odd one out, even when they believe something completely to the contrary. It's called normative conformity. In this case… the interest from the world's media has merely increased that pressure to conform, given the entire planet seems to *want* it to be true.'

'Which is not what can be said of the claims being made by my third guest,' Davy linked smugly, his broad grin suggesting impending ridicule. 'Having spent her previous years encouraging men to have sinful thoughts, she now says she's here to make them see the errors of their ways! Well…I'm glad to see she's come dressed for the occasion!'

The audience howled as Xanthia tried to pull down the hem of her short skirt.

In a nearby green room, a head was buried in exasperated hands.

Davy went in for the kill. 'Xanthia… am I going to hell for my current thoughts, and if so… is it alright to blame you when I get there?'

Xanthia waited for the laughter to subside. 'There is no such place as hell,' she said calmly.

Her vulnerable demeanour turned some of the remaining sniggering into embarrassment. But Davy had no intention of letting the moment go.

'No such place as hell?' He played up his surprise. 'I wasn't expecting *that!*'

Neither was Norman… not least because he'd personally met its caretaker.

'Maybe I ought to believe in you after all,' Davy quipped. 'Hedge my bets!'

'You don't have to believe in me… you simply have to believe *with* me,' she said.

'Wow,' gasped Davy, holding his forehead. 'That's either incredibly deep… or something I might expect to read in a fortune cookie!' He turned to Stump, whose earlier efforts to relax himself were now beginning to kick in. 'I bet that's music to your ears, eh, Stump?'

'Huh?'

'Xanthia telling us there's no such place as hell.'

Stump struggled to remain upright. 'I think she might be mistaken on *that* particular one,' he slurred, before giving up the effort.

The audience erupted hysterically as the rock icon cemented his reputation by sliding off his chair altogether.

'The perils of live TV,' joked Davy, looking around. 'I think we might need some assistance here, please.' A smile twisted his lips as a thought occurred to him while waiting for help to arrive. 'Then again… Xanthia… this could be your big moment. Raising Stump in his current condition would certainly count as a miracle!'

The audience's laughter now seemed tinged with venom.

'I'm not here to do party tricks,' she replied above it.

Norman groaned again.

'But I thought you were claiming this ball of light has given you some sort of super power. Well… this could be your chance to demonstrate it. Though I don't think *you'll* be needing to wear your underwear on the outside. It's clearly visible from where I'm sitting!'

Xanthia tried to reply, but the increased howls of derision drowned her out.

As a camera shot switched to the audience – allowing Stump's body to be removed without further embarrassment – Norman scanned their sneering faces. Not one showed any compassion for her predicament. If there was any, he supposed it was being suppressed by normative conformity. As far as he was concerned, unless Xanthia changed her mind about performing a miracle, the next five minutes were going to be excruciating.

* * *

Reverend Galveston Humbold III formed his lips into a ring of doubt and inhaled his misgivings. 'I reckoned, with righteousness on my side, she'd be easy prey in a debate... but not *that* easy. That Fury fella just ran rings around her! I've seen more fight in a week-old corpse. She was about as effective as a sausage salesman at a sewage treatment facility canteen!'

His assistant lowered the lid of the laptop they'd been studying. 'Praise the Lord, sir. She'll be completely annihilated when it's *your* turn to confront her.'

'You're missing the point, boy,' the reverend drawled. 'A worthy opponent makes victory worthy. Anything less is pointless. I need someone who'll be seen as a serious contender... a credible threat to humanity... someone with whom I can engage in strong and reasoned theological discourse... before I start waving pictures of their private parts about to win the debate. I thought that's what she was gonna be when her blasphemous claims first caught my attention. But battling with *this* docile harlot would be as impressive to my congregation as me ripping up tissue paper.'

'She wasn't helped any by that ex-boyfriend of hers,' offered Steven.

'Another of Satan's protégés, no doubt. But even without the distraction of that long-haired jackass, she'd *still* have failed to land a single, credible punch.'

'At least that means the Devil's lost the first round... which is a *good* thing... isn't it?'

The reverend winced. 'The thing is... the more I've reason to shout against him, the louder I'll be heard. From what I've just seen, I could demolish the threat this Xanthia poses with a whisper no louder than a dinner table fart. While I grant that's good for humanity, it ain't so good for my viewing figures.'

'So, what happens now? Should we look elsewhere for a worthier opponent to focus your attack on?'

The reverend massaged his chin uncomfortably. 'I dunno, boy. The trouble is the die's been cast. I can hardly tell our congregation this coming Sunday that Galveston Humbold III made a mistake when hearing the word of the Lord. Besides... it's obvious to anyone with half a brain she's no angel and needs to be stopped. I mean... did you *see* what she was wearing?'

Steven nodded sheepishly, thinking it foolish to pretend it had escaped his attention.

The reverend winced again. 'Perhaps I ought not be so hasty in dismissing her. There are enough crazies out there on the internet lapping up her story and keeping it in the media's eye. Smartly hitching her wagon to that Stonehenge bunkum has ensured that interest is global... which means I'll be seen by a *far* bigger audience when I finally get to shoot its wheels off.'

'But if she lacks credibility in the first place, sir?'

The reverend acknowledged his dilemma via a tortured grimace. 'Darn it! It feels like I'm stuck between a full cashier's till and the wrong end of a magnum forty-four! She'd be *perfect* if it weren't for the fact she's coming across like the town idiot on their worst day. Hell's teeth... one minute she's trying to convince the public she's their saviour... the next, she's informing 'em there's no such place as hell!' He forced an incredulous smile. 'It's like a snake oil salesman tellin' the crowd they ain't ever gonna get ill!'

Steven raised a finger. 'Perhaps she's playing a very clever game. We know she's working for the Devil, so maybe her inept persona is a deliberate deception. Perhaps she's realised she can carry out his work more easily if she's *not* taken seriously. She's lulling people into a false sense of security. They might be laughing at her... but they're definitely *listening*. That's all she needs. And by denying the existence of hell, she's just given a green light to those on the edge of sinning... and done so without looking like a threat to anyone.'

The reverend's expression froze.

'Sir? Are you okay?'

'Beware of false prophets who come to you in sheep's clothing, but inwardly they are ravening wolves,' he mumbled. 'Scripture... Matthew 7:15.' He stared at his assistant in awe. 'D'ya know what, young Steven?'

Young Steven steeled himself for incoming praise.

'The Lord has just spoken to me through you. That *is* her game. I see it all now. When her misguided disciples... trusting they can have their cake and eat it... finally gorge and puke their way to the gates of Heaven... they'll find those gates slammed shut in their gluttonous faces. And Satan will be waiting... ready to direct 'em to alternative accommodation.' His eyes narrowed. 'I may have vastly underestimated this Xanthia. That libidinous harlot knows *exactly* what she's doing!'

*　*　*

'That went well,' said Norman.

'Sarcasm is the lowest form of wit,' Xanthia lectured him, rubbing the circulation back into feet freshly released from a particularly cruel pair of stilettos.

'No... that's Stump playing for cheap laughs by telling the audience the guy you're sleeping with put up the money for Stonehenge!' he reminded her.

'I think the world would've found out sooner or later,' she sympathised. 'There's too much interest in that side of the story.'

'Shame there's not enough in *yours*,' he returned bitterly. 'Then again... perhaps that's just as well.'

She shot him a sharp look. 'What's that supposed to mean?'

Norman telegraphed surprise at her needing to ask. 'Well...
I have to say... even *I* was underwhelmed by your performance
tonight! As far as I'm concerned, if you're to retain any
credibility whatsoever, the less people who witnessed it the
better!'

'Fewer,' she corrected him. 'Anyway... it was always going to
be one-sided. I knew *that* before I agreed to do the show. I just
didn't count on Stump being there and turning an extremely
difficult task into a completely impossible one. His presence
guaranteed that what should've been a serious conversation
became little more than a joke. I've no doubt that's why he was
booked. You saw what happened. From the moment he passed
out, the audience were baying for further slapstick and as far
from listening impartially as you could get.'

'But there you go! You're still talking about *conversations* and
listening. Surely it's obvious that particular strategy isn't
working. I know you complain you haven't been given a
roadmap for what to do... but tonight was your biggest
opportunity to at least show everyone the power you've been
given. You could've fought back with something that dropped
their jaws... something that needn't have created those negative
ripples you're so worried about. In fact, Stump unwittingly
handed you the perfect opportunity. You could've done
something to help him recover just like you did for me. That
would've stopped the laughter. The host even suggested the
idea *himself!*'

'Trust me, Normy,' she said, standing uncomfortably. 'Davy
Fury was right... getting Stump back on his feet really *would've*
required a miracle.'

Norman read her thin smile as complacency. 'I don't get it,
Xan. What's happening? You let that smug Fury run rings
around you. You could've shut him down at any given moment
with what you know. If conversation is your weapon of choice,
why not have silenced him with a few, clever sentences? But
you just sat there and let him crucify you.'

She looked at him, unperturbed. 'I think you're being
overdramatic. I'm still here, aren't I?'

'But what's the point? Look where *here* is.' He gesticulated wildly. 'We're imprisoned in this lousy room with ridicule as our gaoler. It's only a matter of time before the press get tired of you and move on to their next big story... and then how are we gonna get our message across? What's going on, Xan? Why aren't you worried? You've been watching the same news reports I have... all these strange, ominous happenings. Time's running out. It's obvious what they presage. Every day the other side gets stronger. Take the craze for desecrating spiritual sites that's suddenly swept the planet since I messed with Stonehenge. It's given a green light for every bigot to jump on the bandwagon and promote their poison. Imagine how that makes *me* feel! I've never known so much hatred in the air. The whole world seems to be looking for scapegoats to persecute. It's growing darker by the day. Satan doesn't need to wield a sword himself. He simply whispers in the ear of whoever wishes to hold one for him... like that acne-riddled idiot who stuck a knife in me! Tonight was your big chance to shout back and drown him out.'

Xanthia examined her fingernails and tutted. 'Isn't that typical. I only had these painted two days ago and they're *already* chipped!'

Norman broke from his apocalyptic thoughts and stared at her, open mouthed.

She stared back. *'What?'*

He shook his head... watching her studying what now looked suspiciously like red talons to him. 'If I didn't know better, Xan, I'd swear you were...' He stopped himself. A thought, so alien it would've been unthinkable outside of his anger, had taken advantage of the situation and squeezed past his better judgement.

She looked at him expectantly.

'Forget it,' he said, quickly turning away.

She shrugged and hobbled towards the kitchen area. 'Perhaps if this is getting too much for you, you should think about taking a break from it for a while. I mean... it's not exactly as if I *need* you here.'

'Oh, thanks!' he exclaimed.

'I didn't mean it like that. But a change of environment might do you good.'

Norman thought it sounded more like a ruse to get rid of him so as to avoid further criticism. 'Where do you suggest I go? I can hardly return to France, seeing as I gave away everything to get us to where we are now.'

She dropped two teabags into waiting cups. 'There's something I've been meaning to tell you... and now seems as good a time as any.'

His eyes widened as his anger melted into a pool of embarrassment. 'Oh, God... you're not *pregnant,* are you?' He stared at her in shock. 'Is *that* what this is all about?'

'Forever the romantic,' she sighed.

'Well?'

She looked at him blankly. 'Well what?'

'*Are* you?'

She shook her head... though more from despondency. 'Do you remember being told... after the fire in your bedsit... that a stranger tried to rescue you by climbing onto the roof of a truck parked beneath your window?'

His shock morphed into confusion. 'I'm hardly likely to forget. I've had to live with the guilt of knowing they ended up being carted away in an ambulance while I walked away scot-free. It was an incredibly brave thing to do.'

'Well... wouldn't you like to know who it was?'

Norman peered at her intently, all previous thoughts eclipsed. 'It never occurred to me... you would *know,* wouldn't you?'

'Of course... though the answer might come as a bit of a shock.'

He'd just had one of those.

She grinned playfully.

'Xan?'

'Donald Tucker-Jenkins,' she announced, pouring the kettle.

Norman's jaw dropped. 'The famous *playwright?*'

'The very same.'

'What on earth was *he* doing passing my flat?'

'He wasn't passing. He'd gone there to warn you.'

His jaw dropped even further... which hurt. 'He *knew* about me?'

'Tucker-Jenkins has exceptional psychic abilities and had been receiving messages concerning your activities. He'd been tricked into giving your location and was trying to rectify his mistake.'

Norman struggled to get his head around the fact that, apart from attempting to save his life, the greatest playwright since William Shakespeare had a connection to his efforts to rescue the Universe from oblivion.

Then the penny dropped.

'Shakespeare!' he blurted. 'The sphere of knowledge! That's it! Tucker-Jenkins must've been hit by a fragment when it exploded!'

'Quiet a large piece, actually,' she nodded. 'It's why he writes so sublimely.'

Norman attempted to order his jostling thoughts. 'It all makes sense now... how he suddenly burst onto the creative scene from nowhere!'

'Well... now you know. And now you do... maybe some thanks are in order.'

'Thank you,' he gasped, forgetting his earlier annoyance and trying to process what he'd been told.

'Not me,' she laughed. 'I'm talking about *Donald*. Why don't you pay him a visit and express your gratitude personally? I'm sure he'd appreciate it.'

Norman considered the suggestion. 'D'ya reckon? He must be an extremely busy man.'

'Even if he is, I'm sure he'd like to hear your side of the story,' she pushed. 'After all... he has much to thank *you* for. My guess is you'll *both* find it beneficial.' She prodded the floating teabags with a spoon. 'And while you're there, you can ask him about his previous artistic endeavours with canvas.'

'He paints?'

'Used to. They're no masterpieces… but I'm sure you'll find them interesting. It'll give you something extra to talk about.'

'But what about our work here?'

She shrugged. 'I doubt one day's gonna make any difference. Besides… the whole point is to clear your head. And let's face it… you're certainly not going to win this battle on a muddled one.'

'With you or Satan?' he ventured.

She looked at him sternly. 'Both.'

He weighed up the prospect. Given the thoughts that had been troubling his mind the past few hours, he figured it might be sensible to step away from the madness of the situation for a short while and reassess things from a distance. 'D'ya know what… I think I just might. A change of scenery could do me good. Besides… it'll be great to meet a major beneficiary of all that work I undertook.'

'There you go,' she nodded. 'That's sorted, then. You can go and see him tomorrow. I'll write down the most efficient transport links to his home.'

He squinted warily. 'How do you know he'll be there? You told me you weren't clairvoyant.'

Xanthia tossed the teabags into the bin. 'Knowing Donald… as I now do… I somehow doubt he'll be wanting to go anywhere else in a hurry at this particular moment in time.'

* * *

'Mummy?'

'Yes, Archie?'

'What happened to Granny Mumpstead after she died?'

'In truth… not a lot,' answered his father wryly, eliciting a sharp dig in the ribs from Mummy.

'But I thought Mummy said she'd gone to live with the angels.'

'That's right, darling… I believe she has.'

'So why isn't she doing a lot, then?'

'She probably is.'

'But Daddy says she's not.'

Mummy looked at his enquiring eyes and felt the tug of his confusion. 'We've always said we'd never lie to you,' she explained. 'So, in answer to your question about Granny Mumpstead... Daddy and I believe different things.'

'So, where does Daddy think she went?'

Mummy let Daddy speak for himself.

'I think she's still in the ground, Archie, but asleep.'

'Not asleep, Martin,' said Mummy captiously. 'If we're going to treat him as a young adult and bring Archie up without ever being dishonest to him, you can't tell him you think she's asleep. That clearly *isn't* the case.'

'Mummy's right,' acknowledged Daddy. 'The truth is... Granny Mumpstead doesn't exist anymore.'

'*Your* truth, Martin. Not mine!'

'My truth,' he corrected himself. 'Mummy thinks she's gone to a place no one's ever seen.'

Archie took a few moments to process the information, the workings of his seven-and-three-quarters-soon-to-be-eight brain contorting the cherubic features of his face. 'So which one of you is right?'

Awkward adult looks were exchanged.

'That's for you to work out for yourself when you grow up,' said Mummy... cleverly, she thought.

Archie looked up at them both. 'Is it a game, then?'

'No,' said Mummy. 'It's not a game. We just think you should make your *own* mind up without Mummy or Daddy forcing you to believe what *they* believe.'

Archie's face contorted further. 'Then why don't we find out now?'

'*Sorry?*'

'We could dig Granny Mumpstead up and find out who's telling the truth!'

Given Archie, in his enthusiasm, had said his last comment very loudly, Mummy instinctively glanced around the cemetery in order to make sure any failure in parenting skills on her part hadn't been picked up by others. An older couple at an adjoining plot smiled supportively.

'We can't dig Granny Mumpstead up,' she whispered, turning back in embarrassment and squeezing his hand.

'*Technically*, that's not true,' Daddy pointed out.

'Martin!'

'Just applying the doctrine. We said we'd never edit the truth, no matter how awkward the subject.'

'Oh, right… so what shall we tell him? He can run home and get his little green plastic spade, then come back and start digging?'

'Can I, Mummy? Can I?' shouted Archie enthusiastically.

'*Now* look what you've done!' she hissed.

'You could, Archie,' acknowledged Daddy. 'But I don't think that would be a good idea. As you know… Granny Mumpstead's been dead for exactly a year now, so I don't think you'd be wanting to handle her body.'

'Oh, for *god's* sake, Martin!'

'Why's that, Daddy?'

'Martin! Don't you *dare!*'

'The truth, Fiona. The truth… remember?'

'He's only *seven!*'

'Nearly eight, Mummy!'

'Granny Mumpstead's body is merely a shell, Archie,' she got in first.

'Like at the seaside?'

'No. It's… *was…* just a carrier for her soul. Now that her soul has gone to heaven, she doesn't need it anymore. So her body is slowly returning back to the earth so that trees and flowers can grow by using her…' Mummy faltered.

'As a nutrient supplement,' contributed Daddy.

Mummy glared at him.

'So did we plant seeds in her tummy before we buried her?' Archie asked, trying to make sense of everything.

'We didn't have to,' replied Mummy. 'Her body will decay naturally… like when you see an apple from our tree in the garden that's fallen onto the lawn.'

'Is that why we buried her... so that the birds won't peck at her.'

'Actually, Archie... that's probably *one* of the reasons,' winced Mummy.

'The other being to prevent her becoming a health hazard,' added Daddy.

'Martin! That's enough!'

'He needs to know these things, Fiona. How else do you think he's going to learn?'

'Have some respect, Martin. That's your *mother* you're talking about.'

'*I* don't have a problem with it. As far as I'm concerned, she came from nothing and will return to nothing. It's biology, chemistry and physics simply doing their thing.'

'And who's responsible for *those* things?' said Mummy smugly.

'But, if she's going to rot like an apple, did we bury Granny Mumpstead naked?'

'What?'

'Well... there'd be no point in putting clothes on her if she's going to go all mushy. So was she in the nude?'

Mummy dropped her head and drew a deep breath so as to temper her creeping frustration. '*No*, Archie. We buried Granny Mumpstead in her favourite dress. The one she'd kept in her wardrobe for over fifty years. It was the one she was wearing when she met Grandpa Mumpstead.'

'And where does *he* think she's gone?' asked Archie.

'Hell, Archie,' said Daddy. 'Grandpa Mumpstead firmly believes she's gone to hell.'

'MARTIN! FOR CHRIST'S SAKE!'

Martin raised his hands in righteous compliance.

As he tended to do when things between Mummy and Daddy got a little loud, Archie decided to busy himself elsewhere.

'I know we agreed to tell him the truth, but *that* was taking things too far!'

'Oh... so telling him Mum's gone to heaven – when there's absolutely not *one* single shred of scientific evidence for that being the case – is okay... is it?'

'You told him your father thought she'd gone to hell. What's the difference?'

'Well, if you don't know that, you need to read your bible a little more or you're in for one helluva shock when it's *your* turn!'

'Don't bloody well get smart with me, Martin Mumpstead!'

There was a polite cough from the couple at the adjoining plot.

Mummy mouthed the word *sorry* then gave her spouse a sharp glare. 'What are you doing over there, Archie?' she called out sweetly, seeking to deflect her embarrassment. 'Don't get your clothes dirty.'

'I'm watching the earth bubble,' shouted back Archie, balanced on his haunches and studying the soil of another grave intently.

'It's called a *mound*, Archie,' said Mummy. 'I know it looks a bit like a bubble, but raised earth like that is called a mound.'

Archie looked back and squinted his confusion.

'Come here now, darling, and say goodbye to Granny Mumpstead. It's time for us to go.'

Doing as he was told, he ran back, legs and hair flapping enthusiastically. 'So why are we saying goodbye?' he panted as he got there.

'I told you... it's time for us to go.'

'But Granny Mumpstead isn't here,' said Archie, looking up at his parents. 'You both said so.'

The parents looked at each other.

'Well...'

'Er...'

Archie shook his head and tutted at their foolishness.

Mummy and Daddy turned in awkward silence and started making their way back towards the car, both deep in thought.

'Archie! Don't even *think* about digging it with your hands!' yelled Mummy, who – having realised they were alone – had turned to see her son closely inspecting the soil above his grandma's grave.

'I'm not! I was watching the earth bubble again!' he shouted back.

'*Mound*, Archie,' said Mummy, marching testily towards him. 'I've already told you. It's called a *mound*.'

'Okay. But the earth's not really mounding, Mummy. It just looks like it is because of the hundreds of creepy crawlies squeezing their way out of it. Look!'

The older couple screamed in unison.

'There are ants, the fattest worms I've ever seen and huge spiders and everything!'

Mummy stopped abruptly, having stepped in something sludgy that now appeared to be investigating her toes.

'Was the dress you buried Granny Mumpstead in red?' Archie asked, holding up a wiggling object in his hand.

'Yes,' whimpered Mummy, staring at her foot.

'I thought so,' Archie nodded, peering at the small piece of rotted cloth trailing from the legs of an enormous beetle.

* * *

Swapping the air-conditioned interior of the SUV for the stifling heat outside, Chad Cheadle momentarily felt his breath snatched from him. The midday sun had turned the walled courtyard into a furnace... the steep sides of the narrow gorge in which it lay doing little to alleviate his discomfort.

Sliding from the driver's seat, he stretched his cramped body into something resembling an upright stance and shielded his eyes from the intense glare of the sun.

The temple of Arwan El Kahab was exactly as he remembered it... its dreary façade only rescued from an onlooker's apathy by the addition of a modest, four-column portico, above which resided the fabled window.

Thoughts of him clambering up to it flooded back... along with the elation he'd felt at discovering the perfectly cut channel in the rocks that allowed the last rays of sunlight on a given spring day to invade the temple's gloom and create a mesmerising, magical display of lights.

Except... as with all magic... it had simply been an illusion. He'd managed to demonstrate that an ingeniously cut series of crystals had caused a single, targeted light beam to split into an intricate mosaic of smaller, dancing ones, giving the impression of something other-worldly.

In a dusty repository in London, an even dustier Professor Hummingbone had informed him that the temple's builders were believed to have acquired ancient secrets of geometry and mathematics that would have given them the skills for such a feat. But of greater interest to him was the fact he'd also been informed those same Templar knights were suspected of uncovering deeper and darker truths... the reason for his return.

He'd spent many a subsequent hour researching the enigmatic crusaders and their pilgrimages to the Holy Lands, trying to fathom what it was they'd found and why they'd gone to such trouble to create the elaborate effect at Arwan El Kahab. But so much about them lay shrouded in mystery, he'd come to the conclusion the best way of getting closer to their minds was to use the funds earned from his previous employer to make a pilgrimage of his own.

It felt strange revisiting the site without his old partner. Their playful banter would have provided a welcome distraction on the long, arduous journey to get there. Guilt hung heavily at reliving so powerful a memory without the one person who shared it, but this was something he needed to do for himself. Events at 66 Armageddon Terrace and Stonehenge had taught him that not all lights could be explained away with logic.

Curiously though... it was logic that had brought him to where he now stood.

He studied the coarse, reddish surface of the courtyard and smiled to himself. The sun reminding him that he shouldn't do so for long, he made for the welcome shade of the portico, the crunch of his footsteps sounding crude against the tranquillity around him. That sense of intrusion was compounded as he lifted the large, metal latch on the temple doors and made them groan as he pushed his way into the cool interior.

Eyes adjusting to the darkness, he watched the building slowly give up its secret... a concentric ring of stone plinths sitting eerily silent in the cavernous setting, a larger plinth dominating its centre with equal indifference.

Standing quietly for a few moments, he tested the silence.

Then his thoughts returned to the courtyard.

'I know you're here!' he shouted, his voice violently ricocheting around the walls and rudely shattering the calm.

A handful of startled birds headed for the window.

Having echoed their point, his words tumbled into the stillness.

The temple ignored him.

'I haven't come all this way for nothing!' he shouted again. 'I'm not leaving here until you show yourself! Believe me... I'm prepared to stay for as long as it takes!'

Despite his cannoning words clumsily competing for attention, the message was clear.

He waited for a response.

None came.

Just as he deemed a third attempt necessary, a small movement from the far side of the temple caught his eye.

'Is that you?' he called out in a softer and more conciliatory tone.

Within the gloom, something stirred.

'I come as a friend,' he assured the source of the movement. 'I mean you no harm.' He spread his arms as a sign of peaceful intent. 'I'm on my own.'

After a delicate stand-off, a white, shrouded figure slowly emerged from the edge of the darkness.

Chad exhaled his relief. 'I *knew* you were here.'

'I'm not used to visitors,' offered a voice barely above a whisper.

Though struggling to place the accent, Chad deduced it had spanned many years. 'I hope you don't mind an uninvited one.'

'That depends on why you're here,' came the reply.

'I'm here for answers... ones I've been seeking for a very long time now.'

Once again, Chad found himself having to wait for a response.

'What makes you think I have them?' it finally came.

'Because it's *you* who guard the question.'

The figure cautiously stepped forward. 'You're an American?'

'I am, sir. But please don't hold that against me.'

'I make no judgements,' said the figure, ignoring his visitor's attempt at lightening the mood. Slowly making his way towards the inner circle of plinths, he carefully sat on the nearest. 'I doubt your journey here would have been easy. You've taken quite a risk assuming there'd be someone to greet you at the end of it. Why were you so sure it would be fruitful?'

Chad smiled warmly. 'I'm a private detective. I study clues.'

The old man lifted his head to the level of intrigue. 'And what would *they* be?'

'The courtyard, for one. This place is so well-concealed, I doubt it gets troubled much by anything... not least the effects of the wind. I reckon the narrowness of the gorge must sap its willpower and leave it with very little strength, should it ever manage to make it this far.'

The old man said nothing.

'This isn't my first time here. On a previous visit, I came ahead of numerous individuals and their vehicles. I doubt you'll have forgotten such an intrusion. I've studied satellite images taken since. With so little to disturb them, I expected those footprints and tyre marks to still be visible. But the courtyard was pristine... along with the track leading up to it... which meant only one thing. It was being cared for... just like the crystals embedded in these walls which had been cleared of anything that would've stopped them doing their job that day. Someone was obviously going to a great deal of trouble to keep this temple functional and erase all signs of visitors in order to maintain its secrets.'

The man gently nodded his respect. 'I thought I recognised you. You were the one who stayed behind when the others left.'

'I was.'

'But, you were with a companion. If I remember correctly, he was liberal with his profanities... as well as his bodily gasses.'

'That last bit is why I've here travelled on my own.'

Once more, the old man ignored Chad's attempt at humour. 'It was you who artificially brought the crystals to life and made them dance again.'

Chad smiled. 'And ever since, I've wondered about their purpose and those responsible for creating them. There are so many questions I haven't been able to answer... not least... why all those religious leaders went to such trouble to journey here and witness the effect.'

'So why aren't you asking *them*? Why come all this way to ask a simple caretaker?'

'Because you're not,' said Chad confidently. 'As you've confirmed... you watched my partner and I intrude upon your domain and install our equipment. We even discussed its use. But at no point did you deem it necessary to remove it or warn your guests of our intent, even though it would've been easy for you to do so. I figured there could only be one reason for that. You knew in advance our devices wouldn't be able to capture the *real* reason for their visit. You knew the people inside this temple would be observing something other than what *we* would in our van... something that defied the laws of physics. Those religious leaders didn't come all this way simply to watch an artificial lightshow. Just like an experience people recently had at Stonehenge, what they *really* saw couldn't be captured on camera.' Chad looked at the old man knowingly. '*That's* why I've undertaken such a long journey to speak to you. If you knew all that... you're more than just a caretaker with an overenthusiastic broom.'

The old man nodded sagely. 'Very impressive, young man.'

'The curious thing is... even those who saw something beyond the light couldn't agree on what it was. I remember them arguing. So, my question is... what exactly *did* they see?'

The old man looked up at the daylight squeezing its way through the window. 'Has it ever occurred to you that the reason you don't know is because you're not supposed to?'

'Constantly,' Chad grinned. 'Which only heightens my curiosity. And all that was before I experienced *another* light show... the one I mentioned at Stonehenge... one that knocked spots off the one you guard here.'

The old man swiftly turned his attention back to Chad. 'Is that so?'

'Yeah, it's so... and this one *definitely* wasn't manmade.'

'What makes you so sure?'

'Because it spoke to me.'

The old man studied Chad for a while longer than felt comfortable. 'And what did it say?'

Chad hesitated. 'I know this is gonna sound crazy...' He exhaled his reticence. 'It seemed to suggest I knew all the answers... for the briefest of moments... and then it was gone... with every question I ever had returning. Only... now there are far *more* that need answering!'

The old man slowly stroked his beard. 'And what would you do with those answers if you had them?'

'Well... for starters... I'd finally be able to rest easy,' Chad replied.

The old man snorted. 'I doubt that very much. There are some things it is better *not* to know. Why do you think I take such care to sweep the courtyard?'

'That's precisely what I'm here to find out. You can't experience what I did and carry on with life as if nothing happened.'

The old man feigned surprise. 'Why not? People do it every day. They walk about oblivious to the miracles of life all around them and of the astronomical odds against them being here at all... many even believing it appropriate to *complain* about their lot.'

'You're right... and I admit to having been one of them in the past. But that was before I witnessed what I did.'

After some deliberation, the old man rose and came closer to Chad. Gesturing for his visitor to sit, he settled himself down again on an adjacent plinth. 'You are a very fortunate individual. I wish I'd been privileged enough to see the sphere for myself.'

'The *sphere?* I never used that word. So... you *do* know of it!' said Chad excitedly.

'Of course. We've been waiting a very long time for it to appear.'

'We?'

The old man managed a thin smile, but said nothing.

'The Templars?'

'Among many others. That is why everyone came here the day you and your colleague attempted to eavesdrop on them. They didn't hesitate when invited. They knew time was running out.'

'For what?'

'For what they believe in. For whatever they chose to see on the central plinth.'

'*Chose* to see? I don't understand.'

'It was a call for help to save the Universe from the Universe itself. The power behind it appeared in whatever form it knew they would accept.'

Chad took a few moments to digest what he'd just been told. 'I assume you would've witnessed that spectacle too?'

'I did.'

Chad leant forward eagerly. 'Then... what form did *you* see?'

The old man finally allowed himself a broad smile. 'I saw myself,' he said.

* * *

Donald Tucker-Jenkins remained frozen as the knocking on his door intensified. The postman had already been and he wasn't expecting guests... *ever*. The cats circling around him looked confused, uncertain as to why, if time had stood still, they were still able to wag their tails.

443

'Mister Tucker-Jenkins? Are you in there?' came a voice through the letterbox.

He allowed himself a much-needed breath. *At least it didn't have an American accent.*

'Mister Tucker-Jenkins? I'm led to believe you're at home.'

He paused his breathing again. *Who* had led his visitor?

'I know you're a private man… and probably very busy… but I wonder if I might just have a few minutes of your time.'

The request sounded polite enough. *An enthusiastic fan… perhaps?* 'What do you want?' he called back tentatively.

'A… few minutes of your time,' the voice repeated awkwardly.

'Make it seconds and we have a deal,' Donald negotiated.

There was a brief silence.

'Okay.'

Donald approached the door uneasily. Opening it had got him into trouble before, so he did so with extreme caution.

'Hello,' Norman announced brightly from its other side. 'Have you started the stopwatch?'

'Stopwatch?' mumbled Donald, momentarily disorientated.

'Aren't you timing me?' his visitor smiled, hoping a little brevity might break the ice.

It didn't. Donald stared back blankly.

'I only have a few seconds,' Norman reminded him.

'Then you'd better stop arsing about and get on with it,' retorted Donald.

Norman's smile wavered. 'You once came close to saving my life,' he said, getting straight to the point.

Donald acknowledged the claim with a gracious nod. 'I'm glad you consider my writing that inspirational. Now… if you'll excuse me.' He started to close the door.

'No… *really*,' Norman interjected hastily. 'You tried to save my life… by climbing on the roof of a truck some years ago!'

Donald froze… much to the consternation of the cats again.

'It was me you tried to rescue from that burning building in Armageddon Terrace.' Norman waited for a reaction.

442

When it came, it took him by surprise. As his feet were yanked from the doorstep and pulled into the house, he found himself tumbling on top of Donald, who still had hold of his lapels.

'Yes,' groaned Norman in a state of shock. 'Had I *actually* been in the room at the time, it would probably have gone something like that!' He hadn't expected a re-enactment.

'You never know who's listening!' cried Donald, scrabbling to his feet and slamming the door shut. His eyes bulged as a thought crossed his mind. 'I take it you've come alone?'

'I don't think what *we've* got to discuss is for any other ears,' replied Norman, turning his head away from a cat that was trying to lick one of *his*.

'Don't worry… you can trust Mendelssohn implicitly,' said Donald, referring to the creature. He looked at his horizontal guest apprehensively. 'You know then… don't you?'

'About?'

Donald squinted. '*You* tell *me*.'

'Your sudden creative ability?'

Donald bit a knuckle and squealed.

'Don't worry… Your secret's safe with me,' Norman assured him. He turned his head back towards the cat. 'And Mendelssohn.'

Donald glanced around nervously. 'I can't believe you're actually here in my house!'

'I can't believe I'm on your floor,' said Norman.

'My head's been bombarded with chatter about whatever it is you've been up to for more time than I care to remember. You've caused me incalculable sleepless nights, I'll have you know.'

'And first ones,' Norman pointed out, sitting up.

'I beg your pardon?'

'First nights… of your plays.'

'I'll put the kettle on,' said Donald indignantly, indicating he felt they were scant consolation. 'We've an awful lot to talk about.' He turned and made for the kitchen.

As his visitor stood up and followed, it became apparent the playwright inhabited a world completely different to everyone else… and far more troubled. Swapping the once-grand entrance hall for an adjoining corridor, Norman found himself having to dodge hundreds of small scribbled notes taped to newspaper and magazine cuttings, suspended at head height on strings hanging from its ceiling.

'My filing cabinet,' Donald explained as he did the same.

'Research for your next play?' enquired Norman, trying his best to normalise the situation.

'There isn't going to be a next one,' Donald replied. '*An English Jericho* was my last.'

'Really? Have you run out of ideas?' Norman had no idea how much a chunk of the original sphere of knowledge Donald had received.

'I've run out of *time*,' the playwright answered ominously.

Norman wondered if he was terminally ill. He certainly looked it. With sallow cheeks, matted hair and sunken eyes, he appeared much the same as his publicity photographs. But there was a disturbing weariness about him that took things to a whole new level.

'I *KNOW* HE THINKS I'M MAD!' Donald shouted, disappearing through a door to his left.

Norman glanced down at the cat trailing him, unsure as to which of them the comment had been aimed.

The cat didn't appear to care, having long since given up interpreting his master's outbursts.

Following, and entering an approximation of a kitchen… so filthy, Norman would've previously deemed such a thing impossible… he instinctively retched. He'd noticed a nauseous smell the minute the front door had opened. Finding its source made his eyes water.

'I admit it gets a little stuffy in here,' said Donald, in response. 'But it's far too dangerous to open the windows these days.'

Norman thought it more hazardous *not* to. He also wondered why the oven door had been sealed with packing tape.

Donald abruptly stopped what he was doing. 'I take it you've come in peace?' he asked, his hand poised above the kettle. 'I didn't think to ask.'

Norman considered a sensible assassin would've delayed an answer until *after* they'd enjoyed their cup of tea.

'Only... I took it for granted that anyone those two American agents wanted to harm must be on the same side as me.'

Norman felt reality stagger even further from his comfort zone. Xanthia had filled him in on Chad and Bob's exploits. 'You know those guys?' he exclaimed.

'We're close enough to have wrestled on a number of occasions,' Donald replied. He pulled two cracked mugs from a cluttered sink and ran them under the tap. 'I assume it was you responsible for that ball of light at Stonehenge recently,' he added casually.

Norman's incredulity overflowed. 'You wouldn't happen to know a Xanthia as well, would you?' he gasped.

'I can't say I do,' said Donald, scratching his head. 'Is he a friend of yours?'

'Let's just say... we've done more than wrestle.'

'I make no judgements,' said Donald stoically.

'How come you know about the Stonehenge connection? Besides... everyone else thinks it's a hoax.'

'It looked pretty real to me,' said Donald.

'You were *there?*'

'Of course... trying to save your life for a *second* time. I recognised it as the same thing that struck me the night I clambered up to your window. You don't experience many things like *that* in a lifetime.'

Norman was struggling to keep up. 'It sounds like you've been more involved in my journey than I thought.'

'Which merits a full explanation, wouldn't you say? It would certainly be a great relief to finally put all the pieces together and understand the bigger picture.'

'I obviously owe you that much,' Norman nodded. 'I promise everything will finally make sense and you'll be able to get back to sleeping soundly at night.'

Donald looked at him with a mix of astonishment and horror. 'Are you *serious?* You saw my filing cabinet! What on *earth* do you think *that* was all about?'

Norman hadn't a clue... but hoped he was about to find out.

* * *

'You're not going to tell me you're God... *are* you?' Chad exclaimed. 'Only... when I said I believed you were more than a caretaker with an overenthusiastic broom, I didn't quite have *that* in mind!'

The old man seemed unfazed by the ridicule. 'In our true form, we are *all* God. It's the reason the sphere spoke so strongly to you. As a condensed version of the Universal mind, you instinctively recognised it as part of you and you a part of it. But as soon as it disappeared, your soul found itself returned to more familiar surroundings... that intuitive connection obscured by the distraction of the physical. That is why... unfettered by material shackles... I saw *myself* on the plinth.'

Chad considered the explanation. 'In that case... how come so many of the world's religious leaders didn't do the same that day? Surely they were better placed to understand the nature of God than you.'

The old man placed his hands on his thighs and prepared to stand. 'I wish you a safe journey home. Try not to make too much of a mess of the courtyard when you leave. This summer sun is not conducive to hours of sweeping... especially at my age.'

'Woah!' said Chad, rising anxiously ahead of him. 'We're not done yet. I still have so many questions to ask!'

The old man got to his feet. 'Of course you do.' He met his visitor's impassioned stare with a look of disappointment. 'That's because you don't hear the answers. I thought your experience with the sphere marked you out as someone ready to accept them. I thought perhaps it had sent you here. It appears I was wrong.'

'No... you weren't!' Chad insisted. 'I *have* to know what's going on!'

The old man remained unmoved. 'Your soul already *does* know... but your head is getting in its way. It's an increasingly common trait these days.'

Chad raised his hands in contrition and took a polite step back. 'Okay... you're right. I apologise if my manner of questioning lacked sensitivity. I'm afraid old habits die hard. I'm just desperate for answers. This is all so new to me and against *everything* I've ever believed. I'm struggling with the possibility that the only thing that might make sense of who and what I am is something that doesn't make sense at all! If my head lost your trust, at least give my soul the benefit of the doubt. I'm trying to make amends for a lifetime spent ignoring it. Surely that's worth a second chance?' He looked at the old man imploringly. '*Please.*'

The old man kept his stare.

'You said you thought the sphere might've sent me here. Well... I reckon there's something in that, given I've encountered it on two separate occasions now. That's *gotta* mean something.'

The old Man's expression instantly changed. '*Twice,* you say?'

'Yeah. The first time it exploded. I guess something must've gone wrong.'

'The *second* attempt,' the old man mumbled to himself.

'Second? You mean... there was *another* one before that?'

The old man shook his head. 'It's of no importance.' He studied Chad with a renewed intensity. 'Maybe I was right after all. Perhaps you *are* destined to be here. God does not do coincidences... not on *that* scale.'

Chad resisted voicing his *connection beyond coincidence* mantra, deeming it better to leave the old man to his thoughts.

After some deliberation, a gesture was given for them both to sit again.

The old man drew an authoritative breath. 'The sphere you felt an affinity with at Stonehenge was created to help us in a battle we are currently losing. I believe you've been chosen to help in some way. But, before we proceed further, you must understand this... I am not a teacher. I am a guardian of truths. Arguing against them invalidates the very argument itself. They are above the need for justification. You sought me out... it was not I who sought you. It is not my place to tell you what you must think. But, if you ask me, I will tell you what you *should* think. It is for you alone to appreciate the difference and decide your course of action. Freewill is the greatest gift of spirit. That is one of the truths. But it works both ways. I do not wish to waste my time trying to convince you.' His eyes locked on to Chad's. 'Do we fully understand each other?'

The question returned a nod of compliance.

'Good. Then, we can begin.' He took a moment to settle himself. 'In answer to your initial question... none of the world's religious leaders saw themselves on the plinth because they understandably saw what they have spent a lifetime conditioning themselves to see. It was their *interpretation* of the truth. That does not mean they were wrong. But I am fortunate enough to have access to a source far more enlightening than all their texts and scriptures combined. It is the closest mankind has yet come to the mind of what it calls God.'

Chad leant forward excitedly. 'Is that source here?'

The old man shook his head. 'No. It is kept in a place where it can be more easily accessed.'

'*Kept?* Then do I assume we're talking about a *physical* thing?'

'We are. I'm referring to what the Templar knights named the *Magnum Compendium Secretorum*... an encyclopaedia compiled from a collection of ancient texts containing knowledge passed down from a time when souls were closer to their source and percipient of powerful truths long since forgotten.'

'A book?'

'The greatest of its kind.'

'But wait a minute,' Chad frowned. 'If *that's* the case... how come the whole world hasn't gotten to hear about this... *Magnum*... whatever it's called?'

'The *Magnum Compendium Secretorum*.'

'Yeah.'

The old man's eyebrows rose slightly. 'I think you'll find the clue lies in its title. And it's imperative it remains a secret. Given its contents, it is essential this great treasure is only ever viewed by those who would seek to use it responsibly. Such potent knowledge can be used for evil just as much as for good. Another truth is that we are at the mercy of an ever-changing balance between the two. If the *Magnum Compendium Secretorum* ever fell into the wrong hands, the consequences could prove cataclysmic. That is why it is guarded so carefully.'

'By the Templars themselves,' acknowledged Chad. 'Now everything makes sense. I assume it accounts for those secrets they were rumoured to have discovered and brought to Europe many centuries ago?'

'Your assumption is correct. Tales of the original texts' existence reached the knights' ears when first arriving in the Holy Lands. Said to have been buried in antiquity by their last owner to prevent any misuse after their death, they were believed to have lain hidden for thousands of years. The Templars realised that whoever did such a thing would've been seen in their time as wise beyond the normal abilities of mortals. The knowledge they contained would have also made them *extremely* powerful. Not only would they have been a great ruler, they would have been viewed as a magician by some, possessing the ability to harness spirits, both good and bad. After that individual's demise, whatever great empire it enabled them to build would have quickly collapsed, given that knowledge could no longer be called upon to sustain it.

Scouring the great names of history, the knights concluded there was only one possible contender.'

Chad's widening eyes awaited the reveal.

'The great King Solomon. That is why they spent many years secretly digging beneath the Temple Mount in Jerusalem, a place many believe to be the site of his old temple. In order to provide a smokescreen for their actions… knowing the truth about them searching for something would eventually come to light… the rumour was seeded that they were looking for the Holy Grail and Arc of the Covenant. But what they *really* sought was of far greater value.'

'And explains why the Templars became so powerful, so quickly, on their return home,' interjected Chad.

'And why they were ultimately brought down with even greater speed,' the old man added, the pain of that fall momentarily visible on his face. 'What they were thought to know was considered heretical by those in power at the time, given it was said to amount to a scientific explanation of God.'

'Scientific?'

'A deeper understanding of the principles involved that didn't insist merely on blind faith. Underpinning that excoriation was a fear that if such understanding filtered through to the populace, those claiming authority in God's name would instantly lose their power. That is why the order was given to take the Templars by surprise, before they could prepare and defend themselves.'

'Friday the thirteenth,' nodded Chad, recalling Professor Hummingbone's lecture to him and Bob on the subject.

'Precisely. But though the larger Templar movement was decimated by the gratuitous actions of that day, those guarding the *Magnum Compendium Secretorum* managed to escape with their treasure and keep it hidden. On realising they'd failed to capture the source of the Templars' power, their persecutors set about destroying all references to it, so as not to appear weak and vulnerable. But by erasing knowledge of the *Compendium's* existence from history, they inadvertently ensured its secrets were kept safe.'

'Only known to you.'

'We have guarded that wisdom ever since.'

Chad examined the vast space around him. 'So where does this temple fit into that story? Why go to the trouble of building it in such a remote location if not to hide the *Compendium*? Why bother creating such an awesome effect with the crystals in its walls if so few people got the chance to appreciate it?'

The old man drew an uneasy breath. 'The answer to that lies in the fact not all of the *Compendium's* contents are decipherable. Some of the original texts were written in an obscure and unfathomable code... the means to unlock it rumoured to have been buried elsewhere as a precaution against what are said to be the greatest and most powerful secrets of all being revealed... another example of Solomon's great wisdom. Known as the *Detromunkos*, that cipher has never been located, despite many centuries of searching. Only when the two parts come together will the *Compendium's* full potential be realised. Only *then* might we be able to glimpse the actual mind of God!' His eyes glistened at the prospect. 'That lighting effect you cleverly recreated... though impressive... was but a poor example of the potential contained within the crystals placed around these walls. The sun's energy was not skilfully fragmented merely to provide an annual light show for pilgrims. It was done... utilising knowledge from the *Compendium*... to activate the crystals themselves, much like the stones at Stonehenge when the solstice rays initiated a chain reaction that created the sphere. The competing frequencies focused above this central plinth temporarily produce a confluence of dimensions... allowing the highest beings from the spiritual realm to be directly communicated with. It was hoped they could be persuaded to divulge the parts of the *Compendium* the Templars had been unable to decipher... or the location of the *Detromunkos*... so that those secrets could be used to benefit mankind.'

'And did they agree to help?'

The old man sighed. 'No... and without explanation. Instead, it was said that a new saviour... possessing the gift of all knowledge... would be sent to guide this world to an era of enlightenment.' He looked forlornly at the silent walls around him. 'Despite that individual's failure to appear at the promised time... causing this temple's occupants to abandon their work here... there are those of us who have waited patiently... our hope the only thing to sustain us.'

'Until now,' said Chad, breaking into a broad grin. 'That's what all this is about, isn't it? That sphere of light I witnessed at Stonehenge really *has* given Xanthia the powers she's claiming! Contrary to the ridicule being rained down on her, she's telling the truth!' He shook his head in total disbelief. 'Well, I'll be damned. She experienced the sphere like I did, but has managed to retain what she felt.' He took a moment to process everything. 'So... was it *you* who summoned everyone to that meeting my partner and I were sent to eavesdrop on?'

'Those I serve. They realised the spirit world was in desperate need of help. With paranormal disturbances and abnormal activity increasing day by day, the world's religious leaders realised it too. Everyone could see a time of change was upon us. That's why they agreed to travel to this place... knowing that any message received would be one they couldn't ignore.'

Chad leant forward in anticipation. 'What *was* that message?'

'To use their power and influence to facilitate the collection of works of art containing information necessary to build a second sphere of knowledge.'

'Information?'

'Data encoded within the artworks. Once transferred to a network of computers, it could be used to generate the vibrations necessary for creating that sphere.'

As the long-troubled cogs of his mind *finally* lined up and engaged, Chad dropped his head back and let out a series of startling cries... a mixture of laughter and relief filling the empty temple. 'After all these years... *now* I finally understand what Norman Penkridge was up to!' Grinning from ear to ear, he resisted the urge to embrace the old man. 'He *wasn't* acting out of greed. He *wasn't* seeking material gain. He was attempting something *unbelievably* worthy! And he never gave up... because I assume it was Norman who was responsible for the creation of that sphere at Stonehenge.' He let out a further exclamation of relief. 'Thank *god* I failed to stop him!'

'God will, indeed, have had something to do with it,' the old man nodded.

Chad raised his hands in celebration. 'Which means Xanthia's the one you've been waiting for all these years.'

The old man looked at him in silence.

Chad's hands fell. *'Doesn't* it?'

A pained expression crossed the old man's face. 'The truth is... we don't know. For some reason, she hasn't made contact with us... and time is running out.'

'Are you expecting her to come here?'

'There's no reason why she should.'

Chad registered his confusion. 'Then why are *you* still here?'

The old man sighed with the weight of many years. 'I wish it weren't so. I was hoping to be this temple's final guardian. My dream has always been to enjoy such simple pleasures as greenery again... and to feel a wind that *isn't* sapped of its power on my face before I depart this life. But duty demands I remain until we can be certain this place is no longer needed.'

'And when will that be?'

The old man looked at Chad apprehensively. 'When we know, beyond fine words, what Xanthia *really* intends doing with the immeasurable power she's been given.'

* * *

A rare look of calm transformed Donald's face. Leaning back in his battered armchair, he permitted a half-smile to take advantage of the situation. 'The truth is far stranger than I ever imagined,' he said, shaking his head. 'But just as well it is. I wouldn't have worried *half* so much if I'd known such exalted

431

help was on our side!' He patted the pockets of a threadbare waistcoat to locate his pipe before realising he'd never smoked one.

Insisting on hearing Norman's side of the story before giving his, he'd eagerly savoured every morsel of information imparted… nodding profusely to himself as yet another piece of the jigsaw fell into place.

'I told you it was quite a story,' Norman beamed.

Donald shook his head again. 'They all sensed something big was about to happen. But I had no idea of its magnitude or significance. No wonder the traffic around me was so frenetic!'

'From the spirit world?'

'Of course,' said Donald, looking perplexed. 'I hardly think the village by-pass has anything to do with this.' He gave a sigh. 'I was starting to worry people would think I was mad.'

Norman shot a reflex glance at the man's curious footwear… a stained moccasin and an exploded slipper.

'And you, young man…' He looked at Norman enviously. 'You should feel *extremely* honoured to have communicated with such a formidable vibration!'

'Gabriel?' clarified Norman, no longer able to take anything for granted.

'Whatever,' replied Donald dismissively. '*I'm* forced to make do with a far *lesser* one.' His eyes immediately shot upwards and stared just beyond his frown. 'I'M *NOT* BEING ELITIST! I DIDN'T SAY THERE *WAS* ANYTHING WRONG WITH BEING A FISHERMAN!' He tutted loudly. 'ALRIGHT, THEN… *TRAWLERMAN!*'

Norman waited for the spat to subside. He'd got used to such interruptions… sitting patiently while Donald and his spirit guide traded points over who had been closest to guessing the truth during various stages of his explanation. 'Do you actually *see* him?' he asked, when this particular one was over.

'Whitebait?'

'Yes.'

'Not in the sense you saw your Gabriel. He doesn't possess anywhere *near* that level of influence.'

Norman recognised the signs of yet another fracas about to erupt as Donald's eyes shot skywards.

'I'M SURE YOU WERE... BACK IN THE DAY!' the playwright yelled.

Something was clearly returned.

'IT *WASN'T* SARCASM!' Donald shouted. 'BUT THANK YOU FOR REMINDING ME. I'D ACTUALLY FORGOTTEN YOU *OWNED* THE BOAT.'

Norman wished the bickering would stop. It was *his* turn now. There was so much he wanted to ask and time was pressing.

'I'm awfully sorry about this,' his host apologised. 'Whitebait and I have an extreme love-hate relationship. As in... we love to hate each other to the extreme. Unfortunately, I'm stuck with him. A bit like ugly toes or a Habsburg chin.'

Norman smiled politely. 'Don't worry. I've become accustomed to *far* stranger things by now.'

'Yes... I guess you have,' said Donald. 'I suppose it all initially came as quite a shock. There's so much going on outside our normal lives we're completely unaware of... which is just as well. As the forces assembling against us are daunting, your news has come as a *huge* relief. At least now I can continue my work knowing we've been given someone powerful enough to help us battle those dark energies.' He looked at Norman eagerly. 'This Xanthia of yours... I expect she's busy planning her next move.'

Norman returned a grimace.

Donald's hands gripped the worn arms of his chair. 'Is there something wrong?'

Norman didn't like to say. Speaking aloud an extremely negative thought he'd entertained in a moment of anger, about the woman he loved, not only seemed dishonourable but in danger of making it real. 'Let's just say she's not exactly in a hurry,' he compromised.

'Not in a hurry!' Donald exclaimed. 'What on *earth* is she waiting for? There's very little time left! The world is becoming swamped by evil. I was beginning to fear it was too late altogether!'

'Believe me, I'm with you on that one,' Norman sympathised. 'But, for a reason I've yet to fathom, she doesn't seem to share our sense of urgency.'

Donald's previously found optimism drained from his face and was replaced by a look suggesting he was wrestling with his thoughts.

Norman waited patiently.

After a short time, the playwright's eyes widened. 'Wait a minute!' he gasped. '*Surely* not.' His look turned to one of consternation.

'What's the matter?'

Shaking himself from his thoughts, Donald stared at his guest as if having said too much. 'Don't you want to ask me about the messages?' he swerved.

'Messages?'

'These,' said Donald, pointing up at a further forest of notes hanging from his drawing room ceiling. 'I'm sorry. Perhaps you hadn't noticed.'

Norman could no longer assume Donald was being sarcastic. In truth, he hadn't liked to mention them, preferring to pretend out of politeness that such a thing was perfectly reasonable. 'Your filing cabinet,' he clarified, underlining his willingness to accept the bizarre situation.

'Just one of many,' offered Donald. 'As well as those other messages you encountered in the hall corridor, there are countless more in my study, five of the bedrooms, Nanny's old bathroom… and the driest part of the potting shed.'

Norman wasn't sure how to respond. 'What was wrong with the kitchen?' was the best he could come up with.

'Fire hazard,' Donald explained.

Norman pretended it all made sense. 'I couldn't help noticing the strings have been painted various colours,' he said nonchalantly, as if that was the only strange thing about them.

'It'd be a pretty unusual filing cabinet if they hadn't!' Donald exclaimed. 'How else would I be able to keep track of everything?'

Norman might've had more chance of answering that question if he'd actually understood what it was Donald was trying to keep track of in the first place.

His host signalled for him to stand. 'Go on, young man... pick one. THOUGH NOT A *RED* STRING!' he shouted hastily, with a raised palm and desperate eyes.

Keen to satisfy his curiosity, Norman stood up and did as instructed. Choosing the one nearest his head... suspended on a blue string... he struggled to decipher what was written on it. 'Bomunsa Temple... Seokmodo Island,' he read aloud.

The scrawled note was stapled to an article about the site, torn from a travel magazine.

'Situated off the coast of South Korea and allegedly attacked by vandals,' expanded Donald. 'It's suffered so much damage, experts believe they'll never be able to put it right. Now... pick another... another *blue* one.'

Norman took hold of a corresponding string, careful not to pull it from the ceiling. 'The Tikal archaeological ruins... Petén Jungle... Guatemala.'

'Also reportedly attacked by vandals... as all the sites hanging from strings coded blue have been.' Donald leant forward thoughtfully. 'Though I think it safe to say... I doubt mere *vandals* would've bothered to hack their way through such formidable terrain in that last instance.'

'I'm very aware of these occurrences!' said Norman animatedly. 'Such desecrations are taking place all around the world. I've been following it on the news. My theory is that most are the work of copycats... only the first few having been influenced by Satan. That's how he works... by suggestion. I believe it's his way of attacking people's beliefs and igniting others' prejudices. You turn monuments of faith into billboards for rebellion against it! I think he's trying to recruit an army here on Earth, having failed to have a greater one flood in through the portal at Stonehenge.'

Donald looked at him, unmoved. 'Is *that* what you think?'

Norman nodded.

'And what does Xanthia say?'

'She doesn't,' replied Norman.

Donald cast a brooding glance to where a large section of red strings hung. 'That's what I was worried about.'

'So what do *they* represent?' asked Norman, following his gaze.

'All in good time,' Donald answered awkwardly. 'Now... take a look at the purple ones.'

Accepting he was going to require some patience, Norman examined those nearest him. 'They're just numbers,' he said, looking back at Donald.

'Coordinates, actually.'

'For what?'

Donald rubbed his stubble. 'I'm working on that.'

'And the green?'

'Newspaper reports of unusual occurrences... especially those considered to be of a *supernatural* nature.'

'And yellow?'

'Sayings and quotes that keep gatecrashing my thoughts... just like five years ago... only *far* darker and greater in number this time.' He bowed his head as if struggling with the weight of them all.

Norman noticed one colour in particular vastly outnumbered the others. He turned his attention to a clutch of them. 'What do these black ones represent?'

Donald lifted his chin courageously. 'They'll be the threats.'

Norman thought it best to move swiftly on. 'And *that?*' he asked, pointing to a solitary pink string hanging by the door in the corner.

'My weekly shopping list,' squinted Donald.

As Norman's eyes scanned the room for another colour... other than red... they were beckoned by the hands of a grandfather clock in the corner. 'Is that the time?' he exclaimed in horror. 'I had no idea it was so late! How did *that* happen? I'm gonna miss my train!'

'You've run out of time and must now die!' announced Donald loudly from behind him.

'*What?*' Norman's blood froze as an image of the large kitchen knife Donald had used to cut him a slice of stale carrot cake half an hour earlier flashed across his mind.

'IF YOU MEDDLE IN THE AFFAIRS OF THE SPIRIT WORLD, YOU CAN EXPECT TO BE DESPATCHED TO IT!' shouted Donald.

Norman spun around to see him holding a note attached to one of the black strings.

'You can see the sort of thing I have to put up with,' Donald sighed wearily.

Norman allowed himself a breath again.

'If I've caused you to miss your train, you're welcome to stay the night and catch one in the morning,' offered Donald. 'After all... we still have much to talk about.'

Though such a prospect disturbed him, Norman didn't see he had any choice.

'As all the other bedrooms have been turned over to my filing system, you can sleep in my parents' old room,' Donald suggested. 'The bed hasn't been slept in since they died... but you're more than welcome to be the first.'

Norman looked at him apprehensively.

'Oh, don't worry,' Donald smiled. 'They didn't actually die *in* it! Mind you... I think Mother would've quite liked that. She was always scared of heights. I often wondered if she appreciated the irony in those few, brief seconds before...' He froze in a moment of time, then shook himself from his thoughts. 'Anyway... that was many years ago... before I realised there was such a thing as pain in the world. I think they'll be pleased I'm finally making use of it again.'

'Well... if you don't mind,' said Norman awkwardly.

'No problem at all. I haven't changed the sheets, but Mother was always extremely clean. So I advise you sleep on the left, as Father could sweat quite a bit.'

Norman realised he'd been wrong to assume nothing Donald could say or do could shock him anymore.

'Perhaps I should fix us something to eat,' said Donald, brightening up. 'I'm going to need some energy if I'm to tell you *my* side of the story.'

'And then do I get to know what the red strings represent?'

Donald's cheeriness instantly evaporated. 'You may not want to,' he replied soberly.

Had Norman known that Donald's idea of fixing something to eat was to pour out-of-date tinned custard over the remaining carrot cake, he'd have opted to go to bed hungry.

Consoling himself with the fact that at least he was getting to hear how Donald came to save his life... *twice*... he listened avidly as those circumstances were revealed via equal measures of enthusiasm and anguish. The anguish was exacerbated by Donald's spirit guide constantly challenging the accuracy of his conduit's recollections, in an apparent attempt to build his own part.

When it got to the bit about Donald wrestling with Bob beneath the sphere of knowledge at Stonehenge, Norman asked if he'd been aware of Xanthia standing there when it was transferred to her.

Hearing her name mentioned again, Donald looked at him uncomfortably and replied that he'd been too transfixed by the sphere to notice what else had gone on around him.

'I wish I'd seen it myself,' said Norman. 'It must've been quite a sight.'

'Out of this world,' said Donald. '*Literally.*'

'Quite ironic, really,' Norman mused. 'I did all that work to ensure it happened and missed out on the most important part of all!'

'I think that's still to come,' counselled Donald. 'Talking of which... I think we should get some sleep. We need to be at our best tomorrow if we're to stand a chance of figuring out our next move.'

'Move for what?'

Donald stared at Norman with surprise. 'Countering the red strings, of course!'

'But you still haven't told me what they represent.'

'You're right. I haven't.' Donald's eyes shot upwards to a now familiar place in his thoughts. 'HOW ON EARTH CAN I TELL HIM,' he yelled. 'HE'LL HAVE NIGHTMARES!'

'Donald?'

'All in good time.'

'But...'

'We'll continue this discussion in the morning. It's late.'

At the mention of time, Norman's eyes strayed towards the grandfather clock... then narrowed. 'Donald,' he said slowly. 'Your clock's showing *exactly* the same time as before.'

'I'd be shocked if it didn't,' said Donald, matter-of-factly. 'It doesn't work. I haven't seen its hands move since I was a young man.'

'But I thought...'

Donald looked at him expectantly.

Norman rubbed his forehead. 'Never mind,' he sighed, resigning himself to his fate. It was *definitely* too late to catch his train now.

'That was Father's favourite timepiece,' said Donald. 'He loved and cherished it more than he did Mother. But here's the strangest thing...' His eyes widened ominously. 'The very day after he died, its pendulum stopped swinging and has never swung since!'

Though not considering himself an expert, Norman had owned a few antique ones of his own back in France. 'Have you thought about having the winding mechanism looked at?' he suggested.

Donald stared at him, nonplussed. 'The *what?*'

*　　*　　*

As the constellation of stars Alien One thought looked like an outstretched hand... if you discounted fingers eight and eleven... rose in the sky below the larger constellation resembling a head in profile, he remarked that, with a little

423

imagination, the whole thing looked like someone picking their nose.

Aliens Two and Three looked at him, perplexed.

Picking it for *what?*

Alien One nodded in defeat and admitted they had a good point.

Alien Two shifted uncomfortably and announced he had a problem.

Alien One enquired as to what it was.

Alien Two replied that it was *him*. Everything had been fine until Alien One had decided to introduce the ideas of joking and God. Not only could he now be the butt of something... he realised there was a possibility he could cease to exist if someone he couldn't see took a dislike to him.

Alien One thought he'd already solved that problem by finding a way to placate a vindictive God without resorting to sacrificing each other.

Alien Three agreed that having them constantly affirm out loud that God was better than them was, indeed, a clever solution. The trouble was... it could get a little tedious.

Alien Two agreed. Besides... it was stopping him from doing other things.

Alien One took a long, hard look around the desolate landscape and then back at Alien Two.

Alien Two said Alien One's raised middle eyebrow was unnecessary. He would think of *something*.

Alien Three said at least Alien Two had all the time in the world to do so... minus that spent affirming God was better than them, of course.

Alien Two said Alien Three had clearly missed the point. He *didn't* have all the time in the world. Due to the realisation he was now mortal, he only had a fraction of it. That's why he didn't want to waste any.

Alien One took another long, hard look around the desolate landscape and spent the next three days considering Alien Two's options.

During that time, Alien Two took the opportunity – between affirming God was better than them – to deride Alien One for creating a situation where he had to affirm God's superiority… and appear not to be joking while doing so.

That gave Alien One an idea. He announced that Alien Two could use one of his two recent creations to fashion a career.

Alien Two's eyes lit up. Was he to become God's representative on their planet, ensuring God's superiority was affirmed correctly and sincerely?

As the constellation of stars Alien One thought looked like two splayed fingers rose slowly above the horizon, he shook his head.

No. He could become a comedian.

*   *   *

With Donald resolutely refusing to divulge the significance of the red strings, Norman had opted to lighten the mood before going to bed by following Xanthia's advice and asking to see the playwright's attempts at painting. His curiosity aroused, he was pleased to be indulging in his favourite subject.

'They're really quite good,' he said, rifling through a selection stacked against the far wall of Donald's study. 'You should have them on display around the house rather than hidden away in here.'

'Oh, they're not *that* good,' said Donald coyly. 'I think you're being kind.'

He was right, of course. But Donald had certainly given them his best shot, and there was something about them that grabbed the attention of the beholder.

'Did you go to art school?'

'Never held a brush before,' said Donald.

The admission came as a surprise. 'Other than in conjunction with a dustpan, that is,' Norman joked.

Donald looked at him blankly. 'Nope. Never done that *either.*'

That admission *didn't* come as a surprise.

Norman tilted his head. 'They look vaguely familiar. Were you trying to copy the great masters?'

Donald sniffed indignantly. 'They're all my own work,' he said stiffly.

'I understand. Only… this one looks a little like Gustave Courbet's *The Wounded Man.*'

'Never heard of either of them,' said Donald. 'I simply painted what my muse was trying to convey. It all happened after I got struck by a piece of that sphere of knowledge. Of course, it all makes sense now… my overwhelming urge to express myself in some form or another. But, as you can see… I lacked the finer skills to do it properly in paint. That's why I turned to writing. You've only got to know how to hold a pen. As soon as I discovered *that* outlet, the budding artist in me took a back seat.'

'I can see what bits of inspiration you were trying to convert,' smiled Norman. 'This one looks like an attempt to replicate Klimt's *The Tree of Life*…. and this one… Goya's *Saturn Devouring His Son.*'

'You can have a couple if you like,' said Donald. 'Help you start your collection again.'

Norman didn't know what to say… though "no thanks" was waving hard at him.

'I think I'd have trouble getting them on the train,' he smiled.

'OF *COURSE* HE'S BEING POLITE!' shouted Donald. 'DO YOU THINK I'M A *COMPLETE* IDIOT?'

* * *

Had he known that Donald – when whispering "don't let the bed bugs bite" on closing the bedroom door – had not so much been expressing a polite inanity but an actual warning, Norman would have courteously thanked him for the offer of a room for the night and promptly started walking back to London.

As he stood in front of the mottled mirror examining his itching body, the red bites that peppered his torso seemed to spell the word *IDIOT*… with those on his arms and legs looking suspiciously like the word *DITTO*.

He'd hardly slept a wink… the strangest night time noises having kept him awake for most of it. Even when he'd succumbed to tiredness, his sleep had been peppered with vivid nightmares that had left him feeling drained.

The carpet beneath him seemed little more than its own memory, there being more carpet mites involved in it than actual carpet. Its original pattern long since forgotten, the new one appeared to be on the move.

What had survived of the bed sheet and mattress didn't bear thinking about, thanks to Tucker-Jenkins senior's overactive sweat glands. He'd also cut his toenails in bed, judging from what Norman found embedded in the backs of his legs… their late owner's pyjamas having been sensibly declined when offered by Donald.

Remaining mementos left about the room to commemorate an abruptly curtailed existence had been explored by mice on so many occasions, the resulting droppings now took up more space in the room than its previous occupants ever had.

Norman was glad to leave it, closing the door as quietly as possible so as not to wake his host… his face scrunched tight with the effort.

'I trust you'll be wanting some breakfast,' boomed Donald from behind him.

Norman gripped his chest.

'OF *COURSE* HE WAS GOING TO TAKE A PEEK! WHY D'YA THINK I'VE BEEN STANDING HERE ALL NIGHT?'

'What the fu_! You nearly gave me a heart attack!'

'Heaven forbid,' huffed Donald. 'I *need* you.'

Norman exhaled heavily to compose himself. 'In that case… you ought to start trusting me.'

Donald looked confused. 'What makes you think I don't?'

'You standing here in the corridor all night… worried I was going to take a look at those red stringed messages. I just heard you.'

'Ah,' Donald smiled. 'Hoisted by your own petard! I neither mentioned red nor strings. So you've obviously been thinking about it.'

Norman blushed.

'I think you need a cup of tea,' said Donald, striding off in the direction of the stairs. 'Come on... we have much to plan.'

'Can Xanthia read your mind?' Donald asked, placing an anaemic-looking brew in front of Norman.

'She says she can't.'

'That's not what I asked.'

Norman flicked a disorientated ant from the handle of the cup. 'Why would she lie?'

Donald considered the question. 'Well... there could be many reasons... an innocent one being so that you don't feel uncomfortable when you're around her.'

'And a *non*-innocent one?'

'Do you want a biscuit?'

Having seen the condition of the tin they were being offered in, Norman declined. Besides, he sensed it was being done as a diversion. 'But it's not just reading *my* mind we're talking about, is it? That ability would surely extend to everybody else's.'

'It would.'

'Well, in that case... she *definitely* can't. Not only did she fail to read Stump's reluctance to support her when they appeared together on that chat show... she didn't know he was about to disgrace himself in front of the audience and ruin her chances of being taken seriously.'

'You mean... you *assume* she didn't.'

Norman stared at Donald askance. 'What are you saying?'

Donald looked away innocently. 'Nothing more than you already have.'

'I simply said she didn't share our sense of urgency,' Norman insisted.

Donald stared back at him. 'And you don't find that *odd?*'

'Well... a little.'

418

'OF *COURSE* HE'S HOLDING BACK! I'VE SEEN THE DEEPER CONCERN IN HIS EYES. HE'S SCARED SHITLESS... BUT UNABLE TO SEE THE WOOD FOR THE TREES BECAUSE HE LOVES HER SO MUCH.'

'What wood?'

'*You* tell *me*. You're the one looking for answers.' Donald leant forward assertively. 'Why didn't you stay in London and help Xanthia plan her next move? You clearly think she needs help.'

'I thought it best to get away for a day,' Norman stammered, unsettled by the sudden aggressive line of questioning.

'Was that your idea?'

'Of course!'

Donald interrogated him with a knowing stare.

'Alright... *No*. It was Xanthia's. But she thought it would do me good.'

'And has it?'

'Not really. I'm now more confused than ever!'

'So why send you here if she's all-knowing?'

The question stopped Norman in his tracks. Donald was right. If Xanthia knew absolutely everything, she would have realised that meeting the playwright would be far from the relaxing and refreshing experience she said he needed.

'You say she only has knowledge of everything up until the transference of the sphere,' Donald clarified, giving it some thought. 'Seeing as most of my messages were received *after* that happened, maybe she sent you here to find out how much I know about the other side's intentions.'

'But why not come here herself and ask you directly?'

'Find the answer to *that* and you might hold the key to why she's behaving like she is.' Donald rubbed his chin. 'So... what *exactly* did she tell you about me?'

'That it was you who tried to save my life... and that you have exceptional psychic abilities.'

'True,' Donald nodded. 'Anything else?'

Norman shook his head. 'Well... nothing other than you'd tried your hand at painting.'

'Why would she mention that?'

'She knows how much I'm into my art. She said it would give us something to talk about.'

'I'd have thought she would know we had *enough* to discuss,' said Donald. 'But fair enough.' He scratched the side of his face. 'You seem to be suggesting Xanthia could've known in advance Stump was going to spoil her interview. Surely that would imply she's *deliberately* trying to fail?'

'That depends,' said Donald.

'On what?'

'If she's failing.'

Norman frowned.

'Well… we are clearly agreed on one thing,' Donald pointed out. 'Her silence is deafening, given all that's going on around us. But her failure to effectively respond to the task she's been set is only baffling if that task is what we think it is.'

'And what else *might* it be?'

Donald wrung his hands. 'That's the bit you're not going to like. I have a theory… though heaven knows I hope I'm wrong.' He stared silently ahead, as if a future where that *wasn't* the case was being enacted in front of him.

'I take it this theory involves red strings,' Norman prodded.

Donald broke from the vision. 'Which is precisely why you can't know about them. If she *can* read minds, it'll prevent us testing her.'

'*Testing?*'

'Of course! How else are we going to read *her* mind?' Donald fumbled about on one of the cluttered work surfaces for the remains of a pencil. 'We'll start with the coordinates… those hanging from purple strings. I'll write a few of them down. Your job will be to ask her what their connection is to one another, for there surely must be one.'

'Have you tried researching them on the internet?'

Donald squinted. 'The *what?*'

Norman stared at him incredulously. 'Never mind.'

'Given she knows everything, she should instantly be able to provide you with an answer. In which case, we'll all be winners.

You can go back to trusting her and I'll be nearer to solving my puzzle.'

'What if there isn't one?'

'Puzzle?'

'Connection.'

'Of course there is, you fool!' Donald gesticulated wildly at his world beyond the kitchen door. 'What on earth do you think all those messages are for?'

Norman refrained from pointing out that Donald didn't know the answer to that either.

'They're all part of the puzzle,' said Donald. 'I just have to work out how everything fits together.'

'And if she *doesn't* give me an answer?'

Donald stabbed a finger at Norman enthusiastically. 'Ah... then we'll know she's hiding something and my theory will be proven correct!' The possibility of that caused a look of triumph to illuminate his face.

'And what will that mean?'

'We're all going to die. Now... I just need to find some paper.'

Ducking and diving past Donald's unorthodox filing cabinet on his way to the front door, Norman wasn't sure he *wanted* to leave the crazy world to which he'd become accustomed. Apart from the relief of being able to share his concerns about Xanthia with someone who understood what he was going through, he wasn't looking forward to his return home. It would require him to behave duplicitously with someone he'd been in love with for most of his life, while putting his trust in a man he'd known less than twenty-four hours.

But as that man had come to his rescue on two separate occasions – all thanks to the weirdness that went on in his head – he'd convinced himself it was justified, given the enormity of what was at stake.

Donald seemed happy to return that trust... clearly unfazed by the possibility of his guest taking a peek at any of the notes hanging from the mysterious red strings as he shuffled ahead of him, a retinue of cats hampering his every move.

Not that Norman wasn't tempted. But he recognised there was method in the playwright's madness.

Stopping at the door, Donald proffered a hand that left Norman wondering if had ever encountered soap. 'Good luck, young man... and be extremely vigilant. I fear the odds are heavily stacked against us.'

'Let's hope your theory about Xanthia is wrong, then,' said Norman, gingerly taking hold of the extended appendage.

'We'll see,' returned Donald diplomatically. 'Talking of whom... there's one other thing you must do. It's *extremely* important.'

Norman waited.

'Ensure she stays away from any form of contact with the media until we know what she's up to. We can't trust her with another platform unless certain about what she'll do with it.' Donald tightened his grip... much to Norman's dismay. 'That's absolutely *crucial*... do you understand?'

Norman nodded.

'Good.' Donald finally let go. 'I'll wait to hear from you.' Acting as if what lay beyond the front door was hazardous to his health, he opened it just enough to push Norman through... then opted to say his final goodbyes via a slit no wider than his eyeball.

'Thank you for the use of your parents' room last night,' said Norman, though only because he'd been brought up well.

'You're most welcome,' Donald blinked. 'You're a far braver man than I!'

Norman gratefully inhaled the fresh air and surveyed his surroundings. 'I don't think what's out here is *that* dangerous... not yet, at least.'

'I was referring to my parents' bedroom,' said Donald, through the narrow crack. 'You wouldn't catch me dead in it!'

For the umpteenth time, Norman didn't know what to say.

'It's recently been hosting a particularly nasty energy. Areas like that are usually best avoided. There's no knowing what damage they can inflict.'

'Right... I'll bear that in mind next time.' Norman scratched himself vigorously. 'It's just a shame you didn't give that advice to the bed bugs.'

The crack widened slightly. 'What on earth are you talking about?'

'These.' Norman lifted his shirt to display the mass of bites covering his body.

Donald's eye narrowed. 'That's curious.'

'Why?'

The crack in the door became even thinner.

'Bed bugs require a host to survive... and no one's set foot in that room for over half a century!'

*　*　*

'What is it with these goddamn flies,' cursed the reverend, swatting them away from his face.

Steven pushed his chair back. 'I'll see if I can get some spray, sir.'

'No. Stay where you are. Let's get this meeting finished. These people are costing me money.' Galveston Humbold gave a conciliatory grin to those he was paying. 'Not that they ain't worth every cent, of course.'

Those doing the charging smiled back politely.

'I also need to get home and start preparing my sermon for Sunday's show.'

Steven pushed a folder across the table. 'Here's the research you asked me to do for it, sir.'

'The Evils of Prostitution,' the reverend announced, patting the proffered information. 'There's no greater temptation for the weak of spirit.'

Nods of agreement were offered.

'Especially when it can be delivered to your door,' he elaborated. 'For the Devil's work is surely made easier for the hungry sinner when the risk of being caught shopping for it out in the open is conveniently removed.'

Further nods acknowledged the wisdom of his words.

'I've ensured the evidence pertains to your own residential area,' said Steven keenly, 'just like you requested.'

'Good boy,' winced the reverend, nodding down his assistant's enthusiasm. He quickly turned to the others. 'As I pointed out to Steven... I need to provide proof to any doubters of the extent of this heinous evil. My sermon will stress the fact that if such sin is taking place in *my* neighbourhood, it'll sure as hell be taking place in *theirs*.'

Heads, this time, remained static.

The reverend tapped his fingers lightly on the file, momentarily transported in thought. 'Am I right in believing this contains names and contact details... for verification purposes?'

'Yes, reverend. In accordance with your remit, they're all young girls offering their services within a five mile radius of your house.'

Galveston Humbold III wiped the sweat from his brow. 'Good. Now... let's get down to our main business and the reason I gathered ya'll here.'

Buttocks shifted in preparation.

'As you know, the Lord God Almighty has drawn my attention to an *outrageous* attempt by Satan to infiltrate those of His flock who are of a more gullible disposition. I believe the Prince of Darkness is using an ungodly woman as a Trojan horse for this evil purpose. Hailing from the United Kingdom of England, she's claiming to have been imbued with some sort of heavenly power that'll help save us all from damnation.'

A hand was raised.

'Yes, Marty?'

'D'ya want us to prepare an injunction? Seems like a clear case of infringement to me.'

The reverend grinned. 'Actually, I *don't*.'

An eyebrow rose. 'But Galveston... we went to a lotta trouble trademarking *Saviour of Mankind* under your name. We could strongly argue in the courts that her claim is similar enough in intent to warrant violation of your legally registered rights.'

'You're not listening, Marty. I don't wanna stop her making those claims.'

The lawyer looked at him incredulously. 'Are you saying she's *right* in her asseveration, then?'

'What the *hell's* one of them?'

'In this case... her claim to be able to save us all from damnation.'

'For the record, Marty... *nobody's* gonna be able to save you. You're a lawyer. But in answer to your question... this one possesses about as much divine power as she does morals. Her claim's as phoney as your hairpiece. But I tell ya'll this... the Devil's definitely gotten inside her skin... and I've examined one heck of a lot of it. So... I need her to keep making those *asseverations.*'

Confused heads turned to one another for support.

'Don't worry, I ain't gone mad,' he snorted. 'Far from it. What I've got in mind is a real humdinger. Not only do I intend putting an end to Satan's diabolical scheme... that shameless harlot's gonna take this church global in the process!'

'You want us to *team up* with her?' exclaimed one of the frowning heads.

'Of course I don't!' the reverend scoffed. 'I wanna *stop* her.'

'But I thought you just said you *didn't*,' interjected Marty, scratching his head... carefully.

Galveston Humbold III held the bridge of his nose. 'Alright... I *did*. But, if ya'll just let me explain without these constant interruptions!'

Given the money he was paying them, heads dutifully lowered.

'Appreciate it.' He leant forward enthusiastically. 'Now... having cunningly latched on to that mass hysteria incident at Stonehenge, this Xanthia has momentarily snared herself a considerable amount of media attention around the globe. Most of it's probably down to folks thinking she's wacko and wanting to know what she'll come out with next... but they're talkin' 'bout her, all the same. I figure I need to get myself a little piece of that action. So we're gonna give her a helping hand and ensure she reaches the biggest audience she possibly can! But... having provided her with the oxygen of publicity... we'll then make her choke on it... and hijack that audience in the process! I'm gonna challenge her to a face-to-face meeting, live on TV. If she refuses, I'll claim victory by default. If she accepts... I'll tear her to pieces before she gets the chance to spread any more of her vile poison. Either way, I'll come out the winner. We'll control the showdown by putting it on our own channel and sell the syndication rights to the rest of the world. If you all do your jobs and guarantee this thing's hyped to the max, we'll take this business to a whole new level! So... I want you to throw everything you've got at it, ladies and gentlemen. We can bill it as *The Clash of the Century*.' He momentarily paused. 'No... better still... make that the clash of the *Millennium!*'

'It's the same thing,' pointed out Marty.

The reverend turned and grinned superciliously. 'Oh, believe me, Marty... when it comes to getting people's juices going, there's definitely a difference. And knowing or not knowing that difference is why you're the lawyer... and I'm the one you're working for.'

*   *   *

'So... where have you been?'

Xanthia lowered the handle of her travel case and pushed it against the wall with her foot. She took a while to form an answer. 'When I realised you'd decided to stay over at Donald's, I heeded my own advice and decided to have a small break myself. Didn't you see my note?'

'The one by the kettle?'

'That'll be a yes, then.'

'It simply said you'd be back soon,' Norman pointed out.

She parenthesised a smile with waving hands. 'Ta dah!'

'But it's been three *days!*'

'Which is the perfect definition of a small break, wouldn't you say? Anyway... I'm glad you missed me. But, far more importantly... how was *your* trip?'

He looked at her guardedly, wondering if she *could* read his mind. 'Let's just say it was... *interesting.*'

Her eyebrows rose at the ensuing silence. 'Aren't you gonna tell me *how* interesting?'

He certainly wasn't.

'To be honest, Xan... it was also extremely exhausting. Donald's a very difficult man to have a conversation with, and it wasn't quite the refreshing break I'd hoped for. If it's all the same to you, I'd rather not have to relive it all. Suffice to say... we talked a lot about our past connection... which I guess you know every detail of anyway.'

She tilted her head. 'Fair enough. But there must have been *some* pleasant moments. Did you get to see his paintings, for instance?'

'They were okay,' he shrugged. 'But I see why he decided to take up writing.'

'Inspiration is a curious thing,' she said. 'Its source is always the same, but it depends on what you do with it.'

She looked at him and smiled... which didn't make it easier for what he was about to do.

'Actually... Donald was wondering if you could help him with a small problem that's cropped up during some important research he's been undertaking.'

She nodded. 'Okay. What's he up to now?'

'Attempting to save the world for a *third* time,' Norman replied.

'That figures!' she laughed.

He took a deep breath for courage. 'Just in case *you* don't.'

She stared at him and blinked.

He awaited her reaction.

'Well, good on him... I could do with all the help I can get.' She lurched towards his face. '*Apparently!*' She held his startled gaze. 'As could you, by the way.'

The coolness with which she delivered the last remark unnerved him.

'And what do you mean by that?'

She stood back. 'Well... I take it you've been following the fallout from my TV appearance the other night.'

'Actually... no. As you'll be aware... Donald consigned his television and radio to a pond in his garden, on account of their receivers not being able to affect his mind if they were under water. I've found being out of the loop so calming and relaxing, I decided to stay that way until you got back.'

'Then allow me to fill you in on all the gory details. As you can probably guess... it's been predictable. The tabloids have had their usual sport with me. But a few of the majors decided to run with another story... the fact that Stump let slip it was *you* who funded the Stonehenge project.'

It was her turn to await a reaction.

'Well, they can hardly *arrest* me for it,' he scoffed.

She looked at him awkwardly. 'Actually, they can. Under sections one to five of the 2010 Bribery Act, it would be considered a crime if your payment were deemed to be a sweetener rather than a genuine donation which hadn't required a favour in return... which it *did*, of course.'

He stared back in horror.

'Just sayin',' she shrugged.

He remained speechless.

'Shall I put the kettle on?'

'If it ends up in court, I'll use you as my counsel,' he blurted. 'You'd run rings around the best barristers in the world with *your* knowledge!'

'It wouldn't be allowed,' she said.

'Yes it would. You don't have to employ a qualified legal team. You're perfectly entitled to defend yourself.'

'Correct. It's called litigant in person. But I'm talking about permission from a higher authority.' She rolled her eyes upwards.

Norman assumed she didn't mean the family upstairs. 'But I did it for them!' he insisted... also not meaning the family upstairs.

'Yes. But you weren't supposed to break any laws. You knew that from the beginning.'

'Then, even more reason for you to prove I didn't!'

Xanthia checked herself. 'Okay.' She stood for a few seconds in thought. 'I've just examined the case from every conceivable angle... and you *did*.'

Norman's knees weakened. *Was she being deliberately unhelpful... or just responding in kind to having her abilities called into question earlier?*

'Do you want a biscuit with your tea?'

The question nudged him, as Donald's cake tin came to mind. Would Donald accept her biscuit query as proof she *couldn't* read other people's thoughts? At least that way, he wouldn't need to do what he was about to.

He shook his head and steeled himself. 'About that assistance Donald wanted.'

'Go on, then... What's he after?'

'This.' he pulled the paper he'd been given from his pocket and gingerly handed it over. 'They're coordinates.'

She looked at him contemptuously.

'Yeah... sorry.' He tried to appear as indifferent as possible. 'He needs to know what they represent.'

He waited while she studied them.

'Hasn't he tried the internet?'

'Don't go there. I believe he regards an abacus as a threat to civilisation.'

She chewed her lip nonchalantly. 'Okay. This first one is roughly the centre of a field in County Armagh... give or take a few cowpats.'

'Is there a building there... a monument, perhaps?'

'Nope. Just grass and... well... you know what.'

He made a mental note to check her answer later. 'And the second?'

She stared hard at the paper. 'It's a drainage ditch outside a small village in the state of Uttar Pradesh, Northern India. Nothing remarkable… if you ignore the fact it's full of garbage.'

Norman observed her closely… desperately looking for anything that might suggest she was holding something back.

She blew out her cheeks. 'Then there's a postbox in the centre of Canterbury… a hay barn somewhere in Wyoming. I can be more specific if you like, but trust me, it's in the middle of a lot of nowhere.'

He waited for her to continue.

'The washroom of a bicycle factory in China… a baobab tree in Madagascar… and…' her expression brightened. 'Oh, this one's interesting!'

Norman stepped forward eagerly. 'What is it?'

'It's a bridge in Venice that lovers attach padlocks to in order to show their eternal commitment to each other.'

He watched as she became transfixed by that particular set of coordinates, seemingly transported to the place it represented. Momentarily released from a greater responsibility, the old Xanthia he'd fallen in love with returned as she smiled innocently to herself.

A wave of guilt engulfed him. She clearly had no problem with imparting the information. He chastised himself for entertaining Donald's suspicions.

'Oh dear,' she said, breaking from her warmer thoughts and recoiling. 'This last one's *not* such a happy place.'

'What is it?'

'A grave.'

'Anyone special?'

She looked at him, pained. '*Everyone's* special, Norman.'

'Point taken… I meant *whose*?'

She stared at the coordinates again, then let out a whimper, crouching and grabbing her stomach as if she'd just taken a punch to it.

'Xan… are you alright?'

She raised a hand. 'It's nothing.' She focused on the paper again through a stoic grimace. 'It's the grave of someone called

Alice Mumpstead. She died last year. The anniversary of her death was four days ago.'

He looked at her expectantly. 'And?'

'That's it,' she exhaled, wincing and straightening herself.

'Are you *sure* you're alright?'

She nodded.

His concern quickly overridden by relief at her having cooperated so willingly, he knew the answer she gave next would not only help Donald with his vital research, but prove her loyalty to the cause beyond any shadow of doubt. 'Okay... so, the million dollar question.' A drum roll sounded in his head. 'What's the connection between them all?'

She paused a moment in thought... then fixed him with a stare.

'There isn't one,' she said.

* * *

Alien Two stood apprehensively in front of Aliens One and Three, aware his big moment had arrived. He'd been working on material for a short routine he hoped might launch his comedy career. Though somewhat hampered by a lack of subject matter, it hadn't put him off.

He began by saying hello.

Aliens One and Three made loud gurgling noises as they found the fact he'd done so – having always been there with them – hilariously funny.

Surprised but relieved, Alien Two figured he was off to a flying start. Being a comedian was going to be easier than he thought.

Following up on his success, he asked if they'd come far.

Alien One and Alien Three bent over in agony at the concept of them being anywhere but where they'd always been. Gurgling uncontrollably, they struggled for their next breaths.

Alien Two sauntered about a bit in front of them, waiting for them to regain their composure.

As Aliens One and Three finally sat up and wiped the tears from their eyes, Alien Two delivered his first proper joke.

Wouldn't it be funny if the sky was where the surface of the planet was and the surface of the planet was where the sky was!

Alien Three gurgled a little, though more as a leftover reaction to "have you come far?".

Alien One's face remained blank.

Tough crowd, thought Alien Two.

Deciding a between-joke saunter during silence wouldn't be a good idea, he launched straight into his second rib-tickler.

What's the difference between the sky and the surface of the planet?

His audience stared at him expectantly.

You can't sit on the sky!

A slight snort escaped the corner of Alien Three's mouth… though only because the joke was so bad.

Alien One reacted differently. He felt an overpowering urge to throw something. He was only prevented from doing so by the fact nothing existed to throw.

Alien Two sensed he was losing the crowd and that jokes three, four and five about the sky and the surface of the planet weren't going to help. He'd already delivered his best material.

Falling back on a now-proven formula, he repeated his opening line. *Hello* had certainly worked the first time.

Judging from the reaction it got, his audience didn't do catchphrases.

A curious urge not to be there suddenly gripped him.

Needing to improvise, he looked around for inspiration.

The fact there was nothing to look at didn't help.

The urge to join all that non-existent stuff remained.

His audience waited patiently.

And then something hit him.

It wasn't Alien One, but a thought.

He gurgled to himself.

It was comedy gold.

Alien Two cleared his throat.

Wouldn't it be funny if they spent the rest of their lives saying God was better than them and God wasn't actually there!

The look he was given suggested he might not have much longer to find out.

Was he MAD? He'd just invented *blasphemy!*

Aliens One and Three began rapidly affirming God's superiority so as to distance themselves from the turn.

Alien Two was mortified. It never occurred to him that if God had thought it worth creating him with a sense of humour, that same God wouldn't want him to *use* it.

But not against *GOD!*

Alien Two couldn't see a problem. If God was *that* superior, wouldn't God possess an even greater sense of humour?

Alien Three suggested it might be better if he stick to sky and surface of the planet jokes from now on.

Alien One suggested he get off.

*　　*　　*

'I take it you've come with news,' said Donald through a now familiar gap in his door.

'I have. But I'd rather not discuss it out here.'

Norman was lying, of course. The thought of having to put up with the stench and squalor of Donald's house again didn't appeal. But neither did conversing with half an eye.

'How are those bites of yours?' Donald enquired, that eye narrowing.

'Itching like crazy and getting worse. But what's that got to do with anything?'

'I just don't want you bringing anything untoward into my house,' he replied.

'Despite the fact whatever caused those bites *came* from your house... when you hear what I have to say, you may consider any communicable diseases I could pass on to you an irrelevance... even if it turns out I'm carrying the bubonic plague!'

A bony hand shot from a slightly widened gap and dragged him through it.

'I was more concerned about the cats,' Donald whispered, so as not to alarm them. He looked Norman up and down... as did the cats. 'Well...was I right?'

'About Xanthia?'

'Of course!'

'That depends.'

'No, it doesn't! The test was simple enough. She either cooperated with us by giving you the answers we needed or she didn't!'

'She told me what all the coordinates represented.'

Donald's eyebrows rose expectantly.

'But said she couldn't see a connection,' Norman added awkwardly.

His eyes widening in horror, Donald reeled backwards. 'We're finished!' he cried, grabbing his head. 'I knew it! Our only hope of succeeding against the dark forces has gone! She's working for the other side!'

'Whoa, whoa,' said Norman, raising his hands. 'Aren't you being a little dramatic? Shouldn't we at least consider the possibility there might not *be* a connection?'

Donald stared at him as if he were mad. 'Might not be a connection?' he mimicked. 'Of *course* there is, you imbecile!' He gestured frantically towards the messages hanging from his corridor ceiling and beyond. 'Why do you think the spirit world has been queuing up night and day to pass on these snippets of information to me? They're picking it up from the one, same source... a colossal, negative vibration that's rapidly increasing in power.'

'Vibration?'

'Energy... ripple... it's all the same thing. They're passing on to me whatever they're encountering, in order to help build a picture of what it presages. Those coordinates I gave you are all part of that... so of *course* there's a FUCKING connection!'

Having never heard Donald resort to expletives, the fact he *had* made Norman re-evaluate his own judgement. Not for the first time, he found his mind conflicted. Over the last twenty-four hours he'd managed to convince it that Xanthia was on their side and that everything would be alright. It certainly made life easier. But Donald's profanity challenged that convenience yet again.

'Okay... but what if there's a connection and Xanthia just can't see it?' he proffered positively.

Donald peered at him incredulously. 'Is this the same Xanthia, who has complete knowledge of everything in the Universe, we're talking about?'

'There you go,' said Norman, mustering as much optimism as he could. 'She can still help us.'

Donald dropped his hands from his head and stared at his visitor in amazement.

Norman braced himself for another onslaught and further expletives.

'I like it,' Donald whispered, raising a trembling finger. He looked around wildly for supporting thoughts. 'You might have something there.'

Norman warily kept his eye on the finger.

'Perhaps we could devise a way to circumnavigate our original question and trick the answer out of her,' said Donald, wiggling it in little circles.

'I think we're at cross purposes,' Norman winced. 'I meant... she can help us find the answer as to *why* she can't see the connection.'

Donald's enthusiasm evaporated. 'Oh, god,' he groaned quietly, his shoulders dropping in solidarity with his hopes. 'Even *you* don't believe me.'

'That Xanthia wouldn't want to help us?'

Donald didn't answer. He stared as if a reply was pointless.

'In that case... why don't you ask her yourself?' Norman suggested brightly. 'She's waiting outside.'

Had Donald's eyes widened any further, they would've fallen from their sockets and rolled around the hall floor in a state of permanent horror. 'HE'S SIGNED MY DEATH WARRANT!' he wailed. 'I THOUGHT I COULD TRUST HIM!'

Norman watched in dismay as the playwright ran towards the corridor and started frantically ripping a number of the messages from its ceiling.

'PREPARE TO ABANDON SHIP!' he screamed. 'WE HAVE BUT SECONDS!' He was momentarily distracted. 'YES... *SHIP*. AND FROM WHAT YOU'VE TOLD ME, IF YOU'D HEEDED SUCH ADVICE IN THE FIRST PLACE, YOU'D HAVE ENJOYED A LITTLE LONGER ON THIS EARTHLY PLANE!'

Norman joined him. 'What are you doing? How can you be so certain Xanthia's working against us? You yourself said it was only a *theory*.'

'IGNORE HIM! HIS BRAINS ARE IN HIS PANTS! SHE'S CORRUPTED THE BOY'S LOGICAL MIND!'

'But I'm here to help. Surely you realise I'm the *last* person who'd go against you.'

'You brought her to my house!' cried Donald. 'How on *earth* was that helping?'

Norman tried to calm the situation. 'You don't *have* to see her. It was only a suggestion.'

'You have no idea how dangerous she could be!' Donald wailed.

'You're right. I don't. But given you've refused to tell me everything you know, why *should* I?'

Donald staggered towards him and thrust the messages he'd removed into Norman's hands. 'Because of these!'

Each one had a red string attached.

'If you *really* want to help, start removing the others,' commanded Donald.

'Messages?'

'Red strings!' he yelled. 'Our only hope is that she never gets to see them!'

'She won't,' said Norman, doing as he was told. 'I've asked her to wait outside. Besides... I bet you've ensured this place is more secure than the one I used to house my priceless art collection in!'

'Of course I have,' shouted Donald, hurrying into the drawing room and continuing with his task. 'But that only gives us a little more time. Keep pulling!'

'I still think you're overreacting,' said Norman, following him.

'Your problem is you *don't* think! With the knowledge she has, she'll be extremely resourceful.'

'He's right,' said a voice from across the room.

'Xan... what are you doing here?'

Donald gave a piercing shriek and grabbed his heart.

'I heard shouting. I thought you might be in trouble.'

'He is now,' gasped Donald, falling back into a large chair.

'How did you get in?'

'Through the patio doors.'

Norman looked at Donald. 'You didn't lock them?' he asked in amazement.

'No,' said Donald, not taking his eyes from Xanthia. 'Mother did. They've not been opened since. I never knew where she'd put the key.'

Xanthia held out the item in question. 'Under a flowerpot beside the lawn roller.'

Donald nodded lamely.

'What's going on?' she asked.

'Remember,' Donald hissed out of the side of his mouth. 'She doesn't know about the you-know-whats! They came *after* the sphere of knowledge.'

Norman tried to hide what was in his hands, Donald having already stuffed what was in *his* down the sides of his chair.

'Why don't we all go into the kitchen,' grinned Norman inanely. 'I don't know about anyone else, but I'm gagging for a cup of tea.'

'An excellent idea,' said Donald stiffly, rising eagerly while keeping his eyes fixed hypnotically on Xanthia. 'I also have some biscuits.'

'We'll stick to just tea,' said Norman sensibly.

'What are all these?' asked Xanthia, pointing at the messages suspended on their strings.

Donald gave another squeal.

'They're research notes for Donald's next play,' said Norman, looking her squarely in the eye. 'You're not to read them. That would be considered extremely rude.'

'I wouldn't dream of such a thing!' she said. Grabbing one hanging from a red string, she playfully waggled it at Donald. 'The Devil's in the detail... eh, Donald,' she teased.

Donald looked as if he was about to expire.

'Xan!' Norman admonished her.

'I'm only joking,' she pouted. 'Besides... I thought Donald wasn't going to write any more.'

Donald licked his lips just enough to get them to work again. 'I had a change of heart,' he trembled.

'Just can't ignore that muse, eh?' she smiled.

Donald nodded and returned a weak one of his own.

'So... what was all the shouting about?' she asked, as they negotiated their way towards the kitchen.

'It's how Donald communicates with his spirit guide. He says he's unaware he does it. It can be quite alarming at times.'

'Obviously,' she said.

'I suppose you know he's called Whitebait,' offered Donald, trying to keep the conversation on safer ground.

'No, I didn't,' said Xanthia. 'My knowledge doesn't extend to anything beyond the physical.'

'THANK CHRIST FOR THAT. WE MAY STILL HAVE A CHANCE!' Donald yelled.

Xanthia giggled and patted her heart. 'Ooh... I see what you mean!'

Entering the kitchen, she immediately understood why Norman had used the term *gagging* when referring to partaking of a cup of tea in it.

A cat – busy licking the chopping board – recoiled as Xanthia went to stroke it.

'Don't take it personally,' said Donald. 'He's always like that with strangers.'

She stared at the animal, causing the creature to arch its back and hiss. 'I know. He was mistreated as a kitten. Mrs

Truscott, the woman who sold him to you, used to shut him in a cupboard.'

Donald looked at Norman. 'Remarkable.'

'I told you,' Norman smiled.

'Norman thinks I may be able to help you with something else,' she said. 'If you want me to, that is.'

Donald lifted his chin courageously. 'But he tells me you're not able to,' he braved.

'I can only tell you what I see.'

'And how does that work?'

Xanthia considered the question. 'Well... I only have to focus on something to instantly know all about it. I'm learning not to question too many things going on around me... otherwise I'd end up going mad!'

'THINGS ARE DEFINITELY LOOKING UP!' Donald shouted.

Xanthia's brow crinkled. 'Norman said you thought there was a connection between the coordinates you gave him. But I've focused on them and can tell you categorically that there *isn't*.'

Donald tutted his foolishness. 'Oh, well. I must've got that bit wrong. Not to worry. It's not a big deal.'

Xanthia looked at Norman. 'Are you sure?'

'If *you* say there isn't a connection... then there isn't a connection,' Donald replied.

Xanthia stared at them both, nonplussed. 'But I thought that's why I was here. I was going to take a look at what you've been researching. See if I could help.'

Donald let out a now familiar noise.

Norman pretended he hadn't.

The cat didn't care either way.

'Well?'

Donald placed the blame for any misunderstanding squarely on Norman by staring directly at him and saying nothing.

'Right,' said Xanthia, confused. 'Then... is there anything else I can do?'

Donald puckered his lips. 'Nope.'

397

Norman awkwardly shook his head.

'Okay,' she huffed. 'Then I guess we'll have that cup of tea.'

*   *   *

The two state troopers shuffled nervously as the interviewer proffered a microphone.

'So, you say this occurred in broad daylight?'

'Yes, ma'am. As clear as we're seeing things now.'

'And when was this?'

'Exactly three days ago.'

'And it happened right over there?'

'Yes, ma'am.'

'Could you talk me through it?'

'Well... State Trooper Corrigan and I had been called to an incident concerning an altercation on the knoll beyond that boundary fence which runs along the other side of the road.'

'The Witches Mound?'

'That's correct.'

'So named because the local community once attempted to hang twelve of their number for witchcraft?'

'I believe that's the case.'

'If I understand correctly, the story goes they'd been encouraged to do so by events occurring at that time in Salem, but were stopped at the very last minute. Local folklore has it an angel intervened and – after a fierce argument with the Devil, who admitted to corrupting the villagers' minds – the accused were allowed to go free.'

'That's correct, ma'am.'

'So... tell us what you saw.'

'I saw a figure dressed head to toe in white having a conversation with someone on the very top of that knoll. Both appeared to be shouting angrily at each other and things had plainly gotten outta hand. Trooper Corrigan remained by the car while I went to investigate.'

'As you made that decision, did you have any idea of what you were walking towards?'

'Well... at first I thought it was just some kids messin' around... having dressed up so as to prank anyone who happened to be drivin' by.'

'How so?'

The officer looked at the camera hesitantly. 'I know this is gonna sound kinda crazy to the folks out there... but the one dressed in white appeared to have a huge set of wings risin' from their back. At first, I assumed it was fancy dress... as you would... so didn't think too much of it. But just as I was convincin' myself it *was* kids foolin' about, those wings suddenly unfolded and started movin' in such a way I knew they must be for real!'

'What did you do?'

'I immediately drew my gun, ma'am. I don't mind admittin'... once that happened... I was extremely scared.'

'And you Trooper Corrigan? Did you see the same thing?'

'Exactly as Henry says it was, ma'am. I wasn't close enough to know those wings were for real. But I got to understand *that* part when the figure in white began ascending into the air.'

'Like an angel?'

'*As* an angel, ma'am.'

Both men looked at each other awkwardly.

The reporter whistled her astonishment. 'And what of this *other* figure... the one confronting this angel? What did *they* look like?'

The first officer stared down at his feet. 'That's the equally strange part. There was nothing otherworldly about them. They seemed normal flesh and blood.'

'Like you and me?'

'*Kinda.* Only... in my eyes... more like the type of person who'd be involved in an illicit trade for business on the streets.'

'You mean... dealing drugs?'

He scratched his temple awkwardly. 'More like the acquisition of personal favours.'

The reporter's eyes narrowed. 'Are you saying he looked like... a *pimp*?'

The state trooper shook his head. 'No, ma'am... and, what's more... I never said it was a *he*.'

*   *   *

'Well... what a complete and utter waste of time *that* was!' Xanthia flopped back in the car's seat and loosened the straps of her stilettos. 'I don't know why you bothered bringing me. There are *far* better things I could be getting on with.'

Norman had been thinking the exact same thing. His desire to prove Donald wrong had backfired spectacularly. Not only had he lost the man's trust, he'd also failed to resolve his own doubts about the woman he loved.

'I know things have gotten pretty crazy lately... but that was most *definitely* the weirdest half hour of my entire life!' she exclaimed. 'And why on *earth* did he insist we left by the kitchen window?'

'It's probably connected to the fact he's sensitive about anyone seeing the notes he's written... those for that new play of his.' Norman justified his deception with the knowledge that at least *part* of that statement was true. 'Perhaps he didn't want you sneaking a peek at the ones in the corridor.'

'You mean those ridiculous things hanging from his ceilings?'

Norman nodded, inwardly cursing himself for having raised the subject.

'Well... y*ou've* obviously seen them!' she returned churlishly.

'Only enough to know when to duck.'

'And talking of ducks... what was that weird noise he kept making whenever I came anywhere *close* to asking what he was up to?'

'I warned you he could be unpredictable,' Norman covered. 'You just have to accept his conversations and actions are all part of his eccentricity.'

'It wasn't so much what he said and did that surprised me... it was more what he *didn't*. One minute he's sending you to me with a set of coordinates that are supposed to have some consequential connection… the next, he's pretending nothing matters.'

'Pretending?' fished Norman. *Did she know more than she was letting on?*

'Yes. He's obviously trying to work something important out. I could've helped with whatever it is he needs to know. All he had to do was tell me everything *he* knows.'

Norman tried not to make the same pathetic noise Donald had, as the temperature of his skin rapidly increased.

Turning to stare at him directly, her next words caused his buttocks to weld themselves to the taxi's backseat. 'Do you think he doesn't trust me?'

He struggled to style out his discomfort. 'Perhaps he's uncomfortable in the presence of women,' he squeaked.

'He's uncomfortable in the presence of *anyone*,' she countered. 'Not that he can be blamed for that. It all stems from the childhood he was forced to endure.'

'His parents were cruel?'

'No. Just mad. In fact, his mother *doted* on him. She once sent him off to boarding school wearing a hat she'd knitted to make it look like he had a halo… just in case the other children didn't realise how special he was.'

'And his father?'

'*That* relationship was slightly more problematical. It stemmed from the fact Bostock was mortified by Donald's complete disinterest in ironing boards as an infant. It even caused him to question the child's parentage at one point. He only withdrew the allegation of outside interference when Donald's mother threatened to shoot him with a shotgun unless he rescinded it.'

Norman looked at her aghast. 'She was prepared to shoot her own husband?'

Xanthia shook her head. 'No… Donald.'

* * *

393

'So… Trooper Mitchell… you say this woman you encountered on the Witches Mound refused to explain the circumstances surrounding her being there.'

'She seemed keen not to discuss the matter at all… or the fact the entity she'd been engaging with had simply vanished into thin air.'

'Vanished?'

'Having just risen into it,' added Trooper Corrigan, in case that point had been forgotten.

'But you didn't detain her?'

'We had no legal justification for doing so, ma'am. It's not against the law to argue with someone.'

'Even if that person subsequently rises into the air,' said Trooper Corrigan, pushing the point again.

'It's against the laws of physics,' pointed out the reporter.

'Yes, ma'am, it is. But breaking any of those ain't an arrestable offence either.'

'What about soliciting?'

'Hard to prove when the potential John has simply evaporated in front of your eyes.'

'So you simply let her go.'

'We had to… but not before checking her identity.'

'So, you know who she is.'

'Yes, ma'am.'

'She was carrying verifiable proof?'

'In the form of a passport.'

'A *tourist*?'

'From the United Kingdom, ma'am.'

'And her name?'

*   *   *

'Xanthia!' Norman fumbled for the alarm clock by the side of his bed and attempted to focus on it. 'Xanthia!'

As no answer was forthcoming from a flat comprising only one other room – excluding a bathroom so small you had to be extremely inventive with your knees – he assumed she'd either gone out or was dead.

He rolled onto his back and sighed. 'Half past nine. Why didn't she wake me?'

Rarely allowed the luxury of sleeping beyond her, such out-of-character behaviour favoured the likelihood she *had* died. But the warming embrace of a duvet advised he ignore that possibility a little while longer. There'd be plenty of time to find out. It wasn't as if he'd planned to do anything else that day.

Then again… neither had she.

Still encased in his bedding, he reluctantly shuffled his way into the other room to investigate the reason for her silence.

A cursory glance suggested the lack of a body meant she was still alive and had probably braved the stares and sniggers that would be on offer in abundance at the local convenience store.

It was only as he was shuffling his way back to bed that a further thought struck him.

It wasn't just Xanthia that had been missing from the bleary snapshot. Her small, pink travel case was also absent.

The realisation snapped him from his lethargy.

'Not *again!*'

Once was bad enough. He'd already spent three days on his own before she'd deigned to return without giving any explanation for what she'd been up to. Not that he'd bothered pushing for one. There was no point. She could've simply lied if she didn't want him to know.

So… what *had* she been up to?

More importantly… what was she up to now?

He figured his best chance of finding out lay in the laptop they shared. But a quick trawl of her emails failed to yield any clues. Worryingly… a cheeky search of her deleted folder increased his paranoia. Freshly cleared, it suggested she'd deliberately erased something she didn't want him to see.

Alarm bells ringing, he ignored his moral compass and set about scrutinising her browsing history.

What it revealed left him speechless.

Both he and Xanthia had recently taken to scouring the internet for mention of her name. It was an effective way of gauging the public's reaction to her claims. But the most recent searches – ones she'd undertaken without him – had returned some astonishing results. A host of American websites were reporting her alleged encounter with an angel, as witnessed by two state troopers.

Norman took a moment to digest the information.

Was such a meeting possible? It was at least feasible she could've undertaken the journey in her short time away. Is that why she'd been reluctant to say where she'd been? More to the point... if the angel it was being claimed she'd had a confrontation with was Gabriel... what had they been arguing about?

As he struggled to make sense of it all, the same thought kept waving at him. *If it was nothing more than a silly hoax – perpetrated by someone seeking to make mischief at her expense – why hadn't she mentioned it? Given the traction the story appeared to have gained on the other side of the Atlantic, surely it had been worthy of discussion... even a shared laugh? Why keep it secret?*

Donald's words of warning flashed in front of him.

Was this the smoking gun?

Picturing his last encounter with the troubled playwright, an image hurtled from that memory and struck him like an express train. Sprinting to the bedroom, he flung open the wardrobe and dragged his coat from its hanger. Scrabbling inside a pocket, he pulled out the notes he'd detached from Donald's ceiling shortly before Xanthia had surprised them.

'I'd completely forgotten about these!'

His heart beating faster than was good for him, he spread them out on the bed and stared at their red strings.

So *what* if he read them now? Ignorance of their contents had become an irrelevance. Xanthia could hardly infiltrate his mind and find out what Donald knew if she wasn't there to do so. Besides... this wasn't a game. The fate of the Universe was at stake.

Catching a glimpse of himself in the bedroom mirror, his reflection proffered a suggestion.

Perhaps Heaven had never intended him to be a decoy after all. Perhaps she'd lied about that. Perhaps he still had a greater destiny to fulfil.

Bending down, he picked up the first of the folded notes.

Nodding confirmation to his opposite self that he was justified in doing so, he opened it.

*   *   *

Alien Two was sat with his chin buried in his chest. He hadn't said anything for quite some time and Aliens One and Three were worried.

Alien One decided to intervene and asked if he was alright.

Alien Two said he was feeling something strange, but didn't know what it was.

Alien One suggested it might help if they gave that feeling a name. At least then, it wouldn't seem so mystifying... a bit like he'd done with God.

Alien Two asked him what name he had in mind.

Alien One suggested they call it *disappointment*.

Intrigued, Alien Three asked Alien Two what *disappointment* was like.

Alien Two shrugged and said it felt something like that.

Alien Three asked him to elaborate.

Alien Two said he'd expected a better response to his jokes... and failing to achieve it had left him feeling like he was missing out on something.

Alien Three said, in that case, he *too* had encountered *disappointment*.

Alien One asked him when.

Alien Three replied it was immediately after Alien Two had finished performing his comedy routine.

Alien Two said that didn't help.

Alien Three questioned how he could miss something if it hadn't been there in the first place.

Alien Two explained that once something had been thought of, it was very difficult to pretend it hadn't... a bit like Alien One's God.

Alien One said he had another idea. If Alien Two envisaged the result of missing something as a thing in its own right, he'd then have something to compensate for whatever it was he was missing.

Alien Two said he thought they'd decided to call it *disappointment.*

Alien One explained that disappointment was the *feeling* of missing something... not the actual missing something itself.

Alien Three pointed out you couldn't call something that wasn't there something.

Alien One said you could... and proved his point by naming Alien Two's thing that wasn't there *experience.*

Alien Three said *experience* seemed completely pointless.

Alien One said it wasn't once you'd had it.

Alien Two took a moment to reflect on everything... then announced that Alien One was right. He did *indeed* now have something else he could focus on, which he was happy to recognise as *experience.*

Alien One said Alien Two should be proud of having *experience* of trying to make people laugh.

Alien Two looked at him strangely and asked what he was talking about. As far as *he* was concerned, he now had *experience* of *disappointment.*

Alien Three started laughing hysterically and said that was the funniest thing he'd ever heard.

Alien One suggested, in that case, they also invent a name for what had just occurred. He proposed they call it *irony.*

*   *   *

388

Norman studied the creased piece of paper in his hand. Far from providing him with answers, its unfolding had only deepened his confusion.

Hastily sketched in pencil was what he assumed to be Donald's depiction of a celestial body. Looking like the moon, but with a personality bypass, it wasn't anything he recognised. Having seen the results of Donald's artistic competency... and assuming he still possessed a full palette of paints... it appeared it had deliberately been depicted as ice-white and barren. Instead of adding his signature, its creator had angrily scrawled a large question mark over it... suggesting he shared Norman's bafflement as to what it signified.

The second message was more in keeping with the mystical side of Donald's world. Stapled to a piece of brown paper was a solitary tarot card. Unlike the first message, Norman had no problem deciphering this one's meaning. Not through skilful interpretation of the card's colourfully attired central character, carrying a bundle on the end of a long stick, but because it had the words *THE FOOL* printed in capital letters beneath the hapless traveller.

The claim that a series of random cards could predict the future had always intrigued him. If so, weren't games like *Snap, Happy Families,* and *Beggar My Neighbour* missing the point? Might being dealt *Mrs Bun the Baker's Wife* actually presage a new arrival on the horizon... or finding *Mr Dose the Doctor* in your hand, a warning that you might want to consider putting off trying for one with your partner? It would certainly make keeping a poker face far more difficult if the value of cards you were staring at not only held the prospect of winning money, but foretold the exact time you had left to spend it. As for bridge tournaments... they didn't bear thinking about.

He turned the card over and marvelled at the intricate design on its back, though it still offered no clues.

Messages three to seven should have provided a clearer explanation, given they were notes in Donald's own handwriting. But much to Norman's frustration, only one came close to being decipherable... all having been written in a scrawl reflecting the angst of the man holding the pen. The one line that *could* be read appeared to be a quote from the bible: *"For your merchants were the great ones of the earth, and all the nations were deceived by your sorcery."*

The eighth and final message unfolded to reveal yet another drawing of a planet... the same as the first, he assumed, given its distinct lack of features. But this time it had been depicted in the distance... dwarfed by the monumental void in which it hung... as if the artist had been trying to portray the fact it was trapped in an eternity of silence. Only the eventual collapse of a neutron star might give it a brief moment of relief as it found itself drawn towards the gaping nothingness of a nascent black hole... basking in the knowledge that... finally... there was to be an end to the unbearable monotony of being.

Shaking himself from so depressing a thought, Norman was confronted by another. Having risked peeking at the red-stringed messages, he now found himself more perplexed than ever.

Perhaps Donald was completely mad... and those media reports from America were based on nothing more than silly rumours. Perhaps Xanthia had merely gone away for another of her breaks. You could hardly blame her, given the extraordinary amount of pressure she'd been under.

He shut his eyes to re-evaluate everything.

Perhaps her absence was nothing more than an innocent desire to escape the incessant media circus around her.

The thought momentarily offered comfort... until another forced his eyes open again.

In which case... why not say goodbye?

He looked over at the kettle.

This time, she hadn't even bothered leaving a note!

True... the previous evening hadn't exactly been one of unbridled bliss. Snubbed by Donald... and blaming Norman for having wasted her day... she'd demonstrated her annoyance by spending the remainder of it alone on the laptop. Norman had thought it foolish to object... not least because it offered a

386

respite from further, awkward questions. But that hardly excused such inconsiderate behaviour.

The fact she'd used that time to clear her deleted emails gave him another idea. Scooping up the messages from the bed, he quickly stuffed them back into the pocket of the coat and hurried to the other room.

Sitting in front of the laptop, he cracked his knuckles. A permanently deleted email should hold no fear for a man of his abilities. After all, permanence was relative to a computer. Logically efficient, it saw no point in erasing items when commanded to do so... even from the waste bin. It simply made a note to allow whatever space was no longer needed to be overwritten when the need arose. Whatever Xanthia had chosen to delete might be able to be pulled back from the brink if he applied his skills correctly.

Setting about the task, time passed unmeasured... his complete concentration ensuring his stomach had no say in the matter.

Finally... much to his relief... and his stomach's... the results of his labour started bearing fruit.

A succession of recovered messages began stacking up in front of him.

However... that fruit could not have tasted more bitter.

They appeared to be correspondence to and from the same individual.

His blood froze as he registered the name.

With the room starting to spin, his thinking gave up its exactness as reality took a step back... respectful of the cataclysmic explosion that had just been triggered in his head.

'*Et tu, Brute*,' he croaked, a metaphoric knife in his back causing a pain far greater than the real one recently thrust into his stomach.

He lashed out at the screen in a bid to end his nightmare.

The laptop stood its ground, continuing to display an extensive and mutually effusive exchange between Xanthia and her fellow correspondent.

How could it be?

He struggled to breathe.

Donald was right!

As the irrefutable evidence swam in and out of focus, the revelation became more surreal with every wave of confirmation. His safe world of computers was no more. Even the laptop had turned against him and was taunting him … just like his baying classmates all those years ago… when Xanthia had shattered his world by colluding with them and holding her nose.

Now she'd gone and done it again. Only… this time, it appeared she intended to end his world completely.

A numbing darkness enveloped him.

In a pointless, last-ditch show of defiance, he screamed in anger at her co-conspirator.

'KEVIN!'

To be more precise, he should have added *AKA The Megabyte Master, AKA Ultimate and Unbeatable Supreme Cyber Warrior 2*… but his body had already struck the floor.

* * *

Elbows flew as a jostling swarm of reporters fiercely competed for the best microphone-proffering positions.

The focus of their attention appealed for calm, waving down the frenetic barrage of questions while privately revelling in it. 'One at a time, ladies and gentlemen… please!'

'Reverend Humbold! What d'ya make of the testimony of troopers Mitchell and Corrigan regarding this British woman you've been warning us about?'

'As your words rightly testify,' he nodded smugly, 'I've made my position on that she-devil abundantly clear from the get-go. Those disbelievers who ridiculed my warnings should fall to their knees in contrition and repent of their foolishness! Following her altercation with one of God's most important messengers… after *myself*, that is… it's as obvious as a pole dancer's flatulence that, far from ridding the world of evil, as she claims, this Xanthia intends luring the gullible away from

384

the path of righteousness... like the Pied Piper of... that foreign town... you know, the short-changed paedophile with a flute. Her true colours have been exposed and my exhortations against her vindicated. She is, indeed, the Devil incarnate!'

'Are you seriously suggesting that last bit's the case, though? Following on from the fact the troopers said she was carrying a passport, we managed to obtain a copy of her birth certificate. To our knowledge, nowhere in the Bible does it list Satan's parents as Roger and Brenda Swanson.'

In light of this last revelation... and the growing ridicule he'd been attracting for that part of his claim... the reverend chose his next words carefully. 'I'm glad you've allowed me the chance to clarify the situation. I believe the Dark Lord has taken control of this poor wretch's body. So in answer to your question... she may as well be that loathsome fiend in every way imaginable... excepting his genitals, of course.'

'So... what are you suggesting happens next, Reverend?'

'I'd have thought that was obvious!' he exclaimed. 'I'm suggesting the entire world wakes up to the danger she poses and no longer ignores occurrences like the one those troopers witnessed.'

'Occurrences? Are you implying there have been other such incidents involving this individual?'

'Oh... I *know* there have,' he nodded strongly. 'Many others! Foul deeds perpetrated by this handmaid of Beelzebub while professing to be working for our Lord!'

'Can you give us an example?'

'Well... as a matter of fact, I can. Just yesterday, I was approached in the street by a troubled woman who grabbed me forcefully by the arm. There was such fear in that poor creature's eyes that I immediately knew her soul to be in torment and in need of my renowned comfort and Christian charity... after I checked she hadn't stolen my watch, of course. She informed me that, after seeing a news report on that Witches Mound incident, Xanthia appeared in front of her and instructed her to kill her husband.'

The revelation produced a loud inhalation of shock.

Cameras clicked.

'Where did this happen?'

'Outside my front gate.'

'We meant... Xanthia appearing in front of this woman.'

'She told me it occurred in a dream.'

The clicking abated.

'A dream?'

'That is correct.'

'And did she kill her husband.'

'We didn't get that far. The woman was in emotional turmoil... and I had a golf game I didn't want to miss. But I *do* know what she experienced was irrefutably the work of Satan.'

'How can you be so sure?'

The reverend lifted his head proudly. 'Because the Lord speaks to me.' He raised a hand in anticipation of those his PR team's polling suggested doubted that claim. 'Now... I know there are some confused folk out there who might find themselves questioning my power to communicate with the Almighty... who view this ability He has bestowed upon me with a small tinge of scepticism.' He tilted his head self-deprecatingly. 'And who can blame 'em. It's not *just* ignorance on their part. I often marvel at it myself. After all, I've never claimed to be a saint.' His eyes widened as a thought suddenly struck him. 'Though I'd be happy to accept that appellation if considered worthy enough by His Catholic Holiness the Pope of Rome,' he hastily addressed the nearest camera. 'In truth, I'm just a simple man doing the momentous work for which the Lord has chosen me from the billions of others he has put upon this Earth... a humble servant who He recognised would come across as exceptionally charismatic when seen on TV. By the way... for those not fortunate enough to have partaken of that experience, subscription plans are available on request at *God's Own Cable Network*.'

'When He speaks to you... does He do so in English?'

'Yes, He does,' nodded the reverend earnestly. 'Though I think He could probably speak a few other languages... if He ever wanted to.'

'How d'ya know it's him?'

The question returned a squint. 'Because He says... it's God here... or something along those lines.'

'Is it a booming voice?'

A sign of irritability bracketed the reply. 'Well... I'd go as far as to say it has a certain... *gravitas* to it.'

'And what exactly has He said about this Xanthia?'

The reverend welcomed the questioning getting back on track. 'He's informed me that the Devil has entered her body... his foul and duplicitous intention being to deceive every living soul on this planet into believing she's the saviour of mankind. But heed my words... and *His*, he added quickly... she's a fatal distraction. While pretending to save us all from Armageddon, her real mission is to hasten its arrival!'

'Is that spelt with two d's?'

'You can look it up. It's in the Bible... somewhere near the back.'

'And do we have a date?'

'God wasn't calendar specific. But I can tell ya'll this... it'll be real soon. You'd have to be dumber than a firefly in a firework factory not to have noticed that, ever since this temptress aligned herself to that pagan site at Stonehenge, the days have steadily been getting darker.'

'Isn't that because we've just passed the summer solstice?'

'Don't get smart with me!' he barked, silencing the sniggers. 'And don't take me for a fool. I'm a conduit for divine messages, which you ignore at your peril. This is no laughing matter. There is real evil afoot in the world and it's increasing day by day! You've only gotta turn on your TV to see what I'm talkin' about. It ain't just this sudden destructive spate of fires, floods and droughts we've been suffering... or the hideous swarms of flies and other such soulless abominations that have been plaguing us... or even the fact fruit ain't ripening on the trees, or crops in the fields, as they should. Unnatural occurrences... the likes of which are best confined to horror movies... are now taking place on a regular basis. And these things are happening *everywhere*... from the desert plains of Western

Europe to the deepest oceans of Timbuktu. A darkening cloud of moral pestilence has placed itself over every living thing on this planet. So... you can scoff at my warnings and put what is occurring down to happenstance... or you can join me in the fight to rid ourselves of this insidious evil. I'm calling on every man, woman and child to unite behind the one person who can save this world from impending destruction.'

'God?'

The reverend jerked his head incredulously. 'No... *me!*'

'And how do you intend doing that?'

Galveston Humbold III seized his moment of destiny. It had been presented to him courtesy of one of his PR team, deviously planted in the press scrum.

'By confronting this pernicious impostor head on!' he announced boldly. 'I hereby challenge her to come out from the shadows in which she's been lurking and meet me face to face. Let her pit her claims to be representing the Lord against mine, so the public can see who's telling the truth! Even though my lawyers assure me I indisputably own the trademark... let's put beyond doubt who the *real* Saviour of Mankind is.'

'You say she's been lurking in the shadows... but we've seen footage of her appearing on a British talk show. What's more... she came across as anything but dangerous. What do you say to that?'

'You're right. I've seen it myself... and she was as ineffective as a three-legged barstool. I'm not ashamed to admit that even *I* momentarily questioned God's warnings. But that demonstrates just how dangerous that woman is. As I was thinking, *Galveston... why would the Devil allow one of his own to be subjected to such ridicule...?* God spoke to me and pointed out it was simply a ruse to lure us into a state of false security. Satan knows you don't fight what you don't fear, so he's cunningly sent her as a wolf in sheep's clothing.'

'If Xanthia responds to your offer, will it take place somewhere appropriate... like a mountaintop?'

'I beg your pardon?'

'This fight between the two of you.'

'Well… it ain't like it's gonna get physical… what with her being a girl,' he scoffed.

'It might.'

The reverend took out a handkerchief and dabbed his brow. 'D'ya reckon?'

There were nods as to the possibility.

'I was thinking more like a television studio,' he replied. 'Practicalities aside, I don't like heights. But, if you reckon it'd look better, we could always make it resemble a boxing ring.' He gave the matter some consideration before signalling his intention to leave. 'Well… I thank you all for your attention. Now I must go and pray… and request the Lord gives me enough strength for the battle ahead.'

'Are there any words of comfort you wish to give the public before you do, Reverend?'

Galveston Humbold stalled his departure and stood awhile in thought. 'Actually… there are. For those doubters I mentioned earlier, who find themselves in need of expressing their contrition to the Almighty… it just so happens I've a surplus stock of prayer cushions available at a discounted price. Details are on my website.'

*   *   *

'Donald! Donald! Open the door!' Norman looked about himself frantically before banging on it again. 'Donald… we no longer have time for these silly games!'

He listened as something was shouted on the other side of it.

'She's not with me… I promise. *That's* why I'm here. You were absolutely right about her!'

He listened again.

'I *know* you know you were. But I fear it's worse than even *you* thought it might be!'

Norman scratched the bites on his body, many of which had inexplicably morphed into angry pustules.

'What do you mean, *that's not possible*? If you allow me to show you what I've discovered, I think you'll find it is!'

379

He stuck an ear to the door and frowned.

'*Who's* completely out of touch with reality?'

He frowned again.

'Okay… can you stop talking to Whitebait for a minute…? I need you to open the door. We're in *serious* trouble.'

More words were mumbled from the other side.

'No… you're *not* safer in there alone. Believe me… *nowhere* is safe now!'

The door remained firmly shut.

'Okay, then… I'm sorry you've made me resort to threats… but, if you don't let me in, I'm gonna return home and tell Xanthia the following… *For your merchants were the great ones of the earth, and all the nations were deceived by your sorcery.*'

A yelp sounded, followed by shouting.

'Of *course* I opened them. What did you expect, given the circumstances? Do you think I'm that fool on the tarot card?'

His last utterance caused the door to fly open and for him to be unceremoniously yanked inside. But at least he was getting used to it by now.

'Thank you.'

'What else do you know?' demanded Donald, staring at him in horror.

'A lot more than you.'

'I doubt that!'

'I know Xanthia's working for the Devil and has been stringing us along all the time.'

'OF *COURSE* I OBJECT TO HIS CHOICE OF PERSONAL PRONOUN!'

'Alright… me. I admit I had doubts about you questioning her allegiance. But now I've got actual proof of where it lies.'

'You should've trusted me in the first place, instead of foolishly bringing her here to my house. My attempts to work out what her side was up to were hanging from every ceiling!'

'You're right… it was an incredibly stupid thing to do. But at least she didn't get to read any of it.'

'Because you told her not to… which was as good as telling her we had something to hide!'

'She thinks they're notes for your new play. I made sure of that.'

'NAIVE DOESN'T COME ANYWHERE *REMOTELY* CLOSE!' Donald shouted. 'If she has knowledge of all things before the incident at Stonehenge, she'll know, with my gift, I've never *needed* notes to do my writing... ESPECIALLY AN ENTIRE BLOODY HOUSE FULL OF THEM!'

'I notice you've taken them down,' said Norman, looking around.

'I was hardly going to keep them up there for when she returns to kill me... was I?'

'But you *do* still have them?'

'Thank you for your concern,' said Donald facetiously.

'But do you?'

'Of *course* I do!'

'Thank God for that. We need to put our heads together and figure out our next move. Xanthia's been communicating with Kevin... the kid who tried to kill me. He was supposed to step in at the last minute and receive the sphere of knowledge on behalf of Satan. But Xanthia beat him to it. Only... it's irrelevant. They're both on the same side! They've been sending each other emails... him professing his undying love for her, and Xanthia...' Norman stopped, as an emotion he thought he'd managed to suppress caught in his throat. He looked at Donald hopelessly, his eyes glistening.

Donald's narrowed.

Norman thrust out a hand to request patience while he pulled himself together. 'Xanthia informed Kevin that she couldn't wait to be with him... as no one had ever shown her that level of devotion.' He sucked in the urge to start blubbing like a baby. 'They're planning to meet up in the coming days, but we *have* to stop them. In trying to make sense of everything that's happened recently, I've come to the conclusion their physical proximity to one another might unleash a force we could never hope to compete against.'

Donald's eyes remained narrowed.

'You see… Gabriel told me the original sphere of knowledge was to be given to Shakespeare on his twenty-first birthday, as only *then* would he be spiritually mature enough to receive it. It shattered because it was delivered ten days early. So, what if Xanthia was too spiritually immature to receive the latest sphere? Her scheming with Kevin shows it was clearly never meant for her. She lied. It was meant for *me,* just like Gabriel said. What if – like Shakespeare – she was unable to accommodate it all… just a part? What if the remainder went to someone else… someone who was nearest her at the time? Maybe *that's* why she's been so ineffective. Her abilities are limited. But if Kevin possesses the remaining part, as I suspect he might, their coming together could unlock the Sphere's full potential!' He looked at Donald expectantly.

Donald slowly leant forward, a disconcerted look in his eyes. 'What are emails?'

* * *

The baobab tree had seen it all… or at least, it thought it had. Locally revered, and silently observing the comings and goings of countless generations visiting to pay their respects and seek its help, it had every reason to assume such a thing. After two and half thousand years, nothing surprised it anymore. From heartfelt requests for whatever its Malagasy visitors thought would benefit their lives, to demands for retribution against those who had wronged them… its perceived powers knew no end.

Not that it took any credit for the results. For its greatest wisdom lay in the fact it knew it was just a tree.

It had learned to survive the tropical dry forest by sucking up whatever water it could in the winters and storing it in its impressive trunk so as to endure the unbearably hot Madagascan summers. The fact it had achieved this for so long and stood defiant in such a challenging landscape, gave it a status above the sum of its fibrous parts.

That status made it the assumed home of spirits – both good and bad – and the souls of dead ancestors – only ever good – who were thought to inhabit a hidden realm within.

Each to their own, it had always thought.

Mahasolo and Tsinjo were two such visitors… childhood friends who had been coming to the tree since they were boys. Now entering manhood, they regularly took time to sit in its scant shade and ponder life's mysteries. The ways and whims of girls figured highly in their quest for understanding… the baobab listening patiently, as it did to girls asking much the same questions about boys.

If it could speak, it would tell them all that they weren't as far apart from each other as they thought. Perception dictated one's reality. Change *that* and you instantly changed your world.

Mahasolo wore the cheekier smile, forever using it to influence the more introspective Tsinjo. The two had grown up side by side – brothers without the bond of blood – with never a cross word passing between them.

Which is why their families would never understand what happened that stifling day.

The searing heat was beginning to relent as the sun started embracing the horizon. Mahasolo had been telling his lifelong friend about the new bike he intended to buy. He had almost saved enough money and was hoping the sale of the old one would provide the remainder he needed. Tsinjo listened intently, seemingly happy for his friend.

The flies had been more bothersome than usual, but a sudden gust of wind heralded a swarm so thick it forced the young men to break from their conversation.

The baobab tree felt it too, the tips of its branches violently buffeted, despite all around appearing calm.

As Mahasolo swatted the insects from his face, he noticed Tsinjo staring at him, unperturbed by the invasion. No sooner had he risked opening his mouth to ask Tsinjo what was wrong, his companion calmly leant forward and grabbed him by the throat.

For the first few seconds, Mahasolo thought it was a joke. They had grown up play-fighting, though never in the presence of the baobab. That would've been disrespectful. But the increasing intensity of Tsinjo's grip made any breach of etiquette an irrelevance.

Mahasolo grabbed his companion's forearms, desperately trying to alleviate the pressure on his neck. Unable to do so, he attempted to break Tsinjo's impassive trance by signalling his panic with his eyes. But his friend was looking straight through him. They widened in alarm as the air he needed was denied. His lungs unable to flex, his body shook as the stalemate brought a searing pain.

The last things to occupy his thoughts – before a darkness swallowed them – was how Tsinjo was going to explain what had happened to their families… and the crushing realisation that he was never going to get to ride his new bike.

Tsinjo wouldn't *have* to explain.

That was left to the villagers, who cast theories ranging from a dispute about a girl to the fact Tsinjo had become possessed by a particularly evil spirit said to inhabit the tree.

Not that it mattered.

His lifeless body was found swaying above that of his friend, the belt from his trousers looped around a lower branch of the baobab.

Some say Tsinjo, in a moment of remorse, took his own life. But the shaman from the village insisted that spirits from within the tree – incensed by such disrespectful behaviour – took it upon themselves to punish him as a warning to others.

Only the tree knew what *really* happened. But, having held its silence for two and a half thousand years, it figured the answer was best kept to itself.

*   *   *

Norman stared at Donald incredulously. 'Haven't you been listening to a thing I've been saying?'

'Of course I have. That's why I asked you what emails were?'

'But that's not the *important* bit!'

'Then, why bother mentioning them?'

'Because that's how I found out what Xanthia was really up to.'

'Then, they *are* important.'

'Okay,' conceded Norman. 'They *are* important. But not as important as what will happen if Xanthia and Kevin get together.'

'So… what then?'

Norman grimaced. 'I don't know *exactly*. But certainly nothing good.'

'Then, why have them?'

'Pardon?'

'Emails… Why have such things, if they're nothing good?'

'*What?*'

'I'm asking you what emails are, and you still haven't given me an answer.'

'Oh, for fu_' Norman bowed his head. 'Alright. They're electronic letters that are sent and received on computers.' He cautiously looked at Donald. 'You *do* know what a computer is?'

'Of course I do!' said Donald indignantly. 'Do you think I'm an idiot?'

Norman held Donald's stare long enough to make a point, then reached into the backpack he was carrying. 'Look… I'll show you.' He pulled out his laptop.

Donald jumped back in alarm.

'Don't worry. No one can get at you through it. I somehow doubt you've got Wi-Fi.'

Donald stared at him blankly.

'I'll explain that bit another time.' Balancing the laptop on his knee, Norman fired it up and cued up the incriminating evidence. After persuading Donald to hold the device, and offering some basic tutoring on how to read emails, he waited patiently as their contents were digested.

Becoming more engrossed the further he got, Donald's technophobia quickly disappeared. 'She's clearly as keen to meet him as he is her,' he observed.

'It's her praise for him that cuts the most,' Norman moaned.

'I'm not surprised.' Donald placed a greasy finger on the screen. 'There's a bit here where she says she's finally looking forward to seeing what a *real* man can do.'

Norman rescued his laptop from the impertinent finger and quickly closed its lid 'Yes. Thank you.'

'Just a shame it doesn't say when and where they intend to meet,' Donald frowned.

'That's where I thought you might be able to help. Do you think one of those coordinates you were given might possibly mark their rendezvous?'

Donald considered the idea. '*Anything's* possible, I suppose. But that leaves an awful lot of options. The ones I gave you were just the tip of an extremely large iceberg.' He looked at Norman curiously. 'By the way... you never *did* tell me what they represented.'

'You're right. I seem to remember us getting a little distracted. But there's nothing much to tell. They're all totally unremarkable places randomly scattered around the world. From a tree somewhere in Madagascar to a field of cowpats in Northern Ireland... their ordinariness is why I was taken in by Xanthia's assurance there was no connection. But now I know your suspicions about her were spot on, I trust you when you say there *is*.'

'I seem to remember two American gentlemen realising they'd underestimated my gifts a little too late,' reflected Donald. 'Though, ironically... on *that* occasion, it probably *saved* your life.'

'Well... let's hope we're not too late *this* time.'

'THERE IT IS AGAIN... THAT BLOODY PERSONAL PRONOUN HE INSISTS ON USING!'

'I used it deliberately. We're going to work as a team... equal partners, straight down the middle... you and I together.'

Donald looked skyward and squinted. 'WELL... I ASSUME HE'S COUNTING YOU AS PART OF MY FIFTY PERCENT.'

'That's why I brought my laptop. Not just to show you those emails. It's time to drag dealing with the spirit world into the twenty-first century! We'll play Xanthia and Kevin at their own game by combining *our* powers. There's a reason the Universe gave us the skills we have. We'll input every piece of information from your filing cabinet into my computer and get it to work out what's going on.'

'And how on earth is it going to do that?'

'Far more easily than *we* ever could. Not only will it do so tirelessly, without the need for a break, it won't be swayed by bias. Best of all… computers are *extremely* good at spotting patterns. You provide the data and I'll convert it into a form that can be analysed. Harnessing our skills, we'll make a formidable team.'

Donald considered the proposition. 'I suppose that means you'll be wanting access to my old filing cabinet.'

'I take it that isn't a problem?'

He took a sharp intake of breath.

Norman's eyes narrowed. 'What have you done with the messages, Donald?'

The playwright sniffed awkwardly. 'I hid them in a large plastic drum… for safety.'

'So…?'

Donald pulled a face as if having just sucked a very large lemon. 'What are you like under water?'

It took the best part of two hours to recover the drum from the bottom of the lake in the garden and haul it to the edge. The hardest part had been attaching a rope around it so as to tease it from the muddy clutch of its resting place. It might have taken less time had Donald been there to help. But – flatly refusing to leave the safety of his house – he'd limited his assistance to barking instructions from a small dormer window in the attic. Not that Norman could hear him, given the distance involved. But that hadn't deterred the playwright.

As he rolled it towards the house, Norman was aware of Donald waving frantically behind the glass, pleading for him to get it inside as soon as possible. Not that encouragement was needed. Given what Norman had been forced to wear to undertake the task, he'd no intention of hanging around in the open any longer than was necessary. Bostock Tucker-Jenkins' bathing costume had fared about as well as his bed sheets over the intervening years. It was also intended for someone twice Norman's size... a fact made all the more obvious by its flannel material appearing to have sucked up half the lake.

Relieved to be back in his own, dry clothes – and with the drum cleaned up and lying on its side in the living room – Norman finally removed its lid and scooped out its contents onto the floor.

'First, we'll deal with the coordinates,' he announced, separating the coloured strings into individual piles. 'I began work on a basic program on the way here, which I'll develop as we go along. Once we've entered those, I'll process everything that's in text form. We'll leave the pictures till last, seeing as I need to get hold of a scanner first. I'll assign as many relevant keywords to the latter as possible. But, who knows... their binary codes may prove to have a deeper meaning... like the artworks I had to convert.'

'I haven't a clue what you're talking about, but assume you know what you're doing,' said Donald, completely bemused.

'You can assist me with the sorting... and then with deciphering that appalling handwriting of yours.'

'The criticism is perfectly justified. I blame Mother for never letting me use my dominant, left hand when I was a child. She used to strap it to my waist with a belt to force me to write with the other one. Father always got extremely annoyed with her.'

'I'm not surprised!'

'Yes... he had nothing to hold his trousers up with.'

'Why on earth would she do such a cruel thing?'

'To cure me. She said sinistration was the work of the Devil.'

'I think he's got better things to concern himself with... especially at the moment.'

'Precisely. So I pray all this work will be worth the effort. I must say... it'll come as an enormous relief to finally know what's going on. The meaning behind these messages has been driving me mad.'

Madder, thought Norman, but opted for sympathy instead. 'I know. I sensed your frustration in the question mark scrawled over that drawing of a planet you did.'

'Ah… yes,' said Donald, recalling the artwork in question. 'That particular image was exceptionally bothersome. They insisted on sending it to me over and over again. But, for the life of me, I couldn't figure out why.' Hovering over a number of red strings, he began rifling through them until finding what he was looking for. 'Here's an example. You mean this.' He thrust it towards Norman's face.

Norman recognised the incoming illustration as yet another artist's impression of the celestial body in question… though this one professionally produced and torn from the pages of a book.

'The tenth planet in our solar system,' Donald announced. 'I must say, it took me quite a while to work that bit out.'

'Sorry to disappoint, Donald,' Norman squinted apologetically, 'but I think you'll find there are only *eight.*'

Donald raised an eyebrow.

'Alright… nine, if you don't class Pluto as a *dwarf* planet,' Norman conceded.

'Or ten, if you think Eris shouldn't be called one, either,' Donald added.

'*Eris?*'

'Given it sits out there in the furthest reaches of our solar system with a mass larger than Pluto's, I think that warrants it a little planetary respect. Don't you?'

'To be honest, I've never even heard of it,' admitted Norman.

'Well, you definitely have now.'

'Yeah…. and I can't wait to see what my program makes of it!'

'You won't have to,' said Donald proudly. 'Since scribbling that question mark in ignorance, I've discovered the answer.'

'You have?'

'Things aren't always what they seem. Communications from the spirit world often warrant further investigation. That's because it's down to me how I choose to interpret the vibrations I'm sent. Sometimes I get it wrong... which is probably why I've been thumped so many times. You see... not all entities vibrate as clearly as one might wish. They send their thoughts as best they can... meaning some are open to inaccurate interpretation on my part. As this particular warning kept appearing as the same planet, I knew I must be on the right path. But it was only after searching through a book on astronomy and discovering *which* planet, that I finally realised what they'd been trying to communicate.'

'And what was that?'

'Nothing to do with the planet itself. They were simply trying to alert me to its name... or, to be more precise, who *inspired* that name.'

Norman ran it around his head a couple of times. 'I can't say I've ever heard of anyone called Eris,' he shrugged.

'Unless well-versed in mythology, I wouldn't expect you to. Like all the planets, it's named after an ancient deity.'

'And what did *Eris* represent?'

Donald looked at him apprehensively. 'Strife and discord.'

Norman gulped.

'Precisely,' said Donald. 'I believe the red strings are warnings about the imminent arrival of the Antichrist.'

Norman stared at him in horror. 'If that's the case... what *else* do they reveal about him?'

Donald looked pained.

'What's the matter?'

The playwright shook his head slowly. 'Not him.'

'I beg your pardon?'

'*Her.*'

They looked at each other in silence.

'The minute you expressed your worries about Xanthia, everything fitted into place.' Donald bent down and searched for another red-stringed message from the scattered pile. Finding what he was looking for, he read it aloud. 'AND I SAW

368

A WOMAN SITTING ON A SCARLET BEAST THAT WAS FULL OF BLASPHEMOUS NAMES, AND IT HAD SEVEN HEADS AND TEN HORNS. THE WOMAN WAS ARRAYED IN PURPLE AND SCARLET, AND ADORNED WITH GOLD AND JEWELS AND PEARLS, HOLDING IN HER HAND A GOLDEN CUP FULL OF ABOMINATIONS AND THE IMPURITIES OF HER SEXUAL IMMORALITY. AND ON HER FOREHEAD WAS WRITTEN A NAME OF MYSTERY: "BABYLON THE GREAT, MOTHER OF PROSTITUTES AND OF EARTH'S ABOMINATIONS".'

'*Xanthia?*' gasped Norman.

'Revelation, chapter seventeen,' Donald nodded.

'As in… the bible?'

Donald winced. 'As in… the end of the world.'

* * *

'Mr President.'

'Gus?'

'With respect, sir… I don't think we can ignore the situation any longer.'

Closing his eyes, the president calmly exhaled his frustration.

'The thing is, sir… there's unanimous consensus from every government department that something, somewhere… *somehow…* is going seriously wrong.'

The president pursed his lips and leant back in his chair, aiming his private thoughts at the ornate, oval ceiling above him.

'Sir?'

Returning his gaze to earth, he looked at the man in front of him as warmly as his annoyance allowed. 'I know, Gus. You're only doing your job. You're just the messenger. But, goddammit… why me? Why on *my* watch? I can't help feeling a nauseating sense of *déjà vu* about all this.'

The president's Chief of Staff shrugged his sympathy... glad to be standing in his own shoes and not those of the man sitting at the desk in front of him.

'I mean... just six months into my first term, the world economy takes a tumble and nearly doesn't make it back onto its feet again. Now... just as things looked like they'd returned to normal, and we'd managed to steer this country to calmer waters, the world seems to be encountering an inexplicable malfunction... much of which has an unhealthy unnaturalness about it. What in hell's name is going on, Gus?'

The Chief of Staff gave another shrug.

'I had been hoping to see out a quiet second term and seal my legacy as the leader who helped pull this world back from the brink. But now it seems it's intent on teeing itself up for another nosedive. Only, this time... there's nothing specific we can put a finger on!'

'It may just be a string of unfortunate coincidences receiving disproportionate attention from a news-hungry media, sir. We all know bad news sells. But every indicator we've examined suggests we're heading for an increasingly volatile period right across the board. We're not just talking erratic weather patterns, poor harvests, and this unprecedented increase in insects, parasites and vermin that's been plaguing us. Homeland is flagging up a worrying rise in civil disobedience. Such incidences might be sporadic and containable at present, but they're warning it could escalate to a far more serious level if these negative trends continue.'

The president looked across at the window and frowned. 'What do our people want out there, Gus? Don't they realise how lucky they are to have anything *remotely* like a stable economy to live and work in? A few things go against them and they take it as a cue to rebel against the whole damn lot! I was under the impression events of a few years ago had taught us all an important lesson in life... don't take that stability for granted!'

'As you alluded to earlier, Mr President... it's not just *us* suffering these anomalies. Intelligence reports confirm every single nation around the globe... friend and foe... is encountering the exact same problems.'

'I don't know whether we should take comfort from that or not,' the president smiled wryly.

'The thing is, sir... with the media predictably deciding the narrative, we're in danger of looking outta touch if we don't respond in some way.'

The president drummed his fingers. 'I hear ya, Gus. But respond to *what*? Where do I go with this? The moment the President of the United States officially steps in and puts it on record that there's a problem, the whole thing gets a heck of a lot more real for everybody. What am I supposed to say to our own people that won't create further panic and exacerbate the situation? We certainly don't wanna pour fuel on the fire. And the *last* thing we can afford is for this administration to be painted as alarmist... or worse still... a spooked collective of headless chickens!'

The Chief of Staff wiggled his toes so as to reaffirm the comfort of his own shoes. 'I just don't think we can sit back and do nothing... sir.'

The president sighed heavily. 'No, you're right. We need to wrestle the situation back from the sensationalists and doomsayers. We can't ignore things any longer.' He tipped his head back and stared at the ceiling again... this time at the large, decorative medallion displaying the presidential seal. 'You see what's written up there, Gus... *E pluribus unum*. That used to be this country's *de facto* motto until someone thought a better one would be *In God We Trust* and made it official. Well... I sometimes wonder if they should've left things as they were. I mean... do we *really* all trust in God anymore? From the negative speculation spewing outta the media these days, I'd certainly say *they* don't!' Rising from his chair, he strolled towards one of the large windows offering a view of the gardens and stared out awhile, deep in thought. 'D'ya know what never ceases to amaze me?' he finally said.

'Sir?'

'Here I am... arguably the most powerful man on this planet... and not *once* in all the time I've been privileged to hold that incredibly significant and influential position has God thought it prudent to speak to me. Not even a thumbs up or thumbs down as to how I'm doing. Now... don't ya find that a *little* odd?'

Gus looked down at his feet.

'I mean... he bothered taking time out to have a word with old Abraham... chewed the fat awhile with Samuel... Ezekiel... Saul... Moses... even gave instructions to Noah as to how to build his boat. Now... not that I'm for one minute comparing myself to any of those august individuals... but I do happen to represent well over three hundred million of his flock. So... if he's getting angry with them and choosing this current situation as his way of showing it, don't ya think it might be better if he dropped me a line sometime?'

Gus shifted uncomfortably. 'With respect, sir... I don't think we should bring God directly into the equation when you address the people.'

The president turned sharply from the window and gave his senior advisor a less inviting stare. 'No...? Well, that's interesting...'cos I've got countless religious groups telling me that's precisely who *should* be featuring in this equation! So... do I ignore them and risk increasing their wrath and the vast swathe of voters who hang on their every word... or do I appease them by telling the public that the Almighty is gonna resolve all our problems himself? In other words... am I simply expected to go along with what it says on our currency?'

'I think you need to calm people's nerves. Let them know you've acknowledged the situation and are doing what you can to look into it.'

'It seems to me more a case of needing to calm our *own* nerves,' the president scoffed.

'Perhaps this really is nothing more than a bad collection of coincidences, sir. Perhaps it's simply a case of everything conspiring against us at once.'

'I hope you're right,' sighed the president. 'Because if not... and God decides he still doesn't want to speak to me... being the most powerful man on earth isn't going to mean a darn thing.'

*　　*　　*

The young children watched in silence as the big boy teased them from his elevated position on the see-saw. Straddling its pivot, he was aggressively transferring his weight from one side to the other, causing the small, plastic seats to strike the ground with as much force as possible.

It wasn't fair. This was *their* playground. It wasn't meant for adults.

He gave a sharp flick of his head towards the climbing frame, as if giving permission for them to have their fun on that. But, wise to his tricks, the children stayed where they were. As with the see-saw... and the swings before that... he would only race them to it and seal his victory with a smirk. It was bad enough the bark chippings, which usually protected them from scrapes and bruises, had been carried away by an army of giant ants the previous day. Now, it seemed, they were in danger of losing the entire playground altogether.

Just as they were considering giving up and leaving the boy to his selfishness, a potential saviour appeared in the guise of a lady wearing a large headscarf, who was swiftly making her way towards the mischief-maker. They figured she'd seen what he was up to and would tell him to leave.

On seeing her approach, the boy jumped from his vantage point.

This was going to be interesting.

Confronting him directly, she removed the headscarf to fully expose her face.

They could see she was pretty.

The boy listened intently as she spoke.

When she'd finished, he smiled.

It wasn't what they'd expected.

Nor was the fact the two of them left the playground together, she having covered her face again... him having offered to carry the pink case she'd been trundling behind her.

*   *   *

Steven enthusiastically entered the room. 'Reverend... it's fantastic news! We've got the green light!' The announcement was delivered via a grin as wide as his face permitted.

Galveston Humbold III rose from his chair. 'You've made contact with her?'

'Xanthia made her own approach this morning, having heard about your challenge. She's agreed to meet you face to face!'

'In a debate, of course,' clarified the reverend hastily, the possibility of having to take boxing lessons temporarily muting any celebration.

'Just like you requested. She's not only agreed for it to be televised globally... she says she's happy to leave the arrangements entirely to us.'

The reverend looked shocked. *'Everything?'*

'It's gets even better. She hasn't insisted on *any* preconditions of her own.'

'None?'

Steven shook his head.

The reverend shook *his,* but for a different reason. 'It don't matter if it's hubris or naivety... they're both the traits of a fool. She'll be coming like a lamb to the slaughter.' He clenched his fist ecstatically. *'I will put an end to the pomp of the arrogant, and lay low the pompous pride of the ruthless. Isiah, thirteen, eleven.'*

'Amen to that, sir!'

'Amen, indeed, Steven. This is my moment. This is what the Lord has called me for. I'll tear that wretched harlot to pieces while the whole world watches.' He waggled a finger at the notebook his assistant had opened in anticipation of instructions. 'I want you to assemble the best team of producers, set designers, lighting engineers and publicists you can lay your hands on. This'll be the showdown of all showdowns, so we don't wanna be cuttin' any corners. Money is no object... I'll see to that. We need to make sure she ain't gonna be able to play her *little-miss-innocent* tricks on the public *this* time. I want 'em to see the Devil when she takes to that stage.' He massaged his chin in thought. 'Perhaps we could bathe her in a red light... maybe work some flames into the equation somehow.'

'If we project *artificial* ones behind her, she won't know it's happening.' said Steven, scribbling furiously. 'She won't feel the heat.'

'Oh... she'll be feeling plenty of *that!*' the reverend gloated. 'And here's another idea I want you to work on... While I'm bathed in an *ethereal* light, I want the set behind to resemble those images the shrinks test you with to find out how batshit crazy you are. Ya know the ones I mean.'

Steven signalled he didn't.

'Yeah, sure you do! They make people look at weird inkblot patterns and get them to say what they see. I had it done to me at a dinner party once... just for fun, mind,' he added quickly. 'We all stared at the same one and came up with different things. Some said they looked like playful dragons, kittens or puppies... others, that they were bunches of flowers or black, fluffy clouds.'

'What did *you* see?'

'Two men copulating.'

'You mean the Rorschach Test.'

The reverend clicked his fingers. 'That's the one! Well... I want those things featured on the set behind us. Only... when the ones behind me are viewed from a predetermined camera angle, I want it to look like I've got a magnificent set of wings sprouting from me... like an angel. But the ones behind Xanthia need to give the impression she's possessed of a set of horns. D'ya see what I'm getting' at?'

Steven nodded eagerly.

'We gotta make her look as dangerous as possible. We don't want her fooling the viewers again with those sweet feminine ways women are so practised at.'

'What about some background music to accompany both your entrances... like when boxers make their ring walks? That would *really* set the mood for each camp.'

'I like it!' the reverend grinned. 'Just make sure mine's louder.'

'I'll get on to it right away, sir.'

The reverend halted his assistant's departure as another idea played in his head. 'One last thing before you go. At the end of the debate... when I've finally ground this Xanthia into the dust and the credits get to roll... d'ya think there's any way I can be made to ascend with those wings I talked about into something that resembles the Kingdom of Heaven... but without it looking ostentatious?'

*　*　*

Having spent four days confined to Donald's house, Norman had reaffirmed a truth empirically learnt over the past few years. No matter how bizarre and uncomfortable a situation might at first appear, with enough exposure to it, you quickly became acclimatised to even the most abnormal of scenarios and accepted it without question. Proving Gabriel's point, reality was simply a matter of perspective.

In this particular case, that perspective was akin to observing things from a parallel universe... one where normal conventions of social interaction, common sense and basic hygiene didn't exist. It was also one where being surprised occurred with such frequency that you were actually surprised when you weren't.

The one thing Norman *refused* to become acclimatised to was Bostock and Dyllis' bedroom. Sensibly passing on the prospect of spending another night in it, he suggested he pitch his tent elsewhere.

Which is exactly what he did.

In the garden.

Much to his host's consternation, he'd insisted on camping outside, allowing the playwright his personal space... and Norman the opportunity to breathe fresh air.

Donald vehemently cautioned against the move, warning his guest he would be more susceptible to attack. But sticking to his guns, Norman persuaded his reluctant host to search the attic for a much-loved, childhood relic that had been reminisced about during one of their nightly conversations. Looking like something from Enid Blyton's worst nightmare, the stained, canvas tent had weathered only marginally better than Bostock and Dyllis' bedroom carpet. But it offered a welcome sanctuary from the madness of the house... as well as a bonus glimpse of the stars.

As with the retrieval of the barrel from the lake, Donald refused to step outside and help put it up. As Norman had never erected a tent in his life, it resulted in the production of a geometric shape science has yet to name.

Donald proved far more cooperative when it came to collating the messages he'd received. Enthusiastically deciphering his hastily scribbled notes, he was keen to ensure Norman inputted everything into his laptop as accurately as possible.

Religious texts featured heavily... most originating from the bible. But there were quotes from religions Norman was unfamiliar with and in which he *also* didn't believe. Oddly... a limerick about a young girl from Devizes had been thrown into the melting pot.

There was a young girl from Devizes,
who hated nocturnal surprises.
When some friends, for a joke,
wore white bed sheets and spoke,
she hung herself with their disguises.

When Donald suggested this was probably Whitebait trying to inject a little levity into proceedings – bored with constantly passing on so much doom and gloom – a ten minute argument between alleged poet and conduit had predictably ensued.

Not that Norman could blame the overworked spirit guide if it was. The messages were depressingly dark and apocalyptic... especially those that had been designated a red string.

Less cryptic were the countless images of sites around the world that had suffered differing degrees of desecration. The victims of everything from petty vandalism to wholesale destruction, they were all structures representing peace, love and anything that brought communities closer together... the most bizarre being the burning of a maypole in a small village somewhere along the Welsh border.

More prosaic were the coordinates. Norman inputted them in their decimal degree format... the locations represented to be worked out later and relevant keywords assigned. Donald hadn't exaggerated when saying those he'd tested Xanthia with were just the tip of an enormous iceberg. Had she not told him what they represented, Norman would've assumed they'd all turn out to match the aforementioned sites. But just where a hay barn in Wyoming or a postbox in Canterbury figured in that equation was anybody's guess. As for the washroom of a bicycle factory in China...

Both men worked tirelessly over the coming days, only choosing to stop when fatigue finally blunted their concentration. Though Norman would've happily retired to his tent at that point, his host always insisted he stay awhile and chat. Clearly, having someone to talk to – who *didn't* constantly request milk – came as something of a novelty. Not that the cats weren't important to Donald. But *they* weren't interested in his paintings. To be fair... neither was Norman after the third day... but talking about art provided a common bond, outside of their work, and helped pass the time as conventionally as possible.

It was during one such discourse that Donald sprang a surprise. Announcing he hadn't entirely given up on his painting muse, he offered to do a portrait of his guest.

Thinking it rude to refuse, Norman was also secretly flattered. He'd always envied those immortalised in oil, but had never quite mustered the courage to offer someone a commission to immortalise *him*. No longer able to afford such a luxury, he figured this would be his only chance of joining their ranks.

A stool duly brought for his subject to sit on, Donald eagerly assembled his easel, canvas and paints, and set about his work.

This involved him taking a long, hard look at Norman... then closing his eyes.

Norman waited patiently while Donald sought to make contact with his muse.

Just as Norman thought he might have gone to sleep, Donald opened them with a start and began frantically attacking the canvas in front of him. The speed at which he did so was impressive... barely stopping to contemplate his next brush stroke. Holding his brushes between his teeth, he would occasionally grunt and nod to himself, as if critiquing his own work. But not once during his blitzkrieg technique did he bother to look at his subject again... a fact Norman found remarkable.

With paint flying everywhere, the cats abandoned the room *en masse* before they resembled those multi-coloured, mosaic animal souvenirs frequently found in Spanish gift shops.

As Norman's buttocks were threatening to disown him, Donald finally took a step back and viewed his creation in triumph.

'Is it done?' asked Norman tentatively.

'It is.'

'Can I see it?'

'You must bear in mind it's an *interpretation* of you,' said Donald, as if by way of a warning.

Norman didn't care. He appreciated artists viewed the world through subjective eyes. He was just intrigued to see himself through Donald's. 'This'll be interesting,' he laughed. 'At least I'll know how you *really* feel about me!'

'How my muse feels about you,' Donald corrected him. 'I just hope I've done it justice.'

Standing eagerly, Norman winced as the blood forced its way back into where it should've been in the first place. Waddling over to the easel, he steeled himself for the grand reveal.

Donald proudly beckoned him to take a look.

Norman accepted.

'Oh,' he said quietly.

'What do you think?' Donald beamed.

Norman didn't know where to start.

Perhaps he could've begun by commenting on the fact the artist had chosen to frame his subject using surprisingly dark and depressing colours.

He might even have referenced the fact those colours had been applied with a technique conveying great angst.

Or perhaps he could've suggested that... despite the likeness being remarkably accurate... it would've been even *more* so had Donald not chosen to depict him with his eyes sewn shut.

As for the angry, open-jawed, red-scaled snake forcing its way from his mouth...

*   *   *

Not since the first Beatle boot set itself down on American soil had the arrival of a visitor from across the pond caused such pandemonium. Thousands of people had besieged the airport's terminal in order to catch a glimpse of the person dominating the country's media. *Xanthiamania* was the new buzzword... created and encouraged by Galveston Humbold's tireless public relations team seeking to capitalise on viral stories of their maleficent guest's sensational altercation with an angel.

Any thoughts of braving the baggage carousel completely out of the question, she'd been met at the airbridge by a retinue of sombre-looking officials, accompanied by a well-armed security team... just in case. A curt "welcome to our country" was delivered with as much sincerity as politeness dictated.

Smiling sweetly, she found herself swiftly ushered through a side door, allowing her and her travelling companion an escape from the transfixed stares of fellow passengers.

After a brisk walk in silence through a string of corridors, a further door revealed fresh air, an awaiting limousine, and something as close to privacy as she could now expect.

'D'ya think this is all for us?' beamed Kevin, enthusiastically investigating a well-stocked drinks cabinet, as the driver initiated their getaway. 'I take it we don't have to pay for anything?'

'I think you'll find you'll be allowed whatever you want while you're with me,' she replied.

'Did you see the guns those guys were carrying?' Kevin made shooting actions with his hands. 'Like they think bullets are gonna have any effect against you!'

'They're scared and confused. They're simply trying to protect themselves against something they don't understand. But it's to our advantage they're ignorant of what I can *really* do.'

Kevin's face could hardly contain his excitement. 'You'll show them good and proper, though, won't you, Xan?'

She looked out of the window dispassionately. 'Oh, don't worry... they have no idea what's about to hit them.'

He tilted his head. 'I still don't understand why *I* can't feel anything. You'd think I would, wouldn't you?'

'I told you... you only caught the minutest particle of the Sphere. But it's enough to mean that, with you by my side, I'm invested with that final piece of the jigsaw I needed. *Now* I can begin doing what was planned.'

Kevin played with the air conditioning. 'Has Lucifer made contact with you yet?'

'He doesn't need to. I'm fully aware of what he expects of me.'

'Us,' Kevin corrected her.

She smiled.

'And what do you think Norman's gonna do when he finds out you're here with his coding nemesis?' he smirked.

'It doesn't matter. He's in no position to do anything.' She smiled again. 'You made sure of that.'

'I did, didn't I! I stripped him of everything he had!'

She gently squeezed his arm. *'Everything.'*

'I still don't understand why you didn't let him die, though. He'd served his purpose. I executed my part of the job perfectly. There was no reason to save that creep's life.'

She stared at him unemotionally. 'You're wrong. If I hadn't, alarm bells would've rung the minute everyone realised the extent of my powers. He *was* supposed to be my boyfriend, after all. I simply did what would've been expected of me. I still need to dupe the world into trusting me... just like I did him. He was nothing more than a means to an end.' She ran her tongue over heavily glossed lips. 'Besides... I actually got a kick out of toying with him. He always thought himself so much smarter than me... even *after* he knew I'd received my gift! Well... he won't be thinking that now,' she sneered. 'I consider it payback for all those boring art galleries stuffed with religious sycophancy he forced me to visit while I was playing the game and biding my time.'

'I guess,' Kevin shrugged. 'But what about your confrontation with the angel?'

'Gabriel on the Witches Mound? What about it?'

'Well... that's not exactly helped you fool the public, has it?'

'You're right,' she frowned. 'That whole incident was extremely unfortunate. I wasn't expecting it to happen. But, don't worry. I'll think of something to smooth things over. Having access to the creative mind of every great author who's ever lived, it shouldn't be too difficult to come up with a plausible story. And on the plus side... it's finally given me the serious attention I need.'

'I bet he's furious.'

'Gabriel?'

'Norman... now that you've dumped him.'

'You flatter me. I think he'll end up missing his paintings more than he will me. What will *really* hurt is when he finds out I'm with you.'

'Along with the fact I beat him good and proper with my impenetrable firewall, don't forget!'

She moved her hand to his leg. 'How could I? You demonstrated your superiority over him. And it's no small victory, given how annoyingly gifted he is when it comes to such things.'

'Though... as you say... clearly not as gifted as me,' he gloated.

'You see... that's what I've missed,' she grinned. 'Being with someone who has unwavering confidence in themselves. I can't tell you what an aphrodisiac that is for me. That's why I look back with such happiness on my time spent with Stump... even if he could be a complete pain sometimes. He always lived life to the extreme and never cared about the consequences.'

'Let's not talk about *him*,' said Kevin childishly.

'But, we have much to thank him for,' countered Xanthia. 'He's the reason I'm here in the first place.'

'How so?'

'Well... when I discovered the secret behind his phenomenal success with *Sex Wench,* I figured Lucifer would do the same for me and *my* profile if I avenged him for what Norman had done. Our reception here proves I was right. My name's now on everyone's lips.' She stared wistfully at a giant billboard advertising her upcoming showdown with Galveston Humbold. 'Giving up the excitement of Soddem Hall, as part of that plan, was an *extremely* tough ask, though... especially having to trade it for such an uninspiring bore. It's just as well he had that chequebook of his to ease the tedium. But I knew, if I bided my time and acted the good girlfriend he wanted me to be, I'd eventually be presented with an opportunity to exact maximum punishment.' She gave an ironic snort. 'Mind you... even *with* all that money, he never amounted to anything more than a self-indulgent wimp who constantly struggled to justify his good fortune.' She gazed at Kevin admiringly. 'You, on the other hand, know *exactly* what you're worth and won't allow anyone to stand in your way.' She nuzzled his ear as she squeezed his thigh. 'I can't tell you how energised that's made me feel again. I've missed the excitement of being with an irresistibly confident, bad boy!'

He giggled. 'I got him good and proper, didn't I? I bet denying him access to his precious Templar account cut deeper than that knife I plunged into his stupid stomach!'

She massaged his leg suggestively. 'While I might've saved him from that physical wound... the mental one you inflicted is something he'll *never* recover from.'

Kevin glanced through the privacy screen to ensure the driver's eyes were still on the road. 'Has he tried to gain access to it since?' He placed his hand on hers and dragged it further up his leg. 'I mean... let's face it... I doubt he'll simply give up. He's gonna be even *more* desperate to recover his finances, once he discovers you've left him. He knows it's the only thing that'll make him look *remotely* attractive to a future partner.'

'Stop worrying about him,' she frowned. 'He's an irrelevance now. Besides... you needn't concern yourself about him breaching that firewall of yours. He ceased thinking it was possible after I told him the coding behind it was so devious, even *I* couldn't help him with it. Your idea of having it automatically reconfigure itself every few seconds was genius. *No one* could crack such a thing. Not even you!'

Kevin swiftly removed his hand. 'Don't be so sure of that.'

She looked at him askance.

'You don't believe me?'

She shook her head. 'I know you're good... but no one's *that* good.'

'I am,' he said confidently.

She laughed.

'What?'

'Come on, Kevin. You *know* my abilities. Don't you think if it were possible, I'd have done so myself and reinstated the chequebook? Think what having so vast an amount of money would mean for our mission. To begin with... I wouldn't have to waste time engaging with this evangelical halfwit who's paying for us to be here. With an unlimited budget, we'd have the ability to immediately access and influence the minds of everyone on this planet. And, as an exquisite bonus, we'd have the satisfaction of knowing it was the Templars who helped our Master reign supreme!' She sunk her nails into his leg as she drank in the thought.

'That's why I put a backdoor in my program,' he winced.

Her grip increased. 'I *beg* your pardon?'

'A password that allows me to short circuit my shifting firewall,' he squealed, his eyes watering. 'Once activated, the code would remain static… giving me all the time in the world to gain access to the account.'

She looked at him incredulously. 'Then, how come I don't know about such a thing?'

He shrugged. 'Maybe that bit of knowledge was in the fragment of sphere I received. Who knows?'

Her eyes widened. 'It's more than possible.' She stared at him in disbelief. 'So, let me get this straight… you're *seriously* telling me we might be able to get our hands on all that Templar money?'

'If we had Norman's original chequebook, they'd be powerless to stop us… even when discovering what we were up to. Given the cheques were personally guaranteed by the Archangel Gabriel, they'd be duty bound to honour them, no matter the amount they were made out for. By reinstating the chequebook, we could take them to the cleaners.'

Her open mouth morphed into a stunned smile. 'I *do* have it,' she gasped. 'I took it with me when I left, even though I believed it to be worthless. It was my way of letting him know it was the only thing that gave me pleasure while I was forced to be with him.' She held Kevin's head between her hands. 'This is absolutely incredible! You're even *more* remarkable than I thought. The irony of that chequebook being used to achieve our Master's purpose will reverberate around the Universe for all eternity!' Pulling him forward, she planted a kiss on his forehead. 'You see… I *knew* I'd chosen the right cyber warrior!'

*   *   *

'Have you seen this morning's paper?' Norman thrust it under Donald's nose.

'I have,' the playwright nodded.

'Well... what do you make of it?'

Donald took a few moments to examine what was in front of him.

'Well?'

'I think it's justifiable.'

Norman stared in horror. 'Are you serious?'

Snatching the paper, Donald studied it more closely. 'Yes... I am. It's *definitely* justifiable.'

'Justifiable?' Norman exclaimed. 'How can you possibly think that? I'd say it's indisputably *undesirable!*'

Donald squinted at the newsprint. 'There's no D!'

'What?'

'You'd need a D to spell undesirable.'

Norman looked confused.

'Do I take it we're not talking about the daily anagram?' Donald asked.

Norman grabbed the paper back and stabbed his finger at an article at the top of the page. 'I'm talking about this bit here. It says Xanthia's in America, preparing to appear on a primetime TV show that's going to be screened live around the world!'

Donald let out one of his squeals. 'You can't be serious! That would be *disastrous.* I warned you this must never be allowed to happen. If she gets to spew her poison to a global audience, we're done for! We have to stop her!'

'And how do you propose we do that?'

'By alerting the necessary authorities, of course!'

'But who's going to listen to *us?*'

'I beg your pardon?'

'I said... who's going to listen to *us.* After all... I'm probably about to be charged with vandalising one of *the* most iconic ancient monuments ever... and you...' Norman looked at Donald awkwardly.

'I KNOW... HE WAS GOING TO SAY "*ARE A NUTTER WHO SPEAKS TO THE DEAD*".'

Norman would've used the word *lunatic*... but the point still held.

'You're forgetting one thing, young man,' Donald said stiffly. 'I might shows signs of mild eccentricity from time to time... but I'll have you know my name is revered throughout the world as one of its finest playwrights... and the words I communicate have an enormous effect on people's hearts and minds.'

Norman had to confess he *had* forgotten. Having spent so long with Donald, he'd lost sight of the bigger picture. It was hard to believe that what the man in front of him had to say... on paper, at least... was treated with extreme veneration around the world.

'We need to get ourselves to America as quickly as possible,' insisted Donald. 'I'll get my agent to arrange a meeting with the president.'

'Of your publishing company?'

'Of the United States of America, you idiot.'

Norman squinted. 'Is that *possible?*'

'Of course it is. I *do* have a telephone, you know.'

'I meant... actually getting to see the president.'

'I can make it happen any time I like,' said Donald, matter-of-factly. 'I've met him on numerous occasions. He's one of the most enthusiastic exponents of my work.'

'I had no idea,' Norman gasped.

'I think you sometimes have even less than that,' returned Donald dryly. 'Anyway... let's not waste another minute. We have very few of them left in which to act.'

Norman raised a hand. 'Hang on a second. Aren't you forgetting one important thing?'

Donald gave the question a moment's thought. 'Don't worry. I'll buy a toothbrush when I'm out there. Come on... let's go.'

'But I thought you said it was unsafe for you to leave this house.'

349

'I can't say I'm happy about it,' Donald grimaced. 'But needs must. Besides… I've got a contingency plan. It should at least help protect me for a while.'

'Fair enough,' Norman shrugged, curious as to what that might be. 'I'll pack my bag.'

'Be quick. I'll wait for you in the hall.'

'But don't you have to pack yours?'

'Why?'

'Er… so that you'll have fresh clothes to wear? Underpants… socks… that kinda thing?'

Donald looked at him blankly.

'You're going to ask me *why* again, aren't you?' nodded Norman to himself.

*   *   *

Xin Chen smoothed the crumpled page – long ago carefully removed from a magazine – over the tops of his bare thighs, and leant forward to study the picture on it.

One day the little boat… or at least something very similar… would be his.

His precious wife would lovingly prepare a delicious basket of food, so that the two of them could spend the whole day gently drifting along the river, their feet dangling idly in the cool water as the sun caressed their upturned, smiling faces.

He'd first have to row upstream, of course, and get the hard part out the way. But from that point on he'd be able to sit back and relax… the two of them happily nestled together… enjoying the benefit of the slow current home… far removed from the hustle and bustle of life beyond the passing riverbanks.

Naturally, he'd be of a greater age by then… though he did press-ups every day to ensure his arms would be strong enough to cope with the demand of the oars when he finally got to use them.

He wondered what it would be like rowing his boat. It couldn't be *that* difficult.

He pictured people standing on the bank, admiring the fact an older man could still do such a thing. Perhaps they would clap to spur him on... maybe even cheer.

His wife would be so proud of him... having watched him cleverly save his money so as to give them their dream, and knowing how much he'd sacrificed to make it possible.

It was especially difficult when colleagues invited him to come for a drink after work... or to watch the local football team playing at home. But all that cost money... and boats weren't cheap... not those as beautiful as the one in the magazine.

In truth... his colleagues had all but stopped asking him now. They obviously thought him odd and wanted little to do with him anymore.

But his ostracism would be worth it. He only wanted the best for his wife. That's all that mattered.

He'd finally be able to protect her from those evil spirits his grandmother had warned him about when he was a little boy. The old lady's exhorting eyes and anguished, wrinkled stare had kept him entranced for many an hour, as she spoke of their danger.

Not that he'd ever encountered one in all the years since. But he'd been told they were devious... purposely remaining hidden... working tirelessly behind the scenes to affect his life and hasten his death. So vivid was the tableau of wickedness she'd painted, he'd had trouble sleeping thereafter. Aware of this, his mother had given him an amulet to wear around his neck, promising it would help keep them at bay. Many years later, it still hung on the cheapest of chains, her son having never dared remove it.

It was during one such alarming discourse that he'd discovered those troublesome entities were unable to cross water.

That's why he needed the boat.

It would finally provide a sanctuary from all his years of worrying. But... more importantly... he would be able to give his wife that peace of mind, too.

He'd calculated it would take a little over twenty years to save enough money, provided he stuck to the target he'd set himself. Day-to-day living costs were punishingly high where he lived, and wages for the sort of work he did, pitifully low. But at least it was steady work. People would always ride bicycles.

Mind you... he might not keep that job if he didn't get back to the factory floor. The foreman had already warned him about taking too much time to do what he needed to.

Carefully folding the magazine article into its familiar quarters, he leant down and placed it safely in the pocket of his overalls.

He never noticed the chain from which the amulet hung catch on one of its buttons. Neither did he feel it break as he stood to pull them up.

It was only as he was fastening the final one that he realised the calamity that had just befallen him.

Staring down in panic at the water swirling around an emptying bowl, he instinctively grabbed for where the amulet had been, but felt his fingers meet his palm.

His blood froze.

An image of his grandmother flashed before him... her eyes staring wildly... screaming apocalyptic words of warning from the past.

But it was too late.

His breath shortened as a vice-like grip took hold of his chest... refusing him another.

He fell back against the grubby cubicle door.

The last thoughts that went through his mind were that it was such an undignified place to die... and that forty-seven years had not been long enough.

As his body slumped in the confined space, his head came to rest ignominiously in the bowl of the toilet. It would be the closest it would now ever get to water.

It was half an hour before anyone missed him enough to come and find out what had happened... and a little over a week before no one missed him at all and he was forgotten about completely.

The boat would forever remain an unfulfilled dream... as would the wife he had one day hoped to meet.

*　　*　　*

Xanthia wrapped her arms around Kevin's chest and playfully nuzzled the back of his neck. 'I've always been attracted to talented men. The trouble is, with my gift, it now takes a *very* special man to stimulate me.' She resisted the urge to bite him. 'Luckily for us, age has never been an issue for me!'

'Mum thinks I'm special too,' remarked Kevin, continuing to type on his laptop.

She pulled back slightly. 'That's not *quite* the same thing.' She combed her fingers through his hair. 'I've also got a soft spot for men who don't exhibit fear... those who just get on and do their thing without taking no for an answer.'

'I'm told most women prefer hunks... and I'm not exactly that,' he admitted. 'But brains win over brawn every time, and I'm definitely not short of those.'

She clung to him tightly again. 'I'm still struggling with the fact there's a chance you're about to do something I can't. Even with this gift of mine, I thought it impossible. If we get our hands on that Templar money, our master's victory is guaranteed!'

'I assume we're not expected to spend it *all* on achieving it, though,' said Kevin, trying hard to concentrate on the screen in front of him.

She momentarily released her grip. 'How do you mean, sweetie?'

'Well... I'd like to think we'll be able to spend a little of it on ourselves.'

'Of course we will,' she laughed. 'That's the whole point. We're about to create a world where people can do whatever they want without suffering guilt. I could never understand why Norman was such a slave to it. You see... that's the

345

difference between you and him. You understand there's no one more worthy of the best things in life than yourself. So, yes... we'll take full advantage of our good fortune. After all... what's the point of encouraging the cult of self if we don't practise what we preach?'

'In that case... I'm gonna buy a supercar that turns people's heads. Every man I pass will wish they were me.'

'They definitely will when they see who it is you've got in the passenger seat,' she teased.

'Good point. I'd better make sure it's a cabriolet, then,' he said, without a hint of irony.

'Have you driven before?'

'Of course! I'm an expert at rallycross and formula one.'

'Other than on a computer.'

He shrugged. 'I doubt it'll be any different. And once we've established a state of anarchy, I won't need a driving licence. Learning all those road signs would be pointless anyway. It's not *me* who's gonna be in danger when I encounter old people crossing the road.'

'Won't it be glorious?' she beamed. 'Because of us, people will finally control their own lives. There'll be no more rules. Everyone will be able to do *exactly* what they want.'

'In that case... perhaps I should buy a gun... just in case someone takes a shine to my car.'

'You'll be able to hire your own private *army* if you succeed in breaching this firewall,' she laughed.

'That might not be a bad idea,' he nodded seriously. 'Weakness equals oblivion. It'll be survival of the fittest from now on.'

'I know.' She moved her hands down towards his groin. 'How sweet revenge will taste. I'll take particular delight in seeing the despair of those who've judged me with upturned noses all these years, as they attempt to cling to their crumbling moral high ground. Their anguish will be all the greater for knowing it was self-inflicted. We'll finally put an end to millennia of propaganda, indoctrination and control by those who cast Lucifer as the enemy. The gift of freewill is going to be enjoyed the way he always said it should. When those who cast him out as an angel lose their control over people's minds, he'll take his rightful place at the head of them and reign supreme!'

'Just so long as my mum's alright,' added Kevin. 'I know she can be annoying sometimes… but I don't want her getting hurt.'

'To the contrary,' said Xanthia. 'She'll be so proud of you when the truth comes out. I see it all, remember? I *know* we're fighting for the right side.'

Kevin paused what he was doing. 'So… how *exactly* does that work? I mean… what's it like knowing *everything* that's ever happened, all at the same time… except for the bit of the sphere you say I have, of course?'

'I don't,' she smiled, 'which is just as well. If I *did,* I wouldn't have the mental capacity to put my lipstick on! It's difficult enough for me as it is. I only see what I choose to focus on. That's why I'm constantly battling to limit where my mind goes. It's not dissimilar to you zoning out all the distractions around you so that you can concentrate on what needs to be done. I bet, while you've been typing, you haven't noticed the fan whirring away inside the laptop… or the heat it's dissipating… even less the turbulence in the air it's creating. But have a mind to and you'll be aware of it all.'

'So… you wouldn't instantly know everything about… *me*… for instance?' he asked a little awkwardly.

'Only if I choose to. But it's alright… you can relax. I don't!' Relief softened his stare.

'I know how much you love me, though,' she smiled.

'More than Penkridge ever did, I bet!'

For the first time, a tone of annoyance crept into her voice. 'You have to stop concerning yourself with him, Kevin. He's of no importance. In fact, I'm tired of hearing his name.'

'He wasn't unimportant when the other side asked for his help,' Kevin persisted.

She broke away and frowned. 'Why on earth should that matter now?'

'Because when they were looking for the best computer mind to assist them, they didn't come to *me*.'

'Well… you can hardly blame them,' she snorted. 'You were barely out of nappies at the time.'

'Not quite. So… what did they think was so special about *him?*'

She sighed. 'You *know* I can't answer that. I only have knowledge of matters pertaining to the material world. Even his conversations with Gabriel appear vague and distorted when I try to access them. There's too much vibrational interference for any of it to make sense. Besides… you *were* ultimately chosen… by the winning side, not the losing one.'

'Good point.' His scowl morphed into concentration as he returned to his task.

She leaned in close and gently stroked his hair again. 'Despite me believing it was impossible, you really think you can pull this off, don't you?'

Shrugging away the distraction, he continued his work.

After a period of furious finger tapping, he finally folded his arms and leant back in his chair.

'Now… ask me that last question again.'

'What… about thinking you can reinstate the chequebook and provide us with a source of finance beyond our wildest dreams?'

'Yes. And I don't *think*… I *know*,' he replied smugly… with a grin suggesting he just had.

* * *

Norman had spent the last half hour pinching himself, expecting to wake up at any moment and find it was all a dream. His pyjamas failing to materialise, he expected he and Donald to be rapidly approached by concerned officials realising a ghastly mistake had been made. But at every security checkpoint, he'd been astonished to find himself politely and promptly ushered through.

It was even *more* astonishing and surreal given Donald had chosen to wear a full suit of medieval armour as his "contingency plan" to allow him to leave his house.

While those manning the metal detector at the White House had been willing to ignore the fact their alarm had been sent into overdrive – as the great British playwright waddled through – bemused staff at Heathrow airport had been less accommodating. Donald had been politely ushered into a side room and a private inspection undertaken.

The sight of an irate medieval knight sitting on the back of an electric cart, loudly protesting at his being delayed, had raised many an eyebrow as it beeped its way past those heading for the same flight.

Far happier with the treatment he was being afforded by his American hosts, Donald seemed to be taking it all in his restricted stride... completely unfazed by where he was.

With the last of the security checkpoints negotiated, he and Norman found themselves entering a large, ornate room... two immaculately dressed, white-gloved marines standing guard at a door opposite the one through which they'd just passed. The soldiers' expressions gave little away, except to warn anyone approaching that the person beyond *their* door was of the greatest importance, and that you had little chance of proceeding further... no matter how many great plays you'd written... or the effectiveness of your apparel against ceremonial swords.

Not that it mattered. Just as Norman was awaiting his next surprise, the door in question obliged... and a man familiar to him and the rest of the world strode briskly through it.

'Donald. How wonderful it is to see you. At least... I *assume* that's you!'

Donald flipped up his visor and proffered a gauntlet towards the hand being enthusiastically extended. 'It's good to see you too, Nick,' he returned. 'I appreciate you agreeing to meet us at such short notice.'

'Don't mention it,' beamed the president. 'It's a relief to have a sane mind to talk to in these increasingly crazy times.'

Norman pinched the back of his hand so hard he'd still be reminded of it a week later.

If Norman's brain was struggling to process its incoming signals, the next one blew it completely.

'And Whitebait? How is he these days?'

Norman's jaw fell.

'I always find it difficult talking about his current well-being, given the curmudgeonly old bugger's dead,' Donald replied.

The president laughed.

'LIGHTEN UP, WILL YOU?' Donald shouted at the top of his voice. 'YOU SHOULD THANK YOUR LUCKY STARS YOU'VE BEEN ALLOWED TO COME IN WITH ME.'

The guards didn't flinch.

'It's good to have you both visit me again,' the president smiled. 'And the third member of your entourage... this must be Norman.'

Norman weakly extended his own hand, his mouth still in paralysis.

'It is,' said Donald. 'And we have much to thank him for. There are things that have happened in the past I didn't think I'd ever need trouble you with. But we have entered exceptional times and there's much I must now confide in you.'

'Your people said it concerns these strange occurrences that have been plaguing us and the rest of the world?'

'It does... and they're about to get even stranger and far more deadly if a certain individual is allowed to broadcast from your shores tonight.'

The president looked at Donald solemnly. 'Tell me more.'

'Her name is Xanthia... and she's about to take part in a debate that's scheduled to be televised globally.'

'Ah, yes,' the president nodded. 'I've heard about this. In fact... they've been promoting it so extensively, I don't think there's anyone who *hasn't*. It's with an evangelist we have over here called Galveston Humbold III. Between you and me, the man's a complete charlatan. But he's also extremely popular and a favourite with many of my supporters. I believe he and this girl are going to squabble over which one of them can put a stop to all this nonsense.'

'I wish it *were* nonsense,' returned Donald grimly. 'And, whilst your compatriot might be a charlatan, I assure you this Xanthia is an extremely dangerous and seriously minded individual.'

'But she claims to have knowledge of everything!' the president laughed.

'She has,' said Donald bluntly.

The president waited for Donald's expression to crack and the punchline to be delivered. But when neither scenario materialised, his face dropped. 'Donald... please tell me you're pulling my leg.'

'I've never been more serious. That girl has powers beyond most people's comprehension.'

The president looked confused. 'In that case... why the concern? I thought she's claiming to be able to *save* us all.'

'It's a lie... and worse than that... she intends doing the exact *opposite*.'

'That's what this Humbold idiot's saying.'

'Then, perhaps he's *not* such an idiot,' reflected Donald.

The president frowned. 'But what d'ya want *me* to do about it?'

Donald blinked his disbelief. '*Stop* her, of course!'

'But I can't.'

'You're the president of this country!' Donald exclaimed. 'You're the most powerful man on this planet!'

'I think the Chinese and Russians might want to take issue with that,' the president quipped to those standing around them.

'But you are.'

The president put a confiding arm around his visitor. 'The trouble is, Donald... we have this little thing over here called the Constitution. And part of that gives our citizens the inalienable right to practise free speech. I can't go riding roughshod over the First Amendment just because the great Donald Tucker-Jenkins says I should. It would have me out of office faster than my political adversaries could click their fingers.'

'But you can't just sit back and do nothing,' insisted Donald. 'If she gets to spew her poison to the wider world, we're doomed... including those who might not share your politics. Can't you just take my word for it and have her bumped off?'

'Donald!' The president looked around the room again and gave an embarrassed laugh. 'I think you'll find that's *also* against the rules.'

'Then, at least have her arrested. You *must* be able to detain her for some minor violation or other.'

The president smiled sympathetically. 'Perhaps you should give me a little more information... then we'll see what needs to be done.' He beckoned one of those in the room who'd been patiently standing by. 'Roger... I'm going to spend the rest of this morning with Mister Tucker-Jenkins and his young associate, Norman. I want to hear what they have to say. If they convince me there's a credible threat to this country, I'll need you to action an immediate security meeting with all the relevant departments. So, have them on standby. If it's as bad as Donald suggests, we're gonna need the full team in attendance right away.'

Roger looked at the president and then at Donald's choice of attire. 'With respect, sir... shouldn't we examine your visitor's claims a little more closely before taking such a drastic step?'

The president gave his subordinate a laser stare. 'Do you *know* who we have standing in this room with us at this present time?'

The subordinate had the sense to realise it was a rhetorical question.

'One of the finest minds of the twenty-first century. A man who's finger is so on the pulse of the human condition, that the reading of his words should, in my opinion, be made compulsory in every school in every country of the world.'

He let the point sink in.

'HE'LL COME TO YOU IN A MINUTE.' shouted Donald.

'Furthermore... He has as direct a line to those who are as near to God as we are ever likely to come... whilst we're alive, that is.'

'I TOLD YOU.'

'I'm now going to have that private meeting with him... that direct line... and Mister Penkridge. I don't expect to be disturbed.'

With that, he ushered his three visitors past the white-gloved marines and into the room beyond.

* * *

'Sorry to disturb you, Reverend... but something's come up I think you need to know about.'

Galveston Humbold looked up in shock and quickly stuffed the magazine he'd been reading into the middle draw of his desk. 'Hell's teeth, boy... Didn't that mama of yours ever teach you to knock?'

'She did, sir... and I've never ignored her advice,' his assistant answered awkwardly. 'I guess you must've been too engrossed in your... *study*.'

'Yeah... that's right,' the reverend nodded, fumbling for a pen. 'Those Sunday sermons don't write themselves, you know. So... what can I do for you?'

'It's about Xanthia.'

The reverend leant back in horror. 'You're not gonna tell me she's got cold feet and changed her mind about our televised showdown?'

'Nothing like that, sir. She's safely holed up in the hotel you had me book her into and enjoying our hospitality while she waits.'

'I'm mightily relieved to hear it,' he whistled, wiping his brow with a handkerchief already in his hand. 'There's more riding on this than I care to think about. With the personal finances I've ploughed into this enterprise... that woman *has* to be at that studio tomorrow night!'

'That's why I thought you needed to hear my news.'

337

'Go on, boy.'

'I have a friend with an ear to a very important door in Washington. He's just informed me that the authorities are considering stopping Xanthia appearing on our show tomorrow night... though a decision has yet to be made. Someone has set alarm bells ringing, at the highest level, by suggesting that what she has to say could be extremely detrimental to the health of our nation.'

'Too right!' exclaimed the reverend. 'That someone is me! *I've* been consistently preaching that fact... right about the time everybody else seemed happy to treat that woman as a joke. You need to get in touch with your good friend and tell him to holla back through that door... as loud as he possibly can... that the only *real* way of stopping that child of evil is for Galveston Humbold III to be allowed to peel back her mask and show the world what really lurks beneath!'

'But what if they don't allow that to happen? The word is... ways are being looked at to temporarily detain her.'

'We'll see about that,' shouted the reverend, standing in anger. 'I want you to find alternative accommodation for that woman. Book it in person and make the reservation in your own name. Pay in cash so that it's untraceable. Then tell her there's been some kinda mix up and she's gonna have to swap hotels. Whatever you do... don't give her the option of saying no. If the authorities can't find her, they won't be able to detain her. Not tonight, anyhow. That should give Marty time to come up with some legal mumbo jumbo to stall them, if they're thinking of interfering with the actual broadcast. I also want extra security on the studio doors tomorrow night... just in case.'

'Yes, sir. I'll get on to it right away.'

'Good lad. We've just gotta be smarter and better prepared than the opposition. We don't want them tripping us up.'

Steven looked at the reverend awkwardly.

'What is it, boy?'

'Talking of tripping up... sir.' He directed his gaze towards the reverend's trousers slowly sinking to his ankles.

'Is everyone here?' The president looked to his Chief of Staff for confirmation. 'Yes? Good. So... you're probably wondering why I've called you to this meeting at such short notice. Well... as should be obvious to you all... over the last few weeks we've witnessed a multitude of abnormal occurrences that, through their combined effect, have produced a decline in the well-being of this nation. I'm sure many of you put this down to happenstance and adverse luck. But today I've received information that suggests otherwise.'

Expressions of surprise criss-crossed the table.

'Before I get to that... I'm going to ask Calvin from USDA to put you in the picture regarding issues identified by his department. They give serious cause for concern and illustrate why we need to start taking this matter far more seriously. Calvin... if you'd be so kind.'

'Thank you, Mister President.' Calvin rose and cleared his throat. 'Ladies and gentlemen... The Department of Agriculture has been closely monitoring the fallout from these incidents the president has just referred to, and I can confirm an alarming and exponential deterioration in every single sector of our industry as a direct result of what we're experiencing.'

Concerned muttering filled the room.

'Folks... please,' said the president, waving it down. 'Calvin... continue.'

'Sir. Most alarming of all... we've just recorded a thirty percent drop in food production for the last quarter, which is well below that of even our most pessimistic forecasts. The problem is further compounded by the fact this year's abysmal harvests are not confined to our own borders. Unfavourable weather and unprecedented crop blights have caused equal misery for farmers around the world... along with a worrying increase in local labour disputes... all of which has compromised the global availability of foodstuffs. As a result, it

335

looks unlikely we'll be able to import our way out of this situation.'

His colleagues exchanged looks of alarm.

'I have therefore asked the president to immediately authorise an emergency stockpiling program so that we can guarantee the supply of essential provisions. However...' He glanced across at his Commander-in-Chief apprehensively. 'Initial reports from the markets suggest a number of private companies are *way* ahead of us on this and have already been buying up vast stocks of what we're going to need.' His head shook. 'In fact... they're *so* far ahead of us, you'd think they'd had advance warning of this crisis! But, as we all know... that's impossible. Irrespective of how they managed to gain the upper hand, we now find ourselves at their mercy. We can only hope they'll negotiate fairly when it comes to acquiring those goods.'

'Could we be looking at something similar to what happened five years ago?' interjected one of those in attendance. 'Is it possible someone's manipulating the markets again?'

'It's not feasible anyone could've predicted the extent to which these various catastrophes have hit us, let alone influenced them. We're not talking manipulation of artworks here, remember. These are mostly *natural* occurrences way beyond anyone's control.' Calvin looked at his Commander-in-Chief again and nodded awkwardly.

'Thank you, Calvin.' The president signalled for him to sit and addressed the concerned faces around him. 'Now that everyone's up to date with the seriousness of our position, there's a potential element to this I wish to discuss... one that's been troubling me for quite some time. I believe it's the elephant in the room. So... in light of worrying information I received today, I'd like to address it head on, in order this elephant either be embraced... or shot dead once and for all.'

The Secretary for Agriculture coughed politely.

'Is there a problem, Calvin?'

'With all respect, sir... should we be saying that?'

'What... about *addressing* it?'

'About *shooting* it.'

The president blinked. 'It's a *hypothetical* elephant, Calvin. I appreciate conservation's very much your thing... and political correctness ain't always mine... so, if you found the term offensive, I apologise unreservedly. If you're worried about its welfare, you have my blessing to *hypothetically* lead it from this room and find it a better home... though might I suggest *not* a hypothetical circus, as that's bound to cause offence, too.'

Smirks were quickly concealed beneath bowed heads.

'That won't be necessary, sir,' offered the Secretary for Agriculture self-consciously.

The president nodded his appreciation and refocused... choosing his next words carefully. 'Regarding our trunked friend... is there anyone here who thinks this sudden spate of abnormal occurrences might have a... *supernatural*... cause?'

Those around the table shifted uncomfortably.

'No one?' the president queried the silence.

'I still think we're looking at a series of unfortunate coincidences,' voiced his Chief of Staff.

'I know you do, Gus. But I'm asking if that is *everyone's* opinion at this table.'

The answer came via a consensus of awkwardly nodding heads.

The president drew a troubled breath. 'In that case... could someone please tell me why it was I was required to swear my presidential oath of office on a bible?'

The question produced blank stares.

'I mean... doesn't it say in that good book that we're headed for a cataclysmic showdown presaged by earthquakes in many places and people going hungry? Well... did you know... and I've had the facts checked... that there were more earthquakes recorded last month than in any single one since records began? Now... they may not all have made the headlines... and some might've been classed as tremors... but the figure still stands. So is that *another* one of Gus's coincidences? Or shouldn't we at least be considering the possibility there's a deeper cause to all this? Otherwise, to all intents and purposes,

I might just as well have had my hand resting on a girlie magazine when I took that oath.'

'We definitely shouldn't be saying *that*, sir!' objected the Secretary for Agriculture.

'The point I'm trying to make is... we can't keep repeatedly asking God to bless this country... and believe he has the power to do so... if we're not also prepared to accept the ending we're told he eventually has in store for us. We can't also keep assuming it's not meant for *our* generation, but for some future one that we need never worry about. So... I'm posing the question... what if everything that is happening right now is the start of that apocalypse the bible warns us about?'

The possibility was met with stunned silence... until the Secretary of Defence ended it.

'Calvin's gonna have completely wasted his time saving elephants, sir.'

The president remained grim-faced as he waited for the nervous laughter to subside. 'I appreciate the need to make light of things, Larry. God knows our spirits need lifting. But you might find we'll *all* soon wish we'd wasted less of our time. Because I've been led to believe we're currently under attack from forces you're not going to be able to aim our missiles at.'

'Are you referring to your meeting this morning with Tucker-Jenkins, Mister President?' asked a raised hand, as those around it swapped uncomfortable glances.

'I am, Martin.' The president raised his own to stave off anticipated criticism. 'Now... I know many of you believe he's mad and should stick to writing plays. But what he told me this morning makes a helluva lot more sense to me than an implausibly long string of incredible coincidences. As you know, I've long been an admirer of his work and its ability to shed light on the human psyche. That's why I've quoted his fine words so many times in my speeches. But, I also believe he's been granted a rare glimpse of the fringes of that very power we keep asking to bless this nation. So... unless anyone at this table has an alternative plan for tackling these alarming events… I figure we might as well hedge our bets and go with what he's telling us.'

'What is he suggesting we do, sir… pray harder?'

'His advice is more practical than that, Larry. He's asking we put a stop to the televised debate between Galveston Humbold and this Xanthia woman… the one that's been stoked to near hysteria by the media.'

'But that's tonight, sir.'

'Precisely… which is why I've had to call this meeting at such short notice.'

'Are you suggesting we cancel a much-anticipated religious discourse between two of the media's currently most talked about individuals, *simply* because of an unspecified security concern raised by a foreign playwright?' queried Gus, alarmed at the implications. 'It'll also look like we're giving credence to this ridiculous story about her arguing with an angel!'

'Donald would contest your assessment of that incident… and I appreciate it could exacerbate the already difficult relationship we have with the press. But, seeing as he thought it important enough to break his famous reclusion and come all this way to *beg* me to do it, I think it merits taking that risk.'

'But… on what grounds, Mister President?'

'That's where we need to play clever. I'm well aware we're tip-toeing through a freedom of speech minefield. But I'm sure we can argue this woman… as a media celebrity… is technically engaging in work by having agreed to take part in Humbold's broadcast. I understand she entered this country on a tourist visa… so, surely we can detain her while an investigation is made into a potential violation of its conditions. Now… his legal team will immediately strike back and claim she's *not* being paid… or some other bullshit counter argument. They're too heavily invested in this matter to simply let things go. But at least it'll give us time to work out what to do next.'

'What *are* we going to do next, sir?'

The president shook his head. 'I don't have an answer to that right now. But I know of two individuals trying their damnedest to find one... and we're gonna afford them every resource at our disposal to help speed their work.'

Another hand was raised.

'Excuse me, Mister President... Are we talking about Tucker-Jenkins and his associate?'

'We are, John.'

'Then, sir... I must inform you that his associate is already known to my department... and had I been told in advance that he was going to be allowed to meet with you in person, I would've strongly requested that meeting be refused.'

The president registered surprise. 'You'd better explain yourself, John.'

'Sir. This Penkridge first came to our attention five years ago, when the global markets collapsed.'

'Ah, yes.' The president raised a finger. 'Donald explained about that. My understanding is that Penkridge was trying to nip this whole thing in the bud back then. It's all connected, apparently.'

'With respect, sir... our own findings suggest Penkridge was actively involved in *causing* that crash. But, as he set fire to his apartment and destroyed any evidence, we were unable to progress the investigation further. Without proof... and the crime committed on foreign soil... we were unable to have him extradited for interrogation.'

The president looked shocked. 'Are you sure about this?'

'We definitely are about his involvement, sir.'

'But Donald trusts him implicitly.'

'There's a problem there too, sir. On the day of that fire, Tucker-Jenkins actively tried to stop two of my agents in the commission of their duty, while they were attempting to put a halt to Penkridge's operation at my direct request. It's long been a running sore in my department that he's since enjoyed the worldwide plaudits he has... as well as your own, Mister President.'

The president flopped back in his chair and raised his hands in exasperation. 'Why wasn't I ever told this?'

'We saw no point in troubling you with it, given he was no longer considered a security risk. We believed he was an innocent unwittingly caught in something way over his head. But now the two of them have joined forces, that assumption can no longer be maintained.'

'But it's him who's alerted me to the fact this Xanthia is dangerous and must be stopped!'

'You mean... the same Xanthia who's claiming she can *save* us all... sir?'

The president stared blankly ahead. 'You think *they* might be the enemy?'

'I'm just telling you what we know, sir.'

He exhaled heavily. 'Okay. I appreciate your straight talking, John.' He drummed his fingers on the table. 'Well... that certainly puts a whole new perspective on things.'

'Does that mean you're happy for this broadcast to go ahead tonight, sir?'

The president grimaced. 'I don't know, Gus. From the reports about this woman in the media, it may be wise to err on the side of caution and detain her anyway. But I don't wanna antagonise the constitutionalists and hand the press further ammunition to use against us. I need to make a judgement call on that... and on what we're gonna do with Tucker-Jenkins and this young cohort of his.'

* * *

Having now experienced disappointment, Alien Two asked Alien One if he thought God had experienced it too.

Alien One replied that it was not something he'd considered.

Alien Two suggested he might like to try, as an entity powerful enough to create them might decide to put an end to things if they didn't turn out as expected.

Alien Three asked how they were supposed to know what God expected... if, indeed, God expected anything from them at all.

Alien Two pointed out that it would be pretty pointless creating something that didn't have a purpose.

Alien Three said that if that were the case, why hadn't God told them what that purpose was?

Alien One raised a finger. Perhaps he already had.

Aliens Two and Three looked at him as if God clearly hadn't.

Alien One slowly wagged his finger in time with his thoughts. Perhaps God had sent instructions but they just hadn't noticed them.

Aliens Two and Three looked at the desolate landscape stretching for an unfathomable distance all around and then at each other.

Noting their scepticism, Alien One suggested those instructions might not be obvious. It was possible they existed in a form that needed interpretation.

Alien Three asked why God would make such an important thing so complicated... and, therefore, prone to errors. Surely the easiest way would be to appear in person and inform them directly?

Alien One suggested that perhaps there was a reason God couldn't.

Alien Three apologised for his foolishness and said he thought it was God, the all-powerful, they'd been talking about.

Alien One acknowledged Alien Three's clever fusion of *comedy* and *irony* and said he would name it *sarcasm*. He also admitted he had a point.

Alien Two put forward the idea that it could be a test to see how hard they would try to find and interpret what God wanted of them, thereby indicating the strength of their commitment to, and belief in, God.

Alien One said, if that were the case, he would prefer to refer to such a process as anything other than *a test*, as that could be misconstrued as being rather devious. He suggested a new word that would be free from any negative connotations... *faith*.

Alien Three agreed and said he liked how Alien One always put a positive slant on things. It had produced some interesting concepts that had never existed before.

On hearing this, Alien One began repeatedly slapping his hands together.

Alien Two asked if this action was another new concept. Given Alien One had just received a compliment, was he suggesting it become their way of showing appreciation for something in the future? If so, he would've welcomed them both bothering to make such a noise after he'd performed his comedy routine.

Alien One said Alien Two had fallen into the pitfall of spouting nonsense… or what would now be known as *claptrap*. He was simply demonstrating excitement because Alien Three had given him an idea. As things could be created by positive thoughts… what if the three of them came into being by a positive thought from God?

Aliens Two and Three looked at him in silence.

Alien One smiled back smugly.

After a few seconds, Aliens Two and Three began smacking their hands together.

Alien One announced that he'd changed his mind. He was proud to accept their action as a sign of appreciation.

Aliens Two and Three told him to stop speaking *claptrap*. They were merely trying to fathom what *excitement* was.

Alien One stared at the ground… but not before slapping his forehead really hard.

*　　*　　*

'Tonight… the moment millions of Americans have been waiting for… along with those unfortunate enough to live elsewhere in the world. A ringside seat at the showdown of the millennium… The hottest ticket in television history… A chance for YOU to decide who will be God's chosen one. Sponsored by Gentle Hands Funeral Homes, a subsidiary of the RISE Corporation… in association with Galveston Humbold III Productions… Biblecentric Media… The People's Prayer Group of

America... Scripture Offshore Investments... and Fit-U-Rite Tyres and Exhausts.'

An appropriately apocalyptic-sounding musical introduction accompanied equally appropriate graphics.

Reverend Humbold waited patiently for his cue while the makeup girl applied any last minute touches. 'Did ya'll check the camera angle for those wings I need to have, Steven?' he asked, keeping his eyes shut for her.

'The effect works perfectly, sir... just like you said it would. The subliminal message will definitely hit home.'

'And on her side?'

'She'll look just like the Devil.'

'She *is* the Devil,' the reverend reminded him. 'And I'm no longer talking figuratively. I take it she won't have sight of any monitors?'

'She won't see a thing.'

The reverend brushed his teeth with his tongue. 'Did the hussy take umbrage at me not wanting to meet her before the debate?'

'To be honest, sir... she seemed perfectly fine with it.'

The reverend looked a little put out. 'But didn't she say she wanted to meet *me?*'

'She said there was no point, as she already knew everything there was to know about you.'

He snorted disdainfully. 'We'll see about that... cos I doubt she'd be here if she knew what I have in store for her!'

Steven returned the smirk.

The stage manager motioned for the makeup girl to finish what she was doing and placed a guiding hand on the reverend's shoulder.

'Now... please welcome to the platform... a man who needs no introduction to the good people of America.'

This was true. But just in case potential converts from lands less blessed hadn't done their homework, the reverend had taken the trouble to write one himself... along with the rest of the show's script.

'For the sake of millions of new viewers joining us live around the world... he is this country's best-loved evangelist. A man to whom the American people give their hearts and trust... and not just on Sundays. A religious icon who has dedicated his life to spreading God's word. As loved as he is revered... as humble as he is brilliant... Reverend... Galveston... Humbold... the Third!'

With applause ringing out, the dimmed studio lights slowly increased in intensity as the sunrise fanfare from Richard Strauss's *Also Sprach Zarathustra* set the tone for his triumphal entrance. Arms outstretched, the white-suited evangelist emerged from a cloud of billowing smoke... warmly acknowledging the cheers from the audience as he imperiously strode to his allotted position.

The final crescendo unleashing its uplifting climax, a blinding flash of light illuminated the patterned backdrop behind him. Against the magisterial sound of slowing timpani, his silhouetted, angelic form gracefully lowered its arms.

The rapturous ovation continued until the announcer had recovered from the lump in his throat.

'His opponent tonight couldn't be more different. Alien to these shores... they have never previously preached the word of the Lord. They say they're here to save us all... despite having previously taken their clothes off for a living. But show the wretched creature some Christian hospitality, anyway...'

Leaving the reverend bathed in an ethereal column of white, the remaining studio lights turned red. To the ominously aggressive strains of Carl Orff's *O Fortuna*, Xanthia appeared and stoically walked a gauntlet of booing and hissing... a handful of audience members feeling compelled to rise from their seats to show her a downward thumb... just in case she hadn't got the message.

Unperturbed, she maintained a smile and dutifully took her place, as the warlike timpani of an angry orchestra presaged an end to the psychotic, stabbing choral accompaniment.

Galveston Humbold couldn't believe his eyes... or luck. In contrast to his trademark white suit, his opponent had chosen to attire herself in a black leather catsuit.

Milking the situation, he allowed the catcalling to carry on a little longer before eventually waving it down in an apparent gesture of magnanimity.

'Now... please welcome your host and adjudicator for this evening's showdown... Michael... "Mitch"... Manovich.'

Knowing applause welcomed a face familiar to regular viewers of *God's Own Cable Network*. For those tuning in for the first time, the precise squareness of its jaw risked coming as quite a shock.

A set of obsessively whitened teeth sprang into action.

'A warm hello to our Christian friends out there and all other fellow believers,' he smiled, his fingertips touching so as to impart sincerity. 'Tonight we are set to witness not only the most important event in the history of this planet... but also the most important event in the history of *television*.' He waited for the reverend's words on the autocue to catch up. 'Accordingly... we extend a hand of friendship to the millions of new viewers who are joining us from around the world, no matter their faith, colour, political differences or income bracket. We have all come together as one to observe a battle that will determine the future of mankind... and ladykind, too, if you're a Liberal. While its outcome cannot be predicted... one thing is certain... there can be only *one* victor. One person alone will walk from this studio tonight as the saviour of mankind. The other will be seen for the complete and utter charlatan she is.' He paused – as instructed by the autocue – to let the point sink in. 'So... without further ado... let battle commence!'

A brief musical sting heralded gloves off.

Michael clasped his hands together earnestly. 'Firstly... Reverend Humbold... Xanthia... welcome to the debate.'

Both participants acknowledged the greeting.

'Reverend Humbold... if I can start with you, being undeniably the more recognised figure of the two. You've publicly put it on record... on countless occasions... that Xanthia, here... far from being the one who can save us all, as she claims... is, in fact, preparing to lead us all to Hell. Would you care to elaborate on that truth?'

The reverend swelled his chest. 'I would, indeed, Mitch. Thank you.' He stared directly at the camera moving in on him. 'I need to tell the gorgeous, trusting folks out there in TV land that the woman they see before them is not who she pretends to be. By falsely claiming to have been chosen to save us from the approaching apocalypse, she has unashamedly used and abused our Lord's name, contrary to the second of His most sacred commandments.'

The audience drew a sharp intake of breath.

'Thou shalt not take the name of the Lord thy God in vain,' added Michael, for any heathens watching.

'In asking us to trust and follow her in the ultimate contest between good and evil, I contest she is actually working *for* the Devil... preparing to lure those foolish enough to be tempted by her words away from the true path of righteousness and into the hellish jaws of eternal damnation. Put simply... she is a wolf in sheep's clothing.'

'Well... it's certainly *interesting* clothing,' the host joked.

'It is indeed,' agreed the reverend. 'And I think it shows her true intent. I believe it's no coincidence she's chosen to dress herself from head to toe in black tonight... the official colour of evil.'

The host turned to face his other guest. 'Xanthia... *does* the way you've chosen to dress for this debate show your true intent?'

She leant into the microphone and smiled. 'Yes.'

The audience gasped in horror.

Even the reverend appeared shocked at how easy a victory he might be about to achieve. 'She has been instantly weakened in my presence,' he yelled, in an attempt to gain the credit. 'Her very first utterance has condemned her. The power of the Lord... working through me... is no match for the wicked!'

'Would you care to elaborate, Xanthia?' asked the host, mindful he had another fifty-six minutes of primetime viewing to fill... not to mention sponsors expecting their money's worth.

Xanthia leant forward again. 'Of course. My intention in wearing this outfit tonight is to feel as comfortable and relaxed as possible. I also think it goes very nicely with my shoes.'

'You see... she's playing with us,' hollered the reverend, stabbing a finger at her. 'Her first answer was a blatant assurance to her satanic followers that she intends to perpetrate dark deeds. Her second... a deliberate attempt to obfuscate proceedings.'

'Not really,' said Xanthia calmly. 'I was simply answering the question. And while I'm correcting misapprehensions... I should point out that I've never claimed instruction from *anyone* regarding this task, let alone the reverend's Lord. Besides... even if that were true, the commandment he's referring to isn't what it purports to be. It's merely a convenient invention.' She stood back from the microphone and smiled again.

The reverend looked set to explode, his reddening cheeks taking comfort from the fact that, if they were about to combust, they might possibly be saved by a combination of the sweat from his forehead and spittle from his mouth. 'Ladies and gentlemen... you heard it with your very own ears! She cannot snake her way outta *that* vile utterance. She has cast doubt on one of the most important tenets on which our faith is founded!'

'I haven't cast doubt,' Xanthia countered. 'On the contrary... I've stated a *fact.*'

The audience voiced its outrage.

The host stared at her incredulously. 'You're claiming the second commandment is a falsehood?' he pressed, above the din.

'No. You're still missing the point. I'm *telling* you it is.'

The anger in the studio intensified.

'Okay... let's get this straight... You're standing there in front of our viewers and actually saying the second commandment *isn't* a direct command from our Lord?'

'Well... if you're putting it that way... I'm saying all *ten* aren't.'

The collective intake of breath almost caused the studio backdrop to fall in on itself.

Galveston Humbold was so apoplectic he could hardly speak. But that wasn't going to stop him trying. 'Mine ears have heard the Devil speak, and God hath offered Himself to be my interpreter,' he yelled. It wasn't a quote from the bible... but he couldn't immediately think of an appropriate one... and it sounded good.

'Look,' said Xanthia, trying to calm things down. 'There are many out there who aren't going to like what I have to say. But what I have to say is based on everything there is to know... so, finally the world will be able to look at itself in the truest of mirrors, free from the distortion of prejudices, misconceptions, fears and centuries-old habits. I'm here to tell the truth.'

'The truth?' the reverend screamed, raising a bible that had been conveniently placed on his lectern. 'This is the truth! This is the actual word of God!'

Xanthia squinted awkwardly. 'Well... if we're sticking to the facts... that particular version you're holding up there is a twentieth century revision of a seventeenth century interpretation of a fourth century Latin script that's a disputable translation of a series of earlier, selectively chosen Arabic and Hebrew texts that have, in themselves, all been copied and altered over time to suit the politics and circumstances of the day.'

'This has been purchased from a reputable bible store, I'll have you know!' the reverend retorted indignantly.

Xanthia giggled at the absurdity of the statement.

'You think this is *funny?*' he exploded, waving the bible furiously. 'You think this is a *joke?*'

'Not the book,' she clarified. 'I was laughing at *you*. I know I shouldn't... but I'm only human.'

'I doubt that!' he snorted. 'We've heard testimony from two state troopers that you engaged in a supernatural spat with what appeared to be an angel of the Lord who'd come to call you out.'

'Ah...' said Xanthia delicately. 'I was going to come to that bit later.'

'I bet you were,' spat the reverend. 'After hoping to fool the public into believing your abominable lies. I heard you telling those folks back in the Royal Kingdom of England that there was no such place as Hell.'

'There isn't,' said Xanthia dispassionately, leaning into the microphone again.

'You see,' shrieked the reverend. 'She's even denying the existence of Satan!'

'Oh... he exists alright,' said Xanthia sternly. 'And his power is beyond your comprehension.' Her voice hardened. 'He will have dominance over you and all this world when_'

'Thank you,' interrupted Michael hastily, before she could finish. A voice in his earpiece had just instructed him to shut the conversation down... the producers concerned the hour long bout they'd promised the viewers was shaping up to be an anticlimactic first round knockout. 'I think we're taking a quick commercial break.' He looked to the floor manager for confirmation. '*Yes...?* Yes we are. Don't go away, folks. We'll be back after these messages.'

'Studio off air,' announced the floor manager, as an advert for prayer cushions appeared on the monitors.

'What the hell did ya go and do that for, Mitch,' shouted the reverend, storming over to where the presenter was shuffling his notes. 'You fool. I had her on the ropes. In fact... truth be told... she was in the process of knocking *herself* out. Didn't ya hear her? She just told the whole world the Devil was gonna have dominance over it.'

Mitch raised his hands to signify *his* were washed when it came to any blame being apportioned for the decision. He'd simply followed orders. It wasn't *his* fault the man seething in front of him paid the wages of those giving them.

'Don't bother,' yelled the reverend, angrily striding off in the direction of the production gallery. 'I'll sort this myself.'

Xanthia remained at her podium, calmly observing proceedings. She smiled as the floor manager approached, his raised eyebrows apologising for the distraction of what was occurring in his headset.

'Ma'am... they're requesting you come with me.'

'But won't we be back on air in a few minutes?' she asked, surprised.

His furrowed brow suggested it had now become an order. 'Ma'am... if you wouldn't mind.'

Shrugging, she dutifully followed him... wondering why the studio backdrop had a pattern on it closely resembling a butterfly hovering next to a Viking helmet. Negotiating a maze of corridors behind the scenes, they eventually stopped outside an empty room, its door ajar.

'If you'd like to wait inside, I'm told someone will be with you shortly,' he announced, signalling for her to enter.

Curious as to what was occurring, she did as requested.

It was as she was turning to ask if she should close the door that someone sprang from behind it.

The sting of a needle pricking her neck followed a hand covering her mouth to prevent her screaming.

The last thing she focused on, as darkness swiftly descended, was the molecular composition of liquid anaesthesia.

*   *   *

As the world slowly seeped back, Xanthia savoured the advantages of a befuddled mind. It was like waking *used* to be... not having to think *how* to think and simply luxuriating in the experience of just being.

An alarming memory intruded.

Attempting to focus on her whereabouts, unpleasantly bright lights forced her eyes shut again.

'She's coming round,' announced a voice close to her head.

'What's happening?' she mumbled. 'Where am I?'

There was a short silence.

'You don't know?' asked the voice.

'Is that question meant for me?'

'Yes.'

319

'I have no idea,' she answered weakly.

'You're not able to tell?'

The brusque, anonymous manner of questioning annoyed her. It was irritating enough finding herself waking to such an uncomfortable situation, without bad manners being thrown into the equation.

'Who are you?' she struggled.

'Now that you *must* know, if you possess the power you say you do.'

She braved the lights again and squinted at the voice now directly above her. A blurred face gathered form as she focused on its owner.

A young male in his early thirties, moderately handsome but otherwise nondescript, was staring down at her. As she concentrated harder, his age rose to thirty-seven years, eight months and twenty-four days.

'You look younger,' she said.

'Pardon?'

'It doesn't matter... Brandon.'

The face younger than it actually was registered shock.

Xanthia groaned and attempted to bring her hand up to wipe her mouth, but found the action denied. Instinctively investigating the other hand, she found all movement prohibited. An exploratory attempt to raise her knees met similar resistance.

'She knows my name!'

'I assume that ability is why I'm here,' she muttered. 'I just don't understand these restraints.'

'What else do you know?'

She gave her inquisitor a hardened stare. 'That this whole situation doesn't sit easily with you... unless you've changed your personality in the last few weeks, that is.'

'What's my middle name?'

'Which one?' she sighed. 'You've got two.'

'I know!' he exclaimed with astonishment.

'Good... because if *you* know them, we now have something in common.'

'Go on, then,' he prompted. 'What are they?'

'I'm not a circus act,' she objected. 'So, seeing as you're not going to get a performance out of me... how about you start again and introduce yourself properly? *Then* you can tell me why you've got me tethered to this gurney.'

'You're not in charge here,' he reminded her.

'Neither are you,' she returned. 'You're *far* too junior in rank.'

'Rank in *what*?'

She exhaled wearily. 'Okay... if we must. You're a pathetically junior CIA counter-intelligence operator, having been with them for eleven years, five months and three days... passed over for promotion numerous times because you lacked flair and initiative. Up until the twentieth of last month, you'd become so disillusioned with your lack of progress within the organisation that you were thinking of quitting your job and training to become a website designer. And do you know why you didn't?'

'She knows everything,' he announced loudly.

'Because you *still* lack flair and initiative.'

'It's true!'

'I know it is.'

'I mean... that you have special powers.'

'I have knowledge,' she clarified.

'Of *everything*?'

'Enough to know it's extremely rude to treat a lady like this.' She rattled her restraints. 'So... would you mind undoing these?'

'That's not possible.'

'Yes, it is. What you *actually* mean is... you don't *want* to.'

'You've been deemed a security threat. We can't take any chances. Given your claims, it has to be assumed your power would enable you to possess a complete mastery of combat skills... as well as knowledge of possible escape routes from this building.'

'You're right. I'd favour the ventilation ducts.' She looked about as best as she could. 'I also know this place has an

317

interesting history. Officially, it doesn't exist… despite your organisation having used it many times to interrogate high-value terror suspects. Which begs the question… why am *I* here?'

'I'd have thought that was obvious.'

'You don't believe all that *child of Satan* nonsense Galveston Humbold has been peddling, do you? I'm here to *save* this planet. I've been telling people that all along. If anyone's a danger to the well-being of your country, it's *him*. This is all so unnecessary. I've seen you're a decent human being, Brandon. So, come on… at least let me sit up straight.'

'I'm not at liberty to do that.'

'Why not?'

He glanced up at a camera pointing in their direction. 'I'm not at liberty to divulge that, either.'

'Well… would you kindly tell whoever's in charge I'm happy to have a discussion about things… but *only* if it's going to be conducted in a civilised manner.' She turned her head to indicate further dialogue of any kind was suspended.

'If you mean no harm… why did you announce that Satan would have dominance over this world?'

Forgetting her threat, she looked back at him in anger. 'I was interrupted. They didn't allow me to finish, you fool.'

Brandon demonstrated it was *his* turn to terminate the conversation by moving towards the door. 'Don't worry. You'll have plenty of time to explain yourself during your stay here. We're in no hurry.'

'Michael David,' she announced loudly, in an attempt to stop him leaving.

He momentarily froze.

'They're your middle names. What more do you want to know?'

He banged on the door to get someone to open it. 'You'll find out soon enough.'

'You can't keep me here trussed up like this!' she shouted angrily.

'Yes, I can,' he said, looking back at her. 'And what you *actually* mean is… you don't *want* me to.'

* * *

'Marty… you're my lawyer! You have me regularly deposit so large a pile of dollars into that fat bank account of yours, it's a wonder I ain't developed blisters on my hands from the large shovel I have to use. So, I'm telling ya… of all the problems I pay you to sort, this sure as hell takes priority!'

'They're the government's men, Humbold. You don't mess with these people. You start trying to get in their way and cause them headaches… they'll turn round and sink their claws in you so deep, you'll be crapping yourself about misdemeanours you racked up at *kindergarten*.'

'I'm a man of God, Marty,' the reverend reminded him.

'Yeah… with the emphasis on *man*. You really wanna roll those dice, Humbold?'

The reverend battled his thoughts. 'Hell's teeth… I can't just stand by and let 'em get away with it. They've damned near ruined me!'

'Get away with what? Saving the planet from someone you've been fiercely preaching is about to destroy it?'

'I ain't sayin' they didn't need to detain her. After all… it's *me* who's been telling folks how dangerous that woman is. But she was dangling on the end of *my* line. I was the one that baited the hook. They had no right to barge in and steal her away from me like that.'

'That's a moral argument, not a legal one… and I can't help you with those. That's more your department… allegedly.'

'What d'ya mean, *allegedly*?'

'It's lawyer speak for… I'm not an idiot. Let's just leave it at that, shall we, Humbold?'

Having known each other for many years, the reverend sensibly heeded the advice. 'But even if you're sayin' they *did* have a right to detain her… those knuckleheads could've at least waited 'til the end of my broadcast. Their indecent haste looks like it's gonna end up costing me a truck load of money. I've got angry sponsors calling me up and demanding I hand their portion of it back!'

'Are we talking *Gentle Hands Funeral Homes?*'

'Among others. They said they were hoping for at least a *credible* threat of Armageddon to increase sales of their new interment plan.'

'Don't worry. I'll deal with it,' Marty nodded, scribbling on a notepad.

'And while you're at it… perhaps you could tell those foreign networks that are bellyaching about me filling the remaining fifty-odd minutes of airtime talkin' 'bout my online gift shop, they're lucky I saw fit to offer their viewers a ten percent discount for any disappointment they might've incurred.'

'I'm sure the ingrates will prostrate themselves in contrition once I draw their attention to such generosity,' said Marty dryly, making another note.

'Be firm with 'em, but play it nice. I need to keep these new associates of ours onside so they can help promote my ministry in the future. This battle ain't over by a long stretch.'

'That's why I'm saying you need to concentrate on your fight with Satan… not pick one with the authorities.'

'My battle now *includes* the authorities. They're as bad as he is. I ain't ever gonna forgive 'em, Marty. This is about principles.'

Marty jerked his head in astonishment. 'You've finally *found* some, Humbold?'

'Don't mock me, Marty. I'm tellin' ya… this is about something more important than money.'

'There's such a thing?'

'Hell, yeah. They damn well went and stole my moment of triumph.'

Marty threw up his hands and stared at his client incredulously. 'What are you talking about? You *had* it! Millions of people around the world watched Xanthia fold under pressure and reveal her true hand. *You* did that. The fact she forgot herself and said the things she did, will be seen by everyone who witnessed it as a testament to the pressure you put her under. You won, Humbold... You *won*.'

The reverend shook his head. 'That ain't the point. I needed the public to see a credible fight. I needed to put on a spectacle. That was the whole idea. Besides... they ain't gonna buy the story that she just simply turned tail after five minutes and left the studio. They ain't *that* stupid.'

'Well... forgive me speaking so directly, my old friend... but you've made one helluva living, all the years we've known each other, out of the fact they *are*. Where d'ya think those dollars you object to shovelling my way come from? Now... if you're right... let them voice their suspicions on their own. You don't get involved... understand? That's the advice I'm giving you for all that money it hurts you to pay me. The agents that took her away made it crystal clear... this whole matter's been designated a case of national security, and they'll be looking to extract a heavy price on anyone who gets in their way or makes waves about it in public. You don't take a warning like that lightly... not from *those* kinda people.'

'It ain't in my nature to lay down and roll over, Marty. Besides... I need to know they've got her safely secured and she ain't gonna be allowed to walk through walls... or anything satanic like that.'

Marty looked at him resignedly before slowly shaking his head. 'Not... allowed... to... walk... through... walls,' he confirmed, recording the concern on his notepad. He tapped his pen on the desk and exhaled painfully through skewed teeth. 'Alright. I'll see what I can do. But I'm not promising anything... okay?' He rubbed his chin edgily. 'I've got a couple of contacts who might at least be able to tell us under which legal pretext she's being held. Once we know that, we can look at putting in a challenge. But my guess is they'll deny all knowledge of the incident. You don't place people in a comatose state and take them away on a stretcher for minor misdemeanours. And the mere fact we'll have ignored their warning and raised the matter, will flag up the fact we're prepared to stick our heads above the parapet... and they won't like it one bit.' He eyeballed his client. 'Still… it'll give me a chance to spend some of that money of yours that's accruing in my *fat* bank account.'

The reverend frowned. 'On what?'

Marty picked up his briefcase. 'A good lawyer. I'm *not* a man of God.'

*　*　*

Donald clattered around the holding area, flapping his gauntlets in exasperation. 'But he promised me assistance with this. He was even going to allocate us an expert team of helpers!'

'The president's had a change of heart,' returned the official. 'He no longer wishes to be a party to what you're doing.'

'For what possible reason?'

The question was met with silence.

'This is madness!' cried Donald from behind his visor.

'Furthermore… as your security clearance has now been revoked… I must request the two of you turn around and vacate these grounds immediately.'

'OF COURSE HE MEANS YOU AS WELL,' Donald shouted.

'*Without* any fuss… sir.'

'Just because he had Xanthia removed from that broadcast doesn't mean this thing is over by a long chalk,' raged Donald. 'There are forces at stake here you couldn't *possibly* comprehend!'

'I have no idea what you're talking about,' the official said stiffly. 'I understand the lady you're referring to removed *herself* from last night's broadcast.'

'Oh, right… of *course* she did,' Donald scoffed.

The official remained stony-faced.

'Come on, Donald,' said Norman, placing a hand on his companion's breastplate. 'If they're not going to help us, we're wasting precious time here.'

'But I don't understand. He's a fan!' remonstrated Donald. 'He said I was one of the finest minds of the twenty-first century. He thinks I've got my finger on the pulse of the human condition.'

'No one's questioning your writing prowess, Mr Tucker-Jenkins. I'm sure the president remains an admirer of your work. But he's also a very busy man... especially in this current climate of uncertainty. Now... if you don't mind...'

'You think this *current* climate is full of uncertainties. Well... just you wait!' Donald waddled angrily towards the gate. 'This will have huge consequences! You'll all be sorry.'

Norman smiled politely before turning to follow. 'Donald... wait,' he called out after him. 'Where are you going?'

'Back home to England. We're no longer safe here.'

'But this is where Xanthia is. Perhaps we'll be allowed to speak to her.'

'To what *possible* ends?'

'Well... they're still going to need our help... *eventually*. We need to continue processing the messages, so that we can give them as much information as possible when they realise the mistake they've made. It's only a question of time, once this crisis worsens.'

'Even more reason to return home, seeing as our data's there,' asserted Donald, increasing his stride as much as his metal codpiece allowed.

'No, it's not,' said Norman enthusiastically. 'I brought it all with us.'

The revelation stopped Donald in his tracks.

'What do you think those two extra suitcases I asked to borrow were for? I don't have *that* many t-shirts. I thought we could press on with our task while we're here.'

Donald turned to face him and slowly raised his visor. 'What did you just say?'

'I said I brought the messages with us. We can carry on where we left off.'

Norman watched as the colour drained from Donald's face.

'Donald... are you alright?'

'You naive, reckless imbecile,' the playwright gasped. 'Do you know what you've done?'

Norman's brow creased. 'Yes... enabled us to continue our work while we're here.'

'You've removed incalculably valuable information... our only hope of saving mankind... from the safety of my house.'

'*Safety?* You dumped it in a lake!' Norman exclaimed. 'And Xanthia found the key to your French windows simply by lifting up a flowerpot!'

'I'm talking about safety from the lowest, nastiest, most vicious forms of spirit... those that inhabit the foulest reaches of the netherworld. Why do you think I still live in that crumbling, old house?'

'It's your family home?' Norman squinted.

'That's the reason I don't *sell* it. Don't you think I wouldn't prefer to be in a place that was clean and tidy and boasted all the mod cons? I could have as many houses as I like with the money I've made from my writing.'

Norman looked at him in bewilderment. 'So why *do* you stay there?'

'For *protection*,' Donald answered. 'Don't you wonder why I'm wearing this ridiculous suit of armour?'

'To be honest... not anymore.'

'I need to stop them penetrating my being. That's what my house does. It was built on a site that's exceptionally conducive for keeping those darkest forms of spirit at bay... thereby encouraging the more amicable ones to come forward and communicate with this realm in order to assist it.'

'You're saying that was intentional?'

'Of course not,' Donald tutted. 'Daddy only decided to buy the land because its boundaries resembled the shape of an ironing board.'

'What are the chances of that?'

'I don't know. You'll have to ask the people at the Land Registry.'

'I mean... the fact you have the extraordinary gift of communicating with the dead and fortuitously happen to live in such a house.'

Donald looked about himself, as if questioning his hearing... then back at Norman. 'For a boy the Universe called upon because of his logical thinking, you certainly seem to be displaying a complete lack of it. I was *born* in that house. I grew up in it. Why do you think I am the way I am? It *made* me that way.'

'The house?'

'Yes. I was an only child and Mummy didn't like me mixing with the children in the village. She said I might catch a disease from them that made me common. So, those friendly spirits that inhabited it became my play companions... which isn't as unusual as you might think. Children are sensitive to such vibrations, having not yet been programmed to dismiss them as nonsense. Their imaginary friends are not imaginary at all. I had so many, growing up in that place, I quickly honed my ability to communicate with them... much like one does a language when living amongst its native speakers.'

'But, if your house is built on a site favouring *good* spirits... how come you told me you've been attacked in it by malevolent ones?'

'Because they're now breaking through,' Donald grimaced. 'An entire realm of disgruntled souls on the march and heading this way... and I'm not just talking about Washington, DC. Unfortunately for me... because I'm so receptive to the spirit world, many tend to make a beeline straight for me! If it wasn't for me living on the precise spot I do, I'd be dead by now and experiencing things from the *other* side. It would have been more than whispering voices that assailed me that day I stuck my head in the gas oven to stop it all.'

'You never mentioned that last bit,' gasped Norman. 'I wondered why it was taped up.'

'Well, now you know. And perhaps you finally appreciate why it was mind-numbingly irresponsible of you to remove those messages from the place of sanctuary to which they'd been entrusted. And... for your information... nefarious spirits aren't keen on water... which is why I hid that barrel in the lake.' Donald rocked backwards and forwards on the heels of his sabatons, trying to work out what to do next. 'You say they're in those suitcases you brought with you?'

'Yes... in our hotel room.'

'Then we need to get there as quickly as we can!' Without bothering to look, he stepped into the road, causing a number of vehicles to swerve violently. 'TAXI!' he screamed, sticking out a gauntlet.

* * *

Ethan Menderson was what the locals of his home town in Wyoming called a good ol' boy. He'd also been a bad ol' boy... but that was a very long time ago.

In the time between, he'd discovered God.

That's what had made the difference.

The first half of his life had been spent on the wrong side of the tracks. Not that a train ran anywhere near to where he'd grown up. It was so remote, roads were viewed with suspicion.

Born to a fifth-generation farming family, he'd yearned to break the chain that fate had placed around his prospects. All he'd wanted was to avoid filling the years ahead with endlessly crossing the same fields in a tractor so noisy, he could hardly hear himself think.

Not that those thoughts mattered anyway. Bone-shaken daydreams of something better were forever interrupted by the sickly stench of diesel in his nostrils and the taste of it in his mouth. He grew to despise the all-pervasive odour. It clung to his clothes like a desperate friend refusing to let him go. As the midday sun curled their edges, it gave the sandwiches that temporarily broke the daily monotony an unwanted sweetness... though still more palatable than hours of swirling dust.

His preferred plan of escape had been to visit the vacant homes of people who *didn't* stink of diesel and relieve them of their property, thereby financing his bid for freedom. But he still never managed to progress the dream beyond a wish. The lure of cheap liquor and like-minded company proved a toxic combination... resulting in him swapping the monotony of the fields for the monotony of a prison cell for more times than he cared to remember.

The problem with being released back into so small a community was that everybody knew why he'd been away. Friends eventually dwindled... and those that didn't were those most likely to help him continue the cycle over and over again.

Until old Mother Cartwright.

Bessie... as she had once been known... lived alone and stubbornly kept herself to herself. Her forthright manner towards anyone threatening her privacy led some to point a finger and say, behind hands, she was a witch.

That fabrication eventually wove itself into her sitting on a small fortune her late husband had acquired while panning for gold in nearby hills. Rumour suggested his good luck finally ran out the day he gave her reason to curse him... which ended with the troubled man blowing his brains out in the woodshed. The manner of his death was never in dispute... though the more sensible in the community whispered it was down to a gambling debt he'd refused to honour, and that others had been responsible for pulling the trigger.

Either way, tales of hidden riches made her worthy of Ethan's attention.

As she rarely left her house, he'd gone there after dark, trusting she'd be asleep. But someone should've told him that witches like to work at night... and Bessie proved no exception.

As he slid from the forced window and dropped onto her parlour floor, she was waiting for him.

He stated in court she'd been clutching a broom... leading locals to speculate on whether she'd been looking to defend herself or about to make her escape.

Claiming he'd never touched her, he said she'd simply stared at him... as if reading his soul... then fallen to the ground in front of him.

With no evidence to prove otherwise, the coroner ruled she'd died from a pre-existing heart condition and that it could've happened at any moment. The technicality was enough to spare him a harsher sentence... but not enough to salve his conscience.

Ashamed at what he'd done... and fearing retribution from beyond the grave... he vowed to make amends by repenting his sins and changing his ways.

His sentence finally served, he set about embracing God, his local church, and... less enthusiastically... the familiar smell of diesel. Though just as pervasive, he now considered it the scent of freedom.

As the years slowly bowed his back, the memory of his wayward youth died with those who'd been its victims. Embraced by the community again, he worked hard to retain its trust. Now his dream was simply to live the life he already had.

Finally, Ethan Menderson was a contented man.

So it came as quite a shock when visions of old Mother Cartwright started inexplicably invading his sleep after so many years.

At first... her gnarled, cadaverous face appeared as little more than a fleeting glimpse... a vague memory teasing him from a distance. But as the nights progressed, her shrouded form grew bolder and far clearer... silently floating to the foreground... its haunting presence made all the more terrifying by its numbing muteness. He felt her cold, dead eyes piercing his soul with the exact same look she'd given him before it turned out to be her last.

As if determined to maximise his suffering, she'd recently taken to swooping in on his dreams when least expected, causing him to wake bolt upright in a sweat, fighting to find his next breath.

Sleep was no longer a thing he wished upon himself. Forced to stay awake, his mind began to unravel. Reduced to his knees, he prayed to the God that had rescued him before to intervene on his behalf one last time. Hadn't the slate been wiped clean?

Wasn't that the deal when the pastor had poured water over his head?

But either God wasn't listening... or old Mother Cartwright wasn't listening to God.

As once forgotten tales about her wickedness resurfaced to plague him, his addled mind wondered how long it would be before her risen form attacked him in the *real* world and extracted its revenge.

From that moment on, every breath became a ticking bomb.

Unwilling to close his eyes... and exhausted beyond toleration... a straight furrow proved impossible.

His tractor fell silent.

Having beaten the grave... old Bessie Cartwright had now beaten him.

In a final finger to her torment... and a nod to the bad ol' boy that had put him in that situation in the first place... he refused to give her the ultimate victory of having him do the deed in the woodshed, just like her husband had been forced to do. It was the *hay barn* Ethan Menderson chose to decorate with his brains and the fragments of skull in which it had been encased.

And for the most fleeting of blissful moments... granting an old man his boyhood wish... the overpowering smell of cordite momentarily took away the perennial stench of diesel.

*　　*　　*

Freed from her restraints, Xanthia rubbed her wrists and stared contemptuously at her liberator. 'Am I supposed to thank you for this?'

'You should be aware that the door to this room is securely locked from the outside. Any attempt to harm me or escape will have severe consequences for you.'

'You were never happy keeping your pet rabbit in a cage when you were a boy, Brandon... so, it makes me wonder how you're managing to justify this to yourself.'

'Let's get one thing straight. I'm simply doing my job. And you don't have to prove your ability anymore by demonstrating you know everything about me. I accept you have the talent you say you do.'

'Oh... it's a *talent* now, is it... not a power? Is *that* why I've been unchained?'

'We don't know how you're doing it... but we acknowledge you're able to access a source of information that puts you in an extremely unique position.'

'So, why have me locked in this room when I'm here to help?'

'That's the bit we still need to confirm. Intelligence suggests otherwise.'

'What intelligence?' she scoffed.

'That's classified.'

'No. What you mean is... you're reacting to gossip and hearsay. Haven't I been saying all along that I'm trying to make things *better* for everyone? By keeping me here like this, you're allowing those I have to battle against to have the upper hand.'

'It's that *battle* you say you're engaged in that concerns us. One man's terrorist is another man's freedom fighter. We have plenty of enemies out there who are convinced they're doing the right thing. We need to establish whose side you're *really* on.'

'And how do you intend doing that?'

Brandon glanced up at one of a number of cameras in the room and nodded sharply. Moments later, the sound of the door being unlocked preceded a man of senior years entering to join them.

'Ah...' Xanthia squinted, focusing on the individual. 'Eugene Frederick Pearson... Emeritus professor of chemistry at Stanford University... and a leading expert in the field of electrochemistry and thermodynamics, if I'm not mistaken.'

'I'm impressed,' said the professor, addressing Brandon.

'I expect you've come to ask me about your specialist subject, cold fusion, haven't you, Professor Pearson?' she said.

The man looked at Brandon as if needing permission to reply.

'Think of it as a test of your loyalty towards us,' Brandon answered on his behalf. 'If you really *are* on our side and looking to help, you can prove it by clearing up a scientific quandary the professor tells us has been vexing the minds of him and his colleagues for quite some time.'

'I'm not surprised,' she nodded. 'The physics behind producing a nuclear reaction at room temperature is a molecular minefield when you start examining it closely... isn't it, Professor?'

'Are you doing that now?' he asked excitedly.

'I am,' she smiled. 'And... oh, Professor Pearson... if you could only see what I see!'

He moved towards her eagerly. 'What *can* you see?'

'I see cheap, clean, unlimited power that will benefit the world and see poorer nations able to compete on a more even playing field with those fortunate enough to have had a head start. Wouldn't that be a wonderful thing, Professor?'

His eyes darted towards Brandon.

'The trouble is,' she continued, 'any country possessing the know-how to achieve such a thing will undoubtedly wrap it up in so many patents and protections, there's guaranteed to only be one winner. Now... I don't know about you... but I hardly think that's fair.'

Once more, the professor checked for Brandon's reaction.

Brandon's eyes narrowed. 'Are you playing with us? I thought you were asking us to trust you. Now it's *you* who seem to be struggling with such an issue.'

'If I'm struggling with anything, it's to comprehend why those pulling your strings don't realise there's a *far* greater and more urgent use for my potential,' she retaliated. 'So... instead of keeping me under lock and key and asking narrow questions on science to gauge my intent, I need to be connected immediately with those in power, in order that my words get to be heard and fully understood by as many people on this planet as possible.'

Brandon laughed. 'I think we're a long way from that point! So... why don't we keep it simple to start with? We're looking at a basic trade... a sample of *your* knowledge for *our* trust. Show us you're willing to cooperate on a meaningful level, and we can then start looking seriously at your demands.' He eyed her suspiciously. 'Unless, of course... you *are* playing us.'

'Ask her about the use of palladium?' interjected the professor impatiently. 'Can she at least tell me if we were right to be travelling down *that* path with our approach?'

'Of course I can,' Xanthia answered him directly.

The professor's eyes widened.

'But there'd be very little point. If Brandon's puppet masters, hiding behind those cameras, refuse me access to *their* puppet masters, there'll soon be no paths for anyone to travel down!'

'Information first,' Brandon reiterated.

'That's not going to happen,' she insisted.

'Then, it seems we've got ourselves a standoff.' He signalled for the professor to vacate the room.

'What about amobarbital?' the professor asked, stalling his departure.

'She's already told you,' returned Brandon testily. 'She's not prepared to help with your research.'

'It's a chemical substance used in truth drugs,' he explained. 'Probably better known as sodium amytal.'

'Its use would also be a violation of the Inter-American Convention to Prevent and Punish Torture,' she calmly pointed out. 'If you did so, it wouldn't go down well with the other signatories when I inform them of your actions on my release.'

Brandon looked at her dispassionately. 'Who said anything about you being released?'

Xanthia's mask of nonchalance slipped. 'You know what you're doing here is wrong, Brandon,' she rebuked him. 'That boy who loved his rabbit is still inside you. I can feel his excitement when he dreamt of a career in the CIA, and his pride when taking an oath of allegiance to the Constitution. He swore to uphold it. So... in case you need reminding... that means respecting another person's human rights and includes the words *so help me God* at the end of it. Given I know you still believe in Him, how do you think this whole thing's gonna look in *His* eyes?'

'Correct me if I'm wrong,' said Brandon unmoved, 'but didn't I hear you refuting the validity of the bible during your TV debate with Reverend Humbold? Well… surely that infers there *is* no God… which technically makes that oath invalid.'

'I never said…'

'What's more,' he cut across her firmly, 'you clearly stated Satan was real and would have dominance over this world.'

'I've already explained that. I wasn't allowed to finish the point I was trying to make.'

'Which is extremely convenient… as you've now had plenty of time to concoct an excuse.'

'So, maybe we *should* try amobarbital,' interjected the professor. 'That way we'd be able to establish the truth.'

'That's a clear violation of my rights!' she shouted, jumping from the gurney and causing the two men to shrink back. 'And you'd be playing an *extremely* dangerous game!' She glared at them angrily. 'I warn you… there are things I know that you *definitely* don't want to hear!'

Brandon grabbed the professor's arm and banged sharply on the door. 'I think you've just given us the answer as to whose side you're on,' he responded. 'I think you holding out on the secrets of cold fusion is the *least* of our concerns!'

*   *   *

'I left them right here,' cried Norman, frantically scouring the hotel room for his bags. 'Perhaps the cleaner has moved them.'

A panicked search of the wardrobe suggested otherwise.

'I told you it was a catastrophic mistake,' howled Donald. 'If we don't find those suitcases, there's no hope left. It was our last chance to work out what the other side are up to and figure out how to end this appalling nightmare!'

'I'm so sorry. I really thought I was helping.'

'I should never have yanked you through that crack in my door the first day you sweet-talked your way beyond it. What you mistook for paranoia and madness on my part was simple common sense and sanity. I *knew* I should've listened to the cats.'

'I'll call the manager. They *must* have CCTV.'

'Why would my cats require CCTV? No one's going to bother stealing *them*.'

'The hotel. They'll have pictures of whoever took our bags.'

'What's the point?' Donald wailed. 'Whoever or *whatever* took them will be long gone by now.'

'What if we try to continue our programming without them?' Norman suggested. 'Not having the actual messages doesn't mean we have to concede defeat. Look... I've still got my laptop. And we've already inputted more than *half* the original data.'

'What good's *that* going to be if we no longer have access to the rest of it? It would be like trying to solve a crossword puzzle with only fifty percent of the clues.'

'Maybe you could try and remember what those remaining messages were,' Norman tried. 'It's a good thing we logged the coordinates first. Those *would* be difficult to recall. But the sayings, sketches and pictures you ripped from books and magazines... you *must* be able to remember most of that stuff.'

'Oh, *must* I?' said Donald sardonically. 'I think you have little perception of what goes on in my head at any given moment of the day.'

'Believe me... I've built a very good picture of *that* by now,' Norman countered. 'I understand it won't be easy, but you *have* to try. Gabriel would tell us to think of this situation as a fork. We have two options... give up and let the other side win... or keep fighting... at least until there are no possible forks left. At worst, we'll make victory as difficult as possible for them. As the saying goes... better to die on your feet than live on your knees.'

'You keep my knees out of this,' Donald shuddered. 'I have enough problems with them as it is.'

'Come on, Donald… we can do this. Perhaps Whitebait will be able to fill in the remaining gaps for us.'

'YES… FUNNY HOW HE'S SUDDENLY TAKEN TO YOU,' Donald shouted.

Norman clambered onto his bed and flipped open the laptop. 'Right… no time like the present. The last thing inputted was an article about Native American burial sites you'd torn from a book in your local library.'

'I'm hugely ashamed of my actions that day,' Donald admitted contritely.

'Don't worry. You can make amends by buying them a new one when all this is over.'

'Why would I want to do that?' he exclaimed indignantly. 'That librarian had it coming to her. Whitebait was only trying to help. She kept putting her finger to her lips and shushing us both. How was I to know the Buffalo Bill biography I threw in frustration would miss and strike that old lady whose book she was stamping? I just hope the old dear appreciates it was *me* who insisted they call an ambulance.'

'Is there anything else connected to that subject you can remember?'

'Yes. There was a surprising amount of blood for one so frail.'

'I meant about the Native American burial sites.'

Donald stared awhile in silence. 'Oh, this is hopeless!' he finally blurted. 'Why do you think I wrote everything down in the first place? This isn't going to work. We might as well get on our knees right now.'

'Wrong fork,' said Norman firmly. 'We're not giving up. Let's move on to the stuff you wrote. Maybe *that'll* be easier to remember. Come on… give me something that's in your head… something I haven't already loaded into the program.'

Donald exhaled testily. 'Alright.' He nodded to himself as something presented itself. 'An idiot doesn't realise he's an idiot… because he's an idiot.'

Norman typed it in. 'And do you have a source for that quote?'

'Yes.'

He waited.

Donald looked at him.

'Well?'

'It's from a play called *Bad Breath in Venice*.'

'And do you happen to know the playwright?'

'I should jolly-well hope so!'

'Why... are they a friend?'

'Well... we occasionally have disagreements.'

'Who is it?'

'Me.'

'I beg your pardon?'

'Donald Tucker-Jenkins.'

'You've been given a warning message that comes from one of your own plays?'

'Have I? How extraordinary!'

'No! I'm *asking* if you have.'

'Well, how would I know,' Donald groaned. 'I've already told you... I can't remember anything.'

Norman held the bridge of his nose. 'But you just gave me the saying *an idiot doesn't realise he's an idiot, because he's an idiot*.'

'You asked me for what I had in my head... and I was looking at you at the time,' explained Donald.

Norman sighed heavily and gently closed the lid of his laptop. He stared directly at the playwright. 'Well... I suppose it's always possible that fork only ever had one prong.'

*   *   *

Alien Two asked Alien One where they should look for signs to be interpreted as instructions from God as to what was expected of them.

Alien One replied they could be anywhere and anything.

Alien Two said that didn't help.

Alien One proposed they start by looking where they least expected to find something.

Alien Three asked why.

Alien One explained that it sounded like the sort of thing you should do when trying to locate something enigmatic and mysterious.

Alien Two said, as he didn't know where to find something in the first place, he could hardly start looking in an opposing location.

Alien One surmised... given it was answers they were seeking... the last place they would expect to find them would be already in their heads. So maybe they should start by accessing their deeper thoughts, as that's where the answer to the conundrum probably lay.

Alien Three said, if Alien One thought that's where the answer lay, surely they should look for the complete *opposite* of that... given his last suggestion.

Alien Two, excited that they were now getting somewhere, asked what the opposite of a deep thought was.

Alien One suggested it would be a shallow one.

Alien Two asked what one of those was.

Alien One explained that it would be thinking about things in a superficial way.

Alien Two said he was none the wiser.

Alien One said it would be having thoughts that were considered trivial and lightweight.

Alien Two asked for some examples.

Alien One said his request raised a very interesting point... because what made a thought *trivial* depended on the viewpoint of the person thinking it.

Alien Three suggested they take Alien One's viewpoint, as he was the one who thought about things the most.

Alien One said he considered thoughts of greed, envy, selfishness and spite to be trivial, because they were petty and unimportant. He also thought the same about vanity and feelings of superiority.

Alien Two asked him for some examples of the latter.

Alien One said Alien Two would be having such thoughts if he looked at Alien Three and considered he was cleverer than him... or better looking... or more charismatic.

Alien Two asked whether he would also be having trivial thoughts if he considered himself superior to Alien One.

Alien One said, in *that* particular scenario, he would be having *delusional* ones.

Alien Three said, if God has chosen to hide the answer somewhere among their trivial thoughts, God obviously considered them the most important thoughts of all. Perhaps that meant they should live their lives looking down on any other person who wasn't worshipping their God. Perhaps *that* was what God expected of them.

Alien Two perused the barren landscape and asked what he meant by *any other person.*

Alien One looked strangely at Alien Three and asked what he meant by *their* God. Surely there was only one?

Alien Three explained that... in the ludicrously ridiculous scenario they *weren't* alone in the numbingly vast expanse stretching for an interminable distance all around them... it seemed God expected them to ensure His dominance over a hypothetical Alien Four, Five or even Six... who may *also* have come to the conclusion there was a God who needed worshipping. Only... *they* could have come up with a *different* God.

Alien One fell about in hysterics at the possibility of the numbingly vast expanse stretching for an interminable distance all around them having been created by two separate Gods at exactly the same time.

Watching Alien One helplessly crying with laughter at something Alien Three had said, Alien Two suddenly felt gripped by a wave of envy. It brought to mind his *experience* of failing as a stand-up comedian. What he would have given for such a response to his *own* utterances back then. With envy quickly turning to spite and a desire for retribution, he consoled himself with the fact that... not only could he now add *shallow and trivial thoughts* to his list of *experiences*... his desire to hurt Alien One and Alien Three... if following their logic... must surely be a direct command from God.

Having managed to overcome the brightness of her room and finally get some sleep, the first thing Xanthia recognised, as she was violently awoken, was the sensation of her arms and legs being pinned down while having the restraining straps reattached. The second was Brandon's voice telling her not to struggle and make the situation worse.

With the last restraint in place, the ceiling began to move, as the gurney on which she'd been resting was quickly wheeled out of the room and along a narrow, strip-lighted corridor. A short journey later, a ninety degree jolt saw her entering a far larger room.

'Gentlemen… if you'd like to take your positions,' Brandon announced, as the ceiling came to a jarring halt.

'What is this?' she demanded, trying to raise her head.

'The moment of truth,' he answered.

'Amobarbital,' added a voice she recognised as Professor Pearson's.

'You fools,' she yelled. 'Don't you know you're playing with fire? You have no idea what this could lead to.'

'Your reaction suggests we do,' contended Brandon. 'You clearly have something to hide.'

'I'll fight you all the way,' she warned. 'And you should be thanking me for it. You're about to open a Pandora's box.'

'Doctor Menzies… if you'd be so kind.'

'Wait,' she cried, as a syringe entered her field of vision. 'If you're going to do this, at least permit me the courtesy of seeing those who'll be asking the questions. Surely that's not too much to ask?'

The man holding the syringe looked to Brandon for guidance.

'I see no reason why not,' he shrugged.

Xanthia felt the back of the gurney being adjusted so as to accommodate her wish.

'Well, well, well,' she tutted, as a small group of males standing to one side were revealed. She examined them closely.

'I'm surprised the government have seen fit to employ some of *you* in this affair.'

Her taunt was met with dispassionate stares.

She looked at the man holding the syringe. 'Doctor Menzies... weren't you struck off three years ago for unethical behaviour? Clearly, nothing's changed.'

The doctor in question appeared unconcerned... which was *not* the reaction of Xanthia's next target.

'And Professor Freyer... do your colleagues know the extent to which you cheated during the writing of your doctoral thesis all those years ago? I'm sure they'd also be shocked at the names of the two august individuals who helped you... not to mention the reason why.'

The doctor in question exchanged uncomfortable glances with those beside him.

'Sorry... am I making you all a little uneasy? Only... I thought we were here to establish some truths. For example... Professor Stratton. Now *there's* an interesting hard drive you have on your personal computer.'

'Enough!' shouted Brandon.

Professor Stratton had certainly had *that*. He hurriedly exited the room... presumably to go straight home and wipe the item in question.

'Don't worry, everybody,' she smiled. 'I guarantee any *other* secrets are safe with me... for as long as I'm able to control my own thinking process, that is.'

'Threats are pointless,' Brandon dismissed her.

A few of those in the room weren't so sure.

'We have an important job to do,' he reminded them.

'Ah, yes, Brandon. That's something that's been baffling me ever since we first met,' she mused. 'You'll recall me saying you'd been passed over for promotion on numerous occasions due to your lack of flair and initiative. So, how does someone like that end up being trusted to be the visible face of whatever's going on in this building? That's quite a responsibility, wouldn't you say? Requiring those very traits you seem not to have previously demonstrated. What's further troubling me is why those who've been prepared to overlook that fact prefer to remain hidden. Something's not right here, is it?'

Brandon nodded at the doctor.

Xanthia flinched as a needle punctured her arm and the syringe's contents were dispersed into her bloodstream. Within seconds her look of consternation began to dissipate.

'How long?' he asked.

'It'll be almost immediate,' Doctor Menzies replied. 'I've given her the strongest dose I can.'

Brandon looked directly at her. 'Now listen carefully, Xanthia... I'm going to ask you some basic questions which I want you to answer truthfully. Do you understand?'

Despite fighting her willingness to do so, she nodded.

'Okay. A nice easy one, to start with. What's your full name?'

She hesitated a second. 'Julie...... Mary... Swanson.'

The men in the room looked at each other.

'Is that right?' he asked.

They shrugged.

'You're not very good at this, are you,' she giggled, her head feeling light.

'What brought you here to America?'

'An aeroplane,' she sniggered.

'I meant... for what reason?'

She sighed. 'To take part in a television debate.'

'We're wasting time,' interjected Professor Pearson. 'We need to get straight to business while the drug is having maximum effect.'

'Oh... hello, Professor,' said Xanthia dreamily. 'How are you today?'

'I'm... very well, thank you,' he answered awkwardly.

'That's lovely,' she smiled.

'Go ahead, Professor,' Brandon prodded.

'Right... my first question to you is this... Is cold fusion possible on a practical and economical scale... or, as some might suggest, have we been completely wasting our time?'

Xanthia raised her eyes and returned a look of innocence.

'Well?'

'That's two questions,' muttered Doctor Menzies. 'Because she's unwilling to cooperate, you'll need to be as specific as possible and ask one at time.'

'Actually... if I could interrupt,' she slurred. 'Given my previous encounter with Professor Pearson, I assumed this particular subject would be on the agenda and that I'd be unable to stop myself answering questions on it. So... to avoid pointlessly wasting energy fighting the request, I'm going to tell you everything there is to know about it.'

A burble of excitement filled the room.

'I take it this is being recorded?' said the professor eagerly.

'Too right... you don't want to miss a thing,' she concurred.

'Don't worry,' Brandon assured him. 'You and your colleagues aren't the only ones interested in what our subject has to say.'

Xanthia took a deep breath.

What came out of her mouth was a string of utterances the likes of which no one in the room had ever heard. This wasn't surprising, given she'd decided to impart her knowledge in a dialect last spoken in the mountains north of Mesopotamia, five thousand years prior to the invention of cuneiform writing. She struggled a bit when explaining the ins and outs of catalytically fusing hydrogen... as the language had developed mainly to assist in the trading of sheep and root vegetables... but she persevered, as her brain insisted she tell them everything she knew on the subject.

'Very clever,' said Brandon, when she was finally done... awarding her a begrudging handclap.

'Did you get it all?' she asked. 'Only... the bit about the control of unstable neutrons is *extremely* important... otherwise you could be looking at an embarrassingly large bang.'

'We need to find another way,' advised one of those who'd spent the last five minutes wincing with frustration. 'I was hoping to clear up dark matter and quantum gravity before lunch.'

'I'll have to consult my superiors,' said Brandon. 'Perhaps they can decipher some of what was said.'

'Good luck with *that* one,' she beamed.

'If it's in your head, we'll get it out,' he promised.

'In that case... you're going to have to be far smarter than me... and I've just had a peep at your final year exam results.' She winced and shook her head.

'Get her out of here!' he shouted angrily.

As she was wheeled away, she overheard Professor Pearson propose they try waterboarding... in a voice suggesting he'd only just finished sobbing.

Returned to her own room and left to reassemble her thoughts, the one that kept going through her mind the most was... why... when under the control of a powerful truth serum and in such a vulnerable state... had no one thought it pertinent to ask whose side she was actually on.

* * *

The diner the man had chosen to sit in was as unremarkable as all others of its type. The reason for him sitting there was not.

Those enjoying its menu had the choice of doing so while either occupying a pair of opposing, red, high-backed bench seats that bookended an aluminium table... or one of a row of matching barstools that were not only less private, but advertised the likelihood no one else wanted to eat with you.

The man in question had chosen the former, suggesting to the waitress serving him coffee that she would soon be bringing another cup to the table.

'Can I get you anything else, hun?'

'No, thanks. Coffee's fine.'

She smiled and left him to his wait.

He looked about restlessly, knowing the company he was expecting was of the kind he'd rather not have witnesses to. Sipping his drink, he reflected on how he'd got himself into such a situation.

Just as he was thinking it a mistake agreeing to meet in so public a place, the reason for him taking that risk appeared at the door. Signalling his whereabouts with a raised hand, he anxiously stroked the handle of his cup with the other.

His appointment approached the table and spoke first. 'It's been a while.'

'A little over five years,' the man confirmed.

His appointment sighed heavily at the thought and stared pensively through the diner's window. 'A lot has passed since then.'

'You'd better take a seat.'

His guest accepted the invitation. 'I'd like to say you're looking well... but you're not,' he commented.

'That's because I've been working hard.'

'Yes... I know. That's the negative side of promotion.'

'Another is that it makes this meeting doubly awkward for me.'

'I expect it does. But there's nothing wrong in two old friends meeting up for a lunchtime drink.'

'We're not friends,' the man reminded him. 'In fact... I was hoping to never see you again.'

His appointment smiled. 'Yes... I expect you were.'

'I assumed any business we had together terminated when that business collapsed.'

'Terminated?'

'That it ceased to be relevant.'

'But... as you pointed out... that was over five years ago, and... as *I* pointed out... much has happened since then. Do you know my favourite saying?'

'If I did, you wouldn't have asked,' the man replied brusquely, signalling his desire to get to the reason for their meeting.

'A successful man is one who stands up one more time than he falls down.'

'Then I congratulate you on finding your feet again. Unfortunately... that's clearly come at a price to me.'

'Coffee, sir?'

The appointment looked up at the waitress who was hovering. 'Thank you.'

'And a refill for *you?*'

'I'm fine. I don't plan on staying long.'

They withheld further conversation until she'd departed.

'I bet, when that woman came to work this morning, she never thought she'd be serving coffee to two gods!' the appointment quipped.

'I doubt she did,' the man replied stony-faced. 'Forgive me being so forthright... but as we're both busy men, I'm sure you'll be equally happy to dispense with further pleasantries. I assume it's information you're after.'

'Does that mean you're not interested in hearing that my associates send their regards?'

The man remained silent.

'Many were looking forward to seeing you again, but thought it safer I make this preliminary approach on my own. I'm sure there's increased scrutiny on you, having climbed so high up your professional ladder. It's important for us you remain there. We don't wish to make things difficult for you.'

'You already have.'

The appointment looked away. 'It's unfortunate you feel that way... but business is business.' He took a sip of his coffee. 'I hear your initial telephone conversation with one of my colleagues was about as cordial as this one.'

'It was their request that provoked the atmosphere.'

'Understandable. But we're glad you saw sense and undertook it.'

'Only because it was made clear to me I had no choice.'

'That's correct. You didn't. But, as always... you'll be well recompensed.'

'I'd rather be left alone.'

His appointment shook his head. 'I'm sorry... but that won't be possible... especially given your promotion.'

'And my past.'

'Precisely. Once in the pay, always in the pay... eh... Mister Prometheus?'

It wasn't that Ayush didn't respect the old men of the village. He just didn't want to be like them. Their sun-cracked faces and gnarled, over-worked hands held little appeal to a youth like him. Forever squatting in the sanctuary of the shade and reminiscing about a time when they were as fit and hopeful as he was, they dwelled on moments long gone. He dreamed of the future. They dreamed of the past.

Regularly taunting them about it, he would humorously flex what little muscles he had and dare them to give chase if they were offended.

They never did, of course. With age came wisdom. They knew time would catch him for them... and their revenge would be to smile back knowingly at him from within his *own* memories.

Age wasn't the only thing separating them. Being a progressive thinker, he was desperate to achieve more in life than previous generations from his small village on the northernmost boundary of Uttar Pradesh. Conversations between its inhabitants included a world he refused to believe in. Talk of evil spirits held no place in his modern view of the world. He saw no point in undertaking endless, tedious rituals, like constantly burning camphor to keep unpleasant entities at bay. He simply refused to believe they existed in the first place.

It was a bold stance, given the culture into which he'd been born. Many from the village claimed a malevolent spirit had infiltrated his body and taken control of his mind. But he simply shrugged away their superstitious finger-pointing and narrow-minded animosity.

Why should he fear anything? His parents had named him Ayush... meaning long-lived. So, he would embrace that life... confident that he, too, would reach the age when he'd have time to drink tea and share memories with those whose paths had become interwoven with his. But, unlike the old men of the village... he would do so while sat in a comfortable chair...

away from the constant stench of rotting garbage, and with a full set of teeth.

How he was going to achieve this had yet to be worked out. All he knew was that it would mean leaving the village for one of the major cities, like so many had done before him. But his mother was sick and he was all she had. He would never desert her.

Not yet, anyway.

Those who went never came back. Occasionally they sent money to the families they'd left behind... though never enough. Perhaps they feared, if they returned, they would end up replacing the old men. Only when Mother closed her eyes for the last time, would he pack up what few belongings he had and join them. For now, he would carry on farming their small plot of land, so as to make sure it could sustain them both.

At least... that had been his plan.

He hadn't meant to strike the cow so harshly. He didn't know where the uncharacteristic flash of anger had come from, other than it had been oppressively hot and he was tired. He'd tried shooing it away, but the creature proved annoyingly stubborn. That's why he'd picked up the stick. He appreciated it needed to eat... but not at the expense of him and Mother. He'd worked hard to produce what little crops they had.

Unfortunately for him, his actions against the sacred animal had been witnessed by others... and soon a small crowd grew.

'His wickedness will anger the gods and bring their wrath upon this village!' shouted one of those at the head of the gathering.

'Perhaps he should be beaten by sticks himself,' shouted another. 'It might finally drive those evil spirits from his body.'

'They've made him think he is better than us,' the excoriation continued.

'I've heard he dances around our beds when the moon is full and encourages demons to attack us while we sleep!'

'He never could be trusted!'

'He must be punished... otherwise it will be *us* who suffer the consequences!'

Ayush didn't see the first stone strike him... and barely caught a glimpse of the second. But as he backed away, he tried his best to dodge the hail of missiles aimed at his head.

As more found their target, his adrenalin numbed their impact. He only knew the serious damage they were inflicting by the warm blood blurring his vision and the taste as it trickled into his mouth.

His heart rate rocketing, he suddenly felt a curious sense of detachment... his mind unwilling to accept what was happening. He pictured his mother lying in her bed, blissfully unaware of her precious son's predicament.

The absurd notion that she would intervene on his behalf temporarily flashed through his mind. But, as yet another cruel impact jolted him back to his senses, he realised he was on his own... as would *she* be if he didn't save himself.

Putting his hands up, he pleaded for the crowd to stop.

A large rock forced one of his fingers back... his adrenalin no longer masking the pain as he felt it snap.

Causing an inner strength to explode within him, he refused to accept a reality where ignorance and superstition got the better of him. His name was Ayush. It meant long-lived. He was a progressive thinker. This wasn't a fate he was prepared to accept. This wasn't how his dreams ended. He would turn and run before it was too late... and never come back.

Mother would understand.

Retreating from the onslaught and preparing to flee, he suddenly felt the ground beneath him disappear.

Tumbling backwards into a drainage ditch, the shock of falling further blurred reality.

As he landed among the rotting detritus that apathy had deposited, his determination to escape was overtaken by a panic so severe, it paralysed his body.

He watched with a sickening sense of inevitability as a rock too large to survive was raised above the head of one of those now staring down at him.

As it was released, he screamed out for his mother.

The old men of the village would continue to squat in the sanctuary of the shade and trade memories. But... out of respect for the grief-stricken woman Ayush had left behind... that of the stone's impact would not be one of them.

* * *

Despite the passage of time, being subjected to the collective stare hadn't become any easier.

Mister Prometheus felt it penetrate his soul, as if holding him in the same contempt with which he held himself. But he couldn't let those feelings show. Any sign of weakness on his part would be fatal. The men and women behind the stare didn't tolerate frailty. Power was everything to them. That's why the assembled cabal of ruthless industrialists had adopted the names of ancient gods during their secret meetings... reflecting their superiority over those whose lives they controlled.

Their ranks had grown considerably since he'd last stood before them and sung for his supper. Old and new, they were expecting their money's worth. His eating habits didn't come cheap. At least, Mrs AKA Mister Prometheus' certainly *didn't*... much like everything else she purchased. That's why he'd foolishly accepted their assistance in the first place and agreed to be part of their *Olympus*.

That assistance had come in the guise of an all-expenses-paid holiday for two in the Caribbean. The initial cost of keeping his spouse happy was turning a blind eye to a shipment of arms destined for an embargoed country somewhere in the Middle East. But, had he known how things would escalate, he might've considered divorce a better option. The trouble with accepting your first bribe is that you're just as guilty in the eyes of the law as when accepting all subsequent ones. Thus a second enticement – a complete home refurbishment – appeared to come at no greater cost... unless you were one of those on the receiving end of a surface-to-surface missile that shouldn't have been there in the first place.

From then on, he found himself trapped in a downward spiral. Being corrupted was like opting to lose one's virginity. Having enjoyed the benefits, you couldn't then change your mind.

The collective was only too happy to keep greasing the slippery slope. Having sold his soul, they knew he could no longer use it to raise an objection.

On the plus side... as long as he remained useful, he retained their lucrative patronage.

On the negative... what he was about to impart might seriously jeopardise his relationship with those now looking down on him.

He wasn't just being looked down on in the condescending sense of the phrase. Stood on the floor of a miniaturised, purpose-built arena, he was being imperiously interrogated by those positioned above him.

It wasn't just their meeting place that had required expansion to accommodate their burgeoning numbers. The pool of gods from which they took their names now stretched beyond those of the Greeks, to include deities from *other* ancient civilisations.

Had the arena been a *real* one, Mister Prometheus would've been standing precisely where a losing gladiator might witness a baying crowd sanction their slaying by a collective downward turn of thumbs.

The symbolism didn't escape him.

Appreciating what was at stake, he lifted his head defiantly.

'It's good to see you again,' voiced Mister Apollo, rising from his stone seat and lifting a hand in salutation.

Mister Prometheus avoided returning the pleasantry by replying with a simple nod of acknowledgement.

That symbolism didn't go unnoticed either.

'For those of us meeting you for the first time, we trust this will be a friendly and fruitful relationship,' offered Mister Ra.

'I fear it may not be as fruitful as you might wish,' he replied. He thought it prudent not to cast doubt on the *friendly* bit.

There was a collective frown.

284

'Fear might be a prophetic word if you've not come to us with good news,' boomed Mister Jupiter, another new face. 'We assumed you had this Xanthia woman in your custody. Is this not the case?'

'It is,' he answered.

'Then… are you about to tell us her claim to have knowledge of everything in the Universe is false, as some of us believed it might be?'

'No… I'm not. Incredible as it sounds… she appears to be able to access all there is to know about any subject or individual simply by concentrating on her focus of interest.'

There was a collective ripple of excitement.

'The problem is… she's unwilling to impart any of what she knows.'

There was a collective sense of anticlimax.

'But we thought she was under the impression she's currently a guest of the US government,' contributed Miss Venus.

'She is… albeit involuntarily.'

'So, why won't she assist it when her stated goal is to save this planet?'

Mister Prometheus shuffled awkwardly. 'I have only two plausible explanations for that. The first is… she's sincere in her refusal to favour one particular nation over another, believing the knowledge she has is for the benefit of all.'

There was a collective gasp of incredulity. Unable to comprehend such a notion, there was a collective wait for the second.

Mister Prometheus stared at his feet.

'Well?'

He braced himself for a collective howl of ridicule. 'The other is that she's lying when she says she's been tasked with saving the world… and, as some have claimed… is actually working for the Devil.'

There was a collective silence.

He looked up in surprise at the lack of any objection. 'I really didn't think you'd go for that,' he admitted.

'Neither option concerns this gathering,' announced Mister Apollo. 'Allegiances or intent are of no interest to us. We only seek access to the vast pool of knowledge she has. That is what you were tasked with ensuring.'

There was a collective nod of agreement.

'I assume your employers aren't aware you have her in custody,' clarified Miss Minerva.

'The president agreed to allow her to participate in the televised debate,' Mister Prometheus answered. 'He's under the impression she left that event of her own free will.'

'And those assisting you?'

'The operatives I've used to detain her believe they're taking part in a highly classified operation, and are under strict orders to report only to me.'

'Are you sure they can be trusted?'

'Most definitely. They've been chosen for a specific reason.'

'And what might that be?'

'They are keen to please... seeking promotions previously denied them.'

'Which means you've employed failures and rejects,' pointed out Mister Vishnu. 'Is that supposed to fill us with confidence?'

'It should,' said Mister Prometheus firmly. 'They've been asked to undertake a mission that stretches professional and moral boundaries. Only those hungry for something they cannot attain by conventional means would take such risks and do whatever is asked of them without question.'

'Are they hungry enough to *torture* her?' ventured Miss Venus.

There was a collective wince.

Mister Prometheus shifted uncomfortably. 'Are you telling me... should she maintain her non-cooperative stance, that's how you wish me to proceed?'

'We seek total global domination,' replied Mister Zeus. 'Your job is to get her to provide information that delivers that... by any means necessary. We cannot trade silence. This Xanthia holds the key to technologies that will revolutionise the world. Billions of people will benefit... not just ourselves.

The pain of a single individual is a minuscule price to pay for such an outcome... wouldn't you say?'

Mister Prometheus felt the debasement of his soul reach a new nadir. He wasn't a stranger to employing such techniques when eliciting information from those stubbornly refusing to part with it. But that was on men who'd gladly do the same to him were the tables turned. Violence towards a member of the opposite sex... especially one yet to be judged an actual threat... was anathema to him. Not that he hadn't fantasised about showing Mrs Prometheus who was boss on the odd occasion... usually after she'd shown him it was her.

'If you find such a method unpalatable... must we assume you're no longer up to the job?' enquired Miss Venus, sensing his disquiet. 'Do you wish to have us consider you expendable?'

There was a collective snarl.

Mister Prometheus reflected on his predicament. 'I haven't ruled such methods out,' he answered reluctantly. *Anyone's* pain was preferable to his own.

'We want *everything*,' Mister Apollo reminded him. 'New fuels... materials... medicines... production techniques... farming methods... dominance in nanotechnology, quantum computing and artificial intelligence... all the secrets that science has yet to unlock. Leave no stone unturned. We have provided you with the experts to ask the questions. It's up to you to ensure they get their answers.'

'And if you're smart,' added Miss Minerva, 'you won't need to compromise what little integrity you have left to squeeze such glorious prizes out of this girl. If she has the knowledge you say... simply encourage her to dwell on the pain *others* have been forced to endure when they've claimed to know the mind of God. Focusing on the screams of Joan of Arc, as the flames took hold, should get her to realise martyrdom isn't all it's cracked up to be.'

Mister Prometheus dropped his head. 'You'll have what you want,' he said quietly, as the last vestige of self-respect vacated his body.

*   *   *

Galveston Humbold strode as briskly as two chafing thighs allowed. Pulling down the sleeves of his jacket, he ran a licked hand across what little hair he had left. 'You've put them in the meeting room, you say?'

His assistant Steven confirmed he had.

'And they're here to ask me about Xanthia?'

'They said they have a couple of questions you might be able to help them with.'

'Sounds like it might be the other way around,' said the reverend, pausing as he reached the door.

'Would you like me to come in with you, sir? Only… I should warn you…'

'No, boy,' the reverend interrupted. 'I'll take it from here. You carry on with that research I asked you to do for my sermon on unmarried mothers finding alternative ways to pay their grocery bills. I'll call you if I need any assistance.' He drew a deep breath and entered the room.

'Ah, Reverend Humbold… thank you for taking the time to see us,' offered the young man standing next to a suit of armour.

The reverend squinted in confusion. 'It's no trouble at all… Mister Tucker-Jenkins. It's an honour and a delight to make your acquaintance.' He extended a hand towards Norman. 'I can't claim to have read any of your books, but I hear a lotta people like 'em.'

'*Plays,*' said Donald indignantly from inside the armour.

The reverend blinked and wondered why the person his assistant had called *the greatest living writer in the world* had chosen to bring a bodyguard with him. 'Is this your security?' he asked.

Norman shook his head.

The reverend registered his confusion. 'Then… why's he dressed as a medieval tin soldier?'

'THE MAN'S CLEARLY AN IDIOT!' yelled Donald, flipping up his visor.

280

'Woah!' cried the reverend, lurching back and grabbing his heart. 'What the sweet Mary, Jesus and all the saint's just happened there!'

'Don't worry. He's talking to his spirit guide. He does that a lot,' explained Norman.

The comment produced a look of astonishment. 'His... what?'

'Spirit guide... Whitebait.'

The reverend gave the bits of Donald's features that were accessible a more thorough examination. 'But the man don't look anything *like* an American Indian!'

'Native American,' Donald corrected him firmly.

'I don't care what tribe you come from. You still don't look like one!'

'*This* is Donald,' Norman smiled, trying to resolve the confusion.

The reverend took a moment to process the fact. 'Then who the hell are *you*... his page?'

'I'm Norman Penkridge. Donald and I are working together on an extremely important project.'

'Has it anything to do with King Arthur? Are you a producer and looking for me to invest in your film?'

'No. He's here because Xanthia's his girlfriend,' said Donald.

The reverend's eyes bulged beyond any reasonable person's comfort zone. 'STEVEN!' he screamed at the top of his voice.

'Do you have a spirit guide too?' enquired Norman warily.

'I have a gun!' the reverend cried, backing away from his visitors and hastily frisking an empty suit. 'So, I'm warning you... given you're standin' on my property... with one of you *clearly* dressed for battle... I'm entitled to shoot the two of you dead if I believe you're gonna attack me!'

'How extraordinary,' tutted Donald. 'In England, we prefer to offer our guests a cup of tea and choice of biscuits.'

The reverend shot a panicked glance towards the door, trying to work out if he could cover the distance to it before the younger of the two intruders wrestled him to the ground.

'I think there's been a misunderstanding,' said Norman.

'There certainly has,' the reverend cried, his brow glistening. 'I had no part in your girlfriend's disappearance. I swear on my great-grandmother's life!'

'Disappearance?' frowned Donald.

'Alright… kidnapping. But I ain't the one responsible. You have my word on that.'

'*Kidnapping?*' exclaimed Norman. 'You told your audience she'd buckled under the power of your presence and run from the debate. We watched your show.'

'I know… I know. That's not my fault, either. It was my lawyer's idea… Marty Greenberg. He's the one you wanna kill, not me! D'ya want me to give you his home address?'

'I told you the man was an idiot,' Donald hissed.

'We don't want to kill *anyone*,' said Norman. 'We just want to ask you some questions.'

'And a cup of tea would be nice,' added Donald. 'I'm quite happy to forgo the biscuits… given the circumstances.'

The reverend tried to steady his breathing, despite his mind furiously working overtime. 'Yeah… okay… you want tea… That's a great idea. I should've guessed from the accent. I'll just need to put a call through to my assistant. He's very good at… boiling a kettle. Would you gentlemen allow me to use that telephone over there?' He delicately pointed to the one on the other side of the room.

Donald shrugged.

Inanely grinning his thanks, the reverend gingerly tiptoed his way over to it… mindful not to make any sudden movements. 'I'm sorry about my earlier comment about a gun. It was a dumb-ass reaction on my part. I'm totally unarmed, as you can see. I pose no threat whatsoever to you two good gentlemen.'

'I have to say… it's not something you expect to hear, coming from England,' admitted Norman.

The reverend paused lifting the receiver. 'Really? If that's the case… how the heck d'ya defend yourself over there?'

'We usually resort to sarcasm,' said Donald, demonstrating its use.

The cogs in the reverend's head turned further. 'So... you folks don't have much knowledge about guns?'

'Only the one Father shot pheasants with,' replied Donald.

'How about... handguns?'

'He never managed to get that close.'

'Okey... dokey,' sung the reverend slowly, 'Just one minute.' He put a call through to his assistant. 'Yeah... Steven... it's me. Listen... I need you in here urgently. I've got a problem that needs your help. I desperately need you to bring me a pot of English tea... three cups... and... most importantly of all... so, listen up carefully... a pack of those COLT 45 COOKIES I've got in the right hand, middle draw of my desk... fully opened and ready to serve up to my two guests. Do you understand what I'm sayin'?'

Steven didn't... but the reverend persisted. 'You know... next to the box of those other cookies shaped like BULLETS. In fact... bring 'em both... I'm feelin' kinda peckish.' Replacing the receiver, he smiled wanly at his visitors.

Donald and Norman smiled back.

'Have you come far?' asked the reverend, trying to maintain an atmosphere of normality while he waited for the cavalry to arrive.

'England,' Donald reminded him.

'Oh, yeah... of course.' The reverend drummed his fingers on the telephone. 'I've never been there myself... but I've seen pictures.'

'Next best thing,' said Donald, demonstrating the many uses of sarcasm again.

'I've always been a great admirer of your royal family... Queen Elizabeth and King Philip... Queen Cleopatra... King Kong.'

'*Prince* Philip,' Norman pointed out.

'What?'

'When a Queen takes a husband, they only become a prince.'

'Well... incest ain't exactly in line with the good book,' scowled the reverend. 'But I have heard they're required to interbreed occasionally.'

'Unbelievable,' muttered Donald.

The reverend continued instigating polite conversation about fog, black cabs, Big Ben and a lack of dental hygiene, until being rescued by a knock on the door.

'YOU CAN COME STRAIGHT IN STEVEN,' he bellowed. 'MY TROUSERS ARE FULLY FASTENED.'

Steven entered, carrying a tray supporting three cups, a pot of tea and something covered by a large napkin.

The reverend immediately made for the latter and... having grabbed what was beneath it... spun around and pointed it aggressively at both his guests. 'RIGHT... YOU EVIL, LIMEY MOTHERFUCKERS! GET DOWN ON YOUR KNEES!'

'You obviously take grace very seriously here,' commented Donald. 'I assume we're about to say prayers.'

'You can sure as hell say yours,' spat the reverend.

Donald tutted. 'Fair enough. But I'm not as agile as I used to be... especially in *this* attire. Do you have anything to assist me?'

The reverend looked around the room. 'Actually, I do. Steven... throw this idiot one of our discounted prayer cushions from over there, would ya?'

Steven did as he was told.

'Is that a hippopotamus?' squinted Donald, examining the cheaply embroidered image on the front of it.

'No. That's me,' the reverend frowned.

Donald shook his head. 'No wonder they're discounted. I'm tempted to ask if the manufacturer once made hat stands.'

'Pardon?'

'It doesn't matter. I'm also tempted to ask why you're holding that packet of biscuits the way you are... but nothing in this country surprises me anymore.'

The reverend glanced at what was in his hands. 'WHAT THE HELL IS THIS?' he screamed at Steven.

'I'm sorry, sir,' his assistant twitched. 'We only have that brand of cookies. I looked for the ones you said were in the drawer of your desk... but all I saw was a gun and some ammunition.'

'OF COURSE HE WAS GOING TO SHOOT US,' shouted Donald. 'I BELIEVE IT'S QUITE A POPULAR PASTIME OUT HERE.'

'I might not have a gun,' the reverend warned his guests, 'but Steven here is an expert in martial arts!'

'Tai chi, actually, sir… and I wouldn't say I'm an expert.'

'You are now,' hissed the reverend from the side of his mouth.

'Well, that's good,' said Donald. 'He can calm us all to death.'

'Look… this is ridiculous,' said Norman. 'We're not here to cause any trouble. We simply want to ask you about Xanthia.'

'Why are you asking *me?*' the reverend exclaimed. '*You're* her boyfriend.'

'Not any more,' interjected Donald.

'Thank you,' said Norman awkwardly. 'But I can speak for myself. The fact is, Reverend Humbold, we're on your side… because Xanthia *definitely* isn't on ours.'

The reverend lowered his biscuits.

'Do I assume this means we're skipping grace?' asked Donald. 'Because, if that's the case… can I at least request… before standards of etiquette deteriorate beyond all tolerance… that whoever pours the tea puts the milk in last.'

*　　*　　*

'Is this supposed to scare me?' Xanthia shouted defiantly, as Brandon signalled for the procedure to start. 'You forget… I know what *real* pain is. What you're threatening to inflict on me right now is as *nothing* compared to what I endure every time I focus on each and every one of you fools.' She glared contemptuously at those hovering over her supine body. 'Not only do I feel your darkest torments… I'm burdened by the weight of the billions of agony-strewn paths that have woven themselves throughout history just so you can be standing right here, right now. And what have you chosen to do with that miracle of unimaginable improbability that's been gifted you?'

The room remained silent.

'So don't you *dare* think you can intimidate me. I'm tortured every day. Mine is not a fate I'd wish upon my worst enemies... including you misguided ingrates! What you're about to do is a mere *pinprick* compared to the combined suffering of humankind. And trust me... it's not just the agony of a never-ending sea of individual deaths... or the crushing trail of heartache left behind. It's the relentless, everyday anguish of disappointment... fear... humiliation... loneliness... hunger... depression... unrequited love... injustice... inadequacy... persecution... and everything else that questions the point of existence.' Her stare sharpened. 'But do you want to know what the *hardest* of all is to stomach?'

The majority of those listening were scientists, so of *course* they did. Some had even started taking notes.

'It's the cruelty of one soul to another when professed to be done in the name of righteousness. History is drenched in such sanctimonious abominations. At least when evil is perpetrated for the sake of evil, it doesn't mask itself with hypocrisy. So... if you're questioning my judgement... never mind which side *I'm* on... which side are *you* on?'

Her question wasn't for Brandon or any of those gathered around the gurney to which she was secured. It was aimed at the cameras silently observing her.

The man at the other end of them bowed his head. He already knew the answer. A.K.A. Mister Prometheus was on his *own* side. It didn't matter that he was about to surrender one of the few principles he had left. He accepted the bathroom mirror would become even more uncomfortable now. He'd have to live with that self-inflicted scar for the rest of his life. But at least he'd have a life to live.

As Brandon stared up at him, he could see in the young man's eyes a reflection of his own misgivings. But self-preservation offered a far greater incentive for what was about to take place than simply doing your job. He sensed the young man was begging for his instructions to be rescinded.

It wasn't going to happen. It couldn't.

'Believe me… if you go through with this, you won't ever be the same person again,' she cautioned.

While the comment had been physically aimed at Brandon this time, A.K.A. Mister Prometheus knew it applied to them both.

'You've only got yourself to blame for what's about to befall you,' Brandon retaliated. 'The power to stop this lies in *your* hands. All you have to do is give me something I can take to my superiors to prove you're on our side.'

'You idiot,' she shouted. 'Do you honestly think that's what this is about? Do you think it would make a jot of difference, even if I suddenly acquired a halo and a set of wings? This is purely about what's in my head and nothing to do with why it's there!'

'I have my orders,' he excused himself.

'How very convenient. I'm sure your mother will applaud such loyalty when you tell her what you did at work today. You will tell her, won't you, Brandon?'

'Cloth!' he said sharply.

Xanthia's world went dark as the requested item was placed over her face. She felt her limbs tugging against their restraints as the gurney tipped backwards.

'It's up to you now,' he prompted her.

Flinching as the cloth was inundated with ice-cold water, she gagged as the shock caused her to attempt a deep breath.

That breath denied, her body jerked as if drowning.

She told herself the abuse would soon stop.

After what seemed an eternity, it did.

All she could hear was her heart pounding in her ears.

'Again,' ordered Brandon, before she'd had a chance to grab a sufficient lungful of air.

As a second torrent of water followed the first, her feet instinctively attempted to kick out against the assault.

Just as her lungs felt like they would implode, the cloth was pulled from her face.

She frantically sucked in air to alleviate the searing pain in her chest.

'Okay,' said Brandon. 'You, of all people, must know how this works. Your mind's eventually going to give in to your body. It always does. So… why not spare yourself unnecessary anguish and give me what I need?'

'If I do that,' she spluttered, 'I'll be kept strapped to this thing until there aren't any more patents left to file.'

'You have my word of honour that won't happen,' he promised.

'Your honour became worthless for eternity the minute you demanded the cloth.' she spat back.

'Put it on again!'

Her face covered, Xanthia struggled to draw enough air through the sopping-wet material to prepare for what she knew was coming.

He waited. 'I told you… it's pointless resisting.'

Unable to hold her breath any longer, she exhaled what little she had.

Once more, the sense of drowning caused her body to spasm. Once more, the cloth was removed just at the point she thought she was going to die.

She desperately gulped in air to quell the burning in her lungs.

'Trust me,' he warned. 'Your mind will soon get tired of this. It's never as strong as you think. Not even *yours*.'

'Then… when that happens… death will come as a relief,' she panted.

He glanced up at the cameras again.

'Perhaps we ought to try electric shocks,' suggested Professor Pearson, applying what he hoped would turn out to be Nobel Prize-winning commonsense.

'Though clearly not at the same time,' advised a fellow observer, applying slightly more of it.

'Do the CIA countenance cigarette burns?' offered another.

'*Technically speaking,* we'd be breaking the law by employing such a method,' replied a stilted voice belonging to a Professor Tosspot. '*Technically speaking,* this is a work environment… so… *technically speaking…* a no smoking area.'

Just as Brandon was about to call for the cloth again, he found himself distracted by a commotion on the other side of the door. 'What the hell's that?'

After the sound of frantic shouting, there was a loud yelp followed by an uncomfortable silence.

As those in the room considered whether it was sensible to investigate, their dilemma was nulled by the door bursting open.

'Nobody move or I'll fill you full of lead!' yelled Kevin, wildly waving a semi-automatic firearm at those staring back at him in horror.

'I don't wish to be churlish,' interjected Professor Tosspot in his strangled lilt, 'but, *technically speaking*, bullets are predominantly copper these days, due to that particular element having a greater specific heat capacity and hardness.'

'You're still gonna feel it when it hits your skull, you twat,' shouted Kevin aggressively.

'Well... you say that... but given the time I'd have left for my brain to process sensory signals, *technically spe_*'

'Shut it!' Kevin barked.

'I don't mind you pointing that thing at everyone else,' twitched Xanthia, wafting in and out of his line of fire. 'But would you mind not doing so at me?'

'Don't worry,' he beamed. 'I've got the safety catch on.'

Brandon shot a look at the largest of his colleagues.

Just as the two were telepathically preparing to rush the interloper, half a dozen men clad in a combination of well-worn leather and unwashed denim entered the room.

'We've secured the entire building,' announced one of them. 'Given our location, I reckon it'll be at *least* twenty minutes before they can get reinforcements here.'

'I don't believe it. I *know* that guy!'

'Which one?' demanded A.K.A. Mister Prometheus with alarm, watching the scene unfolding on the monitors in front of him.

'That spotty kid with the attitude... the one waving the gun.'

'Who the hell is he, Papadopoulos?'

'Well... sparing you the pseudonyms he prefers to go by... his real name's Kevin and he hails from London.'

'You mean... in *England?*'

'I do... unless they've moved it since I was last there.'

'Don't get smart with me,' A.K.A. Mister Prometheus warned with a laser stare. 'How come you know him?'

In his shock and excitement, Bob had forgotten their acquaintance had been made during a mission even more *off the books* than the one he was currently engaged in. 'It's my understanding the kid's wanted by the Brits for a murder attempt on Norman Penkridge,' he offered, attempting to remove his foot from his mouth and hobble onto safer ground.

'Penkridge?' barked A.K.A. Mister Prometheus. 'What in hell's name are you doing still sniffing around *that* case?'

'It's purely out of personal curiosity, sir. It doesn't involve agency time.'

'It better not. You've a connection to that name I don't care to be reminded of... and I'm amazed you don't feel the same. The only reason you've been picked for this mission is to give you one last chance to salvage your car-crash of a career... a crash that individual had a hand in.'

Bob was more focused on his colleagues' predicament than his own. 'Shouldn't we be thinking about getting people in there to help our guys?' he said, his eyes darting between the monitors.

A.K.A. Mister Prometheus shook his head awkwardly. 'I told you, Papadopoulos... we're off the record with this one. I can't involve anyone beyond our own, select team.'

'But he could kill them. That kid's a psychopath!'

A.K.A. Mister Prometheus reapplied his forensic stare.

'*Apparently,*' Bob conceded hastily.

'Then, our guys should've taken more care. They knew the risks involved in operating outside the normal boundaries. I don't like it any more than you... but they're on their own, now. They'll have to work this out for themselves.' A.K.A.

270

Mister Prometheus turned back to the screen in front of him. 'What else do you know about this kid?'

'Nothing, sir,' Bob lied.

'And those men with him? Any insight as to who *they* might be?'

'Unless it's dress down day for terrorists, I'd say they're Hell's Angels. I've no idea what the connection is.'

That bit was true. What he also couldn't fathom... given the enthusiasm with which Kevin was waving his gun... was why Xanthia appeared so relaxed in his presence.

'How did you know where to find me?'

'It's a long story,' said Kevin, loosening her restraints. 'I'll tell you later.'

'And who are these men you've got with you?'

He grinned. 'They're the private army you said I'd be able to hire. It's amazing what money can buy.'

'But we haven't got any yet,' she frowned.

'I told them about the chequebook. They've agreed to work for us on the proviso they're paid double when you've made the first withdrawal. They fixed me up with a loan shark friend of theirs to tide me over. You should see the car I've come in!'

A heavily bearded man of considerable bulk, who answered to the name of Tonsils... though only when he wanted to... pointed at Brandon and his cohorts lined up against the wall. 'What do you want us to do with this lot, Megabyte Master?'

'I'm gonna use 'em as target practice,' replied Kevin excitedly. 'They'll be far easier to hit than those bottles you've been getting me to fire at in the woods.'

'Fair enough,' Tonsils nodded. 'But you wanna take your safety catch off first.'

Tutting away his foolishness, Kevin placed the gun's muzzle against the tiled floor and wedged its butt awkwardly between his knees. As he fiddled with the catch, a sudden and deafening burst of gunfire sent him sprawling backwards. Those in the room dived for cover as bullets ricocheted off every available surface.

269

When the last shell casing had finished its death rattle, a tense silence hung in the air. It was broken only by the sound of heavy breathing.

The smell of spent ammunition lingering, Tonsils gingerly raised himself to his knees. 'Do we have any men down?'

'Yes,' whimpered Professor Pearson. 'I think I've been shot in the leg.'

'You don't count. Big Hank… Robbo… Spud… you all okay?'

Those concerned registered their survival.

'Fat Sam… Spanner?'

'Just a slight trouser accident,' reported one.

'Suffering from its fallout,' replied the other from underneath him.

'Sorry about that,' Kevin giggled, scrambling to his feet. 'This thing's lethal.'

'That's the general idea,' Tonsils grunted. 'Perhaps you oughta put the safety catch back on.'

'Is that wise?' shrieked Doctor Menzies from behind what had previously been a perfectly good filing cabinet.

'Line 'em up again,' ordered Tonsils. 'This time… on their knees.'

'They're gonna execute them!' cried Bob. 'We have to do something!'

'I told you, Papadopoulos… this mission can't be compromised. You know how it goes. We're flying under the radar. Our men knew what they were getting themselves into when they signed up for it.'

'What *have* they gotten themselves into?' demanded Bob. 'They might be many miles from here… but they're still operating on home soil. What's so important about this mission that warrants them *dying* on it?'

'The answer is way beyond your security clearance,' returned A.K.A. Mister Prometheus stiffly. 'And if you wanna come in from the cold and get yourself back into my good books, you'd do well to remember that.'

Galveston Humbold daintily slurped his tea, making sure his pinky finger pointed away from the handle of his cup. He understood it had something to do with good manners where his visitors came from and didn't want to appear uncouth. 'I'm not sure what further help I can offer you gentlemen,' he mumbled, through a hail of biscuit crumbs flying from an overfull mouth.

'So... to get this straight... you're saying the government are denying all knowledge of Xanthia's whereabouts,' Norman clarified, 'despite you seeing them take her away?'

'That's what they told my lawyer. But then... that's what he said they'd say. The official line is no orders were issued to detain her and that they suspect her disappearance is a publicity stunt... even having the audacity to suggest I could've had a hand in it myself! Can you believe such downright impertinence?'

'That's why we came to see you. They told us more or less the same thing. They claimed she'd removed herself from the show, but wouldn't elaborate further. If we're to make sense of everything, it's vital we know what's *really* happened.'

'I'm tellin' ya... it's exactly like I said. They drugged her good and proper and carted her away in a comatose state. There was nothing my people could do... being told in no uncertain terms not to intervene.'

'Did they offer proof of identification?'

'Hell, yeah. They flashed bona fide CIA credentials. That's why my security boys were powerless to stop them.'

'Of course they were genuine agents,' interjected Donald matter-of-factly. 'I obviously presented a convincing enough case, as to why the debate shouldn't go ahead, for your president to sanction the action. His government just can't publicly admit to it.'

The reverend lowered his teacup. 'I *beg* your pardon?'

'I told him she was dangerous and needed to be stopped,' said Donald proudly.

The reverend's eyes widened. 'So *you're* the one responsible for ruining my show!' They kept expanding. 'Do you know how much *money* you've gone and cost me? I can't believe you've got the boldfaced effrontery to sit there and eat my cookies!'

'Any reduction in your personal wealth... or *biscuits...* is immaterial,' Donald chomped. 'Besides... I doubt there'll be anything left for you to spend your ill-gotten gains on if Xanthia gets her way. You might not think so now, Galveston... but, believe me... you'll soon realise I've done you a massive favour.'

'*Ill-gotten* gains? And that's *Reverend Humbold* to you!'

Donald's eyes shot beyond his frown. 'Whitebait says he wasn't aware you'd attended a theological college. He was under the impression the certificate on your office wall was purchased via the internet.'

The *reverend-because-it-said-so-on-a-certificate* puffed himself up, ready to refute the allegation... then circumspectly focused on the surface of his tea.

'I just don't understand why *we've* been removed from the loop,' Norman scowled. 'After all... it was *us* who exposed Xanthia as a threat.'

The reverend coughed loudly.

'OF *COURSE* IT'S NOT BISCUIT CRUMBS,' Donald shouted.

'I think you'll find I was ahead of y'all on that,' the reverend remarked.

'Yet you gave her the chance to unleash her poison on a *far* bigger audience than she'd ever had before,' Donald declared.

'Which is precisely what she'd been waiting for,' Norman added. 'You unwittingly gave her the credibility she'd previously failed to achieve.'

'I think you'll find *that* was down to her public altercation with one of God's messengers,' the reverend pointed out, shovelling the remaining cookies into his mouth so as to prevent his guests abusing his hospitality any further.

'That's another thing that's been puzzling me,' said Norman. 'If Gabriel was prepared to risk making an appearance, why didn't he do so in England and warn me about her?'

'*Gabwiel?*' the reverend munched.

'The Archangel. He happens to be a very good friend of mine.'

The reverend's extended pinky curled.

'Perhaps it wasn't him,' Donald suggested. 'Perhaps it was an angel with fewer disruptive vibrations.'

Norman squinted. '*Is* there such a thing?'

Alarmed at Donald's eyes rolling up into his head again, the reverend anxiously examined the sell-by date on the packet of cookies.

'Whitebait says he can't answer your question, as he's never been fortunate enough to mix in such exalted company,' Donald replied.

'But why have the confrontation in America?'

'I'd have thought that was obvious,' the reverend scoffed. 'Less distance for a heavenly being to travel.' He glanced at his watch. 'Now… I don't wish to be rude, but I have an *extremely* important appointment I need to attend.'

'We understand,' nodded Norman. 'It was good of you to see us. But before you go…' He took a deep breath for courage. 'Can you tell us if Xanthia came to your studio alone… or did she have someone with her?'

The reverend nodded. 'As a matter of fact, I believe she did. Not that I saw the young man personally… but my assistant tells me she was travelling with her beau.' Realising the implications of what he'd just said, he winced apologetically. 'Ah… my condolences. Though, if you ask me, you've had a mighty lucky escape.'

'And what happened to this individual after she was taken from the building?' Norman persisted.

The reverend shrugged.

Norman looked at Donald.

'Like I said, gentlemen… I really have to go now. But let me know if I can be of any further assistance. It's certainly been… *interesting.*'

'We're not done yet,' said Donald firmly. 'I've also got a question that needs answering.'

The reverend reversed his attempt to stand and crouched awkwardly. 'I'll oblige if I can,' he said somewhat impatiently.

'How did you know Xanthia posed such a dangerous threat so early on? After all… she'd never given any indication of it… not even to Norman… and they *lived* together! Those who dismissed her claims thought she was either mad or engaged in some kind of publicity stunt. No one actually made such a leap of thinking and assumed she was working for the other side… except you.'

'God spoke to me,' the reverend said earnestly. 'Much like your Whiteboard speaks to you.'

'*Whitebait,*' Donald corrected him. 'And he says he thinks that's highly unlikely. He tells me you've always kept your third eye stubbornly closed.'

'What's my *anus* got to do with any of this?' exclaimed the reverend indignantly. 'And you tell that fella' there in your head… it ain't for *him* to go doubting the words of the Lord… or the people He chooses to communicate them to… or, indeed, the orifice through which He might do it!'

Donald leant forward like a detective about to reach for his handcuffs. 'In that case… Whitebait's requesting you ask the Lord what we should do next… because he says that – for all his trying – he's never got so much as an "I'll get back to you" from anyone *remotely* close to such an exalted level of consciousness.'

The reverend fully raised himself and brushed the crumbs from his suit. 'I'll see what I can do. Now… if you'll excuse me… as I say, I have someone else who's expecting to see me. I don't want to keep them waiting.'

'Are you at least able tell us where Xanthia was staying, prior to taking part in your show?' pressed Norman, as the reverend made to leave.

'I'll get Steven to write the address down for you,' the reverend said curtly.

'I THOUGHT YOU SAID IT WAS HIGHLY UNLIKELY *ANYONE* COMMUNICATED WITH HIM… LET ALONE GOD,' shouted Donald.

'Jeez!' flinched the reverend. 'Is that spirit guide of yours stone-deaf?'

'WELL… *SOMEONE* CLEARLY DOES,' continued Donald, ignoring him. 'I DISTINCTLY HEARD YOU SAY HE'S ABOUT TO GET A DODGY MESSAGE.'

Everyone quietly looked at each other.

'OH,' said Donald contritely. 'MY APOLOGIES… IT'S THIS DAMN HELMET… I OBVIOUSLY MISHEARD THE LAST WORD.'

* * *

Kevin pressed the barrel of his assault rifle hard against Brandon's forehead. 'You might wanna look away, Xan. I think this next bit's gonna get a little messy.'

'The boy's insane!' shrieked Doctor Menzies, kneeling with his hands on his bowed head as instructed.

'Even though you're no longer officially qualified to make such a diagnosis, doctor… wouldn't you consider someone who's trying to drown a person shackled to a gurney to be *somewhere* in that category?' asked Xanthia.

'I wouldn't have allowed you to *die!*' he cried.

'Oh… my apologies… I misread you. You clearly have a *good* heart.'

'Not for long,' taunted Kevin, waving his gun.

'If you're gonna do the deed, I suggest you get on with it,' advised Tonsils. 'They'll have despatched reinforcements by now, so we can't afford to hang around.'

'No problem,' Kevin beamed. 'I'll take them all out in one go. It'll be quicker.'

'Kinder, too,' nodded Tonsils. 'Especially for the one on the end.'

'Oh, I'm not worried about that,' Kevin frowned. 'I just think it'll look more spectacular. I once did something similar in *Cortex Destroyer* and got awarded bonus points.'

'We'll leave you to it,' said Tonsils, heading for the door. 'Best you're on your own when you pull that trigger. One trouser accident is enough for the day. We'll be waiting outside.' He gestured for the others to follow.

'You wanna shoot these cameras out before you do the deed,' advised Spanner, nodding at the ones observing them. 'No point in gifting 'em evidence.'

'Like it matters,' Kevin scoffed. 'And if the footage goes viral, I'll be famous.'

Spanner shrugged.

Xanthia waited until the last man had left. 'I've got a better idea.' She bit her lip in thought. 'On reflection, I think we should let this pathetic bunch of losers live.'

Kevin looked at her aghast.

'Hear me out,' she insisted. 'I've still got to persuade the public to trust me. They're not going to do that if they think I'm responsible for a cold-blooded massacre. We need to be smart and turn this situation to our advantage. Given the majority of people distrust governments and love an underdog, we'll tell the world what happened to me and capitalise on the inevitable outpouring of sympathy.'

'I think that's a splendid idea!' croaked Professor Rawlson from his position on the end of the line.

'I concur,' chipped in Professor Mowbray, next to him.

'So… that's settled,' she nodded. 'We'll lock them in here… and then you can show me what that new car of yours is made of.'

'*Technically speaking…* it'll be alloys, rubber and a selection of automotive composites,' offered Professor Tosspot, unable to help himself.

'Can I kill just one?' pleaded Kevin. 'At least then it'll only be murder and not a massacre.'

'Might I suggest Brandon, if you do?' piped up Professor Pearson. 'After all… he's the one in charge here.'

'Fair enough,' said Kevin, raising his gun.

'No!' shouted Xanthia. 'I *told* you... I need to get the public on my side.' She pulled the barrel away from Brandon's head. 'Let's get out of here. Your friend Tonsils is right... they'll have reinforcements arriving soon.'

Sulking heavily, Kevin did as instructed.

As Xanthia followed him out of the room, she turned to take a final look at the line of shell-shocked faces staring back at hers. 'Don't think you've escaped punishment, gentlemen,' she scowled. 'Because here's a fact I'm happy to give you *without* being coerced. You're all going to have to face the consequences of how you behaved in this room for the rest of eternity... and take it from me... that's an *extremely* long time.'

*　　*　　*

'I only extended the booking on my *own* room,' said Kevin, triumphantly flopping back on his hotel bed. 'It's not that I doubted I'd be able to rescue you... I just reckoned we wouldn't need separate accommodation once I did. Your stuff's in my wardrobe.'

'That's very forward of you,' Xanthia giggled. 'What makes you think I don't still need wooing?'

Kevin rolled to one side and pulled something from under his pillow. 'This... I looked for it in your case.' He held up Norman's chequebook.

'I hope you're not suggesting you're buying *me* with that!' she teased, reaching out for it.

He playfully snatched it away from her. 'I did what you asked me to do.'

'You did,' she smiled, kneeling on the bed and demanding it with a click of her fingers.

He handed it over. 'So... I believe that means we can now have sex. I think I've finally earned it.'

Opening the chequebook, she ran her finger across its stubs. 'I think you're in for a bit of a shock.'

261

'Don't worry,' he grinned. 'I've watched a lot of porn. I know what to expect.'

'I don't think you do,' she smiled back.

He looked at her eagerly. 'So... what happens now? Is it me who makes the first move?'

'I think you'll find I'm the one in the driving seat,' she replied.

He drew nearer. 'I'm okay with that.'

'I somehow don't think you will be.'

'No... really. I'm used to my mum telling me what to do.'

'I actually feel *sorry* for you,' she said, her smile waning.

'There's no need... she can't control me now.'

'You should've been stronger.'

'Easier said than done. She's a pretty formidable woman and not easily swayed.'

Xanthia gave him a look of pity. 'Then, it's a shame you didn't inherit that quality.'

His grin wavered. 'Xan?'

'I've seen the forks you've chosen to take in life... none more catastrophic than the one Satan presented to you.'

'Forks? What on earth are you talking about?'

'It's what Norman calls those decisions we're faced with that ultimately determine the direction of our lives.'

'Why are you mentioning him?' said Kevin pettishly.

She looked him in the eyes and winked. 'Because... I *love* him.'

Kevin's face twitched. 'Is this some sort of joke? If it is... I don't find it the least bit funny.'

'Life's like that,' she said. 'You need to grow up and face the fact it's serious at times... and *always* very real. It's not the shoot-'em-up computer game you seem to think it is. People aren't expendable targets, put on earth for you to improve a score... no more than emotions are things you can win and bank. You have the most pathetic soul I've ever encountered... so the Devil's welcome to it when you find this fantasy game of yours eventually logs you out.'

Kevin stared at her, confused. 'I don't understand... What's going on here?'

She stared straight back. '*You* work it out. After all... you're always boasting how clever you are.'

His eyes slowly widened. 'You were... *playing* me?'

'Of course... which wasn't too difficult, let's face it. I simply allowed you to believe I was the avatar you'd constructed for me in that ridiculously childish mind of yours.'

'But what about our plans? We had it all worked out. You need me to help you win the fight. Are you saying there isn't going to be an Armageddon?'

'Oh, *that* bit's real. The only difference is I'm here to stop it... just like I've been telling people all along.'

'But that's because you're tricking everybody,' he floundered. 'Just like you tricked Penkridge.'

'Not *everybody*. Just you.'

Without being able to hit a pause button, while struggling with what to say next, '*why?*' was the best he could manage.

'For this,' she smiled, waving the chequebook. 'Saving the world doesn't come cheap. That's why the Templars set their account up in the first place. A lot of people went to a great deal of trouble over many centuries to amass this amount of financial muscle. Of course... with my gift, I'd eventually be able to replicate that kind of wealth. But we don't have the luxury of time. That's why I needed you to reverse the damage you'd done. From the minute I focused on your ingenious firewall, I realised you'd coded in a password-secured backdoor that would allow you to reinstate the chequebook. Because, after you'd despatched Norman, you planned to steal it and use it yourself. That's all you were to me... a password I couldn't see. The Devil's insistence that he was with you when you created it produced too great a vibrational interference for me to view the event clearly. He knew *exactly* what he was doing. In fact... he's the one who should take credit for me not being able to reverse your work... not you.'

'The *idea* was still mine!'

259

'If only you knew how unattractive your hubris makes you. Ironically... it's also been your undoing. Asking you directly for help would've raised suspicion. So I played on that arrogance and waited for you to strut into my trap.'

'But I rescued you today! That's gotta count for *something*. You're only here because of my tenacity!'

'I admit that was impressive. How on earth did you know where to find me?'

'I asked a taxi to follow the van they took you away in.'

She blinked with incredulity. 'That's *it?* I thought you said it was a long story. I was at least expecting yet another inflated account of your brilliance.'

'I could hardly say it had been that easy in front of Tonsils and his gang, could I? They need to respect me.'

'I think they just need you to pay them,' she laughed.

Kevin's look of abandonment morphed into a scowl. 'I bet this was Penkridge's idea.'

She gazed at him introspectively. 'To the contrary... he doesn't have a clue. I couldn't risk your side knowing my real intention. Gabriel had told Norman they observed everything he did. If I'd explained what I was *really* up to, they'd have alerted you and ruined my plan.' She let out a heavy sigh. 'That's been the toughest part to live with... knowing he's out there doubting me.' She waved the chequebook again. 'But this should help make up for it.'

'He isn't gonna beat me!' Kevin shouted. 'I should've pushed that knife even further into him when I had the chance!'

'Well, there you go,' she smiled. 'That's *another* mistake you've made. You really need to up your game, Kevin. He's definitely looking like the number one in my book.'

'Oh, don't worry,' he snarled. 'He hasn't won yet. You're forgetting... that thing you're holding isn't worth the paper it's printed on. All I have to do is cancel it a second time and reactivate my rolling firewall. You'll both be back to square one!'

'You might find that a little difficult,' she grinned. 'Once you'd kindly unblocked the account, I wrapped a firewall of my own around it. Trust me… with my skills, there's no *way* you'll be able to get beyond it and mess things up again.'

Baring his teeth, Kevin lunged for the chequebook.

Instinctively channelling the skills of a Shaolin master, she deftly sidestepped his advance and assisted his forward momentum with a graceful combination of hands and feet. It would be the only time in his life that her opponent would find a trouser press in a hotel room useful. Fortuitously placed, it stopped him investigating the contents of a minibar without having to open its glass door.

'I'd stay on the floor, if I were you,' she advised. 'You'll find this sort of stuff's a lot harder without a games controller in your hand.'

'What are you gonna do… call the police?' he wheezed, clutching his abdomen.

'While that might see you go to prison for what you did to Norman, there are punishments awaiting you that are *far* more fitting.' She stepped over his body to retrieve her suitcase from the wardrobe.

'Like what?'

'Well… you sold your soul to the Devil, for starters. That really *is* a fate worse than death.'

'And the others?'

'They're waiting for you the minute you leave this room. When I opened the chequebook just now, I made sure you hadn't used it to make a withdrawal. Not only will you have some explaining to do to the hotel manager when he presents you with the bill… Tonsils and his friends are expecting payment for their services, too. And… as for that loan-shark friend of theirs… well… the best of luck with *that* one!'

'But you still need me,' he insisted. 'You told me my presence completed your power. You said I have the missing piece of the sphere.'

'I think you have a missing part of your brain,' she laughed, heading for the door. 'It was all part of the deception. Aside from your propensity for committing evil, there's nothing special about you whatsoever.'

'You can't leave me like this,' he cried. 'This isn't fair! The Devil promised we'd be together.'

'Well, he was right. We were... albeit briefly.'

'But he suggested in *other* ways.'

'I think you'll find he's not the best person to trust,' she said, opening the door.

Kevin stared in horror. 'Does that mean we're never gonna have sex?'

She gazed at him pitifully and took a sharp intake of breath. 'Knowing what your private army has gotten up to in the past... I think it's more accurate to say... *you're* never gonna have sex.'

*　　*　　*

It was a standing joke between the two men that... having walked every field in County Armagh in pursuit of rusty nails, discarded ring pulls and twenty years of disappointment... they'd never been let down.

Today would be no exception... or so they thought.

As they swept their metal detectors in lazy unison, the dream of a treasure hoard had long since morphed into an excuse to get away from their spouses and talk about a world where they were expert lovers, political geniuses and master tacticians in every sport known to man. Their adeptness in so broad a category of subjects was made all the more remarkable by the fact that every other person on the planet... according to them... was a complete and utter eejit.

During those years, they'd divided the spoils from the hoard of gold they were about to discover so many times, the mathematics no longer made sense. It wasn't just friends and relatives who were going to benefit. The community in which they'd grown up, married and raised their children would also thank them for their generosity. They would respectfully decline having the new hospital wing they were going to fund named after them. The attention they received from the media for unearthing such an historic and valuable find would be fame enough. Local charities would also be winners... as would the regulars at their local drinking establishment. Even the archaeological world would praise them... lauding their honesty and integrity in properly declaring their hoard.

All that was needed was that elusive pot of gold.

In the meantime... as long as the worthless detritus they regularly unearthed made them howl with laughter once the dirt was brushed from the anticipated treasure... they considered themselves rich enough.

Éogan ran as fast as the roughly ploughed field and the weight of his sword allowed. It would only be a question of time before his pursuers were upon him. He wouldn't fight. No point in risking death. They weren't looking to *kill* him... only take him prisoner. His value lay in being alive. Ransomed back to his family, he'd be left to explain why he'd been foolish enough to cross into a rival clan's territory without a retinue of men for protection.

Not that his father would've sanctioned his journey. Those neighbours, once a useful ally, were now a sworn enemy.

But it wasn't just years of peaceful co-existence that had been abandoned in the diplomatic divorce. Éogan had lost the opportunity to see the girl he'd hoped to marry. Her father was as stubborn as his own. Their betrothal... arranged to strengthen a valuable alliance, but having blossomed into so much more... had been cruelly annulled, thanks to a drunken argument over the misappropriation of a few head of cattle. The young lovers... caring little for politics and everything for each other... found themselves stranded on opposite sides of a bitter dispute... hostages to the egos of two fractious and obstinate warlords.

But Éogan refused to accept the decision of others. He was his father's son, in that respect. Orlaith was the love of his life and he wished for no other.

They'd arranged to meet in secret and abscond. Starting a new life far away, they'd be masters of their own destiny and live the dream they'd promised each other.

Whether through fear or a misguided desire to protect her mistress, it had been Orlaith's maid who'd betrayed their hopes... leaving Éogan to brave a leap from a window in order to make his escape. But not before the woman he'd vowed to be with forever had forced her cherished bracelet into his hand. Once belonging to her grandmother, it contained a breathtaking array of opals, garnets, emeralds, rubies and sapphires skilfully inlaid in an exquisitely engraved band of gold by the finest craftsmen in the land. Refusing his offer of the equally magnificent torc from around his neck, she'd insisted that... while the two of them were apart... those individual pieces should remain together as an eternal reminder of the beauty of their combined love for each other.

Watching him disappear through a veil of tears, she yearned for the day he'd eventually return with the bracelet... along with a ring for her finger.

As he ran, Éogan's ears pounded with the sound of his heartbeat against the heavy draw of his breath. But it didn't stop him hearing the dogs in the distance and the shouts of angry men following. His legs were getting heavy and he knew they wouldn't carry him much further. Realising time and topography were against him, he stopped and threw back his head, bellowing to the sky.

The dogs momentarily paused their barking... then resumed with increased vigour.

He drew his sword and thrust it into the ground, repeatedly stabbing at the soil. Loosening just enough, he sank to his knees in exhaustion and hastily scooped out a hole with his bare hands.

Rather than see it confiscated as spoils of his capture, he removed the torc from his neck and threaded it through Orlaith's parting gift... bending its dragon-headed ends together until the two pieces became one. Carefully placing this representation of their commitment to each other in the hole, he quickly covered it with the discarded earth and marked the location with three white stones.

If fate decreed they were to be together again, he and Orlaith would return one day and retrieve it. If not... the two pieces would remain forever hidden... symbolising a love that was now entwined for eternity and could never be broken.

The strength of the signal took the two men by surprise. Having just finished solving the third world debt crisis, they were close to calling it a day. With the discovery of a rusty hinge... half a dozen bottle tops... the broken blade from a penknife... and thruppence ha'penny in coins dating back no earlier than George VI, there was only so much excitement two men could take.

They were also in danger of getting soaked. Out of nowhere, the sky had darkened to such an extent, only a raucous murder of crows was making use of it. The men hadn't dressed for such an unseasonable downpour.

Passing their detectors back and forth over the patch of soil, they discussed whether to leave it for another day. The problem was... if they postponed their investigation and marked the spot, it might be dug by others before they returned. A less obvious marking might mean them not being able to locate the site themselves.

With one eye on the clouds, the decision was taken to dig.

His companion standing by, ready to test the piles of earth as they were removed, the other hacked at the ground with his spade to break the stubborn soil.

As he did so, he found himself overtaken by the strangest feeling. The harder he thrust, the more his legs became leaden and his breathing difficult.

A dog howled in the distance.

'You alright?'

'The weirdest thing.'

'Is it your heart?'

'I dunno.'

'Then kindly remove yer hand from it and put it back on yer spade. I don't wish to be getting soaked!'

Spurred on by adrenalin, his companion resumed his efforts until he'd done enough to allow the use of a trowel. Dropping to his knees, he hastily scraped away the looser earth.

The shape of their find was the first to reveal itself.

'I reckon it's a horseshoe.'

'It's come from a fair-sized beast, if it is.'

It was the glint of gold that finally dropped their jaws... as bright and mesmerising as the day it had been placed in the ground.

Mouths agape, they watched in silence as the rest of their discovery slowly revealed itself.

'I think we're agreed that's more than a soddin' horseshoe!'

'What d'ya reckon it is?'

'It's our dream... that's what,' gasped the digger, sitting back on his haunches in wonderment.

'Look at that thing. I've never seen such an object before. And look at what it's made of. It's gotta be worth an absolute fortune!'

'We've definitely unearthed something of historical importance. We need to record it properly before removing it from the ground.'

'What? Are you kiddin' me? Have you seen the anger in those clouds? They're about to blow and drop half the friggin' Atlantic Ocean on top of us! I reckon it'll be accompanied by an uncomfortable amount of thunder and lightning... and we're stood in the middle of an open field with enough metal on us to build a friggin' pylon. Let's just pull that thing out the ground and get back to the safety of the car.'

'No way.'

'What?'

'We can't do that.'

There was a difficult silence.

'Are you for real?'

'We always said we'd do things properly if we ever hit the jackpot.'

'We've said a lotta things over the years. The landlord at the Crosskeys thinks he's in line for a new speedboat.'

'What's wrong with you? This is the moment we've been dreaming of. We've finally dug up treasure. So, if you think we're not safe here, we'll backfill the hole and report it to the authorities. They can arrange for someone qualified to come and take over. It'll still be *our* find. We're the ones who'll get the credit... not to mention a share of its value.'

'A *share?*'

'God willing.'

'You're bringing *Him* into the equation? If He were on our side, He wouldn't have sent those ominous clouds!'

'Well... someone a little lower down the ladder, then. I think it's the Secretary of State who makes the final decision on whether it's officially classed as treasure.'

'I *know* it is. That's what concerns me. D'ya not think we're entitled to *all* of it? After all... it's *us* who've been trudging up and down these damn fields for the last twenty years, not the Secretary of friggin' State!'

'That's not how it works. You know that.'

'Look... if it wasn't for you and me, this thing would've remained hidden in the ground for eternity. We deserve to be recompensed for its full value... not a poxy share.'

'Money's not the issue, here. We're not talking gold coins. Look at the craftsmanship that's gone into that torc alone. That didn't hang around the neck of the local farmer. I reckon this thing could be of historical importance.'

A flash of lightning lit the sky.

The man's companion grabbed the spade and raised it to shoulder height. 'Get away from that hole... or so help me.'

'Are you *serious?*'

'Deadly. Now... either hand that thing up to me or move away and let me at it.'

'This isn't right!'

'Neither is needlessly giving up what I've been dreaming of for years.'

'You're crazy! You'll never be able to sell it. That torc is unique. No one will touch it with a bargepole!'

'Maybe not.' The man leant down and yanked it from the ground. 'But the bracelet's definitely gonna make *someone's* eyes light up.'

A crack of thunder shook the air.

'What are ya doing?'

'What d'ya think? Separating them. Don't worry… you can have your precious torc and some column inches in the local newspaper. I just want the bracelet. No one need ever know they were together. You'll be able to bask in your moment of fame and glory and I'll have my money.'

'But they *were* found together. They *both* belong to the nation.'

'Not anymore.'

'Wait! You're gonna break them!'

'No… see… the torc's bending easily. Besides… I'm only putting it back to how it used to be.'

'YOU CAN'T!'

'HEY… GET OFF ME, WILL YA!'

'I WON'T LET YOU DO THIS! GIVE THEM BOTH TO ME!'

As the two men held on to the objects, a blinding flash of light terminated their argument.

It wasn't until the next morning that a local walker saw what she thought were two dead animals lying beside each other in the sodden field.

The doctors said it was a miracle that one of the men had managed to summon the inner strength to survive the ordeal and remain conscious throughout the bitterly cold night… unlike his less fortunate companion.

The torc… considered to be one of the finest of its kind ever discovered in Northern Europe… can be seen on display in the men's local museum… next to a large plaque naming them both… and thanking the survivor for his generosity in donating his entire share of the proceeds from its valuation to the local community.

The bracelet is kept hidden from the authorities in the safe of a private collector... who happens to live just streets away.

Poor Éogan and Orlaith.

So near... and yet... so far.

* * *

The taxi driver waited patiently as one of his passengers struggled to extricate the other from the back of his cab. 'Do I assume from the medieval attire you're from somewhere in Europe?' he addressed the suit of armour, once it was standing upright. He'd thought it best not to enquire during the journey, as having to keep a conversation going with a lunatic, while negotiating traffic, could be quite stressful.

'England, actually,' said Donald, lifting his visor.

'That'll explain the Australian accent,' the taxi driver nodded. 'Are you related to Ned Kelly?'

Donald looked at him incredulously.

'The outlaw,' the taxi driver explained. 'He liked wearing tin suits, too.'

'No, I'm not! How much do I owe you?'

The taxi driver shrugged his indifference. 'Twenty dollars.'

Donald handed him two ten dollar bills.

They induced a look of disdain. 'I appreciate you're not from these parts, sir... but it's customary to give the driver a tip in this country.'

'Oh... I do beg your pardon,' apologised Donald profusely. 'Just a second.'

Expecting him to reach for his wallet again... wherever that might be kept... the taxi driver looked on in bemusement as his fare awkwardly leant back and stared up at where his forehead had just been.

'You okay, sir?'

'*I* am,' Donald assured him. 'But... oh deary me.'

'Sir?'

'I've have a message for you from the other side.'

249

Confused, the taxi driver glanced at the empty sidewalk across the road.

'Rather rude,' Donald tutted, believing he was being ignored.

'You wanna explain, sir?' said the taxi driver, looking back at him, perplexed.

'I'd have thought it was self-explanatory, young man. I possess psychic abilities.'

The taxi driver made a strange shape with his mouth. 'O...k...a...y.'

'You'll need to drive *extremely* carefully over the next few days.'

'What?'

'YOU'LL NEED TO DRIVE CAREFULLY FOR A WHILE,' shouted Donald, assuming the man to be hard of hearing as *well* as short on manners. He quickly raised his eyes. 'OF *COURSE* I'M NOT TALKING TO YOU, YOU IDIOT! NOT ONLY DO YOU NOT HAVE A CAR... YOU DON'T EVEN HAVE *ROADS!*'

Completely bewildered, the taxi driver looked across at the empty sidewalk again.

'According to my sources... you'll need to be *extremely* vigilant over the coming days,' Donald advised him.

The taxi driver's mouth contorted even more than the first time. 'Are you talkin' 'bout... an *accident?*'

'Well... I doubt it'll be deliberate,' squinted Donald.

'Wait a minute... let me see if I'm hearing you correctly. You're actually tellin' me I'm gonna be involved in... a *crash?*'

Donald nodded as sympathetically as three and a half kilograms of helmet allowed.

'*Where*, exactly?'

'Ah... now that's the part they're always annoyingly vague about. But, by the look of things, I believe they're showing me something resembling a traffic light.'

'Sir?'

'A stop light,' contributed Norman, observing the driver's consternation.

248

'We have both,' the driver addressed his other fare facetiously.

'Well... you're probably going to have one less now,' said Donald bluntly.

'Is it bad?'

'It *is* rather bent.'

'I meant the *accident!* Am I gonna be hurt real bad?'

Donald winced.

The taxi driver's eyes bulged. 'I ain't gonna... *die*... am I?'

Donald held his gauntlet out flat... then rocked it ever so slightly.

'You *serious?*'

'Not a thing I would ever joke about,' Donald replied, grim-faced.

The taxi driver stared at both his fares in disbelief.

'Anyway... have a nice day.' smiled Donald politely. He turned to leave.

'Hey! But what about a tip?' the taxi driver yelled.

'I just gave it to you,' Donald returned, without bothering to look back. 'You'd better drive carefully over the coming days.'

'Nice one,' Norman sniggered, as the two of them made their way towards the hotel they'd been deposited outside. 'That'll teach him! Did you see the expression on that poor guy's face?'

Donald looked up at the sky. 'THIS SUIT MIGHT BE FASHIONED FROM WELL-TEMPERED STEEL. BUT, GIVEN MY BONES ARE *NOT*... AND THE FACT IT WAS NEVER MY INTENTION TO BE *ENTOMBED* IN IT... YOU COULD'VE AT LEAST WARNED ME *BEFORE* I GOT INTO THAT UNFORTUNATE IDIOT'S ILL-FATED DEATHTRAP!'

The hotel foyer was surprisingly busy. A black sign supporting a row of white letters welcoming the Association of American Saucepan Manufacturers explained why.

Norman gazed about anxiously. 'Do you think Kevin will still be here?'

'I certainly hope so!' Donald retorted. 'That boy's our only lead. It's *imperative* we get him to tell us what Xanthia's planning to do next.'

'I think it's going to be rather difficult.'

'Not once he knows we've located him. He'll *have* to talk. With his cover blown, the threat of an extremely long prison sentence should be incentive enough for him to start singing like a canary.'

'I meant difficult for *me*. The last time we met, he thrust a knife into my stomach... remember?'

'From what I saw in those emails you showed me, he's simply an immature and naive young man who's become so obsessed with getting the better of you, he's got himself way out of his depth. If you offer to drop the charges in exchange for what he knows, he'll be able to walk away from the mess he's in and start afresh.'

'But what if he doesn't want to? What if my theory about him receiving part of the sphere of knowledge is correct? His being with Xanthia would enable her to become the Antichrist those red strings warned you about!'

'Well... they're *not* together, are they? That's the reason we're here. Granted... if she were in close proximity, our lives would certainly be in grave and mortal danger.'

'Normy!' shouted someone from the far side of the foyer.

Donald frowned. 'I didn't know you had connections in the world of saucepans.'

'I don't!' Norman froze as he saw who it was frantically trying to get his attention. 'It's *her*,' he choked.

Following his stupefied gaze, Donald caught sight of Xanthia waving excitedly. 'OH, SWEET JESUS!' he bellowed, his eyes shooting skywards. 'YOU DON'T THINK *THIS* MIGHT'VE BEEN A MORE APPROPRIATE WARNING TO GIVE WHEN I STEPPED OUT OF THAT BLOODY TAXI?'

'What's she doing here?' Norman gulped.

'Coming straight this way,' squeaked Donald.

'Is that a *gun* she's waving at us?'

'Well... I don't think it's a packet of biscuits this time.'

'What are we gonna do?'

'Smile and be nice,' Donald hissed. 'Remember... she doesn't know we know what we know.'

'I know she's here with Kevin.'

'No, you don't,' said Donald through gritted teeth, a rigid grin plastered across his face.

Xanthia could hardly believe her eyes. 'Normy... I certainly wasn't expecting this! What on earth are *you* doing here?'

'Ditto,' he offered stiffly.

He felt a swift kick to the side of his foot.

'I know,' she grimaced. 'I'm so sorry. I should've told you I was coming to America... but I couldn't. It's a *very* long story.'

Norman refused to replicate Donald's ridiculous grin. 'Not even a note?'

His ankle took another swipe.

'Donald... will you stop kicking me... especially with *that* footwear. She's not stupid.'

'No, I'm not,' said Xanthia. 'And neither are you. You *know* the other side have been watching my every move... which is why I couldn't tell you what I've been up to.' She turned to Donald. 'Interesting threads, by the way, Donald. Are you expecting a fight?'

He squealed.

'I know *exactly* what you've been up to,' said Norman furiously. 'There's no point in lying. I managed to recover your deleted and mortifyingly salacious email exchange with Kevin!'

'Oh, Norman,' she groaned, her shoulders collapsing. 'I'm *so* sorry you had to experience that part of my deception without knowing the truth. I was hoping to keep it secret until I could give you this to explain.' She held out the chequebook, her eyes craving his forgiveness. 'Against all the odds, I've managed to get it reinstated!'

'I was right about it not being biscuits,' remarked Donald.

'It was Kevin who cancelled it and put that firewall around the account so you'd be unable to change what he'd done. Trust me... he was the only one who could reverse the damage. That's why I wrote those ridiculous emails. I needed him to allow us access to the finance we so desperately require. It was *essential* he thought I was on his side... along with those who'd encouraged him in the first place.' She grabbed Norman's arm. 'I know how much it must hurt... but that deluded teenager has unwittingly given us the ability to get my message out to the entire world. And you were absolutely right... it won't be a second too soon. So, you see... I *wasn't* ignoring your concerns about my lack of commitment... I was simply having to play an *extremely* difficult game.'

Norman gave Donald an awkward look.

'You don't believe this rubbish, do you?' Donald scoffed. 'She's playing you, boy!'

'I have to say... it *does* sound plausible,' Norman vacillated.

'Of course it does. You said it yourself... she's not stupid. She knows we've rumbled her and is desperately trying to formulate a plan B. The cheek of it! She's even suggesting you help promote her corrupt agenda!'

Norman squirmed. 'But what if she *is* telling the truth?'

'Of *course* I am,' She bounced excitedly on her toes. 'Look, Normy... I've got us the chequebook back!'

He turned to Donald again. 'She's got us the chequebook back.'

'You stupid boy. She didn't know you'd be here. We've probably caught her leaving to cash one of its cheques... unless you think she was looking to buy some saucepans with it.'

'Normy knows I don't do cooking,' said Xanthia, holding up her immaculately manicured nails.

'*That* bit's true,' he nodded.

She glanced about uneasily. 'Look... can I suggest we go somewhere a little more private... especially with Donald dressed the way he is?'

It was now obvious that a foyer full of stunned faces was staring at them.

'We do a deluxe range with rubber grip handles, if that's of any help,' offered one of those faces. 'You'll find they're kinder on the hands.'

'We're safer staying here,' hissed Donald in Norman's ear. 'She won't risk doing anything while there are others around as witnesses.'

'Isn't that the girl from the TV debate the other night?' piped up one of the delegates. 'The one that's been plastered all over the news?'

'I believe you're right,' said another. 'She's even wearing the same clothes.'

'I haven't had a chance to change yet,' Xanthia pointed out politely.

A number of noses in the foyer crinkled.

'I was kidnapped,' she explained.

'Thanks to my connections,' said Donald loudly. 'It was me who warned the president about her.'

'I don't even *know* you!' insisted the president of the Association of American Saucepan Manufacturers, from over by the lifts.

'Yes, you do,' interjected his wife. 'I believe that's Donald Tucker-Jenkins inside that suit of armour… the famous author!'

'*Playwright*,' Donald corrected her.

A round of admiring applause rippled through the foyer.

'Oh… good grief,' sighed Norman, bowing his head in disbelief.

'Would you mind if I had a picture taken with you?' asked the Association's president, stepping forward. 'We'll put it on the cover of next month's trade journal.'

'As a matter of fact, I *do*,' Donald replied curtly. 'This woman is about to facilitate the end of the world as we know it. If we don't stop her, the lifetime guarantee on some of your members' pans will be far shorter than anticipated. She is, in effect, the Antichrist!'

The man's eyes widened. 'In that case… would she mind if I had a picture taken with *her*?'

'That might not be such a good idea, honey,' whispered his wife. 'You know how sensitive your nasal passages can be, and she's just told us she hasn't changed her outfit in so many days.'

'We really do need to go somewhere private,' Xanthia insisted, pulling on Norman's arm.

He nodded.

'Don't listen to her!' yelled Donald. 'She's already poisoned your mind! That's what she does! Don't be the fool on that red-stringed tarot card you took a peek at. They couldn't have sent us a clearer warning!'

'I just think it wouldn't hurt to hear the full story,' he countered. 'What's the worst that can happen?'

'I have people conversing with me on a daily basis who will *happily* answer that!' Donald exclaimed. 'And before you start believing she's the *old* Xanthia… I have one word to say to you.' He fixed Norman with an intense stare. 'ERIS!'

Norman flashed a look at her.

'The Goddess of strife and discord?' she frowned.

'Well… I'm not talking about the planet,' Donald scoffed.

'*Dwarf* planet, actually,' she tutted.

'Told you,' said Norman smugly.

She tugged his arm again.

'Don't ignore the red strings!' Donald quaked, his eyes trying to hook Norman's. 'You saw how many warnings I was sent regarding that name.'

Norman looked at Xanthia. 'It's true.'

'I haven't a clue what you're talking about,' she scowled.

'Thank goodness for that,' Donald cried. 'There's hope for us yet!'

Torn in two, Norman hesitated.

'Look, Normy… I know this has all come as a bit of a shock and that Donald thinks he's trying to help… but you *have* to believe me.'

Like a five-year-old putting off a trip to the bathroom, he squinted his pain.

She tightened her grip on his arm. 'We don't have time for this. You *have* to make a choice… and it's the biggest fork you'll ever face in your life. So… you better get this right! Who's it gonna be… him or me?'

Norman looked back at Donald.

'I've already come to your rescue on two occasions,' Donald reminded him. 'Now it seems I'm doing so for a third. But, get this wrong, and... believe me... there won't be a chance for a fourth!'

His face distorted with agony, Norman turned to the delegates for impartial advice.

The whole of the foyer shrugged... which was understandable. Decisions involving the fate of the Universe were clearly outside the Association of American Saucepan Manufacturers' remit.

He turned to Xanthia again.

She tilted her head. 'Well?'

Eyes glistening, he cringed apologetically.

'Normy?' she blanched.

He'd made his choice. 'Sorry, Xan.'

* * *

Norman stared bleakly out of the taxi window, oblivious to the heroic attempts of its driver to weave in and out of the heavily congested traffic.

'It's imperative we get back to Washington as quickly as possible,' said Donald. 'With that kind of financial muscle at her disposal, we *have* to get the president to listen to us before it's too late. I just don't understand why they let her go.'

Norman didn't respond.

Leaning forward, Donald addressed the driver. 'Can't you get us to the airport any faster? I promise the tip at the end will be well worth your while... and of a *monetary* kind.'

The driver shrugged. 'Sorry, mister. I'm doin' the best I can. Not only has there been a plague of oversized rats running amok in the city today and disrupting traffic... there's been an accident at the lights a little way ahead that's caused extra tailbacks. I passed it on the way down.'

'Traffic lights, you say?'

'Yeah.'

Donald flipped up his visor. 'Was it serious?'

The driver looked at him in his rear view mirror.

Donald raised his eyebrows expectantly.

The driver winced.

* * *

'Is this everything?' asked the president, studying the open suitcases in front of him.

'Everything they brought with them, sir.'

'And you've analysed the contents?'

'Every scrap of paper.'

'So... do we know what it's all pointing to?'

His national security adviser nodded. 'As far as we can ascertain, the various cuttings and scribbled notes are a record of past and future targets... mixed in with a large number of hand-written threats, which we assume the two men are planning to deliver to corporations or individuals. In the case of those locations already known to be attacked, great care has been taken to detail the extent of the damage caused. While many of the scribblings bear the hallmarks of Tucker-Jenkins' eccentricity and are written in his own hand... Penkridge's DNA is all over them. It's damning evidence of both men being engaged in a systematic campaign of global disruption. We think they're seeking to capitalise on this run of natural disasters that have been occurring, and create panic in the general population for personal gain'.

'So you think they *are* playing the markets?'

'We can't be certain... but it seems to fit with what John over at Langley told us. He's convinced Penkridge is a bad apple, having been in charge of the case involving him and that international art fraud.'

'Do we have *proof* of his guilt this time around?'

'We haven't been able to connect either man as yet to this suspicious trading of essential supplies that's taken place. But it's only a matter of time. We just need to complete our understanding of the unique and inventive coding system they've utilised to conceal what they're up to.'

'Do these coloured strings have anything to do with that?'

'They're part of it, sir. It appears black strings have been designated to threats intended for individuals as yet unidentified... and blue strings to physical targets we know have already been attacked.'

'Like Stonehenge?'

'Except, in these other cases, it's gratuitous vandalism rather than a well-organised propaganda stunt. I've asked my British counterpart for a copy of the file they're building on Penkridge over that particular incident, to see if we can sort the fact from the fiction. As it's impossible for him and Tucker-Jenkins to have been personally involved in every attack recorded here, we believe they're employing a worldwide network of associates... probably the same one Penkridge used to acquire those artworks John's team investigated.'

'Has that case been reopened as I requested?'

'I'm told he's dealing with it personally.'

'Any developments I should know about?'

'I've called a number of times, but he's been absent from his desk these past two days. I'll make sure to follow up on it as soon as he returns.'

'Good. I wanna be kept abreast of any developments.'

'Of course, sir.'

The president studied the contents of the cases again. 'And these other colours?'

'As far as we can ascertain... notes coded purple are coordinates for future targets... though many appear totally illogical. I fail to see how a bicycle factory in China has any strategic value... but I'm confident our guys will work it out. Those coded green are media reports of unnatural occurrences... providing yet another link between what's been happening and our two suspects.'

'Excellent. And the significance of the red strings?'

'Again... we're still working on those. But it's the solitary pink string we believe to be the most significant of all.'

'How so?'

'Standing apart from the others, we believe it's the cipher for unlocking the meaning behind the more enigmatic notes. We've got our top cryptology guys attempting to break it. But it's proving a tough task. They tell me our suspects have gone to an incredible amount of trouble devising an original and sophisticated code, which is why they've so far failed to crack a single piece of it.'

'Can I see it?'

'I've prepared a copy for you, sir.'

The president studied the piece of paper he was handed. 'What do you think *aubergine* and *carrots* refer to?'

'That's where we think they've been *particularly* devious. Our guys don't know if they should take the first word at face value or substitute it for our American equivalent... *eggplant.* It further demonstrates Tucker-Jenkins' and Penkridge's determination to hide what they're up to. This linguistic ambiguity creates numerous, additional cryptic permutations, which only complicates our efforts. As you can see... the same problem occurs with their use of the word *courgettes* instead of *zucchinis.*'

'And *quarter pound of mince?*'

'We're working on it, sir.'

The president handed the paper back and strolled over to the window. 'I'm so disappointed in Donald,' he said, shaking his head. 'I feel like I've lost a good friend. I can't believe he's gotten himself involved in all of this... or, indeed, understand what he hopes to gain from it. I doubt he needs the money. How such a gifted individual can illuminate the world's problems with such clarity, and then seek to exacerbate them by destabilising it to the point of recklessness is beyond me. He clearly has an axe to grind that doesn't come across in his writing. I guess that's the nature of genius. It's unpredictable.'

'He's definitely that, sir.'

'Do we know where the two of them are right now?'

'In line with John's advice, we've had eyes on them since our last meeting. They flew out of Washington yesterday... probably after discovering their cases had been removed and realising the game was up. But I've just received information they're on their way back.'

'What were they doing?'

'We know they met briefly with Galveston Humbold... before going on to have a meeting with Xanthia in the lobby of a hotel.'

The president turned from the window. 'They knew where she was?'

'Which is more than we did.'

'Or Galveston Humbold. His legal team have been haranguing my staff over her sudden disappearance and accusing us of being involved. Our security agencies assured me they had nothing to do with it, in accordance with my instructions to allow her to take part in that ridiculous debate.'

'At least we now have her on our radar.'

'But what the hell were the three of them doing at this hotel? Do we have any idea?'

'Intel suggests there was an altercation between them, stemming from an attempt to realign loyalties. But I advise we proceed with caution on that interpretation of events.'

'Why so?'

'Because Tucker-Jenkins was heard to inexplicably utter the word *biscuits* on two separate occasions... yet another Anglo-American lingual divergence. Given the word *cookies* would've been equally odd in such circumstances, we think they were communicating in code.'

The president massaged his chin. 'This meeting... was it just the three of them?'

'Actually, sir... there *were* others present.'

His brow furrowed. '*What* others?'

'The Association of American Saucepan Manufacturers... and the hotel receptionist.'

'Is there a link?'

'All we know is... at one point, Penkridge requested their advice on what seemed to be an important decision.'

The president clenched his fist. 'In that case, I want that association rigorously investigated and a report put on my desk by this time tomorrow.'

'Does that include the receptionist?'

'Don't be so ridiculous.'

'Yes, sir.'

'If they're seen to have any involvement in this matter... *whatsoever*... I'll immediately have them proscribed a terrorist organisation.'

'Eminently sensible, sir. In the wrong hands, a boiling saucepan can be an extremely dangerous weapon.'

'As for Tucker-Jenkins and Penkridge... see to it they're detained the minute their plane touches the ground. We can't allow unhinged deviants like that to wander around freely. Despite the international shockwaves it'll cause in Tucker-Jenkins' case, I want him and his cohort behind bars and wearing orange jumpsuits for the rest of their lives! It's imperative we guarantee the safety of this nation... along with the rest of the world. Do you understand?'

'Crystal clear, sir. I'll liaise with the Department of Justice to ensure it happens.'

'Good... and then arrange for me to meet with this Xanthia in person. I'm keen to hear *her* side of the story.'

His national security adviser let out a noise akin to a small mouse realising they'd just bumped into a very large cat. He stared at the president aghast. 'With respect, sir... do you think that's wise?'

'Of course it is... I'm the president!' He glared at his subordinate. 'How could it be anything but? Regardless of whether or not she has the miraculous power she claims, she's been living with Penkridge for the past five years, so *must* know what he's up to. Perhaps she had a Damascene moment at Stonehenge and now feels the need to come clean and spill the beans. Maybe *that's* why she's claiming to be able to save the world... and also why *they've* been trying so hard to stop her talking. Let's at least hear what she has to say about this whole affair, once its ringleaders have been neutralised. I want you to make contact and invite her here to the White House.'

*   *   *

'You complete imbecile, Prometheus! How could you let such a thing happen?'

A collective wail of anguish sounded.

It wasn't the insult – or anger with which it had been delivered – that bothered its recipient. Nor was it the superfluous use of the word *complete*. After all... in Mister Prometheus's eyes, you were either an imbecile or you weren't. It was the fact his honorific had been omitted from the tirade that left him in no doubt as to the precariousness of his situation. He gazed up at the myriad of faces glaring down at his and knew their patience with him had just run out.

'You held the most valuable asset in the Universe in your hands and allowed an acne-riddled adolescent with a handful of unwashed thugs to steal it from under your nose!' exploded Mister Zeus.

'While you looked on and did nothing!' yelled Mister Indra.

'There was little I *could* do,' Mister Prometheus fought back. 'My operatives were taken by surprise by heavily armed men.' He considered their personal hygiene irrelevant. 'The reason my team was so easily overrun is due to the fact I've been forced to operate clandestinely.'

'Forced? How so?' demanded Mister Apollo, his face flushed with fury. 'Are you suggesting this calamity could in any way be of *our* making?'

'I'm saying... given the difficult position you've put me in, I couldn't risk drawing attention to my mission. Employing more men, or mobilising reinforcements, would've done just that and been professional suicide.'

'That "difficult position" pales into insignificance compared to the one you're in right now,' hissed Miss Minerva through narrowing eyes. 'Perhaps suicide might've been the easier option for you to consider.'

There was a worrying collective nod of heads.

Mister Prometheus knew the owners of those heads had ruthlessly clawed their way to the top of powerful empires by methods it would be best not to dwell on. Only a fool would dismiss such an outburst as hyperbole.

'There is only one way for you to seek redemption and save that incompetent skin of yours,' boomed Mister Atlas. 'You must throw further thoughts of caution to the wind and utilise every morsel of your power and influence to have this girl tracked down and brought before us. When that finally happens, she will remain in *our* custody... and... trust me... we will not display the weakness in prising those secrets from her that you have.' He rose angrily. 'Now... go from here and find out where she is!'

Mister Prometheus stood his ground and took a deep breath for courage. 'I *know* where she is,' he said, steeling himself for the backlash.

It arrived amidst a collective dropping of jaws.

'YOU KNOW?' thundered Mister Hermes, his face turning an alarming shade of purple.

'If that is so... why have you *dared* to come here and give an account of your failure instead of immediately rectifying the situation?' raged Miss Artemis in disbelief.

Mister Prometheus knew they weren't going to like his next utterance, either. 'Because she's now being monitored by every government agency... including my own. So, unless you have the same influence over those bodies as you do with me, it'll be impossible for my team to get remotely near her without drawing attention to themselves... and by default, me.'

A collective groan anticipated what was coming next.

'Regrettably, we don't,' responded Mister Atlas, sitting down heavily. 'The heads of those other agencies have proven to be of far higher moral character than you.'

Mister Prometheus deflected the low blow by telling himself that *they* weren't married to Mrs AKA Mister Prometheus.

'Why their sudden interest in the girl?' demanded Mister Ra. 'We were under the impression it was only *us* who knew the truth behind what she's capable of.'

'It's *who* has taken an interest in her that's awoken the intelligence community,' Mister Prometheus replied soberly.

There was a collective look of knowing-but-not-wishing-it-to-be-so.

Mister Prometheus knew confirming their worst fears would seal his fate. There was only one reason they'd brought him back into the fold, and he'd just allowed that reason to escape his clutches. The minute they realised redemption was beyond him, he would be expendable. But if they didn't hear the news from him, it would reach their ears sooner or later. He drew a martyr's breath. 'The President of the United States has requested a one-on-one meeting with her at the White House.'

A collective howl of torment accompanied a collective flailing of hands.

'Once they discover what she can do, she will never be allowed out of their sight!' wailed Miss Venus.

'We have just lost the chance to dominate this planet for an eternity!' thundered Mister Zeus.

There was an eruption of frenzied consternation.

'We had the answer to every scientific mystery in our hands!' cried Mister Bacchus.

'She would've opened up a world of unimaginably lucrative commodities,' wept Miss Anuket

'Cheap, limitless energy was within our grasp,' groaned Mister Tsukuyomi. 'We could've made even *more* money by selling it at the same price as we currently do.'

'She could have unlocked the secrets to materials that self-heal and save the consumer having to re-buy a product!' exclaimed Mister Quetzalcoatl. 'We would've patented the knowledge and made sure no one got to use it!'

'We would've owned the rights to technologies that reversed global warming… enabling us to demand whatever price we chose from the world's governments for their use,' lamented Miss Epona.

'But for your incompetence, we could've held this planet to ransom,' bellowed Mister Anubis. 'You've just lost us the opportunity to become *real* gods!'

'ENOUGH.' shouted a voice from the highest tier of aspiring deities. It cracked through the air with an authority that brought immediate silence.

As its owner stood, Mister Prometheus sensed a collective shrinking back, even from those he considered to be the strongest. Looking for the source of that nervous apprehension, he was astonished to find the deep, rich voice belonged to a woman.

With a mesmerising combination of menace and elegance, she slowly stepped down through the hastily parting bodies towards him, her wolf-grey eyes burning into his with an unbroken gaze. Dominating a long dress of purple and scarlet, her flowing, black hair cascaded over a scintillating necklace of gold and precious jewels. He was, at once, in love and terrified.

Reaching the front row, she stopped... though merely as a courtesy to those seated there.

Finding his mouth devoid of moisture, Mister Prometheus ran his tongue around the inside of it so as to allow it to function. 'I don't think I've had the pleasure,' he managed, as one corner flickered uncontrollably.

Her eyes darted towards the tell-tale sign of subordination. 'I rather think you're being polite,' she said icily.

He was... but he was also being truthful. The rest of the gods had faded into his peripheral vision.

Her piercing eyes reattached themselves to his, sending long-forgotten shockwaves through his body.

'If the President of the United States of America gets to see what this girl can do, we will all be finished, Mister Prometheus. Do you understand?'

Fixating on the lips that had just wrapped themselves around his name, he wondered what it would be like to feel them brushing softly against his. His heart quickened as he imagined the warmth of the breath that would tease from between them.

'You needn't fear her imparting information detrimental to your collective businesses,' he assured her. 'Xanthia made it abundantly clear she's not interested in taking sides. I give you my word they won't be able to force her to talk any more than my own men could. I've been involved in enough interrogations during my lifetime to know when a subject would rather die than give up their secrets. I can categorically guarantee… Xanthia is one such individual. She poses no threat to your commercial interests whatsoever.'

His interrogator's eyes narrowed. 'You really *are* an imbecile, Mister Prometheus. Not only has your incompetence deprived this collective of the chance to dominate every technology imaginable and become unassailable… you look to have brought it to the brink of ruin for a *second* time!'

Delivered with such cutting malevolence, Mister Prometheus found the insult strangely arousing… which surprised him. Mrs AKA Mister Prometheus never had that effect when chiding him for his many inadequacies around the house.

'How so?' he objected… though with nowhere near the depth of tone and forcefulness he'd intended. The strangled utterance came out as a pathetic squeak.

'How so?' she cruelly imitated him, doubling his embarrassment. 'Haven't you previously assured us this Xanthia has knowledge of *everything?*'

Given the trouble his mouth had got him into, he thought it best just to nod.

'One must assume that encompasses those grey and darker areas this collective has involved itself with… which includes paying *you.*' She let the last bit sink in, just in case it hadn't. 'So… given this girl is claiming she wishes to save the world… and make it one predicated on *righteousness*… do you *still* maintain she isn't a threat to every single one of us here?'

The question hung awkwardly.

Mister Prometheus realised he couldn't argue against such a prognosis... his end much nearer than he'd thought. His fate looking well and truly sealed, he shrugged pragmatically. 'It still doesn't change the fact there's little I can do about it now,' he offered.

'Not true,' Mister Atlas shouted from behind her. 'You can have her killed!'

His outburst produced a collective call for retribution, loudly voiced through angrily clenched teeth.

Mister Prometheus tried to decipher the inscrutable stare of the woman in front of him as calls for blood rained down on him from every direction.

As the demands reached fever pitch she raised a hand. 'SILENCE... ALL OF YOU!'

The command was instantly obeyed.

'It seems the fate of this girl is in your hands, Mister Prometheus,' she said coldly. 'So, consider your next answer *extremely* carefully.' Her eyes bored into his with even greater intensity. 'Are you absolutely *certain* there's nothing you can do to rectify this situation?'

Mister Prometheus painfully shook his head. The truth had been hard enough to impart the first time. Now it hung like a weight that would drown him.

'Then, my colleagues are right. If *we* can't own the hen with an ability to lay golden eggs, we need to ensure it doesn't cluck for anyone else. After all... the consequences of *that* wouldn't bear thinking about.'

Mister Prometheus countered the idea with silence.

'Don't think such a solution comes easy,' she continued. 'I, too, hoped to profit greatly from what was in that girl's head.'

For a moment her unforgiving stare wavered.

'But sacrifice her we must,' she said, recovering her authority. 'The damage she could do far outweighs any benefits we might've hoped to gain.'

Resigned to his fate... and Xanthia's... he dropped his head.

'Come now,' she sneered. 'I'm sure it won't be the *first* time you've had to carry out such an unpalatable order. And, on the positive side… at least you'll have earned all that money we pay you.'

There was a collective sense of good housekeeping.

He stared at her lips again and wondered how things so beautiful could utter words so heartless. Not that it made her any less attractive.

'More importantly,' those lips continued, 'I might be persuaded to look more favourably on you when it comes to *your* future, Mister Prometheus.'

That part of the deal *did* appeal to him… in more ways than one.

He selfishly nodded his compliance.

'Good. But before you go from here to execute our orders… and our uncooperative chicken… is there anything you wish to ask, so that there be absolutely no doubt in your mind when you come to sanction her extirpation?'

Mister Prometheus studied the multitude of faces around him. He found their total compliance to the woman in front of him strange, given they belonged to some of the most ruthless and opinionated individuals on the planet. But that wasn't the issue exercising his mind. 'There *is* one thing that's been intriguing me,' he ventured, drawing another of his breaths-for-courage. 'When it was stated earlier that only this collective knew the veracity of Xanthia's claims… how was that so?'

The thinnest of smiles finally cracked her steely veneer. 'Maybe there's hope for you yet, Mister Prometheus. Maybe you're *not* such an idiot after all.'

'And the answer?' he braved.

'Is not for your ears,' she answered frostily. 'Now… leave us! The next time you stand here, we will expect confirmation that our problem has been terminated. If not… we will terminate the reason for it existing in the first place. Do you understand?'

He did. Not that he'd had any doubt such a situation would be so. He knew, the very first day he'd sold his principles for an easier marriage, that a time of reckoning would eventually follow. What he didn't know, back then, was how the woman he'd sold them for would be so far from his thoughts when that moment finally arrived.

'Before I go…' he chanced. 'We still haven't been formally introduced.' This was true of many of the unfamiliar gods sternly looking down on him. But *they* didn't have features so sharp they'd cut his heart.

The nostrils at the end of those features flared. 'I am Miss Eris,' she announced haughtily. 'And I promise… you will not forget my name.'

*　　*　　*

'Donald Tucker-Jenkins?' The gentleman at the head of the small greeting party placed a hand inside his jacket.

'It is I,' said Donald, bowing his head as best he could. 'But if you'll excuse me, I'm not of a disposition to give autographs today. It's been quite a harrowing one and I've much work to do. So, if you good people will excuse me…'

The gentleman in question whipped out a small wallet and proffered its contents directly in front of Donald's visor. 'FBI.'

'Ah… at last!' he exclaimed, examining the badge being thrust at him. 'I see the president has finally come to his senses! I knew it would only be a question of time.' He nodded his relief to Norman. 'Unfortunately, that time is now even scarcer than it was. So, we've no more of it to lose. I trust you have a fast car.'

'You're under arrest.'

Donald's helmet jerked. 'I *beg* your pardon?'

'For the preparation of acts of terrorism… designed to commit blackmail, impede the workings of our government, and cause harm to the citizens of this country and its infrastructure.'

Donald scanned the remaining faces through the small slit in his visor. 'Is this some sort of joke?'

Noting they were equally as grim as the one behind the badge, he quickly concluded it was not.

'I suggest you and your companion come quietly, sir. Given your celebrity status, I'm sure you don't wish to make a scene.'

'I'M A PLAYWRIGHT, YOU IMBECILE. CREATING SCENES IS WHAT I'M FAMOUS FOR!'

Unsure if Donald was addressing the arresting officer... or objecting to identical advice from his spirit guide... Norman wondered how it was remotely possible *not* to create a scene while dressed in a full suit of medieval armour.

'Cuff them!'

'Them?' exclaimed Norman.

'Norman Penkridge, you are being detained for the same offence.'

Before he could post an objection of his own, a pair of handcuffs was smartly attached to his wrists.

'This is outrageous!' yelled Donald, as his gauntlets were wrenched from him in order to expose his own. 'Whatever happened to the land of the free?'

* * *

'Miss Eris!'

The individual being called turned from the car she'd been about to enter. 'What's the meaning of this?' she scowled. 'We're now *outside* Olympus. This approach is most irregular. I've said all I have to say to you.'

Mister Prometheus held up his hand in apology. 'I know... but we need to talk.'

'We already have!'

'In *private*.'

She glanced at the chauffeur holding the door, then back at her waylayer. 'What could possibly make you want to take such a risk?' she glowered.

Mister Prometheus lowered his hand. 'I have something I believe you might want to hear.'

Her frown bought him the time he was looking for.

'I think it could be of *great* interest to you,' he pushed.

'Am I to assume it wasn't for the ears of my fellow gods?'

'That's precisely why I'm here,' he nodded. 'They know *some* of what I have to say... but not all. And I doubt they'll have shared what they *do* know with you.'

Her frown deepened. 'How so?'

'Because you're new to Olympus... and those who enjoyed its first incarnation are not the kind to give away anything unnecessarily.'

She stared at him in silence for a moment. 'Isn't your position among its current incarnation precarious enough as it is, Mister Prometheus?'

He no longer cared. The woman in front of him had blinded him to all other considerations. 'I'm aware this is a dangerous move on my part... but trust it'll make you see me differently.'

She cocked her head. 'To what?'

'The others.'

'You mean... the *collective?*'

'They're a collective in name only. Their meetings are nothing more than a convenient council of self-interests. Those involved masquerade as a unified group merely so as not to get in each other's way. Their pretence of unity is as much an illusion as the pretence of them being gods.'

'You don't think I know that?' she snorted.

'I do... and I believe you have a self-interest that outstrips even theirs,' he ventured bravely.

Her head slowly tilted back. 'Now you *are* living dangerously, Mister Prometheus.'

He didn't care about that either. 'I'd prefer it if you called me John... now that we're alone.'

The chauffeur pretended to take an interest in his shoes.

'I think it extremely foolish for a man in your predicament to be highlighting his mortality,' she responded coldly.

'I'd rather you *did* see me as just a man,' he chanced, oblivious to the unlikelihood of that ever happening.

Her eyes narrowed. 'Are you *flirting* with me, Mister Prometheus?'

He was... but it was so long since he'd done such a thing, he was unsure as to what to do next.

226

'This information you say has been withheld from me...' she assisted him. 'You might consider our collective disingenuous, but aren't you forgetting I'm one of them? Why take such a risk?'

'Because I think you're *more* than them,' he replied.

She turned to get into the car. 'Flattering my ego will not save you, Mister Prometheus. I suggest you get on and do the one thing that might!'

'I also think you wanted *far* more from Xanthia than they did.'

She froze.

'You were right earlier... I'm *not* a fool,' he expanded. 'I've spent my life spotting tells and reading beyond what comes out of people's mouths. For one so confident of their authority, I sensed your hesitation when issuing the order to eliminate her. So I asked myself... why?'

She turned to face him again. 'And what was the answer?'

'I don't know... but it has something to do with more than just a loss of new technologies and innovations.'

The lips that had so entranced Mister Prometheus parted slightly as the tip of a tongue showed she was contemplating her next question.

'I'll save you the trouble,' he offered. 'When the collective assigned me a list of experts to assist in the interrogation of the girl, I did background checks before agreeing to those individuals working with my team. As expected, they were all ideally qualified for the task in hand.' He looked at her knowingly. 'Except one.'

She gave a nod for him to continue.

'Professor Cottingham... more qualified in his field than all of them put together... though someone whose expertise lay in a subject completely outside the collective's scientific remit. But that wasn't the most intriguing part about the professor's illustrious CV. I discovered it included studying in England under the tutelage of one of his discipline's greatest minds... a renowned academic two of my agents had dealings with in the recent past… Professor Hummingbone… a leading authority on Templar history.'

She looked at him dispassionately. 'Why assume this *Professor Cottingham* has anything to do with me?'

'Because, for one so influential among the collective, your voice was suspiciously absent from their combined outrage over the loss of technological opportunities… despite telling me you'd hoped to benefit greatly from Xanthia's abilities. So I came to the conclusion those benefits lay *elsewhere*… perhaps in a direction Professor Cottingham could assist you with.'

She allowed herself a half-smile. 'I now see why you've reached the position you have in your *own* field of expertise, Mister Prometheus. I congratulate you on such astute powers of observation.'

'Does that mean you wish to hear what it is I have to tell you?'

She stepped away from the car door and signalled for him to get in. 'If it pertains to the Knights Templar… I most certainly do.' Her smile broadened as her eyes zoned in on his. '*John.*'

*   *   *

'Mister President… your guest is here.'

The president straightened his tie and pointlessly adjusted his cuffs. 'I'm ready. Show her in.'

His Chief of Staff hovered at the door. 'Are you sure you don't want someone in here with you… just in case?'

The concern raised a smile.

'Don't worry, Gus. I know where the panic button is.'

'As you wish, sir.'

Awaiting his controversial visitor, the president reflected on reports that had crossed his desk that morning. Providing extremely uncomfortable reading, they ranged from the contamination of a major water supply in Oregon by toxic algae to an unidentified parasite causing herds of cattle to bloat and keel over. It didn't help that it was all happening against an ominous backdrop of increasingly disruptive protests, as people sought to vent their fears and frustration over the multitude of adverse situations now occurring on a daily basis. He just hoped the woman he was about to meet might shed some light on the campaign behind them and assure him that things would now be returning to normal, given its ringleaders were safely behind bars.

For her own part, Xanthia had notified the White House Office that she'd taken the precaution of depositing a letter with a third party detailing her recent ordeal... and that if she failed to return from the meeting it would immediately be released to the press. They, in turn, hadn't a clue what she was talking about. If they'd had *their* way, she wouldn't be allowed anywhere near the most powerful man in the world.

It wasn't just the president who rose as she entered the room. His eyebrows joined the rest of him... then stretched a little further. He was used to people dressing a little more conservatively when awarded a private audience... especially when it included the additional honour of taking place in the historic oval office.

'I do believe my wife was wearing one of those the very first day I met her,' he said, by way of a polite introduction. 'Though I think I'm right in saying... she wasn't wearing fishnet tights.'

Accepting the hand being offered, Xanthia kept hold of it and tutted. 'That's just typical of a man.' She gave a look of admonishment. 'She was *actually* wearing floral-patterned culottes. But, picking up on the fact you didn't like them, she chose to wear a miniskirt on your *second* date.'

Attempting to let go of his hand, she found the action denied.

'Now you mention it... you're absolutely right!' His mouth fell. 'How on earth could you know that?'

She shrugged away his surprise. 'It's a gift... which is what I've been telling everyone for weeks. It's also why I assumed you wanted to see me.'

Her hand remained a prisoner.

'And her earrings?'

Xanthia's eyes narrowed. 'That's a trick question, isn't it?'

He waited.

'Alright... she wasn't wearing any. She'd forgotten to put them on and spent the first hour of your date constantly apologising about it... so much so, you insisted on taking her to a nearby jewellers and buying a pair.'

Finally releasing his grip, the president gazed at his unorthodox guest in disbelief. 'Well, I'll be... that's truly astonishing! I've never mentioned that fact to anyone in my life! It's a private memory shared only by the two of us.' He checked his thoughts, having had them yanked well beyond his comfort zone. 'So, it's true... you clearly *can* do what you say you can!' He shook his head in stupefaction.

Xanthia thought it best not to add that his wife had preferred a completely different pair and thought he had an appalling eye when it came to choosing such things.

'I always make sure to buy her a new set on the anniversary of us meeting,' he said, in a daze.

Xanthia pictured his long-suffering wife and smiled politely. 'I know.'

'Yes... yes... I suppose you would,' he stammered.

She acknowledged the chair he was about to fall into. 'Shall we sit down, Mister President? Only... you look like you might need to.'

Taking her advice, he beckoned for her to occupy the seat opposite him, his mouth agape.

'This meeting will go down in history,' he pronounced, once he'd managed to process what had just occurred. 'Such an ability is a blessing for mankind. I do believe God has finally answered my prayers.'

'I wish God would answer mine,' she grimaced. 'Some divine assistance wouldn't go amiss right now. I've never felt so alone.'

The president's eyebrows... having got as close to the ceiling as an incredulous forehead permitted... plummeted, along with the rest of the face to which they were attached. 'I don't understand. Hasn't He sent you? After all... I've been asking Him for help long enough! I was under the impression it's the reason you received your extraordinary gift in the first place.'

'Another thing typical of a man,' she huffed.

He stared blankly.

'Assuming God is male.'

The president squinted. 'But… it says so in the bible… *doesn't* it?'

'Of course it does. It was written by men.'

'Hang on a second…' His eyes bulged and shot towards Xanthia's miniskirt. 'You're not gonna tell me…'

'God's neither male nor female whilst being both at the same time… if that's of any help,' she explained.

'Not really.'

'Look… if you're going to insist on using the G word in our discussions, just accept It's neither a He, a She, or even a They. It's everything that has ever been, is and will ever be at exactly the same moment in time… except there *is* no time. You'd do better to think of God as an intelligent, quantum energy, and accept that's as close as you'll ever get to understanding It. After all… It exists in a combination of dimensions even *I* struggle to get my head around.'

The president shifted uncomfortably. 'I'm afraid you've lost me already. Furthermore… it's not what I was expecting to hear from you.'

She shrugged. 'You and the rest of the world, it seems. And therein lies my problem. Everyone wants me to confirm their particular version of whatever they've chosen to believe in… if believing anything at all, that is. Otherwise, they think I'm a liar and blasphemer.'

'Or playing for the other side,' the president said slowly.

She smiled. 'I hardly think you'd be standing here alone with me if you *really* thought that.'

He kept his stare. 'Maybe. But there's a thorny issue I need to broach before we go any further. It's the reason I doubt you'll have received the warmest of welcomes from my staff… and why I'd put money on there being an awful lot of anxious faces on the other side of that door right now.'

'Am I right in thinking it's got something to do with me and what appeared to be an angel?' she pre-empted.

'Are you telling me it *wasn't* one?'

'I don't know,' she grinned. 'I wasn't there.'

'But we have two state troopers who've testified you were.'

'I know. They even examined my passport to confirm that fact. Which was very convenient, don't you think?'

'For whom?'

'Well... if I tell you that Trooper Mitchell is a second cousin of the woman who cleans the apartment for Galveston Humbold's head of PR, you'll no doubt be able to join the dots yourself. I don't know whether Humbold was involved in the deception... or if it was simply a case of someone doing their job as enthusiastically as possible for him... but I saw no point in objecting until I'd gotten myself onto his show. Publicity works both ways, of course. Let's face it... it got me a far bigger audience than I'd managed up to that point... including this one with you.'

The president didn't respond.

'Unfortunately, I was never given the chance to challenge him about it.' She looked at her host sternly. 'Which brings me to a thorny issue of my own that we need to discuss.'

'Go on,' he nodded.

'Before I agreed to this meeting, I used my gift to focus on you and discovered a good and relatively honest man, well-deserving of the office he holds.'

The president raised an overworked eyebrow. '*Relatively?*'

'I doubt you'd have got this far in politics without the odd transgression,' she winked. 'But don't worry... everybody's guilty of that. So... other than a few professional peccadilloes... I think you're a pretty okay guy.'

'That's very kind of you,' he laughed. 'I'm glad so expert an examination of my life stacks up to such a favourable assessment!'

'So... I'm assuming it wasn't you who had me kidnapped.'

The president's jollity morphed into shock. 'You *were?*'

'I thought so,' she scowled. 'There's more going on than even *I* know about.'

He telegraphed his confusion. 'Wait a minute... is such a thing possible? I thought you had knowledge of *everything*. I thought that was the whole purpose of your gift.'

'Only up until the point I received it. Anything after that is as much a mystery to me as it is to you!'

He took a moment to process the fact. 'Okay... I understand. But you clearly know what Tucker-Jenkins and Penkridge have been up to. You can't be surprised they wanted to stop you talking, given the threat you posed to their operation. I expect it was *them* who had you kidnapped.'

'Don't be ridiculous,' she laughed. 'Donald's simply led Norman astray. My detention had nothing to do with them. It was the result of *far* more disturbed minds.'

'Well... I guarantee it wasn't anything to do with my government. And I think your boyfriend's history suggests he's capable of more than you're willing to admit. I've seen evidence of his involvement in these troubles we've been experiencing, and it goes way deeper than simply being "led astray". If anything, I believe your boyfriend has corrupted *Donald*.'

'I somehow doubt that,' she scoffed. 'And, for the record... he's my *ex*-boyfriend... *apparently*.'

'Then, you'll have no misgivings in helping us build a cast-iron case against him and his accomplice. We need to ensure the two of them are incarcerated for the rest of their lives.'

Xanthia stared at him in disbelief, 'Incarcerated?'

'Yes... and it's imperative they remain so.'

Her shock intensified. '*Remain?*'

'Of course. I had your ex and Tucker-Jenkins arrested yesterday.'

Her eyes widened in direct proportion to the gulf in each other's viewpoint. 'On what possible grounds?'

The president narrowed his. 'You need to ask? You *know* the lengths they've been going to to destabilise this planet.'

'Excuse me,' said Xanthia, shaking her head as if to reboot her thoughts. 'Are we talking about the *same* Norman and Donald?'

'Pray God there's only one such pairing!' the president exclaimed. 'We most definitely are. Our security agencies are in possession of evidence that they've been co-coordinating a worldwide campaign of disruption and terror. What I now need is for you to fill in the gaps and furnish us with information that will enable us to return things to normal... and as quickly as possible.' He leant forward eagerly. 'These abnormal weather patterns we've been experiencing... not to mention numerous plagues of everything you can think of that's ungodly. Are they just a coincidence they've sought to exploit... or do they somehow have a hand in those, too? I know Donald claims to be able to talk to the other side... but is it possible he can actually *influence* it?'

She blinked heavily. 'Mister President... whatever Norman and Donald have gotten up to without my knowledge, I can guarantee you this... they have *nothing* to do with what's happening to this planet right now!'

The strength of her assertion took the wind from his sails. '*Seriously?*'

She nodded firmly.

The colour drained from his face as the thought of his problems *not* being over replaced his previous, more comforting ones. 'Then... what *is* happening to this world?' he flinched.

Her expression darkened. 'If you want the easy answer... it's finally reaping the seeds it's sown.'

Personally, he would have preferred an even *easier* one... ideally providing him with a target he could bomb.

'What we're experiencing is the other side of that quantum energy I spoke about earlier. It's all a question of balance. Whilst the metaphysical mechanics behind it are too complex for the human brain to comprehend, it basically boils down to a battle between opposing vibrations... positive and negative... or good and evil, by the time the strongest of them manifest in this physical realm. What we're experiencing are the climactic moments of a critical tug-of-war that's been raging for eons.

The problems you refer to are the result of that darker force finally gaining the upper hand.'

The president gripped the sides of his chair and wished he wasn't currently in it, so he could at least steady himself by sitting down. 'But you're here to help restore this balance... *aren't* you?'

She gave a hesitant nod. 'That was the idea.'

His head jerked. '*Was?*'

'I don't think Heaven thought this one through,' she sighed. 'The power I've been given was intended for a time when people were more willing to accept they were part of a grand design. My words would've been taken as the truth. Unfortunately, the truth now appears to be whatever each individual deems it to be... and while, paradoxically, that is a manifestation of God's quantum design, it can only be considered the correct path to follow if it resonates in accordance with the fundamental force behind everything.'

The president's brow creased. 'Gravity?'

'No,' she frowned. '*Love.* It's the yardstick by which everything should be measured. It also happens to be the solution to this mess we're in. Not a love of self, of course, but of one's fellow man... though ultimately it's all the same thing. Suffice to say... if your version of truth doesn't resonate with it, then it's not what it purports to be.'

The president raised a hand. 'Hang on a second.' He looked at her incredulously. 'Are you *seriously* telling me that all we need to do to solve these problems we've been having is to get people to...' he struggled to complete the sentence for fear of sounding foolish, '*love* one another a little more? Surely it can't be *that* simple?'

She shrugged. 'Actually... it *is*... which makes this predicament we're in all the more shameful. You only need take a moment to imagine how things would be if all thoughts and actions were based purely on such an obvious and noble yardstick. Hungry mouths would become a thing of the past... as would tears cried in anger or regret. Suspicion would be consigned to history, along with its consequence... fear. Trust

217

would be seen as a pleasure not a risk... strangers viewed no differently than neighbours... and the colour of people's skin would be no greater a deal than the colour of their eyes. Just *imagine* such a world... and then consider the energy that could be redirected towards its betterment, rather than wasted on its divisions. And while you may struggle a little with this one... nature would be kinder to us, too. There's more going on there than you think.' She looked at him and smiled. 'So... yes, Mister President... in answer to your question... it really *is* that simple. All it requires is love.'

He stared at her in silence, as if needing to hear it confirmed yet again before he could believe it to be true. She watched him slowly digesting her words, until he realised for himself that it was.

Leaning back in his chair, he gazed at the ones inscribed on the ceiling above him. '*E pluribus unum,*' he muttered. 'And there was me thinking God hadn't answered my prayers.' He gave an ironic snort. 'He *had!*'

Xanthia's eyes narrowed.

'Apologies... *It* had,' he hastily corrected himself. 'The answer was staring me in the face every time I raised my eyes to question the silence.' He repeated the words, much louder. '*E pluribus unum...* Out of many, one. Those words up there might refer to the creation of this single nation from many states, but I guess we need to apply that doctrine of oneness to the whole of this *planet!*'

'That's what it would take to save it,' she confirmed.

After an intense period of contemplation, he stood up imperiously, much like a president should when about to make a momentous and historic announcement. 'If what you're saying is true, we need to make sure you get that message across to the rest of the world as soon as possible! I personally guarantee, from this moment forward, you'll have the entire resources of the most powerful country on Earth at your disposal. Just tell me what you need and you'll have it. There's nothing in my control that won't be made available to you. I promise that whatever's in that incredible head of yours will be

216

put to maximum use. You're no longer on your own, Xanthia. We're now a team... and we'll be a winning one at that! Together, we'll restore that all-important balance.' He looked at her triumphantly, his face reflecting the fact destiny had decreed he be the man who possessed the foresight to see past her pink miniskirt and fishnet tights. Utilising the power vested in him, he'd unite the world and forever be remembered as the president who saved it during its greatest moment of peril.

She, in return, winced apologetically.

'Is there a problem?' His chest deflated, as the prospect of future scholars discovering his name cleverly concealed in the quatrains of Nostradamus appeared to be in doubt.

'You could say that,' she said quietly.

'Well... what is it?'

She sighed heavily. 'Having used this "incredible head" of mine to assess the situation from every conceivable angle, I've now come to an inescapable and irrefutable conclusion.'

He looked at her expectantly.

She shook her head. 'It can't be done.'

*　　*　　*

The brutal sound of his cell door slamming shut sent a tidal wave of despondency coursing through Norman, and seemed the overture to a future devoid of hope. According to those responsible, his life was over. Their interpretation of *evidence* found in his luggage sounded plausible even to *him*. What chance of convincing a judge that Donald really *could* converse with the dead, and that everyone had simply got the wrong end of the stick?

The fate of the Universe had been cruelly wrenched from his hands and there was nothing more he could do... quite literally. *His* fate would now be determined by others. The only fork he was ever likely to encounter would be of the plastic variety... his only choices being whether it was worth wasting his time stabbing somebody in the prison canteen with it or not.

His body shook as he relived the trauma of the last twenty-four hours. God forbid the convulsions it would go through when he finally got round to considering those that stretched ahead.

Having spent the night in a cramped holding cell, he and Donald had been transferred to a maximum security facility the very next morning. Boasting depressingly high walls topped with razor wire, they were ominously interspersed with armed watchtowers containing grim-faced guards. Processed by unsympathetic wardens who preferred chewing gum to conversation, their silence was more than made up for by the harrowing noises coming from the corridors beyond. A subsequent, humiliating walk along them had been accompanied by the aggressive banging of metal cups against steel bars... not to mention a surprising amount of wolf-whistling, which he presumed was aimed more at him than Donald.

Ironically, he'd never felt so popular.

His alleged partner in crime had shuffled defiantly ahead, determined to maintain what dignity was left a man of his renown. Divested of his protective suit, he'd kept his head held high... along with a chain attached to the larger one manacling his feet.

The dishonoured playwright hadn't got off to the best of starts with those threading it through straps attached to an obligatory jumpsuit. Failing to understand their charge's relationship with his spirit guide, they'd initially looked on in bemusement as he'd vociferously taken Whitebait to task for pointing out that orange clashed with his skin tone. But before Norman could intervene on his behalf and explain, they'd deemed a baton strike to the back of the legs preferable to a polite request to wrap the argument up. Given his constant complaints about his knees, Norman was surprised Donald could walk at all after that.

Their destination turned out to be separate cells, something Norman considered a mixed blessing. While he could now wallow in his misery alone, he'd strangely miss Donald's company.

Perched on a thin, unforgiving mattress, he drew his knees into his chest and buried his head between them. At least it offered the pretence of privacy... a security camera situated in the top corner of his cell, presumably there for his own protection. Not that there was any point in causing himself harm. The world was about to end shortly anyway. Perhaps it would be better if it happened as quickly as possible... preferably before he was called upon to take a shower.

He brooded on what that end might look like.

Would the apocalyptic visions of Revelation really take place? Would the sun become as black as sackcloth and the moon the colour of blood? Would a blazing star called Wormwood fall from the sky and poison the rivers? Would a great beast with ten horns and seven heads really rise from the sea? Would the plagues of flies, locusts and other nuisances the world had been experiencing increase to such an extent they'd become unbearable? Would people struggle for a direction in which to run as thunderbolts rained down from a sky rent asunder by the appearance of four men astride four horses?

Or would everything resemble a cheap, Hollywood B movie, with the dead rising from their graves and roaming the streets as Zombies? After all... many were claiming it was already happening.

More depressing than that... perhaps the world would simply continue tearing itself apart until it had unpicked the final thread in the fabric of society and Satan's creed of selfishness ruled supreme... finally making it a place no sane individual wanted to inhabit.

And what would mark the definitive end? There could hardly be an official announcement. At what point would the news channels switch off the lights and call it a day?

He gripped his legs tighter and comfort-rocked himself. Whatever happened... it wasn't going to be pretty.

Not that it mattered. He wouldn't see it anyway. His cell didn't even have a window.

He groaned at the irony. Tasked with saving life itself... and given the myriad scenarios that could've resulted... he'd managed to end up in one where he wouldn't even be allowed to witness the results of his own failure.

How pathetic was that?

Out of the billions of people who'd inhabited the planet through countless millennia... mere specks in the unimaginable vastness of the Universe... it would ultimately boil down to it being *his* fault that it all ceased to exist. Norman *Pooey* Penkridge would be the name on the lips of every entity in Heaven as they cursed him in its final moments.

How had it happened? What fork could he have taken differently that would've prevented things turning out the way they had? How was he to know he shouldn't have trusted the only person he'd ever loved... or that going to the aid of what he thought was a friend in need would result in a knife being plunged into his stomach and destiny turned on its head? What words of wisdom could that little old lady on the park bench possibly offer him now?

As the memory of that meeting with someone he assumed to be Gabriel flooded back... he thought about trying to summon the archangel one last time.

Not that he held out much hope. Numerous attempts since their last encounter hadn't elicited so much as a fluttering feather.

If he *were* successful, he'd ask him to explain how things had gone so badly wrong. If powerful and all-knowing, how had God allowed it to end up like this? He appreciated Armageddon had long been foreshadowed... but even the *Book of Revelation* promised a happy ending for those who passed muster. Why couldn't God intervene and stop this atrocious nightmare? It was as equally baffling as God failing to prevent those natural disasters that brought untold misery and pain to the millions who suffered them. He always marvelled at the flawed logic of disaster survivors repeatedly thanking their maker for being saved, instead of cursing that same God for putting them in that position in the first place!

He drew his head from his knees.

'Gabriel,' he mumbled quietly, assuming he didn't need to shout. He looked up at the ceiling, despite that also being unnecessary. 'So… what happens now?'

His question returned silence… much as expected… although he *had* rather hoped for the sudden appearance of a hop-on chariot and a temporary hole through which he could make an escape.

'I appreciate you materialising could disturb the fragile balance and advantage the other side… but, let's face it… what have we got to lose? Things couldn't be much worse! So… how about throwing caution to the wind and having one last chat… just for old time's sake?'

He waited.

Nothing.

He waited some more.

Still nothing.

'Much as I thought,' he sighed, swinging his legs from the mattress.

Just as he was standing to stretch them, the solitary light in his cell flickered.

He held his breath, not daring to take another.

It flickered again, more violently this time.

'Gabriel?' he gasped.

His cell door began rattling.

'I *KNEW* IT!' he yelled ecstatically. 'I *KNEW* YOU WOULDN'T ABANDON ME!'

The rattling increased.

'GABRIEL!'

The door flew open.

'Towel,' grunted a guard, tossing a stained one onto Norman's bed.

Norman looked at the flickering light.

The guard acknowledged it with a curt nod of his head. 'Get used to that. They do it all the time in this place.' Retreating, he slammed the door shut.

Norman stood in dazed silence.

He now knew how the world would end.

It would come from the extinction of the last ray of hope... the crushing of the last positive thought... when an eternal, impenetrable darkness finally obliterated what little light remained.

* * *

'What do you mean, the balance can't be reset?' recoiled the president. 'That's why you're here, isn't it? I thought you were given this gift to save us all!'

'I was,' nodded Xanthia. 'But I've come to realise that such a thing is impossible.'

'*Impossible?*' The president's eyes widened. 'It can't be! If what you say is true, we're all going to die!'

'We're all going to cease to exist,' she corrected him. 'There's a massive difference.'

'Not from where *I'm* standing!'

'That'll be going, too. The moment the karmic evolution of souls ceases to be a possibility, God will simply... *evaporate,* for want of a better word... along with everything else.'

'*Evaporate?* But... God is... *God.*'

'Yes... and It's part of everything and everything a part of It. Hope is a powerful determinant in that equation. It's what holds it all together. The moment we are no longer able to become one again... that's it.'

He stared at her in horror. '*That's it?* You mean... absolutely *nothing?*'

She nodded.

'But it can't be!'

'With respect, Mister President... I think we're going round in circles.'

'But I don't understand... it doesn't make sense. Why on earth would those assisting these dark forces you speak of wish for such a situation? What's in it for them? Surely they'll cease to exist, too.'

'They will.'

'Then, why?'

She puffed out her cheeks. 'Greed would be a good place to start. Their souls have forgotten time is an illusion. They're only focused on the present, because that's where the pleasure they crave lies. You can dream of and reflect on glory, but power is felt in the moment. As far as *they're* concerned, the future is for others, so of no importance to them. Once a soul is distanced from its source, it loses its perspective. They've become blind to the consequences of their actions.' She looked pained. 'It was my job to open people's eyes again. But having glimpsed the complexities of human nature and seen its innumerable flaws, I now accept such a thing is impossible. Nothing I can say or do would make enough difference to the way our species thinks. We've strayed too far from the truth and reached the point of no return.' She looked at him apologetically 'I'm sorry.'

Mouth agape, he tried to think of something presidential to say. *Not on my watch* sounded good, but highly inaccurate given what he'd just been told. If the woman in front of him couldn't see a way out of the crisis, he'd keep that soundbite for the press. At least they wouldn't be around to vilify him when it turned out he'd lied.

'How long have we got?' he gasped, praying she wasn't going to look at her watch.

As she opened her mouth to speak, the door burst open.

'What the hell...!'

'Mister President... I need you to step away from your visitor... immediately!'

Rapidly alternating his focus between two men pointing handguns at Xanthia, he refused to do as requested. 'What's the meaning of this?'

'Special Agent Patterson, sir,' shouted one.

'And Special Agent Rodriguez, sir,' barked the other.

'I know... I recognise you both.'

'We're under strict orders to remove this individual from your presence, sir.'

'Whose orders?'

'Mine, Mister President,' panted his Chief of Security, swiftly entering the room. 'I'm sorry for such a dramatic entry, but we've just received intelligence that your visitor planned to do you harm today.'

'Well... she's definitely upset me, if that counts.'

'*Serious* harm, sir.'

The president looked at Xanthia sitting innocently in her pink miniskirt and fishnet tights, then back at his Chief of Security trying to catch his breath. 'What was she gonna do... *flirt* me to death?'

'The warning was unspecific, sir... but it's come from the very top. In fact, it was delivered directly to me by the CIA's Chief Operating Officer himself.'

'John?'

'Yes, sir. He was adamant the threat be neutralised immediately.'

'I trust that doesn't mean you're gonna shoot her... at least not here in my office.'

'No, sir. He's requested we hand the subject over to his department for interrogation.'

'And he's *certain* of this threat?'

'According to him, the warning's come from a highly reliable intelligence source. Such is the danger she poses, he's only entrusting the prisoner's transfer to a personally handpicked operative for security reasons. They're on their way now to take custody of her.'

The president stared at Xanthia incredulously. 'I don't believe it. She had me fooled.'

'Excuse me,' said Xanthia, raising a hand. 'Don't I get a say in this?'

'Not anymore!' The answer was delivered by the president's Chief of Staff, storming through the door to join the others. 'If I'd had my way, you wouldn't have been let in here in the first place! Mister President... I trust you're okay?'

'I'm fine, Gus, thank you. And it seems I owe you two gentlemen an apology. I should've listened to you both when you tried to warn me about this girl.'

'I'm just glad we were able to act in time, Mister President. Who knows what she had planned.'

'Well, *I* certainly don't... and I'm all-knowing!' Xanthia interjected.

'Remove her!'

Holstering their guns, the agents yanked her to her feet.

'I told you... there's something else going on here that needs to be investigated!' she shouted, as she was roughly manhandled out of the room.

As the door shut on her protestations, the president collapsed into his chair. 'Thank God, Gus. The Almighty might not have sent us that woman, but He *definitely* delivered us a saviour in John. That man's diligent efforts might've just saved this entire planet. For the briefest of moments, she had me believing it was pointless trying to put a stop to all this nonsense.'

'That would clearly have been in her interest, sir.'

He snorted his relief. 'She even had me believing God wasn't male!'

'Pure evil, sir.'

'That man has definitely warranted his position. Such outstanding service won't go unrecognised. We owe him big time. I'm gonna award him the Presidential Medal of Freedom as soon as we clear up this mess.'

'God?'

'No... *John!*'

His Chief of Staff looked at him awkwardly. 'That might not be for a while yet, sir.'

The president scanned the man's expression. 'More bad news?'

'I'm afraid so. We're getting reports of street protests escalating to worrying levels in the capitals of a number of our allies... as well as our own cities. This global plague of disillusionment is spreading much faster than we thought and getting seriously out of hand.'

'That's because people are scared, Gus. They know something's wrong. The trouble is… they expect us to have the answers.'

'We do, sir. They're currently incarcerated not far from here. Whatever Penkridge and Tucker-Jenkins are responsible for starting, they can help us stop. I propose Xanthia isn't the only one our intelligence agencies interrogate… but we'll need to ramp it up a notch with *those* two. We have to get inside those degenerates' heads by any means necessary. The sooner we understand the structure of their organisation, the sooner we can set about dismantling it and reversing the damage they've caused.'

'Are you suggesting what I think you're suggesting?' the president grimaced.

'We need to employ *extra* measures, sir. You know they won't be giving up their secrets easily.'

'That may be so. But authorising what you're referring to never sits easy with me… even with the most hardened of terrorists… you know that.'

'I do, sir. But such an extreme procedure is only used on a *needs must* basis… and if ever there was a time to justify it, it's now.'

The president chewed his lip. 'I doubt a man of Donald's age will survive the process.'

'That doesn't mean we shouldn't try, sir. Whatever happens, we know he'll talk and give up his secrets. They always do. Besides… he's not the man you thought he was.'

'He'll be even less that person if I agree to your request.'

His Chief of Staff remained unmoved. 'Extraordinary situations require extraordinary measures, Mister President.'

The president exhaled wearily. 'Okay, Gus… you've convinced me. You're right. It's imperative we get a handle on this thing.' He nervously made a fist. 'Put the call in to those who need to know… and may God have mercy on those two… and forgive *me*.'

* * *

'From Red Square to Tiananmen Square and… as you can see behind me… here in Parliament Square… over-stretched and exhausted security forces are doing their best to contain the waves of protest that have erupted around the world. It's as if a dam holding back the grievances of the entire planet has finally burst and flooded our major cities.' The reporter turned to the tide of protestors passing his vantage point opposite the Houses of Parliament and proffered his microphone at one holding a sign advising DON'T DRINK THE WATER. 'Excuse me, madam… can I ask what you're hoping to achieve here today?'

The lady in question stopped her chanting and took a moment to confirm she was holding her sign the right way round. 'I don't want people to drink the water,' she said, slightly perplexed.

'And why would that be?'

'Because the government have added something to it that's causing people to hallucinate and imagine all these nasty things that are supposed to be happening.'

'But to many, the occurrences you're referring to are worryingly real,' he pointed out.

She looked at the reporter as if he were an idiot. 'That's because they're drinking the water!'

'And the gentleman with you…' he quickly moved on. 'His sign says… STOP THE TAXIS.'

She glared at her companion contemptuously. 'Ron… I *told* you it was spelt with an *E,* not an *I.*'

'Is Ron your husband?'

'Regrettably.'

'So it seems the two of you have different reasons for being on this march today.'

'Yeah… mine is based on sound facts gleaned from internet forums.'

'And your husband's?'

'He wanted a day off work.'

'Do Ron's employers know what he's getting up to in his spare time?'

'It wouldn't surprise me.'

'Why's that?'

'He works for the Inland Revenue.'

The reporter blinked his dismay. 'Can I ask what evidence there is for the claim you're making?'

'Yeah, of course. It's that article with over three million likes on social media that's recently gone viral.'

The reporter waited for her to elaborate.

She stared at him blankly.

He filled in the awkward silence. 'Some might say it's just another of these conspiracy theories that are currently trending... whipping up tensions and driving people to vent their anger... many violently, in some reported cases.'

'*Taxes* are real,' interjected Ron. 'Believe me, *I* should know.'

'So is water,' she pointed out.

'I don't condone the violence, by the way,' said Ron, leaning in earnestly towards the microphone.

'SMASH THE RICH!' yelled a passing protester, seeing the camera as an opportunity to promote their grievance to a wider audience.

Ron stuck up a thumb. 'Right on, brother!'

The reporter faced the camera again. 'So, as you can see... it appears everyone here has wildly differing concerns and fears about the current plight we find ourselves in. I've seen banners calling for everything from the immediate removal of those in authority to demands for cheaper burials and greater pest control. Many even believe we're witnessing the start of the Apocalypse.'

'THAT'S BECAUSE THEY'RE DRINKING THE WATER!' shouted the woman, from behind him.

*   *   *

'I don't suppose you're going to tell me what's going on?'

The agent into whose custody Xanthia had been delivered glanced at her dispassionately in his rear view mirror, then back at the road taking them out of the city.

'The silent type, eh?' she shrugged. 'Though we all know *that's* not true.'

He didn't respond.

'You know these handcuffs were totally unnecessary,' she said, rattling them behind his head. 'It's not as if I've got anything to escape for. There's nowhere to run. We're all headed for as bleak a future as any of us could imagine. I'm just curious to know where you fit into it all.'

He maintained his silence.

'I mean... you being the one driving me right now seems one helluva coincidence. That *alone* peaks my interest.' She stared out of the window. 'What was it your partner always used to say?'

Her question caused his eyes to reattach themselves to the rear view mirror.

She nodded to herself. 'Ah, yes... there it is... always look for the connection *beyond* coincidence.'

The car swerved.

'Oh, come on,' she scoffed. 'Don't tell me you didn't think I could read you like a book. I doubt they'd have entrusted me to someone who's not aware of what I can do.'

'We know what you can do,' said Bob, breaking his silence. 'It's what you *intended* doing that's caused alarm.'

Her eyes shot to the mirror. 'Intended? That's an assumptive use of the past tense. Should I be worried?'

He quickly focused on the road again. 'Don't read too much into it. I was referring to the fact you're no longer free to do it.'

She stared at him suspiciously. 'But I'm only in that position because of intelligence that's blatantly false. So, back to that coincidence. I'm thinking... what are the chances of someone... within feet of me when I gained the ability everyone seems so concerned about... being the very person now driving me in this car? And, if that's not intriguing enough... when it comes to a connection with my ex-partner, they have an *extremely* interesting history.'

Bob glanced in the mirror again. 'So does *he.*'

'You tried to prevent him saving the Universe... not once, but twice,' she rebuked him.

'Is *that* what he was doing?' Bob scoffed. 'Now you sound just like *my* ex-partner. He's also had his brains scrambled by those lights at Stonehenge.'

'But it wasn't just Stonehenge, was it? The two of you also saw them outside Norman's bedsit that time you were sent to kill him. Or have I read too much into *that* assignment, too?'

'Look, lady... let's get something clear... I'm just doin' my job. I admit there's a heap of craziness going on right now that I don't pretend to understand. But if you can read me like a book, you'll know why I seized the chance to be back on a team that's working to put a stop to it, without questioning how it's done. So... if you wanna talk coincidences... how come you got rescued yesterday by the same freak that stuck a blade in your boyfriend's gut... or *ex*-boyfriend, as you're now calling him? You didn't seem that worried when that lunatic burst through the door waving a semi-automatic weapon all over the place.'

'You *saw* that?'

Bob averted his gaze.

'You were on the other end of those cameras!' she exclaimed. 'You're involved in my kidnapping!' She tugged anxiously at her handcuffs. 'Something's wrong here. The president gave me his word the government had nothing to do with it... and I know he's an honest man.'

Bob kept his eyes on the road.

'But you're definitely CIA... just like Brandon.' She struggled to make sense of her predicament. 'That means there's more to my abduction than a single agent doing a bit of freelance work on the side. The fact there are *two* of you throws up yet another connection beyond coincidence. But to what?'

Her captor wasn't going to answer that.

He didn't need to. As she focused on his history, one branch in particular jumped out at her. She leant forward eagerly. 'Prometheus. Now... *that* looks interesting!' She concentrated on the name. 'Is *that* what this is? Is he up to his old tricks?'

Bob hadn't a clue what she was talking about.

'Your boss is working for others,' she announced hurriedly. 'You need to stop what you're doing. This is not an official assignment. If you think it is, you're being used.'

'Is that so?'

'Yeah, it's so. I think your boss has gotten himself embroiled in a situation he can't get out of. I believe he's being paid by others to do this. What's more… he's prepared to sacrifice you and Brandon, and whoever else he's involved, just to satisfy his ends. He's dragging you into something you really don't want to be involved in. This mission is not what you think it is.'

Bob's eyes locked onto hers in the mirror.

She watched him absorbing what he'd been told.

'Are you certain about this?'

'Of course!' she nodded animatedly.

'Let me get this straight… You're telling me the Chief Operating Officer of the CIA is on the take? Is *that* what you're saying?'

'He's done it before, so I doubt he'll have changed his habits.'

Bob squinted. 'You want me to stop the car?'

'No… I need you to take me back to the president! It's imperative he knows what's going on!'

Bob nodded slowly. 'Fair enough. I'll make a turn at the next junction.'

Xanthia sunk back in her seat and exhaled a huge sigh of relief. 'That explains it all… including my interrogators happily turning a blind eye to ethics. It appears every one of them has sold their soul for personal gain or glory. I sensed all along it wasn't for patriotism or the common good.'

Bob studied her in the mirror. 'This thing you do… you can see *everything* there is to know about someone… the actual thoughts they've had… stuff like that?'

'If I want to,' she replied. 'The trouble is… you risk opening a can of worms. There's a danger of going down paths you really shouldn't. After all… I'm only human and just as curious as the next person.'

'So… if I asked you what a certain individual thought of… *me,* for instance… you'd be able to take a peek.'

'Of course. But as I said… I wouldn't advise it… particularly in *your* case.'

He ignored the slight. 'But you *could*.'

'In principle.'

'So… take Chad Cheadle, for instance.'

'Your *connection beyond coincidence* colleague? What of him?'

Bob drummed his fingers on the steering wheel. 'I dunno… I was just curious to know what he thought of me… deep down.'

Her eyes widened. 'You'd seriously wanna go there?'

He exorcised his embarrassment with a laugh. 'Yeah… actually, I would.'

She shook her head. 'Well, it isn't going to happen. Like I told you… it'd be a can of worms.'

The car slowed.

'Interesting.' She leant forward again and glanced at the car's indicator, then out of the window. 'Are we taking the scenic route?'

'I love trees,' said Bob, pulling onto a smaller road heading towards a heavily wooded area.

'No you don't.'

He put his foot down.

'What's more… we're going in the wrong direction.'

As far as Bob was concerned, that depended on one's destination. *His* had been preordained. He might have entertained doubts about the man who'd given him his instructions, but it wouldn't be the first time he'd put loyalty above personal misgivings in his line of work.

Xanthia turned in alarm as the road they'd left rapidly disappeared behind them. 'Haven't you been listening to a thing I've said? Where are you taking me?'

Bob kept his attention on the road.

'You're not gonna tell me?'

'Can of worms,' he mumbled.

Having sped its way between thickening forest for a couple of miles, the car slowed again.

Xanthia's heartbeat quickened. 'There's nothing here,' she said nervously, aware of the remoteness of their location.

Turning onto a rough, narrow track, Bob headed directly into the dense tangle of trees. As the terrain grew increasingly unsympathetic, he finally brought the vehicle to a halt.

'I guess this means your boss has given up on interrogating me,' she said stoically.

Bob exited the car without saying a word and opened her door.

'How gentlemanly,' she nodded. 'Most unlike you.'

'We'll go on foot from here.'

She flashed a look of incredulity. 'Have you *seen* what I'm wearing on my feet?'

'If it's a problem, take 'em off.' He grabbed her arm. 'It's not far.'

Hastily removing her stilettos, she hobbled beside him, struggling to keep up as he hurried her along. They hadn't gone far before they came across another abandoned vehicle.

Bob looked about anxiously. 'This way,' he said quickly, increasing his grip and yanking her sideways into the undergrowth.

She stumbled on, doing her best to keep pace with him, her feet becoming numb with pain. Just as she thought she wouldn't be able to take another step, they entered a small clearing.

Bob stopped and loosened his grip.

Xanthia froze as she spied a freshly dug hole in the ground just ahead of them, a spade stuck in the mound of earth beside it.

'I assume that's for me,' she said quietly.

Without answering, he prodded her towards it.

Determined not to show weakness, she stoically shuffled ahead until she was standing at its edge.

'Not that it makes any difference to me, but it'd be kinder on you if you got in,' he said unemotionally.

'You're right,' she whispered in a daze. 'I don't wanna ruin my clothes, do I?'

He waited while she slowly lowered herself into the makeshift grave.

'I guess there's no point in appealing to your better nature,' she muttered, the last words catching in her throat.

'Like I said, lady… I'm just doin' my job.'

'I know,' she said, dropping her head. 'I just wish I'd been able to do mine.'

*　　*　　*

Corbin Deadwood held up the letter and offered it towards the gaping mouth of the postbox.

It wasn't a letter he'd ever intended writing, but a man could only be pushed so far.

He poked it into the waiting aperture, knowing as soon as he let go, a catastrophic storm would be unleashed, forever changing the lives of those whose names and details he'd entrusted to a first class stamp.

Not that he felt he'd been left with much choice. From his point of view, it was a matter of justice… albeit somewhat rough. Seeing as *his* name had been dragged through the mud, he didn't see why those responsible should remain spotless. Hence their enumerated names on an enclosed list.

The annoying thing was, it needn't have come to this.

It had all started with Mrs Speckleman… name number five and lighter of the touchpaper. Why couldn't she have simply minded her own business?

Ronald Cramborne, Chairman of the Parish Council and name number six, also shouldered a fair proportion of the blame. He could've simply had a quiet word in the ears of names, two, three and four on the list and suggested they let the matter drop. There was certainly no need to involve the police.

The trouble was… once the editor of the local newspaper got hold of the story… name number seven… the genie was out of the bottle.

He'd told Mrs Speckleman from day one... clean anywhere you find dirt... but don't EVER go into that particular room. He'd even stared at her so hard when he'd said it, her eyeballs had quivered. Failure to comprehend a simple instruction had ruined everything.

Forty-seven years he'd been the village postman. Three more and he'd have received a clock. Now the red postbox was staring at him like he was a civilian. As soon as his letter dropped, control of its contents would be out of his hands. After all, he'd been forced to suffer the indignity of handing in his special postbox key in front of smirking colleagues. Not to worry... most of them were on the list, too.

There'd be no going back once his fingers release their grip. Lives would be irrevocably changed... especially his.

Bloody Mrs Speckleman!

He'd tried to convince her that the large pentagram he'd drawn on the floor was the outline of a new tool shed he was thinking of building... and that he was only standing in it to see if there would be enough room for his lawnmower. To be fair... it probably didn't help that he was naked... nor that said lawnmower was being represented by the severed head of a pig.

If her eyeballs had quivered before, you should've seen them at *that* point!

But it was the amount of screaming she did that *really* sealed his fate. Had she been a little more British and toned it down, name number one on the list wouldn't have taken advantage of an unlocked side door in the belief *"someone was being horribly murdered as I passed by in the street, your honour".*

Unfortunately... name number one was the brother-in-law of name number eleven... who happened to be married to name number six, the aforementioned Ronald Cramborne... so a full investigation was duly convened. Apparently, Parish Councils didn't take favourably to trusted members of the community having a slightly different theological bent to theirs. They could also be extremely vocal when it came to pressing charges.

Personally, he didn't see the problem. He'd always delivered their letters on time... even the vicar's... *curse his name*... number eight on the list. What did it matter to *them* what he got up to in his spare time? It had all been done behind closed doors... until Mrs Speckleman yanked *that* particular one open, of course. Some people played golf... name number twenty-two far more often than his wife... name number twenty-three... would like. His own pleasure just happened to involve ritual sacrifice.

Not that humans were involved. Being a Satanist in rural England required maintaining a sense of proportion... and a bit of patience. The suffering of others would eventually come when his Lord and Master took control.

With that dream in mind, he'd kept his head down, so as not to draw unnecessary attention to himself. That meant carrying out his duties as efficiently as possible, being suitably polite to everyone he met, and regularly checking in on lonely members of the village who regarded his visits as a godsend... which was a bit ironic, really. Admittedly he'd dipped his hand in few badly concealed savings tins, but ceremonial candles didn't come cheap... especially when you had to have a whole ring of them to summon anything half-decent from the netherworld.

But Mrs Speckleman's quivering eyeballs had put paid to all that.

While the judge rejected the charge of indecent exposure... and a lesser one of cruelty to animals... the damage had been done. According to his former employers, he'd lowered the public's expectations of the British postal service... which took some doing.

The final ignominy was having his P45 delivered through his letterbox by someone else.

Most of the other names on his list hadn't been *directly* involved in the scandal. They'd simply not given him their support when he needed it the most. Lifelong friends and acquaintances had rapidly distanced themselves, as if he couldn't be trusted.

But, in fairness... he couldn't.

If only they'd known the half of it.
Mind you... they would soon.

He loosened his grip and allowed the letter to slip to the very tips of his fingers.

Devil worship hadn't been his *only* guilty secret in life. Having never found a companion who found wearing shorts to work in winter attractive, he'd filled his lonely nights revelling in the secrets of others. It was amazing what you could discover if you carefully steamed open their correspondence before they got a chance to read it themselves... or before it reached the depot. It presented a fascinating window on the world... a cross section of humanity's failings and flaws exposed for all to see.

Take names forty-seven and sixty-one, for instance. These pillars of the community had been cheating on their respective partners... forty-eight and sixty-two... for the last five years. Professing undying love for one another, their private missives left little to the imagination.

Number seventy-four had clearly committed mortgage fraud. The figure given to the Inland Revenue relating to taxable earnings was nowhere *near* the amount claimed on his loan application form.

As for eighty-nine... what an eye opener *that* had been! Demonstrating an unhealthy fixation with a lunchtime newsreader, they'd regularly written to tell them so... explicitly detailing what was planned if they ever came face to face. At least, he'd *surmised* it was name eighty-nine. Though the letters were always anonymous, he believed he recognised the shaky handwriting.

And then there were those plainly wrapped parcels designed to keep their contents secret... unless you possessed a very fine scalpel and broad selection of packing tapes with which to make good your inquisitiveness. You'd be amazed at what you could order online... especially when sourced from abroad.

It was all there in the letter... forty-seven years of accumulated secrets with corresponding names... meticulously recorded in numerical order.

Addressed to printers in a neighbouring town, it contained instructions to distribute the salacious details in booklet form to every single person in the village... his final finger to its inhabitants being to have it delivered courtesy of the postal service.

He pictured Mrs Speckleman's eyeballs upon receiving hers. With luck, she'd live every day of the rest of her life burdened by unbearable guilt... becoming a husk of her former self, until remorse and self-loathing caused her heart to shrivel to a point it could no longer continue beating. He hoped her final thought on Earth would be of the blood-stained room into which she'd so foolishly intruded... and the torment that it all could have been so different if she'd simply shut her mouth and... if offended by the blood... got to work with a mop and a bucket of bleach.

The letter hung precariously...

... as did his thoughts.

Despite his voyeuristic pastime, he wasn't a bad man... Satanism aside... and clearly not by the standards of those it had involved. If he held on to the letter and withdrew his hand now, the local community could go on living as it always had, blissfully ignorant of the apocalypse he could've unleashed. He would have proved himself a *far* better person than all of them put together.

More to the point... he would save himself from going to prison for a *very* long time.

He stood a moment in contemplative silence.

A chill wind caught the side of his face.

He smiled... and released his grip.

* * *

Xanthia recognised the sound behind her as that of a Sig Sauer P226 being cocked. A firearm favoured by many CIA operatives, it would at least do its job efficiently. She also knew – having studied the man holding it – that although he'd hesitate slightly before pulling the trigger, he'd complete his task. He wasn't a bad man... he'd just forever struggled to become a better one.

She closed her eyes.

At least he believed he was doing the right thing. That should count for something.

She used the remaining seconds to rapidly appraise her life.

Prior to Stonehenge, everything she'd ever cared about or considered important now seemed ridiculously trivial and an unforgivable waste of time... or, as Gabriel had once admonished Norman... of *being*.

Everything, that is, except Norman himself. That was the only bit she'd ever got right. She pictured their last meeting and stifled a sob. The bullet that would terminate her squandered existence was irrelevant. His lack of trust in her when she needed it most had made the future pointless... even if she *could've* succeeded in securing one for the world she was about to leave.

There *was* one positive, however. At least she'd avoid the impending mass rush for the exit.

Except... the exit would no longer be there... or what lay beyond.

Ordinarily, dying wouldn't have fazed her. Having been privileged to glimpse the enormity of the wonder that was life, she understood it was nothing more than a single point along an unimaginably vast and incredible journey... just one more *tick* before another *tock*. But the battle in which she'd become embroiled would silence that pendulum for eternity.

Not that there would even be silence... or eternity, if one was being pedantic. *Nothing* would be left.

In fact... not even the *concept* of nothing.

A tear forced itself from beneath an eyelid.

She wondered if she'd be allowed to feel it hit her cheek.

After a slight hesitation, Bob drew a determined breath and applied his finger to the trigger of his gun.

Xanthia heard the sound of a Sig Sauer P226 being cocked...
...which confused her.

'I wouldn't do that if I were you,' warned a voice loudly.

Keeping his gun trained on his target, Bob turned his head towards the threat. '*Chad?* What the friggin' hell are *you* doing here?'

'Pointing this gun at you,' came the steady reply.

'I can friggin' see that! I was just wondering... *why.*'

'I think the answer's pretty obvious... don't you?'

Bob gave a flick of acknowledgement towards Xanthia. 'What... *really?* You're gonna shoot me, if I shoot her?'

'If you're stupid enough to pull that trigger... yes.'

'For what it's worth,' interjected Xanthia hastily, 'having studied Mister Papadopoulos in some detail, I believe he *may* be.'

'I know,' nodded Chad. 'That's why he needs to understand I *will* do what I threaten if he chooses to ignore me.'

'Oh, c'mon,' Bob snorted. 'Are you outta your mind? Apart from the fact it's *me* you're pointing that thing at... you're interfering in a high-level operation here. There's a sound, logical reason for what's going on here. I'm following orders. You, of all people, should appreciate the importance of *both* those things.'

'I'm not interested. You've got yourself on the wrong side. You can thank me later, but right now you need to lower that gun and hand the girl over to me.'

'No I don't,' returned Bob brusquely. 'It's *you* who seem to have lost the plot. You might not be working for the agency anymore, but *I* am. I've been given a chance to come back in from the cold, so I'm not gonna allow you to mess things up for me. I've got a job to do.' He tightened the finger on his trigger.

'I'm warning you!' shouted Chad, tensioning his arms. 'You pull that thing and I swear I'll do the same!'

'What...' scoffed Bob, 'after all the years we've spent together guarding each other's backs? I don't think so!' He returned his attention to his target.

'Knowing what Chad *really* thinks of you, I wouldn't roll that dice if I were you,' Xanthia offered quietly, her head still bowed.

Bob wiped his mouth. 'What are you talking about?'

'Well... you asked me in the car... and I warned you it was a can of worms.'

Chad's trigger finger tensed.

Bob turned his head and focused on the raised veins in his old partner's arms. *'Really?'* he groaned.

Chad nodded without breaking his stare.

Bob rolled his jaw. 'Then I guess we've got ourselves one helluva standoff... cos I ain't backing down.'

'Me neither,' Chad affirmed.

'I believe we could be here for some time,' Xanthia sighed, not daring to move.

Just as a watching bird in the trees above thought a cinematically themed warble might be appropriate, the stalemate was broken by the sound of yet *another* Sig Sauer P226 being cocked.

'Not necessarily,' said a voice directly behind Chad. 'Put the gun down, Cheadle.'

'Thank Christ!' exhaled Bob. 'I was wondering where you'd got to, sir.'

'Ah... Mister Prometheus,' Xanthia muttered.

Unfazed, Chad kept his firearm focused on Bob. 'As my ex-partner pointed out a few moments earlier... I don't work for the agency anymore... *sir*... so there's little point in you issuing me an order.'

'You're right, you don't,' said AKA Mister Prometheus calmly. 'Which is why I won't have a problem putting a bullet in the back of that idiotic, civilian head of yours. You're getting in the way of important government business here, Cheadle. You know I can't allow that to happen.'

'See... I told you,' confirmed Bob. 'C'mon, ol' buddy... do the sensible thing and lay down your weapon. You must realise how important this job is if it's being personally overseen by the main man himself. Don't worry... we'll sort this out. I'll personally make sure you walk away from this thing unscathed. I give you my word on that.'

'You should listen to Papadopoulos,' AKA Mister Prometheus advised. 'Not least because it's the first time I've ever heard anything sensible coming out of his mouth. He's right. We'll put this episode down to a simple misunderstanding and you'll be free to go from here and get on with your life without repercussions. You have my word on that, too.'

Chad kept his gun on his target. 'Here's where we're stand... Bob, your head is currently a *what's-left-of-our-friendship* away from being scattered all over this clearing and providing food for the worms. If mine goes that way first, my motor reflexes will guarantee it won't do so alone. So... as you rightly pointed out... we've got ourselves one helluva standoff.'

Sensing destiny on its side, the watching bird ruffled its wings and opened its beak to sing.

It was stopped again by the sound of a fourth gun being cocked.

Xanthia recognised it as a Colt 45... which made a change.

The others recognised it as an unexpected complication.

'Excuse me for intruding upon this lil' ol' forest gathering of yours,' drawled its owner, 'but I'm here to re-establish rightful ownership of what is... in the supreme judgement of our dear maker, the Lord himself, God Almighty... rightfully mine... having had it so *discourteously* snatched away from me in the first place.'

'Galveston Humbold?' queried AKA Mister Prometheus, unable to see the person threatening the back of his head, but recognising the voice and appalling syntax.

'In the flesh... and with the addition of some mighty useful firepower in my right hand. So... ya'll be wanting to stand *exactly* where you are.'

'Reverend Humbold. What fortuitous timing,' beamed Xanthia. 'I never thought I'd be so pleased to see *you* again! You're right... we never did get to conclude that discussion of ours, did we?'

'We didn't, ma'am. My moment of glory was stolen by those who seem intent on hastening the Lord's judgement on you. Not that I blame 'em for that last part, mind. But you and I have unfinished business, and I'm here to right an egregious wrong. I suggest you climb yourself outta that hole and make your way over to me. Then we'll leave these gentlefolk to sort out their differences... as we will do ours.'

'Seeing as we're both here to *save* a life, does that mean I can put my gun down?' grimaced Chad, the weight of his arm beginning to tell.

'No, it don't, young man. You're doing just fine keeping that unwholesome-looking fella at bay, while this one in front of me does the same to you and maintains a convenient status quo that'll guarantee me a safe exit.'

'You idiot, Humbold,' barked AKA Mister Prometheus. 'There's no way you're getting away with this! You're wilfully interfering in government business. This could see you put away for life!'

'Well... that's strange... because, according to that government of which you speak... they've officially informed my legal team they have no knowledge of this jezebel's whereabouts. So... apart from opening a sack of snakes I doubt they'll thank you for... I fail to see how you're gonna make *that* charge stick in a court of law. Furthermore... what it seems you were intending doing here to this unfortunate creature ain't exactly constitutional, is it?'

'Who told you we'd be here?' demanded AKA Mister Prometheus angrily.

'I was guided by God,' the reverend announced proudly.

'I somehow doubt that,' AKA Mister Prometheus scowled.

'Well, if you want specifics... I have an ear to the goings on in Washington. As soon as I heard the president of this fine nation was to be presented with my stolen property, I got myself on the first available flight to claim it back. And it appears I did so just in time. For the good Lord saw to it that I arrived at the gates of the Capitol just as she was being driven from them. I simply had my taxi driver trail the car. In fact, the man's waiting now, a little way down the track. So... seeing as the meter's still running... if you gentlemen will excuse us...' He signalled for Xanthia to join him.

There was the sound of a Sig Sauer P226 being cocked.

The rotor blades of the Sikorsky S-92 had little respect for the carefully manicured courtyard fronting the temple at Arwan El Kahab. Before the whirlwind of sand and debris had been given a chance to settle, its door slid open to discharge four heavily armed men to form a protective arc in front of it. With the blades finally coming to rest, the remaining passengers alighted into the thinning cloud of dust.

'Let's get this over as quickly as possible,' hissed Miss Eris, clicking her fingers impatiently.

Her bodyguards headed for the temple.

'It's as unimpressive as Prometheus said it was,' she glared, giving the building's façade a contemptuous once-over. 'They really *didn't* want people coming here, did they.'

'All clear inside!' shouted one of the men, having unceremoniously forced the temple's door open with his boot and briefly recced its interior.

'I doubt that very much,' she returned. 'After what I've been told occurred here, such a place won't be without its guardians. What's more… I've completely wasted my time coming all this way if it is.' She made a fist. 'FIND THEM!'

*   *   *

Reverend Humbold froze as he felt the cold barrel of a gun pressed against the nape of his neck. 'I take it you're not the taxi driver taking umbrage at being kept waiting?' he ventured delicately.

'Correct,' came a curt reply.

'I *thought* it a bit extreme,' said the reverend. 'Especially for a man who'd shown such interest in purchasing one of my discounted prayer cushions.'

'For a place I assume was chosen for its remoteness, this clearing is proving surprisingly popular,' remarked Xanthia, slowly turning her head to address the latest arrival. 'Hello, Brandon. Fancy bumping in to *you* here.'

'I wondered where the hell you'd got to,' said Bob tetchily. 'My friggin' arm feels like it's about to drop off!'

'Mine won't stop shaking,' concurred AKA Mister Prometheus, much to Chad's consternation.

'I thought I heard another vehicle and stayed out of sight... just in case,' said Brandon.

'Good lad.' AKA Mister Prometheus supported his outstretched arm with his spare hand. 'It appears all that training we gave you has finally paid off... unlike Cheadle, here, who's gotten sloppy since he left us.'

'How d'ya figure that?' squinted Chad.

'Well... I can't believe you thought it was *me* who used that spade over there,' AKA Mister Prometheus snorted.

Chad shrugged. 'I *didn't*.'

'Then who do you think dug that goddam hole the girl's standing in?'

'The same person who told me you'd be here.'

'What?'

'I was talking to Chad... *sir*,' clarified Brandon. 'As I was saying, I decided to remain hidden until I was sure we weren't gonna get any more interruptions.'

'Good call,' Chad nodded. 'I somehow don't think I'd have been allowed to walk away from this mess once the reverend had said his goodbyes. I know too much.'

'What the hell's going on?' exclaimed Bob.

'You've been outplayed,' Chad grinned. 'Like I said earlier... you've got yourself on the wrong side.'

Xanthia addressed Brandon. 'Seeing as you now appear to be playing on the *right* one... why the sudden change of heart?'

'I realised I still had one,' he answered, 'and that yours was far bigger than mine. The fact you intervened and saved my life... despite all I'd done to you... proved you weren't the monster everyone was making you out to be.'

'I told you the boy who cared for his rabbits still existed,' she smiled.

'Not for long,' yelled AKA Mister Prometheus. 'You're both finished! I don't know how the two of you think you're gonna get away with this... unless you're planning on putting me and Papadopoulos in that goddam hole!'

'Personally, sir... I wouldn't have suggested that as an option,' Bob winced.

'What does it matter now, Papadopoulos? If that girl goes from here, *I'm* finished!'

'Sounds a little extreme,' said Chad. 'So, why would *that* be?'

'None of your goddam business, Cheadle!'

'Or the government's, I suspect,' offered Xanthia. 'I think you'll find your old boss has reverted to his previous habits and been doing a little freelance work of his own.'

'Enough of this,' shouted AKA Mister Prometheus in exasperation. 'Let's all just pull our triggers and get this over with.'

'Whoa!' yelled Chad and Bob, their eyes bulging in unison.

The reverend passed what the others mistook to be wind. 'Hang on a goddam moment,' he yelled, 'In the name of Mary and the sweet baby infant Jesus... let's just take a few seconds to think about what we're doin' here! This wretched girl ain't worth dying for. You can have her cursed soul.' He dropped his gun. 'I'm recanting ownership. Take her... she's yours.' He put his hands up in the air. 'I ain't ready to meet my maker right now. I'll spare you the finer details... but I'd appreciate being able to change my underwear before I do.'

'She's not going anywhere,' insisted AKA Mister Prometheus, stiffening his arm. 'The moment that girl is seen again in public, I'm a dead man.'

Bob looked at Chad.

Xanthia carefully raised a finger. 'I might have a solution.'

All eyes turned to her.

'Seeing as there are some out there who have clearly taken an extreme dislike to me, given this hole I'm standing in... *and* managed to convince your government I'm implicated in a plot against it... I'm not sure I *want* to be seen in public again for what little time is left. So... why don't Chad, Brandon and myself leave you two gentlemen to fill in your hole as planned? You can tell those paying you that your mission was a complete

186

success. No one needs be any the wiser and we all get to walk away from this mess unscathed.'

Bob eyed his boss as the proposal was considered.

Sighing heavily, AKA Mister Prometheus lowered his gun. 'What the hell... I'm getting too old for all this, anyway.'

On seeing him capitulate, Bob did the same.

'That's settled, then.' Exhaling her relief, Xanthia turned to climb out of the redundant grave.

'Wait a minute...' said Bob, stalling her escape with an outstretched palm. 'What about the reverend, here? What's to stop him blabbing with that overactive mouth of his as soon as he leaves this place? After all... he hasn't exactly built his career on keeping it shut.'

'That's for you to figure out,' said Chad, stepping forward and offering Xanthia a helping hand. 'But perhaps you might want to take into consideration the fact you've now got yourselves a very convenient, empty hole.'

*   *   *

Miss Eris contemptuously studied the temple's interior, ignoring the cry of pain from the body that had been roughly thrown to the ground in front of her.

'We caught him trying to hide,' said one of those responsible for the throwing. 'We're pretty certain there's no one else here with him.'

Examining the stonework, she addressed the figure sprawled at her feet without bothering to look at him. 'They've left you here to cope on your own?' she asked, surprised.

'It's not a question of *coping*,' he answered, defiantly raising his bruised face from the dirt. 'My duty is not a burden.'

Miss Eris finally gave him her attention. 'Well, old man... I think you'll find *that's* about to change.'

'There's nothing here for you,' he returned, sitting himself up and trying to staunch the blood coming from his nose. 'Unless you've travelled all this way for advice, that is.'

She snorted her disdain. 'And what would it be if I had?'

185

He looked up stoically. 'That you cannot win against someone who is prepared to sacrifice their life for their cause.'

She studied him in silence, then leant forward. 'Is *that* what you think you're about to do?'

The old man said nothing.

'No. You misunderstand me,' she smiled. 'I have no intention of killing you... not yet, anyway. If I did that, you'd no longer be of use to me.'

'My allegiance can't be bought,' he countered, 'and you'll find nothing of value here.'

'Oh, I already have.' She delicately placed her foot on one of his hands and cruelly applied her weight to it. *'You!'*

The old man stifled his pain as the sickening crack of bones made those in attendance wince.

'I accept that what I'm *ultimately* looking for might not be here,' she continued. 'Though keeping it concealed in such a remote and secretive location might be considered a prudent move.' She looked about again. 'Perhaps it's buried under one of these ridiculous plinths. Is that what I'm supposed to do... guess which one?'

'You can search under as many as you like,' returned the old man. 'The only thing you'll find is dirt.'

'I've already found that,' she laughed, grinding her foot into his shattered hand. 'Your side is in its death throes. Mine is poised to take control. I just need to ensure I have a seat at the head of the table when it does. The treasure I seek will guarantee I do.'

'Then you will fail in that quest,' grimaced the old man through tightly clenched teeth. 'The *Magnum Compendium Secretorum*... for we both know that is what you seek... will forever be beyond your reach. I told you before... you cannot win against someone who is prepared to die for what they believe in. I will *never* divulge its whereabouts.'

'Well, I hardly thought you would... *voluntarily*.' She gave him a smile. 'But at least your last statement tells me you know where it is. It seems my journey here was worth it after all.'

'Go to hell!' he shouted defiantly.

'I won't have to,' she gloated, placing her head close to his. 'It's coming here.'

The sound of the temple's door opening reverberated around the cavernous interior. The old man watched as two men entered carrying a large, metal chest. Affording its contents the greatest respect, they carefully placed it on the largest of the plinths and stood back.

'So... now we've established you *do* have the answers I seek in that stubborn head of yours, the question is... how do we get them out?'

'You're wasting your time,' countered the old man valiantly. 'Death does not scare me. It's *dishonour* that would torture my soul for eternity. Do what you must... but you'll never have possession of the *Compendium*.'

'Oh, bravo!' Her laughter ricocheted around the temple and mocked him with its echoes. 'I'm sure your predecessors were equally courageous while guarding its whereabouts. You do them proud. But here's the thing... they were right to assume they could chose death over disclosure. You, on the other hand, have been burdened with one unfortunate disadvantage.'

He looked at her warily.

'Progress,' she smirked.

His attention switched to the metal chest on the plinth.

'Oh, no... that comes later,' she teased. 'I'm talking about *science*. I'm afraid it's made your ancient values of honour redundant.' She acknowledged one of her retinue standing nearby. 'So, why don't I introduce you to one of its exponents?'

The man in question stepped forward.

'I'd like you to meet Doctor Menzies.'

The doctor tipped his head in acknowledgement.

'If you're wondering which particular field of science Doctor Menzies is expert in... it involves the use of amobarbital... or sodium amytal, if you'd prefer.'

The old man's eyes widened as he grasped the implications.

'I thought that might wipe that pained martyr's look from your face,' she gloated. 'He might have been thwarted by the cunning of your precious Xanthia, but I doubt a man of your lesser intellect possesses the ability to answer in forgotten tongues. So, let's not waste any further time. Doctor Menzies… you have what you need?'

The doctor held up a black bag. 'I do indeed.'

'Then, I suggest you get to work.'

*   *   *

Donald studied the heavily tattooed arm that had just deposited something onto his plate and wondered if *Mum* and *Phyllis* were one and the same, given love was being professed to both in identical design. He then turned his attention to what had been deposited.

'Am I supposed to *eat* that?' he asked indignantly.

'You can do what you like with it, buddy,' the owner of the arm responded. 'But if you don't move on in the queue, I'll find a use for it myself… thereby saving the majority of your colon the effort.'

Sagely heeding the advice, Donald waited as another curiously pictorial appendage dolloped a second unrecognisable concoction next to the first.

'Don't say anything,' whispered Norman, behind him. 'Our accents stand us out enough as it is.'

'I've never feared being different,' sniffed Donald stoically, marching off to find a space at one of the many benches lining the canteen.

'I can't believe what's happened to us,' groaned Norman, hastily joining him. 'I'm living my worst nightmare. Not only am I facing a future where the only thing I can do all day is stare at blank, pictureless walls… there's not even enough room between them to swing a cat.'

'You'd be surprised at how little space you actually need to do that,' said Donald matter-of-factly. 'And don't worry about the future. Seeing as we're now confined to this place, I doubt there'll *be* one soon.'

'You seem remarkably calm about it,' Norman scowled. 'Doesn't such a thought horrify you?'

Donald considered the question. 'If you want the truth... I feel like a great burden has finally been taken from my shoulders. I've been living with the responsibility of deciphering what's been going on between this world and the next for more years than I care to remember. I don't know whether it's the thick walls and metal door of my cell... or the fact those in the spirit world know I can no longer be of assistance... but they've suddenly stopped bothering me... except *one*, of course.' He lifted his eyes in annoyance. 'I've spent the last few hours luxuriating in relative equanimity and resigning myself to our fate. As to that of the Universe... it's out of our hands now. You just have to accept there's nothing more we can do about it. If the President of the United States can go from thinking I'm one of the greatest writers of truths... to believing I intended heaping such unparalleled misery upon the world... there's absolutely no hope for the human race... let alone you and me. All our efforts have been a complete waste of time.'

'We can't just give up,' Norman declared. 'That's why... while you were happily enjoying your solitude... I tried summoning Gabriel.'

Donald froze, his fork poised above the unidentified item on his plate.

'Needless to say, it didn't work.'

The fork dropped.

'When I realised he wasn't coming, I told myself that was how the Universe would end... on the extinction of the last vestige of hope. But then a thought occurred to me. It meant that, as long as there *is* hope, it doesn't have to be that way. If Gabriel taught me one thing, it's that positive thoughts can overcome *anything*. And he's absolutely right. I never gave up on finding that missing piece of the first sphere of knowledge... even when he himself said it couldn't be done. And I never gave up when it came to resolving all the problems surrounding Stonehenge. What's more... positive thinking also got me Xanthia!'

Donald's eyes narrowed.

'Okay... so, that last bit hasn't gone so well. But what I'm saying is... why should I give up now?'

Donald looked about himself in bemusement. 'Because you're going to be incarcerated in here for the rest of your life... however long that may turn out to be?'

'Then I'll escape,' said Norman in hushed tones.

'ESCAPE?' scoffed Donald loudly.

'Shhhhh!'

'And how are you going to do that?'

'I have absolutely no idea.'

'And clearly even less about what you'd do if you actually succeeded. You're forgetting... we no longer have my messages to help us, thanks to you... and Xanthia has sole control of your chequebook.' A thought struck him. 'Who knows... perhaps she used it to get the president to change his mind about me. After all... everyone has their price.'

'I don't!' Norman objected. 'I gave up everything I owned to ensure the Universe could continue... remember?'

'You did... and I'm sure you'll be well-recompensed when you finally transition to the other side. No grubby, lower levels for you, my boy.'

'They'll be no levels for *anyone,* if we fail!'

Donald nodded sagely. 'You're right. I was forgetting. I always assumed death would allow me to put faces to those who've been using me as a conduit all these years. I was even looking forward to meeting Whitebait in his natural habitat. But that'll all be denied me now.' He gave the matter some thought. 'Then again... regarding that cantankerous old trawlerman, perhaps it's for the best!'

Norman looked about anxiously as he spotted the telltale signs of an impending altercation.

'I'M SURE THE FEELING *IS* MUTUAL.' Donald yelled.

The noise in the canteen faltered.

'OH, REALLY? WELL... THAT'S HARDLY SURPRISING, IS IT? YOU'VE *ALWAYS* TAKEN THINGS THE WRONG WAY... EVER SINCE THAT DAY YOU FOISTED YOURSELF UPON ME!'

There was a pause.

'YES... *FOISTED.* AND FOR THE RECORD... I WASN'T INFERRING THAT *YOU* WERE PART OF THE GRUBBY, LOWER LEVELS.'

The canteen fell silent.

'ALRIGHT... THAT'S VERY HONEST OF YOU. AND THERE WAS I BEING DIPLOMATIC!'

'Prisoner Tucker-Jenkins... shut up and eat your food,' barked one of the guards through a bullhorn.

'Or what?' snapped back Donald testily, without the need for one. 'Are you *also* going to bypass my colon, just like Phyllis's lad over there with the illustrated ape arms?'

Norman sunk back into his bench

'Phyllis is my probation officer,' the ape in question corrected him.

'Then, it's a shame she didn't think to enrol you on a cookery course!'

'Right... that's it,' roared the guard, drawing his baton and storming towards Donald. 'You're about to have yourself a spell in solitary.'

'CHANCE WOULD BE A FINE THING!' yelled Donald, the remark tilted at Whitebait.

The canteen watched in amusement as Donald was yanked to his feet and roughly frogmarched away.

'IF YOU DO MANAGE TO KEEP YOUR INTENTION TO LEAVE THIS ESTABLISHMENT HIDDEN FROM THE GUARDS AND FINALLY EXECUTE YOUR ESCAPE PLAN' he shouted back at Norman, 'I HOPE YOU'RE RIGHT ABOUT THE POSITIVITY BIT.'

* * *

Reverend Humbold eyed the gun he'd hastily dropped and wondered how quickly it could be retrieved and pointed at the two gentlemen with whom he'd been left alone.

'I wouldn't try, if I were you,' advised AKA Mister Prometheus, reading his mind. 'You'll never make it.' Having sensibly retained hold of his own weapon, he demonstrated the fact by aiming it at his outmanoeuvred target.

'Now, just a second...' winced the reverend, pulling a silk handkerchief from his pocket and mopping a glistening brow. 'I fully appreciate why you might be of the mistaken belief I'm disadvantaged at this particular moment in time. But remember... I'm not here alone.'

'I know things got a little confusing a short while ago, but Papadopoulos is on *my* side,' pointed out AKA Mister Prometheus.

'I meant... we're being watched.'

Bob surveyed their surroundings and squinted. 'Are we to assume your taxi driver is an expert in camouflage?'

'I'm talking about the Lord God Almighty,' the reverend boomed with sudden confidence... the mystery observer's identity revealed in a tone implying They shouldn't be messed with. 'He is with us right now.'

'I don't see his gun,' said AKA Mister Prometheus dryly.

'But you'll feel the full power of his wrath,' the reverend hollered, stabbing his finger aggressively. His pink appendage wasn't as convincing as a gun, but he thought it was worth a try. 'For you will be made to atone for your sins, come judgement day.'

AKA Mister Prometheus shrugged. 'I can't see that one more of *those* is gonna make much difference.'

The reverend locked eyes with his opponent as he desperately tried to think of another strategy. 'It's not too late to repent of those sins,' he suddenly cried, lifting his hands skyward, 'For He will cleanse your soul and make it pure again. So... come join with me right now. Sink to your knees in humble contrition and beg the Lord's forgiveness.' As if to sell the suggestion, he helpfully demonstrated what was required... though it appeared to involve less a sinking and more a controlled lowering.

AKA Mister Prometheus turned to his bemused subordinate. 'Do you know what, Papadopoulos... I think on *this* occasion I'd be doing the Lord a favour.' He aimed his gun at the reverend's head.

'Sir?' interjected Bob hastily.

'Not now, Papadopoulos. Let's get this thing over with and get the hell outta this goddam place.'

'But you can't shoot a man in cold blood!'

'Oh... believe me, Papadopoulos... being in the presence of this particular individual, my blood has never felt warmer.'

'But he hasn't done anything wrong.'

'You mean... apart from holding a gun to the back of my head and threatening to remove it from my neck?'

'I was guided by God,' wept the reverend, clasping his hands for mercy.

'Well, if that's the case... and you're as innocent as Papadopoulos seems to think you are... you'll be rewarded with a place in Heaven. What more could someone of your profession wish for?'

The reverend fell forward and prostrated himself. 'Forgiveness?' he sobbed loudly.

'I'm not happy about this,' Bob said uneasily.

'You don't have to be. This isn't about you, Papadopoulos. Sometimes fate decrees we do things we're not comfortable with. You know I'm right. After all, you weren't so concerned about eliminating the girl.'

'That was different. It was part of our mission.'

'So is this. We're protecting its integrity. If you can't see that, maybe I need to reconsider your future.'

'You might want to reconsider yours,' said the reverend boldly, standing up and showing them the end of his retrieved gun.

'Oh, for Christ's sake.' AKA Mister Prometheus held the bridge of his nose.

'Thou shalt not blaspheme!' the reverend shouted angrily. 'You don't wanna offend me any further than you have. It's one of our Lord's sacred commandments.'

177

'So is *thou shalt not kill*... which is why I assume you've left your safety catch on.' AKA Mister Prometheus swiped the weapon from the reverend's trembling hands.

'I trust you'll understand I was guided by God in that last threat, too,' he squeaked.

'Enough of this. Get back on your knees and say what prayers you have to. I'll give you thirty seconds to make your peace.'

Mumbling incoherently to himself, the reverend did as he was told.

'Okay... time's up.'

'No... *please* don't!' Lunging forward, he fastened himself to AKA Mister Prometheus's legs and hugged them tightly. 'I'll pay you! I'll do anything you want! Just tell me what would please you most!'

AKA Mister Prometheus struggled to free himself.

The reverend clung on in desperation.

'Excuse me,' came a voice from the edge of the clearing.

AKA Mister Prometheus quickly hid his gun.

'I was wondering if you'd be much longer. Only... the meter's still running and I'm nearing the end of my shift.'

Unable to believe the Lord had answered his prayers, the reverend ecstatically released his grip. 'Oh, dear God... I'm coming now!' he shouted eagerly, attempting to stand.

AKA Mister Prometheus placed a firm hand on his shoulder. 'You're not going anywhere,' he hissed. 'You take care of the taxi driver, Papadopoulos. I'll see to this idiot.'

The reverend stayed where he was... as did Bob.

'Did you hear me, Papadopoulos?'

'I did, sir... and this *definitely* isn't right!'

AKA Mister Prometheus scowled irritably. 'Must I do them *both* myself?'

'It wouldn't normally be a problem,' called out the taxi driver, seeing a lack of action. 'But it's my daughter's birthday and I promised her I wouldn't be late. You know what it's like when they're little. It's a big deal for them.'

Bob locked eyes with AKA Mister Prometheus.

The bird in the tree above finally grabbed the opportunity to unleash his cinematically themed warble.

After a tense few seconds, AKA Mister Prometheus released his hand.

The reverend gingerly got to his feet.

'You can count yourself *extremely* lucky, Humbold,' whispered AKA Mister Prometheus aggressively. 'But I promise you this... if you *ever* mention what happened here to *anyone*, I will personally ensure you never get to preach again. And, next time... God won't be given the opportunity to answer your prayers. Do you understand?'

The reverend nodded obsequiously.

AKA Mister Prometheus gave the smallest flick of his head. 'Okay. Get outta here.'

As the reverend scrambled his way to safety, AKA Mister Prometheus turned to his subordinate. 'So, Papadopoulos... what happens now?'

*　　*　　*

'Who would've thought,' laughed Miss Eris, shaking her head in disbelief. 'What a novel place to keep something hidden. Mind you... I suppose it's the *last* place you'd think of looking for such an invaluable treasure. But... thanks to you... it won't be there for long.'

The old man groaned, his spirit broken.

'You see... it wasn't so painful, was it?' She looked about the temple. 'Though you might find this next bit is.'

He no longer cared what fate had in store for him. The secrets he'd carried for the best part of his life had slipped from his lips like mumbles from a troubled dream.

'Now you finally get to see what's in the box,' she teased.

Eyes struggling to stay open, he watched as the men who'd placed it on the central plinth carefully removed its lid.

'We suggest you retire to a safe distance, ma'am,' said one of them. 'There's always a risk attached to this initial phase of the operation.'

175

'You're right,' she nodded. 'We'll wait for you and your men in the Sikorsky. I'll tell the pilot to start its engines. I think an aerial view is going to be quite spectacular.'

'Are we not taking this gentlemen with us?' enquired Doctor Menzies, as she signalled for him to accompany her.

'I don't see how he can be of any further use to us,' she replied. 'Besides… there's not enough room for him.'

The doctor looked at her uncomfortably. 'Aren't we at least going to carry him outside to a point of safety?'

'And leave him in that unbearable sun?' she smiled. 'Doctor Menzies… there's a cruelty in you I find most attractive!'

'But, aren't we?' he frowned.

She shook her head. 'I believe our friend's sole reason for existing vanished at the same time as the contents of your syringe. I think, therefore, it would be more merciful if we left him here… don't you? At least, that way, he'll get to enjoy a ringside seat. Now, Doctor… let's leave these men to their work.'

The coordinated explosions that ripped the temple apart did so with such ferocity, not a stone was left standing. The courtyard that had been so carefully swept for centuries would remain strewn with rubble for however many were left.

*   *   *

'How can I be of help, gentlemen?'

The two men, smartly attired in black suits, stared at their inquisitor dispassionately.

'We've come to borrow two books from your prison library,' said one.

The governor's eyebrows rose just enough for it to be noticed.

'Is there a problem?' enquired the other.

'No, no, gentlemen. No problem at all. It's just that_'

'Ah, ah!' the first cautioned, raising a finger.

The governor's lips pursed.

'Shall we start again?'

The governor dutifully nodded.

There was a pause. 'We've come to borrow two books from your prison library.'

The governor responded as if reciting from a script. 'I trust your library ticket is up-to-date?' he asked robotically.

'It was renewed last fall,' came the prompt reply.

The governor exhaled testily. 'And what books would you like to borrow?'

'We're interested in anything by Norman Penkridge and Donald Tucker-Jenkins.'

The governor broke from his scripted exchange. 'Is this some sort of joke?'

'I beg your pardon?'

'I asked you gentlemen if this is a joke.'

The men in suits looked at each other uneasily.

'We insist you keep to the protocol,' instructed one.

'To hell with the protocol,' returned the governor, throwing up his hands.. 'It's bad enough we have to go through this goddam charade every time you request a loan of one of my inmates. But you might've bothered to coordinate this particular one with your own department... especially given the high celebrity status of one of those "books" you're wishing to borrow.'

'With respect, governor... the protocol is there for a very good reason.'

'I'm fully aware of the reason. I'm not exactly gonna get a request like yours in writing, *am* I? And I sure as hell don't expect you to be flashing any official paperwork at me to prove who you are and what you do. But now we've said enough to establish this request is genuine, and that I accept your authority to remove those men from my care, I think we can dispense with the cloak and dagger bullshit and safely move on. Though God knows I wish you'd return my prisoners in the state in which they're lent out to you. Some are sent back to this place no longer knowing who they are!'

'Governor! That part of the conversation did not happen. Walls have ears. So I suggest you keep to the protocol if you wish to remain in charge of the ones you've been given responsibility for.'

'You can threaten me as much as you like, sonny... but your protocol don't allow for a situation such as we've got here.'

'And what situation is that?'

The governor drew a calming breath. 'I don't have those particular "books" you want in my library.'

The men in suits looked at each other, confused.

'Are you telling us we've been sent to the wrong institution?' asked one.

'I'm telling you those books are already out on loan.'

'But they can't be,' exclaimed the other.

The governor delicately raised his hands to suggest they not only *could*, but *were*.

'You'd better explain yourself, Governor!'

'Very well,' he obliged. 'Between you and me and any ears these walls may have... someone's already beaten you to those books. They came here this morning... just like you... and requested they take them out.'

'And you simply obliged?'

'Of *course* I did.'

'But *why?*'

'Because I believed they were from your department.'

'*Believed?* Why the hell didn't you initiate the protocol to establish their authority? That's the reason it exists!'

'I did,' insisted the governor indignantly 'I followed the correct procedure, just as I've been instructed. Each statement and response given was word perfect... not a single syllable outta place. Everything was *exactly* as it should be.'

The larger of the two men stood and paced the room uncomfortably. 'I don't understand how that can be. No one else has been sent here from our team... so what you're telling us doesn't make sense. How could an impostor know the protocol and what to say? Such a thing is *impossible.*'

'Impostors,' said the governor, stressing the plural.

'There were two of them?'

'A man and a woman.'

'A *woman*?'

'I know,' nodded the governor. 'I was as surprised as you, given the nature of your work. But I guess the fairer sex can be just as cruel and ruthless as men.' He squinted awkwardly. 'No offence.'

'The ramifications of this don't bear thinking about!' exclaimed the one still seated. 'Not only has a colossal breach of security taken place... we now have two *extremely* dangerous individuals at large. The consequences could be catastrophic!'

'Knowing what these two men are accused of, we must take immediate action to ensure their recapture,' affirmed his colleague. 'Governor... we'll need a full description of those responsible.'

The governor tilted his head in thought. 'Well... when it comes to appearance... neither was as sharply dressed as the usual *bookworms* from your department... which I have to confess, *did* strike me as odd. I just assumed you guys were having a dress-down day.'

'This woman, in particular... did she have any distinguishing features?'

'You mean... apart from the obvious?'

There was a curt nod.

'Well... it was a little hard to tell, given she'd chosen to wear a scarf over her head... not to mention an enormous pair of dark glasses.'

'You didn't find that odd?'

'No more than having to pretend I'm a librarian,' replied the governor with pointed sarcasm.

'And her companion?'

'The same thing.'

'He wore a *scarf*?'

'I was referring to the glasses.'

'Both of them... wearing sunglasses indoors... and you considered that perfectly normal behaviour?'

'With respect, gentlemen... I don't consider *anything* your department does as *normal* behaviour. I merely assumed it was part of the uniform. You're a law unto yourselves and an understandably secretive bunch. I mean, let's face it... it's not as if you're ever going to send out Christmas cards.'

'I trust you'll have a record of these interlopers on CCTV?'

'Of course. There are numerous cameras between here and the main gate. You're more than welcome to take a copy of everything we've got... though I wouldn't pin your hopes on it being *that* useful. I've been requesting an update to our system for years. It's like watching an overused 1970's porn video cassette through a jar of Vaseline. Not that I know what that's like, of course.' He drummed his fingers on the desk. 'Now... seeing as that's as much help as I believe I'm able to provide... you gentlemen will have to excuse me. It's time to undertake my daily inspection. It's important I check the *other* books are exactly where they should be... all lined up nice and neatly on my shelves and strictly adhering to the Dewey Decimal System.'

*   *   *

Had Donald been able to press himself any further into the rear corner of the car without causing himself serious injury, he would have.

'Surely you believe me now,' said Xanthia addressing him from the front passenger seat. 'I've come to your rescue, haven't I? If I were as evil as you seem to think, I'd have simply let you rot in jail. Without our intervention, there's no *way* you and Norman would've ever seen freedom again. And believe me... given what the agents Chad and I impersonated get up to on a regular basis, that would've been the *least* of your worries!'

Donald chose to say nothing, his bulging eyes doing his talking for him.

'You have to admit, she's got a point,' Norman conceded. 'Twenty-four hours ago I was lying on a cold, hard bed convinced life was over. Now look at us... we're *free*.'

'Not quite,' cautioned Chad from the driver's seat. 'You'll now have every law enforcement agency in this country hunting you down. As far as the authorities are concerned… us springing you like we did has simply sealed your guilt.'

Donald let out one of his private squeals.

'And don't think you're off the hook with me, either,' she said, flashing Norman a reproachful stare. 'I've merely corrected an injustice, that's all.'

'Which means they'll also be after the two of you,' he pointed out. 'You're now as guilty as us in their eyes.'

'I was anyway,' she shrugged, 'thanks to Galveston Humbold's over-imaginative PR team and a little bit of high-level corruption. But it's not a problem anymore. They think I'm dead… or will do, soon.'

Norman looked at her in astonishment.

'It's a long story. I'll explain later.'

'We need to think about changing this car,' advised Chad. 'As soon as they realise we weren't who we claimed to be, this thing will be more dangerous to be sat in than Bonnie and Clyde's Ford Deluxe when the authorities finally caught up with *them*.'

Xanthia inhaled sharply and grabbed at her chest. 'For all her bravado when she was with him, she was so frightened in those final moments, you know,' she wheezed.

Chad momentarily took his eyes from the road and looked at her, stunned. 'Really? You can do that? You can *actually* put yourself in another person's shoes?'

'I can… and, trust me… my view of history will never be the same again! That's the curse of this gift. I see it all… which is why I'm *trying* to see less and less. Perspective plays havoc with your judgement. It starts to blur the line between what's right and wrong. So… let's change the subject. Turn right at the next exit and take the second left.'

'Why? Where are we going?'

'The home of someone called Edith Halshore. She's a creature of habit and will be playing bridge at her neighbour Jean's house right now. She naively hangs the keys to her Buick

169

on a hook in an unlocked garage. It's always topped up with gasoline in case of an emergency. Having just spent a few moments in *her* shoes, I reckon she'll agree this *is* one. And, in case you're wondering... seeing as I still have enough judgement to know where that line between right and wrong is, we'll slip a note through her mailbox promising she'll be more than generously reimbursed as soon as we get our finances sorted.'

* * *

To any reasonable alien, there was only one thing worse than sitting on a planet with absolutely nothing on it... and that was sitting on a planet with absolutely nothing on it except a feeling of ill will.

In the case of Alien Two, there were *two* things worse... sitting on a planet with absolutely nothing on it except a feeling of ill will... and sitting on a planet with absolutely nothing on it except a feeling of ill will and being unable to do anything about it.

Despite it being God's wish he hurt Aliens One and Three, he hadn't actually managed to work out how.

His main problem was that Alien One seemed to be the ideas man... and Alien Two could hardly ask *him*.

Unperturbed, he concluded that God would appreciate his dilemma and provide him with a solution. In the meantime, he'd just have to sit and wait.

Alien One had been busy staring out into the vast sky, the way he always did before announcing something profound. Having concluded his pondering, he said he'd been considering Alien Three's hypothetical second god scenario. Instead of finding it hilarious, he now realised it couldn't be dismissed, as to do so would invalidate his original logic behind the *first* god coming into being.

Despite Alien Two's delight at Alien One no longer finding Alien Three funny... proving comedy wasn't as easy as one might think... he couldn't simply ignore God's command to make them suffer.

Alien Three... *also* delighted that Alien One was no longer laughing at him... adopted a smug look.

Alien One immediately wiped it off his face by saying there was a *but*.

Alien Two glimpsed the hand of God in Alien Three's sudden disappointment.

Alien One stated you couldn't have two supreme beings at the same time as that would be silly. The clue was in the name.

Alien Two agreed... not only to please the *one* supreme God... but to add to Alien Three's discomfort. A win, win, in his book.

Alien One suggested there were two possible solutions to the conundrum. The first being... no god was all powerful. It had been a mistake to make that assumption in the first place.

Alien Three asked him what the second one was.

Alien One looked at Alien Three awkwardly and replied he might have a little trouble getting his head around it.

Alien Three tutted and said he wasn't Alien Two.

Alien One explained it entailed accepting everyone inhabited their own individual universe, the state and rules of which could be affected by thoughts... but that those universes existed together in a way he had yet to devise. Suffice to say... he would be doing a lot more staring at the sky in the coming days.

Alien Three said that... given he didn't have a clue what Alien One was talking about... the first option sounded more plausible.

Equally confused, Alien Two said Alien One was a tiresome idiot who was just trying to make out he was cleverer than them.

Alien One's face contorted with pain.

Alien Three asked him what the matter was.

Alien One replied that Alien Two's comment had really hurt him.

167

Alien Two broke into a broad grin. He *knew* God wouldn't let him down.

*   *   *

Norman leant back against the warm bonnet of the Buick and marvelled at the behemoth of a building in front of him, as the final rays of sunlight brushed shadows across its tired Art Deco façade. 'What on earth *is* this place?'

'Headquarters,' announced Chad, 'as well as home, for the time being.'

'Headquarters?'

'We'll come to that bit later.'

Norman squinted at four enormous chimneys sprouting from its roof. 'I assume it's a factory of some sort.'

'A disused power station, actually,' said Xanthia.

'I admit it's unconventional,' Chad nodded, 'but there's no way we can risk having you stay at any place that has my name attached to it. The minute those we've given a bloody nose to work out my involvement in your escape... and they *will*... they'll have surveillance on every location I've ever visited or think I'm likely to. This place is conveniently off grid in more ways than one. They won't *dream* of looking for us here. We can rest safely and plan our next move.'

'You don't think a nice, quiet, out-of-the-way hotel would've been better suited?' remarked Donald stiffly.

Chad looked at him askew. 'You kiddin' me? Do you know the stink the arrest of the world's greatest, living playwright has caused... not to mention the reason for it happening in the first place? You and Norman are now the hottest topic of conversation in the media since Xanthia's arrival on these shores. The extra news you've slipped your chains is gonna have everyone looking out for you and hoping to catch a glimpse. On top of which, your mugshots will be on every check-in screen in this country. You need to understand how serious your predicament is.'

'I know *exactly* how serious it is, thank you very much!' he retorted, eyeing Xanthia nervously.

'Being here at least buys us some time,' said Chad.

'For what?' Donald sulked.

'Saving the world. We can now all work together as a team.'

'I think that's an *excellent* idea,' enthused Norman.

'Talking of which... there's something I haven't told you. I thought I'd wait for the appropriate moment... and this seems as good as any. We won't be alone in our task. I've been put in contact with the folk behind that magical chequebook of yours. The Templars are a global network of powerful and influential individuals willing to assist us in more ways than finance. All they're waiting for is a call to arms from Xanthia.'

'It gets even better,' said Norman excitedly.

Xanthia didn't respond.

'We'll talk more about it later. But first, we need to get ourselves inside. My colleague Brandon's waiting for us. I'll come back and dispose of the car.'

'This colleague of yours... he's obviously someone you think you can trust,' said Norman, as they headed towards the building.

'Yes... I'm curious to know how *that* particular alliance came to be,' remarked Xanthia. 'Despite our initial interaction, he's certainly proven more affable than your *previous* partner.'

'I got a call outta the blue,' Chad explained. 'Brandon told me he was having a crisis of conscience. He wanted my advice. Our paths had briefly crossed at Langley, where he says he remembers me as having a reputation for always trying to do the right thing.' He shrugged. 'Funny... I simply thought I was doing my job until I discovered the two were incompatible! Anyhow... he figured I'd make a trustworthy confidant. Having just returned from an extremely enlightening trip, where someone else had come to that same conclusion, his call couldn't have been more apposite... not to mention *timely*, in your case, Xanthia. When he explained what he was up to, I instantly knew it stank, having been in a similar situation myself. It was one of his boss's so-called *off-the-record* ops that

165

not only put an end to my career, but nearly put an end to Norman. Given the lengths I knew he'd go to in order to maintain its secrecy, I realised you were in mortal danger. When Brandon told me he'd been tasked with buying a spade, it was clear we needed to act immediately. The rest you know for yourself.'

She linked her arm around his. 'I'm truly grateful for everything you've both done. Not only for selflessly putting *yourselves* in danger... but for finding us this sanctuary.'

'Headquarters,' he grinned.

She was about to gently suggest he might want to lower his expectations when Brandon appeared, enthusiastically beckoning them through a side door in the building.

'The plan worked, then,' he beamed, as they followed him inside.

'Like clockwork,' confirmed Chad.

'Welcome, everyone! I trust you'll make yourselves at home here.'

Given the scale of decay and detritus confronting them, Norman figured Donald would have no problem doing just that. All the place lacked, to complete that homely touch for the playwright, were a few random bowls of rancid milk strewn across the floor and the ever-present stench of cats' urine.

Despite the less-than-satisfactory conditions, Norman was impressed. They were standing in a debris-strewn corridor that wove itself around a colossal central hall... an awe-inspiring space whose sole purpose had been to house the beating heart of the building... or *four* hearts, to be precise. These once-proud turbines – now entombed as rusting hulks – had proven too big to be removed by metal scavengers or souvenir hunters. Everything else had been fair game. Rooms adjoining the corridors had long since been divested of their purpose... with wires now hanging pointlessly from control panels stripped of their dials, and vandalised furniture mingling with sections of fallen ceiling littering the floors.

'Chad and I figured, not only would this place have an infinite number of places to hide, we'd get ample warning if disturbed.' Brandon whistled loudly so as to allow the competing echoes to demonstrate his point. 'You just need to be careful where you tread. Most of what's around us has very little holding it together!'

'A metaphor for this group, I'd suggest,' muttered Donald sourly.

'We'll need to get hold of some basic provisions, of course,' added Chad. 'Food, camp beds, blankets... that sort of thing. Brandon and I haven't exactly had time to prepare for this stay, so don't expect miracles. Bank cards would be instantly traced, and the cash we *did* manage to withdraw before coming here won't last long.'

'Well, don't expect me to be of any help with that side of things,' warned Donald. 'Having been labelled a terrorist, they've frozen my assets. There's no chance of me being able to fund us.'

'None of that's a problem,' said Norman positively. 'Xan... I take it you still have my chequebook?'

'*Your* chequebook?'

'*Ours,*' he acquiesced.

'*Mine,* actually,' she corrected him. 'You made it perfectly clear you didn't want any part of it... remember?'

He conceded the point with a gracious nod. 'All the same... I assume you managed to hang on to it?'

'Of course I did. What do you think bras are for?'

'In that case, if Chad and Brandon's pooled finances can stretch to a second-hand laptop and some form of portable internet connection, I'll use my hacking skills to set up an American bank account under a pseudonym. Assuming they'll have frozen my bank account too, we'll courier a healthy cheque to my old friend, the Provider, and get him to deposit it into his own account and make an international bank transfer to my new one. That should keep us ticking over for a while. We'll be able to get whatever we want after that.'

'Perhaps someone could show me to my room whilst you're sorting it out,' said Donald. 'It's been quite a stressful day and I'd quite like to get some rest.' He looked up at the crumbling ceiling. 'FOREVER THE DRAMA QUEEN. I FAIL TO SEE HOW ON EARTH IT COULD POSSIBLY APPLY TO YOU *TOO*. YOU'VE BEEN DEAD FOR OVER A HUNDRED YEARS!'

Brandon waved his hand at the surrounding squalor. 'Take your pick, Donald. As you can see, there are many options. You might have to improvise a little regarding a bed until we get that side of things sorted, but you won't find yourself short on space.'

'As for us... we need to talk... *alone*,' said Xanthia, giving Norman a look that suggested it wasn't going to be a pleasant one. 'But perhaps it's best left 'til the morning. Like Donald, I'm exhausted and would rather have that conversation on a clearer head.'

'I think that's eminently sensible,' he concurred sheepishly. 'Though I doubt *I'll* get much sleep tonight, given what I believe you're going to say to me.'

'Oh, you have no idea,' she said. 'And I promise you this... it'll be far worse than you can *possibly* imagine.'

*   *   *

'Tell your mistress that Galveston Humbold the Third wants to see her... *immediately!*' barked the reverend unsociably close to the maid's face.

'Is she expecting you?' the poor woman flinched.

'At this time of night? I hardly think so!'

'Who is it, Claire?' came a voice from atop an ornate, cantilevered staircase that wrapped its way around part of a magnificent entrance hall.

'It's that man from the television, madam. The one who's always asking for money so that you'll get to meet Jesus when you die.'

'You mean... *Galveston Humbold?*'

'That's what he said.'

'At this time of night?'

'He said *that* as well.'

'This is most irregular,' Miss Eris scowled, hurriedly descending the stairs.

'Shall I let him in?'

Not bothering to wait, the reverend barged past the maid. 'I don't intend debating the issue!'

'Do you want me to call security, madam?'

Miss Eris strode purposefully across the chequered hall, like a queen about to annihilate a pawn, and fronted her unexpected guest. 'That won't be necessary. We'll be in the drawing room. Go and put some coffee on.'

'This late, madam?'

'Just do it!' She stared at the reverend coldly. 'I wasn't sleeping anyway. I'm suffering from jet lag.'

'You'll be sleeping even less when you hear what it is I have to say,' he drawled through a mouth angled to imply impending shock.

'This better be worth my time,' she hissed, ushering him into the drawing room. 'What do you mean coming here to my private residence? Our relationship is strictly business.'

'That may be. But, seeing as I was unable to arrange a meeting with you at your offices… and no one had the courtesy to tell me why, I thought I'd bypass your minions and come direct.'

'I've been away attending to matters in far more exotic climes. I've only just returned, so you're fortunate to have caught me. But now you have, you'd better explain yourself before my maid returns with our coffee and an all too keen set of ears.'

'With pleasure… though I doubt you'll find that particular turn of phrase appropriate in this instance.'

'I'm listening.'

'It's about that child of Satan… Xanthia.'

Miss Eris stuck out a hand. 'Stop right there. That girl's of no importance to me anymore.'

The reverend reeled back in amazement. 'Of no *importance*? But you said she'd come to destroy the world!'

'She'd come to destroy *my* world,' Miss Eris corrected him. 'But, now I'm about to have delivered into my possession something that makes her an irrelevance, I no longer need her services.'

The reverend's face contorted further. '*Need* her? What in the name of Christendom are you talkin' about? No one *needs* evil like that.'

She sighed with the lateness of the hour. 'Oh, come on Galveston... you *know* she isn't the wicked monster you've been making her out to be. You exaggerated for effect to line your pockets and enhance your reputation. There's nothing wrong with that. But please don't tell me you've started believing your own hype.'

'I *might've* coloured things up an incy-wincy bit,' he conceded awkwardly, 'but you're the one who told me she was up to no good.'

'I told you she was a threat to you... and to me... and she was.'

'That's exactly what I'm sayin'! It was *you* who brought her to my attention. You came to me and said I should warn the folk of this country that she was a godless harlot who was peddling blasphemous claims.'

'Because I knew it would be good for your ratings... and I was right, wasn't I?'

'I won't deny that. And I can plain see why you chose to do so. Your RISE corporation has benefited big-time as a major sponsor of my shows.'

'Any publicity generated was simply a bonus,' she dismissed the comment.

'*Bonus?*' The reverend squinted incredulously. 'If you believe that girl *ain't* dangerous, what in tarnation *other* reason could there be for persuading me to have her spout her vile falsehoods to the good people of this nation?'

'Like I told you... I *needed* her. She might not be evil, but she definitely possesses the powers she says she does. Sorry to shatter that over-inflated ego of yours, Galveston, but you were nothing more than a worm on my line. You were simply a means of luring her to a country where I could access the knowledge in her head. My corporation might be international and its influence global, but what I had planned for her was far more easily achieved on home soil.'

'Well, as you've raised the subject of soil… I take exception to being likened to something that wriggles on its belly through it! So you might wanna recant that egregious insult and *then* ask me why it is I've bothered calling on you at such an unsociable hour.'

'I was hoping you'd get to that bit,' she yawned.

'Okay… well here's *another* bonus for ya. It's news that'll make you wise up to the *real* threat that girl poses.' His neck twitched in direct proportion to the alarm he believed he was about to unleash. 'She really *is* as dangerous as I've been telling people. So much so, our government don't just wanna deport her or lock her up… they've figured the safest option for the well-being of this country would be to stick her in a hole in the ground… permanently. Now… it don't get more serious than *that* when looking to defend this nation's security. Furthermore… if *that* don't raise your heart rate a little… she's currently out there running amok in this beautiful and sacred land of ours!'

Miss Eris glanced at a marble casement clock on the mantelpiece. 'Not anymore,' she said casually. 'I've had her dealt with myself.'

'*Dealt with?*' the reverend snorted. 'I doubt that. Even those dumb-arsed feds haven't been able to put a stop to her.'

'What are you talking about?' she frowned.

'Those government thugs who stole her from my show… well, it seems they've *really* gone and messed things up. It was bad enough they had to stick their snouts in my business, just as I was on the brink of saving the world by annihilating that temptress and making her utterances an irrelevance.'

Miss Eris raised her hand dismissively. 'Before you go any further, Galveston… I watched that whole, sorry debacle. Take it from me… I knew full well that girl would tear you to shreds. You can count yourself lucky I spared your blushes by having

159

her removed before she crucified you in front of your gullible viewers and ended that sham career of yours forever.'

Her outburst brought such an awkward silence, the clock on the mantelpiece winced as it was obliged to move its minute hand.

'You did... *what?*'

'Oh, you needn't thank me, Galveston. My reasons were purely selfish. Having Xanthia appear on your show not only guaranteed her whereabouts, it provided the ideal environment for having her taken by surprise and seized. It was the *last* thing she was expecting that day.'

The reverend stared in complete stupefaction. 'You mean... it was *you?*'

Miss Eris nodded.

'You wouldn't happen to be in league with an imbecilic writer from the Kingdom of United England who goes around masquerading as a tin soldier... *would* you?' he drawled slowly.

'Not unless he also masquerades as a god,' she answered. 'You see... I managed to persuade certain associates of mine... who *do*... to exert their influence and have her detained. I convinced them her head contained valuable ideas well above a fridge magnet slogan telling us to love one another. While they saw their actions as a research and development opportunity, I was after *far* more profitable truths. That girl possessed the ability to unlock secrets I knew would give me unrivalled power over everyone and everything on this planet!'

Still struggling to process the betrayal, the reverend watched dumbfounded as the woman responsible closed her eyes and temporarily appeared to forget she had company. Her quivering facial features suggested she was savouring the thought of such a glorious prospect. He'd seen similar expressions of ecstasy before, but usually in movies you wouldn't want your children to watch.

'Would you kindly close that mouth of yours,' she said, when done. 'I believe you've just dribbled on my carpet.'

He did as he was told.

'Regrettably,' she continued, 'that troublesome girl refused to cooperate. It appears she was smarter and more resilient than I anticipated.' She looked at him dispassionately. 'So I agreed to have her eliminated.' She glanced at the clock on the mantelpiece again. 'The deed will have been done by now. I think it safe to say we can *both* sleep soundly tonight.'

The reverend's left eyebrow rose in objection.

Miss Eris honed in on it. 'What's *that* supposed to mean?'

'Well... assuming the Federal agents your "associates" managed to persuade to steal her from my show were the exact same ones who had her standing in that hole I just talked about, not more than twenty-four hours ago, I'd say they either ain't reported back yet... or they've been mighty economical with the truth if they have. And if you're wondering how I can be so sure... I was actually there with them when they tried to bury that she-devil! What's more... the guy in charge of the whole fiasco was looking to do the same to *me* so as to cover up the fact he'd let her slip his clutches.'

Miss Eris' face fell. 'Not for the first time,' she muttered through clenched teeth. 'Prometheus... you incompetent imbecile.'

The reverend's ears caught the name. '*That's* the name Xanthia uttered before I intervened.'

'I don't doubt it.' growled Miss Eris. 'I *told* him she would know everything about us!'

'Prometheus is one of your so-called *gods?*'

'He was supposed to put an end to her interfering.'

'Well... you should've kept to your side of our arrangement and left that to me. I might only be a mortal in your eyes, but at least she wouldn't be free to do whatever she likes. Those fools you hired didn't even have the commonsense to see she was lying when she professed a desire to fade from public view so as to facilitate her escape. I've never seen such gullibility. But she can't fool me!'

Miss Eris made a downward sweeping gesture with her hands, as if brushing her annoyance with Prometheus away. 'None of this matters anymore,' she said, taking a deep breath and turning to face the door. 'Now... where's that maid with our coffee?'

The reverend struggled to comprehend her indifference. 'How can you be so relaxed about this whole affair? That girl didn't just *escape*... she was *rescued*... by two men who seemed to have a worryingly close connection to those federal henchmen you'd tasked with killing her. So, if *that* don't set alarm bells ringing for you and your god-masquerading associates...'

Miss Eris spun angrily and fixed him with her wolf-grey eyes, her sudden change of countenance instantly chilling the room. 'How *dare* you lecture me on how I should react or what I need fear!' she spat. 'Your naive, pathetic, backward, little mind has no comprehension of what will shortly come to be. That girl is no more than an annoying fly in the ointment. But she's finished. For I'm being guided by a force that will crush whatever opposition she cares to put up against it. Its coming has been predicted for millennia, as has my part in those ancient scriptures. I am about to have delivered into my possession a treasure so great it will render her powers worthless. It will enable me to unleash the full potential of that glorious force and give me control over every living thing on this Earth! People will eat when I say they eat... starve when I say they starve... dance to every tune I care to play. Not even the heavens will be able to stop me.' She closed her eyes. 'I will no longer have to masquerade as a god... I will BE one!'

The reverend wondered if she was going to pull another one of her special faces.

'So... where does that leave *you*, I wonder?' she said ominously, slowly opening them again.

He pulled his own face.

'Don't worry,' she sneered. 'There *is* still a job you can do for me. I haven't finished with you yet. You're going to be my mouthpiece. The world is about to change forever. The public will need someone reassuringly familiar to prepare them for their journey... and I've now given you the perfect platform for

156

doing that. Aside from the fame you've always craved, you'll be suitably recompensed, of course.'

He stared at her open-mouthed.

'Carpet!' she reminded him.

*   *   *

'I can't get over the sheer scale of this place,' marvelled Norman, from a walkway overlooking the four gigantic, slumbering turbines below.

Sitting eerily silent among the sprawling decay, their only role now was to remind the curious trespasser of why such a cathedral-like space had been built in the first place. Any pretence of activity was down to random, flickering shafts of light taking advantage of the vast expanse of shattered roofing above and dappling their rusted ironwork.

'Did you manage to sleep?' enquired Brandon.

'Not a lot,' he yawned.

'It'll be better when we get some beds.'

'It wasn't the hardness of the floor that kept me awake. It was the thought of all the explaining I'm gonna have to do to Xanthia this morning.'

Brandon smiled. 'She found it in herself to forgive *me*. I'm sure she'll do the same for you.'

Norman sensibly removed his weight from the corroded rail on which he'd been leaning. 'By the way... have you seen Donald this morning?'

'Not since he took himself off last night. He told me he wanted to be alone.'

'I guess that's to be expected, given it's his default setting. I think it's gonna take him a while to come to terms with things. He just needs time to sort it all out in his head.'

'From what Chad's been telling me... that's a pretty busy place at the best of times!' laughed Brandon. 'I understand it gets quite crowded.'

'I know. So much for him being alone. I doubt *that's* ever gonna happen!'

'Talking of privacy...' Brandon signalled Xanthia's approach. 'I guess I'd best leave you two to it.' He winked and made a diplomatic departure via the opposite end of the walkway.

'Good morning,' said Norman as she reached him.

'I think you'll find it *won't* be,' she replied.

He thought it best to counter the comment with a look of contrition, consoling himself with the fact that at least his sleepless night appeared to have been warranted. 'I know you're angry with me, Xan... and totally understand why. But you can't blame me for thinking the way I did. I'd had Donald constantly bleating in my ears about how dangerous he believed you to be... compounded by that fake news story of your altercation with someone I assumed to be Gabriel. Seeing those emails between you and Kevin simply tipped me over the edge.'

'Therein lies the problem,' she grimaced. 'Tipping points. Yours wasn't the only one.'

He looked at her blankly.

'We've always known the battle ahead would boil down to a struggle for supremacy between positive and negative vibrations,' she said.

'We *have*,' he drew out cautiously.

'We also knew those vibrations were finely balanced... the reason Gabriel couldn't materialise and help. That meant there was little time for dithering *or* margin of error.'

He immediately spotted an opportunity to get off his back foot and gain the initiative. 'Which is precisely what I've been telling you for ages. So, let's draw a line under what's previously happened. It's essential we put any negative events behind us and move on.'

'Well... it's a shame you didn't follow your own advice in that hotel foyer the other day,' she cut him down. 'Because the fork you took there turned out to be that other tipping point I referred to... but one of *far* greater consequence.' Her eyes locked onto his, so as to steady him for her next utterance. 'In a nutshell, Normy... it's over... and I'm not just talking about our relationship. We've been defeated. It was the point at which negativity finally triumphed and our battle was lost. There's no point in fighting anymore. It's simply now a question of waiting for the end.'

He laughed nervously. 'No point in fighting? What are you talking about, Xan? Don't be daft. How could *one* stupid moment be such a definitive point? It was nothing more than a silly misunderstanding.'

She gave a look that suggested otherwise.

'Oh... come on!' he remonstrated. 'You can't be serious. I was confused at the time. It's obvious I've now changed my mind about you. I was wrong to think what I did. I'll shout it from this gallery if you like and send out all the positive vibrations needed to atone for my error. Surely that's all that matters? We need to move on and turn the balance back in our favour while we still can... before it's too late... as a team... you, me, Chad... Brandon... even Donald, if we can get him to come to his senses.'

Her expression remained the same. 'You're not listening. That's what I'm saying... it *is* too late.'

Norman was unsure how to respond. The best he could do was a half-smile that felt totally inappropriate given her reaction to it.

'There's no going back,' she confirmed stony-faced.

'Yes there is,' he snorted. 'The other side don't get to win simply because of one foolish moment on my part. If I inadvertently created a negative vibration which tipped the scales against us, I'll tip them back in our favour with as many *positive* ones as it requires. Just tell me what to say or do. That's the nature of balance... it can shift either way.'

She shook her head. 'This one can't, Normy. Not anymore.'

He peered at her incredulously, '*What?*'

'I don't think you fully understand. The tipping point I'm referring to isn't of an irreversibly calamitous change in the Universe's spiritual equilibrium. Precarious as it is, such a thing has yet to occur. It would be hubris indeed to think that you, Norman Penkridge, had also been given the responsibility for determining *that*. The tipping point I'm talking about is the instant you made me realise there's absolutely nothing I can do to prevent it happening. Being privileged... and cursed... to experience mankind's thinking from every conceivable angle, I've come to the inescapable conclusion it can't be saved... *ergo* an apocalyptic outcome is inevitable.'

He stared at her askance. 'Xan... what on earth are you talking about? You know that's not true! Why do you think so much effort went into producing the sphere of knowledge in the first place? It was done so everything *could* be saved. You're supposed to use it to put things right.'

She returned a look of anguish. 'That's what I'm telling you... the very thing that was created to help me do just that is the exact same thing that's allowed me to see it's impossible. The fork you took the other day finally confirmed it.'

His eyes widened. 'Hang on a second. You're not blaming *me* for you thinking we should simply give up.'

'It's not a question of blame, Normy... *or* giving up. It's a cold, hard fact. Like you said... the sphere of knowledge was gifted to a mortal because it was believed they'd be better placed to understand their own kind and use its power to change things for the good. But there was a major flaw in that plan. It assumed mankind *could* be changed. You may not want to accept it, but, having braved the darker recesses of its collective mind, I now know it *can't.*'

She was right. He didn't want to accept it... *any* of it. 'If Gabriel could materialise, I think he'd have something to say about that,' he objected forcefully.

'I'm sure he would,' she shrugged. 'But as much as he once failed to grasp the concept of time, it seems his spiritual form makes him unable to comprehend just how powerful the lure of ego is.'

Norman didn't see it made any difference. 'Even if so... there are millions of people out there who *haven't* lost a connection with their soul. They live fair, honest, decent lives. That must count for something... otherwise this battle would've been over eons ago.'

'I couldn't agree more. The world *is* full of good people, all as appalled at what's happening around them as you and me. But it's no longer enough. Because there are others seeking to take advantage of a glaring anomaly in the struggle between positivity and negativity.' She stepped closer and grabbed his arm. 'Remember the Devil telling you in Stump's bedroom that it was an uneven playing field we'd been given?'

He was hardly likely to forget.

'Well... what he *didn't* say was that it's weighted very much in *his* favour when it comes to good versus bad. You only have to look at it logically. An entire drinking well is made unusable by a single drop of poison... but the smallest vial of toxin cannot be purified by a single drop of water. That one-way arrow of inequity is inherent in every situation you can think of... even thoughts and actions. A spotless reputation can be tarnished forever by one foolish moment... but a life of wrongdoing can't be assuaged through a lone act of charity. Even a cathedral built over centuries, that's stood proudly for countless more, can be easily reduced to rubble in a few explosive moments of madness. And I shouldn't have to remind *you* that a priceless work of art – crafted by a lifetime of skills – can be rendered worthless in a matter of seconds.'

Norman winced as he recalled the fate of the unfortunate Turner.

'Even nature itself isn't immune to that unfairness. A tree spanning generations can be uprooted in the blink of an eye by an angry gust of wind... and an entire forest ravaged by flames from a single spark. I won't *begin* to bore you with entropy and the laws of thermodynamics... but, suffice to say... the odds have always been heavily stacked against the survival of the Universe and everything in it.' She splayed her arms. 'Yet... here we are... making this life we've been given all the more remarkable... and any self-destructive tendencies the human race has, all the more unforgivable.'

He stared at her in shock.

'So you see... as great as the power behind such an incredible gift is, that anomaly is why it doesn't take much for a few lost souls to cause disproportionate mayhem in the world. Their actions are like that single drop of poison... contaminating everything that's good. It's also why the devil stands on the brink of annihilating the very power that created him in the first place.'

'Well... at least it clears up *that* little mystery,' exclaimed Norman. 'I never *could* figure out how he'd been allowed to get this far. I mean... he was only supposed to *test* us!'

'Yes... and it appears we failed.'

Norman chewed his lip. 'But hang on a second... *that's* the bit I refuse to accept.'

Xanthia thought he might.

'Despite that anomaly, there has to be a host of people out there operating on the cusp between good and bad,' he insisted. 'Their vibrations must constantly fluctuate between those two states, meaning they ultimately contribute to *neither*. If we could win just a *fraction* of those over to our side, surely it would be enough to tip the balance in our favour.'

'Which was precisely my plan,' she nodded. 'While never assuming it would be easy, it transpired my cautious pessimism was wildly optimistic. Many of those you talk about are the people you pass in the street and assume to be just like you and me. But here's the thing, Normy... I've seen beyond those socially manicured expressions and it's not a pretty sight. Everywhere I've looked I've ended up battered and bruised by festering anger, hidden jealousies, repressed desires, greed and unbelievable levels of selfishness... all cloaked by a perceived normality. From the pettiest one-upmanship to the deepest, darkest thoughts that must even frighten those who have them... you can't begin to imagine the chaotic swirl of negative forces at work in some people's heads. I had no idea! *That's* what we're now seeing surfacing around the world. The gloves are finally off. People have become emboldened as they find their negative feelings validated by the selfish actions of others. That poison I talked about is spreading exponentially.' Her eyes momentarily brightened. 'But, despite all that... I *still* believed I could make a difference. That's why reinstating the chequebook was so important. I knew fighting such an uphill battle wouldn't come cheap... but was confidant it could be done.' For a brief moment her thoughts drifted to a world where she'd achieved that dream... until the sudden flight of a bird from the rafters broke her from it. She looked at him forlornly. 'And then you went and made your choice on that crucial fork of yours... and I realised... I was *wrong*.'

He stared at her in stunned silence.

'I figured if someone who loved me as much as *you* did no longer trusted what I had to say, what chance anybody else? If a person fortunate enough to have been counselled in the ways of Heaven and the power of positive thinking by none other than the Archangel Gabriel himself could get it so badly wrong, what hope the rest of the world?' She met his eyes with a sadness that cut into his soul. 'That... Norman... was *my* tipping point.'

He swore he felt the whole of Heaven sigh with her. Mouth agape, he gazed in stupefaction at the shattered remains of the once proud power station and wondered if there could ever have been a more apposite place to receive such devastating news.

She watched him carefully processing the facts, knowing how hard the thought of failure being laid at his door would hit him. She hadn't done it to be unkind. The truth was the truth.

He seemed to know it too. Far from objecting to her judgement, he continued wrestling with what he'd been told. When finally done, he took a deep, decisive breath.

'Xan... if you think I've gone through everything I have in the last five years just to throw in the towel and admit defeat, you've got another thing coming!' He clenched his fist. 'I've been stabbed... metaphysically disembodied... almost burnt alive... *twice*... made homeless... *twice*... thrown in jail... forced to give up every possession I've ever owned... and, worse than all of those combined... endured a night in Bostock Tucker-Jenkins' *stained-with-god-knows-what* bed sheets! So... let me tell you this... and any of those dark forces who care to be listening in. There's no *way* a red-scaled, foul-breathed, smirking, cloven

149

excuse of a shit vibration… and everything he represents… is going to get the better of me… Norman Penkridge. I'll be the first to admit I'm as guilty as the next man of letting some of that poison seep into my thoughts and cloud my judgement. But it's never stopped me from aspiring to be *better*. So, I refuse to believe it's not the same for many of those vibrationally challenged individuals who've shocked you into submission. In which case… there might just be a glimmer of hope.' He looked at her resolutely. 'And while there's *that*… I, for one, won't be giving in!'

She shook her head and sighed heavily. 'Gabriel was right… you never were much good at listening, were you?'

* * *

Alien Two had opted to sit alone… purposefully distancing himself from Alien One and Alien Three. It was so small a distance, they actually hadn't noticed. But in Alien Two's head, the gulf between them was immense. *He* hadn't let his thoughts become corrupted by *ideas*. He was quite happy to accept God was responsible for everything that was mysterious… instead of looking for ridiculous alternatives like *answers*.

To make matters worse… Alien One and Alien Three had downgraded their declarations that God was better than them to an apathetic movement of their lips… usually while staring at nowhere in particular.

During that staring, Alien One appeared to be doing even more thinking than usual.

Alien Two and Alien Three awaited another pronouncement.

When it came, it would've blown their socks off, had they been wearing any… or, indeed, had the kind of feet on which to put them.

Alien One said he'd solved the question as to which of the two *more-than-one-supreme-being-conundrum* options was correct.

Alien Three asked him what the answer was.

Alien Two... having already deemed both of them blasphemous... only listened so as to know which one God would expect him to punish Alien One for.

Alien One blew their non-existent socks off by replying that it was both.

Aliens Two and Three looked at each other uncomfortably.

Alien One said he didn't blame their scepticism. He'd had a hard time getting his head around the concept too. But if you accepted that reality was of your own making... but shared alongside others... it was possible to have a situation where two gods were all powerful at exactly the same time... as well as *not* all powerful at exactly the same time. You could even have a reality where there were no gods at all, while appreciating that there *were*. It would simply be your point of view according to your reality... much like his perception of what should be deemed *trivial thoughts*.

Alien Three looked at Alien Two again in much the same way as the first time.

Alien One said he didn't blame their continued scepticism.

Alien Three said that... curiously... the concept was such a difficult one to comprehend, it had made his feet sweat. It was therefore just as well they weren't being covered by anything.

Alien One said... if his theory was correct... there would be a reality somewhere where they actually *were*.

Alien Three looked at Alien Two yet again.

Alien One said their continued scepticism was beginning to annoy him.

Alien Two said probably not as much as Alien One was annoying *him*.

Alien One said their annoying each other proved his point. If they just accepted that each person was expressing their own version of reality... and was perfectly entitled to do so... all three of them could go back to existing in perfect harmony.

Alien Three asked if he'd come up with a name for such a situation.

Alien Two said it would be more appropriate to ask if he was mad.

Alien One replied he'd decided to call it *perspective*.

Determined to carry out God's command and hurt Alien One yet again... Alien Two told him his idea was completely stupid. Insulting him had certainly worked the previous time.

Alien One smiled and said it didn't matter, as in his own reality it *wasn't*.

Tilting his head approvingly, Alien Three offered an appreciative nod of respect.

Alien Two found himself speechless... though he assumed *God* would have something to say on the matter... from *Its* perspective.

* * *

'I was hoping Donald would join us,' Norman addressed the impromptu meeting. 'But it seems he's chosen to hide himself away. We'll just have to formulate our next moves without him.'

'The first must be to get you online as quickly as possible so you can put your finances in place,' Chad suggested. 'Brandon and I will source that second-hand laptop and internet connection you asked for... but, seeing as we also need some basic provisions, it'll clear out what little funds we have. If your plan doesn't work, we're in trouble.'

'Don't worry,' Norman assured him. 'Once I get my hands on those two items, we'll be able to buy whatever we want.'

'Then may I put in a request for an enamel, roll top bath,' chipped in Xanthia. 'Though, if truth be known, I'll happily settle for a shower unit. Do you think they deliver to derelict power stations?'

'There's no need for sarcasm,' he frowned. 'This is serious business.'

'I wasn't being sarcastic,' she objected. 'We're all minging... can't you tell?'

'I think you'll find we'd need a supply of water for either of those luxuries,' smiled Brandon.

She shrugged. 'Not a problem. It shouldn't come as a surprise that I know *exactly* where the utility company's stopcock is and how it can be turned on again. The same goes for reinstating the electricity supply to this place. If we're going to stay here for any length of time, we might as well do so in comfort.'

'The electricity supply?' exclaimed Norman. 'You're not suggesting we get these turbines operational again, are you?' He kicked at the pipework of the one they were standing beside.

'No need,' she replied. 'This place was built so it could draw power *from* the grid, not just provide it. If production was ever disrupted, that power would've been needed to perform what's known as a black start. Despite much of that equipment having been vandalised or removed, the main facility for doing so is relatively intact. It's just a case of cleverly patching it up by using what's around us.'

'And you can *do* that?' Chad whistled.

'No. You boys can. There's no way I'm ruining these nails.' She flashed them to make her point. 'But if you follow my instructions to the letter, Norman will be able to recharge his laptop as many times as he likes... and we'll all be able to get close to one another without causing offence.'

Brandon rubbed his hands enthusiastically. 'Now we're cooking!'

'We'll be able to do that as well,' she said. 'So you might want to add an oven to that shopping list of yours.'

'And what's the plan after that?'

She turned to Norman. 'Yes, Norman... how are you going to save the Universe once we're spotlessly clean and well fed?'

There was an awkward silence.

'Wait a minute,' interjected Chad. 'I'm a little confused. Surely that's *your* department, isn't it, Xanthia?'

She smiled sympathetically. 'Though you and Brandon have kindly provided us with this safe, if unconventional, haven... Norman has been somewhat optimistic in suggesting our actions here can be anything more than a case of basic survival. As this meeting was at *his* insistence, I think it best if I let him explain.' She gave a nod of encouragement. 'In your own time, Norman... if you wouldn't mind.'

He held her stare for a moment.

'Xanthia thinks it can't be done,' he announced. 'There... are you happy now?'

'Hardly,' she tutted.

'The chequebook side of things?'

'The *whole* thing,' he elaborated.

'What... you mean... saving the Universe?' exclaimed Brandon. 'But that's the reason for us being here... isn't it?'

'She's come to the conclusion her powers are insufficient to change the way the world thinks... at least... not enough to make a difference.'

Chad turned to Xanthia. 'Please tell me this is an example of your British humour.'

'I'm afraid it isn't,' she replied solemnly. 'I'm deadly serious.'

'But that doesn't make sense. Not from what I've been told. I have it on good authority everything that's ever happened in history has been a stepping stone towards this precise moment in time. It's the decisive battle. The final showdown. Armageddon. We *have* to win!'

'Precisely,' concurred Norman, glad to have a supporter in his camp.

'And regarding that authority,' Chad continued, 'as mentioned yesterday... I've a direct line with people ready to assist us in whatever way we need. They've been waiting and preparing for this moment for a very long time.'

'The Templars. Yes, I know,' Xanthia nodded. 'And you're right... they've certainly demonstrated an inordinate amount of patience. After all... they've had to put up with Norman spending a considerable amount of their money on his hobby over the last few years.'

'I was only doing what Gabriel said I could,' Norman protested... though the excuse sounded lame, even to *him.*

'They countenanced it by figuring Heaven might still have a use for him,' she added.

'They figured correctly.' he responded.

144

She stared at him askance. '*Really?* Then what *exactly* are you going to do?'

Everyone looked at Norman.

'Build another sphere of knowledge,' he announced proudly. 'A *fourth* one. Only, this time, it's going to be applied to the person who should've received it in the first place.'

She blinked heavily. 'William *Shakespeare?*'

'Of course not! I'm talking about *me*. If people weren't prepared to take you seriously, because of your colourful past and the way you've chosen to present yourself, they certainly won't be able to level that excuse at me. I'll turn the one quality I've always excelled in to my advantage.'

She squinted. '*Obstinacy?*'

'My blandness. I'll use it as the gift it was clearly meant to be. I'll appear all things to all people. From Atheists to Zoroastrians, as you once put it… they'll find it easy to imprint their individual expectations on me. Then… having gained their trust… I'll become the new saviour Gabriel said the sphere was designed to create… someone who shines so bright, detractors will be struck dumb.'

'Well, you've certainly left *me* speechless… and you haven't even *started*,' she scoffed.

His narrowing eyes singled her out for his next comment. '*This* new saviour won't be averse to performing the odd *miracle* to make everyone sit up and take them seriously.'

'Them taking you seriously *will* be the miracle,' she countered.

'I'm going into battle, Xan… with Chad's Templars behind me… and I don't intend to lose.'

'Then, it's a shame Donald doesn't still have his suit of armour to lend you,' she mocked. 'You'd *really* have shone brightly in that!'

Chad raised a hand before the bickering deteriorated. 'Wait a minute… Aren't you forgetting one thing, Norman? For all the help the Templars can give us, you're now a wanted man.'

'He's forgetting more than that,' Xanthia insisted. 'He's forgetting everything I've ever told him!'

'To the contrary... I've taken onboard every single word. Despite that anomaly you warned me about, I merely think a different approach is needed. Besides... there's no way I'm sitting back and doing nothing.'

'You can wander around in a beige robe and sandals and convert water into an entire range of cocktails, if you like. But apart from an adoring few, you'll be ridiculed and vilified by the rest of the world. It's grown too cynical. *Whatever* you say or do, you'll be dismissed as a charlatan and trickster. Look what's happened to me. The only benefit is you'll see what I see and realise I'm right.'

'But, Xan... he's got a point,' interjected Chad. 'We can't just hang around and do *nothing*. Who knows... the combining of your powers might make that crucial difference. At least it's worth a try.'

Norman looked directly at her. 'Actually... worst-case scenario... it might be worth more than that.'

'Like what?' she shrugged.

'Phase cancellation,' he offered.

She shrugged again.

'Well... didn't you once tell me the hardest thing about having your ability was being able to hang on to the real you... and that seeing the world from everyone else's perspective meant you struggled to keep your own?'

'Why do you think I've insisted on dressing the way I do,' she said. 'It's the only part of the old *me* I have left. If I let go of *that* part of my identity, I'll be saying goodbye to myself completely. I thought *you* of all people would understand.'

'Alright... so I admit I could've done better on that score,' he acknowledged. 'But here's the thing... wouldn't you like your old self back and be able to return to how you *used* to be?'

'Of course... with certain caveats, that is.'

'Such as?'

'Being able to use the word *caveat*, for one,' she answered.

'So... what if I might be able to offer you that?'

'How's could it be *remotely* possible?' she derided him.

He smiled. 'Like I said... phase cancellation. It's when two_'

142

'I know what phase cancellation is, thank you very much,' she interrupted testily.

'Of course... sorry. So, you'll appreciate it's just possible that vibrations from a fourth sphere of knowledge might react with those you received from the third and cancel some, or even all of them, out. Surely that's enough incentive for you to humour me and help build the thing.'

'But that only highlights yet another flaw in your plan,' she pointed out. 'If phase cancellation *does* occur, the vibrations you're hoping to receive will be cancelled out too! *Then* where will we be?'

He looked at her lovingly. 'In a world where at least *you'll* be happier for whatever time is left... and that's good enough for me.'

She stared at him, completely dumbfounded... and wanted to tell him he never ceased to have that effect on her. But practicalities came first. 'Look... even if I *were* prepared to help... how on earth do you intend creating this fourth sphere of yours?'

'I'm glad you asked,' he grinned. He stretched out his arms triumphantly. 'Welcome to *Ark Two!*'

Nonplussed, the others surveyed the dereliction around them.

'We're gonna fill this place with as many computers as it takes to recreate the vibrations from my original scans and set them all in motion... simultaneously. Admittedly, that's one helluva lot of computers. But it's not as if we're short on space. We need to be totally self-sufficient... no more relying on outside help in the form of distributive computing. We can't afford to risk anything being tracked back to us here. We'll take delivery of the computers at source from as many different outlets as possible, so as not to raise suspicion.'

'But aren't you missing one glaringly obvious problem?' she asked.

He kept his grin. 'No.'

'Well... I think you'll find there's the little matter of those original vibrations. Much of the binary data you outsourced no longer exists. I can tell you for a fact… it's long-since been overwritten or ended up in landfill during the intervening years.'

'I'd be very surprised if it hadn't,' he said.

'Well… assuming you're not proposing acquiring the original artworks again and starting from scratch… where are you planning to get it from?'

His grin broadened. 'You!'

'What?'

'Think about it, Xan… you have knowledge of *everything*. All you have to do is access that data and input it into a computer terminal.'

She stared at him in disbelief. 'And there was I just beginning to love you again. Are you *mad*? Do you know how many individual digits that entails?'

'I'm perfectly aware of the size of the task,' he replied.

'No, you're clearly not! We're talking billions and billions of separate noughts and ones… all having to be typed without a single digit out of place. Not *one* single mistake or slip of my finger during the entire procedure.'

His grin hovered awkwardly. 'I was hoping you might be able to channel a skill that would help.'

'What… that of an ambidextrous, time-warping, ninja typist, you mean?'

'*Something* like that.'

'At this moment in time, I'm channelling the skills of a psychiatrist,' she glowered, 'and, believe me… it's not looking good for you.'

The remnants of his grin left him to sort the problem out on his own.

'Distributive computing,' Chad nodded heavily. 'So, *that's* what you were up to back then. Well, I'll be damned. Our investigations established you'd uploaded a heck of a lot of data to random ISPs… but we thought it was a smokescreen for what you were *really* up to, seeing as none of it made sense.'

'In its rawest form, it wouldn't,' said Norman. 'Without any accompanying code to give those binary digits context, they would've simply appeared as garbage.'

'Is that what you're after now?' asked Brandon. 'This "garbage" you uploaded?'

'If Xanthia's unable to help... every single piece of it.'

Brandon gave the matter more thought. 'In that case... just how good *are* your hacking skills?'

'As good as mine,' admitted Xanthia, 'and that's saying something.'

'So, between the two of you, d'ya think you could access the servers of the NSA?'

'The National Security Agency?' She visualised the problem and whistled. 'That's a tough one. Though... wait a minute... I *am* seeing see a couple of potential backdoors that look ripe for exploitation.'

'And am I right in assuming this information required is still on their servers? After all... the fact the CIA were able to examine it suggests it was scooped up by the NSA when first transmitted... despite originating from overseas.'

'Naughty, naughty,' tutted Norman.

Xanthia concentrated harder. 'All I can say is that it *was* up until the morning of the summer solstice.'

'Then it's unlikely to have been erased in the meantime... especially being part of a previous investigation. Stuff like that's usually archived in case it's ever needed again. '

'Excellent logic,' said Chad.

'That solves our problem, then.'

'Not quite,' Norman winced. 'You see... there's a bit missing.'

'And where do we look for that?'

'You can't. It went up in smoke with the rest of my bedsit. Hubris made me hold on to that particular piece of data. I wanted the satisfaction of triggering the final piece of code myself.'

Xanthia rolled her eyes.

Norman kicked the turbine's pipework again in frustration. 'Damn!'

'Do you mind?' came a faint voice. 'That's the *second* time. Any more and I'll be in danger of losing my hearing!'

'Donald?'

'Well... you're in trouble if it's not,' declared the muffled reply.

'Where are you?'

'I'd have thought that was obvious!'

The others stared in bemusement as a maintenance hatch on the turbine slowly creaked open.

'It was lovely and quiet in there until you started your banging,' said Donald, awkwardly clambering out. 'Someone with an entrepreneurial spirit has kindly removed the copper coils and left a space that's afforded me the best night's sleep I've had in years. In fact, I can't remember a time when I've *not* had a single voice badgering me for something or other when trying to doze off. It seems even Whitebait can't penetrate this amount of metalwork.' His eyes immediately shot upwards. 'OH... SO, NOW I'M NOT PROTECTED AND YOU'RE COCK OF THE WALK ONCE MORE, YOU THINK YOU CAN START HASSLING ME AGAIN. WELL... BE WARNED, TRAWLERMAN... I'VE NOW FOUND THE *PERFECT* ANTIDOTE TO YOU AND YOUR TIRESOME JABBERING... AND IF YOU DON'T TONE IT DOWN, I'M CLIMBING STRAIGHT BACK INSIDE.' He examined the stares confronting his. 'Do you think I'd be able to arrange to have this thing transported back to England if we ever make it past Armageddon?'

'If Xanthia's to be believed, you won't be that lucky,' said Norman. 'She's insisting there's nothing we can do anymore to win that battle.'

Donald stared at her suspiciously.

Chad put a hand on his shoulder. 'On the positive side, Donald... we're getting a bath.'

'I should hope so,' he sniffed. 'I've always been a firm believer that cleanliness is next to godliness.'

* * *

'Gus… these demands are ridiculous!' railed the president, his hand shaking as he studied the paper he'd just been handed. 'There's no way we can accede to what's being asked of us here.'

'They're only doing what corporations like theirs have always done, sir… trying to profit from the markets.'

'But they're acting as a goddam monopoly on this. How has that come about?'

'We don't know, sir… but they're clearly aware they have us over a barrel. Our strategic stockpiles are running dangerously low… and the fact we weren't able to build them up before realising what was occurring, means we'll soon be in the position of not being able to take care of our own citizens.'

'Then I'll issue a presidential decree and requisition everything these self-serving, opportunistic parasites have hoarded! We can't have the tail wagging the dog at a critical time like this.'

'With respect… that might not be as easy or as prudent as you think, sir.'

The president eyed his Chief of Staff incredulously. 'Prudent? What the hell are you talking about?'

'Well, sir… many of the corporations responsible for issuing that demand have been extremely astute in the legal structuring of their businesses. Most have positioned themselves within the jurisdiction of foreign governments, all of which would dearly love to get their *own* hands on these dwindling commodities. Given that much of what is on offer has yet to reach these shores, any rash action on our part would be seen as nationalistic and provide those governments with an excuse to apply similar measures, thereby requisitioning those supplies for themselves. The whole thing could trigger an international crisis of unimaginable proportions.'

'This *is* an international crisis of unimaginable proportions! It's occurring right now!'

'Even so, sir… I don't think we should be looking to exacerbate it. We need all the friends we can get at a time like this.'

'But these leeches aren't just looking to increase their profits… they're also demanding a seat at the top table. They're actually looking to have a say in the way this nation of ours is governed!'

The Chief of Staff looked down at his shoes. 'Again, with respect, sir… many would claim they've been doing that for years.'

'Not at *this* level, Gus… not so blatantly. This goes beyond aggressive lobbying or political sponsorship. It violates the very principles of democracy itself.'

'But at least it would temporarily get us out of the mess we're in. Maybe we could sell it to the public as a purely advisory role.'

'Not with the title they're demanding.' He read from the paper. 'Chief Executive of State. That sounds like a direct challenge to *my* position!'

'Whatever name they wish to put on it, you'd still be in charge, sir.'

'I don't seem to be in that position *now,* Gus. God *help* us if I agreed to this. We'd quickly find ourselves on an extremely slippery slope.' He threw the paper onto his desk. 'No. This can't happen. It's unthinkable.'

'Shouldn't we at least *talk* to them, sir… see how far they're prepared to negotiate on that last point?'

'But who would I be negotiating with… this proposed *Chief Executive of State* themselves? Do we even know who that might be? Have they put forward a name?'

'I don't have that information at this stage, sir. But do you want me to at least see about putting a meeting together? It doesn't mean we're agreeing to their terms.'

The president's expression changed. 'Hang on a minute… you don't think it's *Donald,* do you?'

The Chief of Staff's eyes widened. 'Tucker-Jenkins?'

'Let's face it… that would make sense of a demand that goes far beyond profiteers simply taking advantage of the markets. Perhaps this is all connected to him and that Penkridge fella.'

The president momentarily switched thoughts. 'Talking of which... has there been any news of those two yet?'

'I'm assured every possible resource is being employed to have them recaptured before they can do further damage. With so much heat on them, they won't be able to remain at large for long.'

'Maybe they don't intend to,' said the president, as another thought struck him. 'Perhaps they intend to brazenly turn up here!' He explored the idea. 'Could it be Donald's allowed himself to become embroiled in this whole sordid affair just to achieve a position of political influence? Perhaps he feels his writing hasn't had a great enough impact on the world and he wants to have more.' He picked up the note he'd discarded and studied it in greater detail. 'Having said that... I doubt he's written this himself. The content might be highly dramatic, but the syntax lacks creative flair.'

'Who knows, sir.' said his Chief of Staff respectfully. 'Regardless of the note's author, it doesn't alter the fact Tucker-Jenkins is *responsible* for this mess.'

'I know, Gus. But it would certainly go some way to explaining much that's been baffling me about his behaviour. If this *is* him, he's clearly gained the backing of some extremely powerful people. These demands aren't without substance. As you say... they really *do* have us over a barrel.' The president tipped his head back in frustration. 'She might've been playing for the other side, but that Xanthia girl was right when she said there are people in this world whose greed leaves them incapable of seeing beyond the moment. Well, I promise you this... I swear to God, when we finally get ourselves out of this nightmare, I'll make these blinkered, bloodsuckers pay... *whoever* they are.'

'In that case, Mister President... we'd better make sure we secure that future and find out. With your permission, I'll set up a meeting.'

*　　*　　*

'Mind if I join you?'

Xanthia gave a half-smile and patted the floor on which she was sat. 'Be my guest. The seating isn't all it should be… and the view isn't much better… but other than that…'

'It was the company I was after,' said Chad, settling down next to her.

She drew her knees tight into her chest. 'I fear you might be disappointed with that bit, too.'

'I doubt it,' he smiled. 'You're an incredibly strong woman. I'm full of admiration. Norman's just been filling me in on all the gory details.'

'You mean, regarding what I've seen in people?'

'Yeah… and all I can say is that if *I'd* experienced one fraction of what you have, I reckon I'd have found myself being strapped to a gurney by a load of men in white coats.'

She turned and faced him. 'I *was*… remember?'

They stared at each other for a few seconds then burst out laughing.

'Oh… I've missed that,' she giggled, wiping away a tear and grabbing his arm. 'It's been such a long time since I've been able to let go of all the serious thoughts in my head and just enjoy the moment.'

He let her bask in that feeling a little longer before chancing his next remark. 'Perhaps there's *still* a way you can do so in the future.'

She put her smile on hold. 'Are you saying what I think you're saying?'

'I'm saying there's a very good reason we shouldn't give up.'

She let out a groan. 'Not *you* as well? I thought *Norman's* pig-headedness was bad enough!'

He placed his hand on hers to stop it pulling away. 'Just hear me out. Perhaps there's something you may not have taken into consideration when you came to your decision… something that you weren't aware of and haven't yet focused on. That's possible… isn't it?'

She looked at his hand dispassionately. 'All I can say is... to make me change my mind, your *something* would have to be ridiculously obscure and *spectacularly* powerful.'

'I think you might've described it perfectly,' he grinned.

She studied him curiously. '*It...?* Am I to assume we're no longer talking hypothetically?'

'I'm told it's very real.'

'That's *spectacularly powerful* as in *beyond normal human expectations*,' she qualified.

'I believe it may be.' He carefully released his hand.

She left hers where it was.

'What if I told you it's not just money, influence and manpower the Templars can offer us? What if they were able to provide a resource far greater than all those three combined?'

She stared at him for a few seconds then dropped her shoulders in disappointment. 'You're talking about their *Magnum Compendium Secretorum*, aren't you?'

'I am,' he confirmed, shocked by her negativity. 'You already knew about it?'

'Absolutely not... but I do *now*.'

'And you don't think it can make a difference?'

'Not from what I've just seen. Sure... it contains truths and formulas far in advance of normal thinking... and I can see why the Templars considered it a potent resource. It's what helped propel them to such meteoric heights after their return from the Holy Lands.'

'I know. But I've been told it contains much *more* than that. My understanding is it holds incredibly important and powerful secrets.'

She nodded respectfully. 'It *does*. It answers questions that have perplexed the finest minds since Socrates... including answering probably the greatest mystery of them all.'

His eyes widened. 'The meaning of life?'

'No. Why two people always yawn at the same time.'

Chad struggled to reconcile her casual attitude to the *Compendium* with the old man's veneration of it back at Arwan

El Kahab. 'Doesn't it contain things that could be considered magical?' he persisted.

'I'm sure much of its contents appeared so to a medieval mind,' she shrugged.

'So you're saying it *doesn't*?'

'*Everything's* explainable,' she smiled. 'You just have to be able to see beyond the conjuror's handkerchief.'

'But what about the *Detromunkos?*'

No sooner had the question left his mouth, a look of abject panic registered on her face. Clutching her chest, she made short, sharp whelping noises as if struggling to breathe.

'Xanthia!'

Shaking her head wildly, unable to communicate, her widened eyes locked onto his. She grabbed both his arms and squeezed them to the point of pain.

Attempting to clamber to his feet to summon assistance, the force of her grip held him down.

'What is it? How can I help?'

Her eyes rolled up into her eyelids.

'Shall I get Donald? Maybe he'll know what to do!'

She shook her head again, her face contorted in agony. As he watched helplessly, she slowly relaxed her hold.

'It's okay,' she gasped, trying to steady her breathing. 'I'll be alright. Just give me a minute.'

'What the *hell* happened?'

'I'd rather not talk about it,' she grimaced, 'Besides... there's no way I could put it into words.'

'Did you see it... the *Detromunkos?*'

She winced sharply at its mention and desperately shot her hand out to stop him uttering the word again.

'I need to know, Xanthia. I reckon it has a crucial part to play in all this. The Templars say it's the key to unlocking the most powerful part of the *Compendium*. That's why they've been waiting so long for someone like you to come along and help them with it. It's a vitally important cipher.'

'I know what it is!' she shouted.

'Then, why not use this incredible gift you've been given to assist them?'

She gritted her teeth and looked at him angrily. 'THAT'S THE *LAST* THING I WOULD WANT TO DO!' she screamed.

* * *

Xanthia gazed up from her hunched position on the floor. 'This feels suspiciously like an inquisition,' she said, warily observing those warily observing her.

'It's nothing like that,' Chad assured her. 'We're worried about you, that's all. I've called the others because it's only fair they're aware of what's going on.'

'*Nothing's* going on,' she insisted.

'Well, for starters... you scared the hell outta me.'

'*You* were scared,' she retorted. 'Try being in *my* shoes!'

'Chad says the Templars need your help with something and that you don't want to give it,' said Donald bluntly.

'Something they believe could save us all... the *Detromunkos*,' Chad reminded her.

'Will you stop mentioning that damn thing,' she recoiled. 'It causes me the most excruciating pain every time you do!'

Donald tutted. 'How very convenient.'

'Shut up, Donald.' Norman admonished him. 'Xanthia's clearly got her reasons. We just need to let her explain in her own time.'

She nodded appreciatively. 'Thank you.'

'But we don't *have* time,' insisted Chad.

'You'd be begging for even *less* of it if I gave the Templars what you want me to!' she exclaimed. 'We don't know when the end will come... months, weeks... maybe only days from now. But come it most definitely will. But if I were to replicate that...' She hesitated.

'Shall we call it the *D word*?' brokered Brandon. 'Would that help?'

'*Thing...*' she continued, 'and it ended up in the wrong hands, you'd all wish that end to come as quickly as possible... but you'd be doing so for eternity.'

Her inquisitors looked at each other, confused.

'As things stand, when the spiritual balance finally tips, it'll create the metaphysical equivalent of a black hole, towards which anything positive would be drawn and annihilated. Nothing could escape that fate or reverse it. But it's immaterial. At the very moment it occurs – with the karmic progression of souls no longer possible, and the *reason* for everything becoming null and void – it will all cease to exist. If it's any consolation... you won't feel a thing.'

'Just like being dead, then,' nodded Brandon.

'Do you want to know how many spirits I'll now have queuing up to take issue with you on that?' Donald groaned.

Her countenance darkened. 'However... if what Chad would have me replicate fell into the wrong hands... we'd be forced to endure a never-ending nightmare beyond all imagination!'

'How so?' squinted Norman. 'What exactly *is* this Detro_'

She shot out a hand again. 'Please!'

'The Templars say it decodes part of a book in their possession called the *Magnum Compendium Secretorum*,' Chad answered for her. 'It contains wisdom and secrets handed down from the ancients.'

'Really?' Donald suddenly exhibited interest. 'It wouldn't happen to explain why two people yawn at the same time, by any chance, would it?'

'Yes... apparently.'

Donald bowed his head in respect.

'The Templars believe the coded section to be the most significant part of all.'

'Oh, it's *certainly* that,' Xanthia confirmed. 'It provides access to powers beyond the comprehension of ordinary mortals... which is precisely why it was concealed using a cipher. Containing secrets from an age when sages were attuned to a universal wisdom, it details powerful spells that would prove catastrophic for mankind if used with ill intent.'

'*Spells?*' scoffed Brandon.

'Incantations designed to create specific vibrations that interrupt and affect the balance of that at which they're targeted,' she elaborated. 'At a quantum level, we're nothing more than packages of energy vibrating in a universe made up of other such packages... be it the people around you, a single cell or the largest neutron star in the cosmos. A hex is simply one such package created using vocal intonations to influence another. The more vociferous and targeted that incantation, the greater the effect those vibrations have.'

'The walls of Jericho,' acknowledged Donald.

'Precisely. The trouble is... by their very nature, those spells are riddled with inherent dangers. As everything is connected to everything else, upsetting the balance of one situation can adversely affect that of another... and so on, and so on. There are spells within the coded section of the *Magnum Compendium Secretorum* that are so powerful, they risk causing an unstoppable chain reaction of vibrations that could produce catastrophic fissures in the boundary between the physical and spiritual realms. If that were to happen, every dispossessed soul and negative entity would seep through and contaminate the earth plane. The suffering would be unimaginable. But that would not be the worst of it. With Satan having triumphed and usurped God's position as Supreme Being, not only would the infallibility of love no longer be a truth and God cease to be, the Universe would automatically continue to exist without Him under its new deity... meaning the pain and suffering would too. With the boundary between the physical and spiritual realms breached, there'd be no death to rescue anyone from the torment. Like the madness of a Hieronymus Bosch painting, we would literally be living in Hell on Earth... but for *eternity!*'

An uncomfortable silence accompanied the stares of horror.

'Sounds like it's just as well the Templars *didn't* find this... you-know-what,' Brandon shuddered.

'But you do know where it is, don't you, Xan?' Norman pushed her.

She shook her head. 'As a matter of fact, I *don't*. That's the strangest part. I should be able to see it... but I can't. It doesn't make sense. It's like the object itself has simply vanished from the face of the earth and its footprint been erased.'

'Then, who had it last?'

'The Templars believe it was King Solomon,' answered Chad. 'That's how they figured where to dig for the *Compendium*.'

'That's an assumption on their part,' she cautioned. 'Suffice to say, we should be extremely grateful that *someone* exercised great wisdom in ensuring the two parts remained separated.'

'So... is *that* what all this was about?' asked Norman. 'The reason you refused Chad his wish?'

She nodded.

'Well... given what I've just heard, your decision seems eminently sensible,' said Brandon.

Norman placed his hands in his pockets and shrugged. 'I agree. In which case... nothing to see here.' He turned and left.

'I'm off to my turbine,' said Donald, departing in a different direction.

Brandon raised his hand in a gesture of farewell and did the same.

Chad grimaced apologetically at Xanthia and slunk back down beside her. 'Sorry I put you through that... but you can't blame me for trying. Not giving up is what I do for a living. I ruthlessly plough on until a problem's solved. And, for one glorious moment, I thought I had the answer to ours.'

She flashed a look of irony. 'I know... just like Norman. Except *his* single-mindedness stems from his disastrous childhood.'

'He had a tough upbringing?'

'*Tough* is somewhat of an understatement. *Seismic trauma* would be more appropriate.'

'You've taken a peek at it?'

She blushed slightly. 'Let's just say... I couldn't resist the tiniest of ones. But even if I'd managed to stay my curiosity, I already knew much of what he'd gone through. As crazy as it sounds, I was there at the time and played a part in it,' She matched his incredulous stare. 'I know. How's that for karmic blowback? Being a child myself, I had no idea how damaging the endless taunts he was subjected to would be. Let's face it… even *adults* rarely stop to think about the consequences of their actions. It was only when I chanced those few, stolen moments in his shoes that the reality of what it had done to him truly hit home.' She sighed. 'That man has spent most of his life making himself as invisible as possible in order to avoid encountering further pain. Escaping into a world of computers spared him having to deal with anything involving emotions. An adolescent fixation with me was the closest he got… a conveniently impossible fantasy he assumed was way beyond his grasp. And then it all changed… including that last bit. Not only was he given a responsibility beyond the experience of anyone who's ever lived… he suddenly found himself immersed in a world where everything was about expressing those very feelings he'd been trying so hard to avoid! Paradoxically, it's why he became fixated with art. By immersing himself in tangible expressions of other people's emotions, he could finally experience a world that was new and exciting, without risking his own. The only person he's ever done *that* for is me.'

'He obviously cares for you a great deal,' said Chad. 'It was touching how he considered you might benefit from him creating another sphere of knowledge, even if *he* didn't.'

'Oh, don't be fooled by that,' she scoffed. 'While I may figure *somewhere* in the equation, he wants to do it because he's desperate to exorcise his previous failings… as *well* as save the Universe. He thinks it would right a wrong and fulfil a stolen destiny… a destiny that would justify the pain he's suffered and make everything he's gone through worthwhile. *That's* why he'll refuse to give up, no matter what I tell him.'

'He's even more complex than I thought,' Chad confessed. 'It's good to finally get a handle on what makes him tick. He's been a bogeyman in my life for so long, to make sense of everything, I've dressed him in all kinds of assumptions…

including his blandness... as he himself put it... being an ingenious disguise to throw people like me off the scent.'

'No... I promise you that bit's real. It's what goes on beneath that's truly remarkable to behold. It takes quite a person to survive everything *he's* had to in life and still remain positive. Like you, he's definitely not wired to quit.'

Chad offered a pained look. 'Then, it's a shame he's gonna have to.'

She smiled. 'Oh... I wouldn't bet on it, if I were you. The chances are he'll use that logical mind of his to find a solution to his problem and build that sphere of his. And if he does, I'll help him all I can.'

'But you said there was no point. I thought we'd finally established that.'

'You're right... there isn't.' She stood up carefully and brushed the dirt from her skirt. 'But I still love him, despite everything that's happened between us recently. So... I'll be doing it because he *needs* me to.' She stared at a point nowhere in particular. 'Besides... I rather fancy this *phase cancellation* theory of his, and the glorious possibility of having the old me back for whatever time we have left.'

*   *   *

Alien Two's hatred towards Alien One had increased to such an extent it now consumed his every passing thought. It also consumed a lot of his stationary ones, as well.

Paradoxically, it provided welcome relief against the eons of nothingness that had preceded it. He remembered telling his nemesis he'd be deliriously happy if some other *thing* existed to break the tedious monotony of existence.

Well... his wish had been granted.

How great was God!

Hatred gave him a purpose. It was also far easier than being a stand-up comedian. You couldn't *fail* at hating someone. More to the point... it could be used to demonstrate loyalty and devotion to the One that had given it to him in the first place.

126

Well... it *could*... if only he was able to work out *how*. Having announced that everyone had their own perspective, Alien One had made insults not only subjective but... *ergo*... completely pointless.

How was he supposed to hurt him now?

Alien Two waited for a sign... or better still, action... from God.

Alien One was still sat there, smugly enjoying his own *perspective*.

Alien Two waited a little more.

He waited a little more... again... patiently.

He waited a little more... again... a little more... though with less of the *patient* bit this time.

As a certain set of stars eventually dipped below the horizon, Alien Two felt something he recognised as *disappointment*.

Perhaps, he concluded, hatred wasn't so dissimilar to being a stand-up comedian after all.

Observing Alien One through narrowing eyes, he assumed he'd been contemplating something that would mess with their lives again. Why had he insisted on questioning things in the first place? Everything had been perfectly fine as it was... if you excluded millions of years of interminable boredom. Now they were expected to cope with such things as *disappointment, experience, joking, irony,* and *claptrap.* Oh... and he'd almost forgotten... the biggest change of all to their lives... *G_*

Alien Two suddenly felt gripped by a combination of what Alien One would later term *guilt* and *fear*. Not only had he foolishly created *blasphemy* during his unsuccessful comedy routine... hadn't he just transgressed again?

Putting his hands together in contrition, he begged forgiveness for including God in the same thought as one that referenced things he was expected to *cope* with. He hadn't meant it the way it may have seemed. Sure... it sometimes took considerable effort to be absolutely certain God wasn't being offended all the time... and there were days when...

Damn... and *again?*

To atone, he promised to hurt Alien One as much as he could... with or without God's help.

Studying the object of his ire staring into space, trying to make sense of everything, Alien Two noticed Alien One's brow had become heavily furrowed... as if the burden of doing so was adding an uncomfortable weight to his shoulders.

It gave him an idea.

Adding *more* weight to them would surely increase that discomfort.

Affirming loudly that God was better than them, he launched himself at Alien One.

* * *

'This better be worth it!' said Donald irascibly, clambering down from the sanctity of his turbine. 'For the first time ever, I've found a way to introduce a little peace and quiet into my life, and these meetings are playing havoc with that *me* time.'

'You'll be able to have as much of it as you like,' Norman smiled, 'if I manage to recreate a fourth sphere of knowledge.'

'Well... I thought we'd already established that isn't going to happen,' Donald retorted, looking to the others for support.

'*You* might have,' said Norman. 'But I think I've found a solution to our problem.'

Brandon's eyes lit up. 'The missing digits?'

'I think I know how we can obtain them.'

Xanthia winked at Chad.

'The answer came to me as I was reflecting on a time, back in England, when Donald showed me his paintings. I remembered thinking his attempts reminded me of famous works of art.'

'YES... AS IT HAPPENS, I *AM* OFFENDED BY HIS USE OF THE WORD *ATTEMPTS*.' Donald shouted skyward.

'Having given the matter some thought, I figured it was because he was accessing the same chunks of inspiration those original painters used... but receiving *his* from the second sphere.'

'You think it fractured in the exact same manner?' said Chad, incredulously.

'Bits of it, at least. Xanthia will be able to give us a definitive answer on that.'

She focused on the moment of its destruction. 'Well, who'd have thought it... you're right! It seems parts of it *did*.'

'There you go! So... I wondered if Donald had ever attempted to interpret the piece responsible for inspiring the Turner that was destroyed.'

'THAT'S *TWICE!*'

'Because, if he *had*, it might just contain the information we require, even if poorly transcribed.'

'THE BOY NEVER STOPS DIGGING, DOES HE?'

'Excellent logic,' nodded Chad. 'In which case... all we need to do is get hold of that painting and digitise it. It's certainly worth a try. What have we got to lose?'

'My creative integrity... apparently,' Donald sniffed.

Brandon frowned. 'How are we gonna get it delivered from Donald's place to here without blowing our cover?'

'Don't worry,' said Xanthia. 'It's not a problem you need worry about.'

'You have a solution?'

'Nope.'

'Then, how are we gonna do it?'

'Simple,' said Norman. 'As Xanthia's clearly aware, we're *not*.'

'*Why?*' Chad squinted.

'Because Donald assures me he never painted anything *remotely* resembling it.'

Chad turned to Donald. 'Are you certain?'

'One hundred percent, dear boy. I've never been a fan. I blame the cataracts. His, not mine.'

'In that case... are you suggesting that piece of inspiration might still be out there?' Chad struggled.

123

'I can confirm it's not,' said Xanthia. 'The fragment in question wasn't replicated during the second sphere's destruction.'

Chad threw his hands up in the air. 'Then, what's this all about?'

Norman grinned. 'It's about how we can access the *original* vibration in the manner Donald *would* have, had it been duplicated.'

'But that's already been used,' said Brandon, equally confused, 'by William Turner.'

'Precisely,' Norman beamed. 'And that's exactly how we're going to get it back! Remember Xanthia telling us she could put herself in the shoes of historical figures and know exactly what they were thinking and feeling at any given point in time? Remember when she briefly accessed Bonnie Parker's last moments with Clyde Barrow in their car? Well... all she needs to do is put herself in Turner's shoes at the precise moment he accessed the inspiration for his painting and replicate it by channelling the very skills and emotions he possessed at that time.'

'An exact replica,' muttered Xanthia, nodding.

'I doubt it even has to be exact,' said Norman, 'just so long as the vibrations you encode are transmitted to the observer. Gabriel used two completely different works of art... a Mondrian and some music by Schoenberg... to test the calibration of my decoding program. To be successful, they needed to generate the same binary digits. He told me it wasn't how individual pieces looked or sounded that mattered, it was how they captured the inspiration that produced them. If Picasso had been in front of a block of stone with a chisel in his hand – instead of an easel and some paint – *The Weeping Woman* may well have turned out to be a statue instead of a painting.'

'If it's the picture I'm thinking of, he'd probably have opted for an angle grinder,' said Donald.

'Oh... and before anyone says it's a waste of time,' pre-empted Norman, directing his comment at Xanthia, 'at least it'll give us something to do. For those of a negative disposition, just think of it as a way to keep ourselves entertained until the lights go out.'

'I'm in!' enthused Chad. 'If only for the pleasure of experiencing that sphere again. Whatever happens after that is in the hands of the gods.'

'Possibly not the ones you're thinking of,' muttered Xanthia, as an image of Mister Prometheus and his associates briefly gatecrashed the party.

'You can count me in, too,' said Brandon, raising his hand.

'You seem to be forgetting one important fact,' interjected Donald. 'As Chad has made abundantly clear... we're currently the most wanted individuals in this country. While I commend your fighting spirit, Norman... and for ignoring Xanthia's blatant attempts to deceive us into thinking we should simply give up... I'm beginning to think she's right in this particular case. I mean... let's face it... you're hardly going to be seen as "beige" once the American government put their propaganda machine into overdrive. They've already labelled you a terrorist, for goodness sake.'

'Believe me, Donald,' said Norman defiantly, 'I'm well used to name-calling. And even if I *can't* win the public over to my side, at least I'll have up-to-date knowledge of everything... unlike Xanthia. That means I'll be able to access and interpret those messages you received *after* our adventure at Stonehenge. We'll use that information to finally put a stop to this whole thing!'

Donald stood a moment in thought. 'In that case, you have my full support... if only to allow you the chance to atone for the egregious sin of losing those messages in the first place.'

The others turned to Xanthia for her reaction.

She opened her mouth to speak.

'I haven't finished,' Donald tutted, holding up a finger.

She waited politely.

'THAT'S GOOD TO HEAR. I'M GLAD WE FINALLY AGREE ON *SOMETHING*.' He nodded calmly. 'Whitebait says he's in, too.'

'As I was about to say,' she proceeded. 'As soon as Norman has our finances in place, I'll need a full set of oils, brushes, canvas, and a very sturdy easel.'

* * *

'Forgive my surprise... but you're not the person I was expecting to see,' the president greeted his guest soberly.

'Is that because I'm a woman,' asked Miss Eris, ignoring his outstretched hand.

The president withdrew it. 'I make no distinction.'

'We have much to discuss. My colleagues and I are eager to progress things as quickly as possible.'

'I'm glad you appreciate that's all this is at the moment... a discussion,' he pointed out.

'You can place whatever label you like on this meeting,' she said haughtily. 'The outcome will be the same. You will cede an element of power to our collective.'

'I beg your pardon?'

'Forgive such bluntness... I have neither time nor desire for diplomatic pleasantries. And please don't insult me by pretending your predicament isn't as serious as you know it to be. The long-term complacency of you and your predecessors has brought about this moment. It is *my* side who now have the upper hand. If you wish to interpret our demands as that of an occupying enemy, I should point out it's one that cannot be defeated militarily. Furthermore... collectively existing beyond the reach of any one nation's legislation, we cannot be subjugated by punitive laws. Any call for multilateral action against us will not only increase our ire but also garner no friends. Your *real* enemies are those who would rather work with us than against us in order to maintain their own stability. Hunger is a powerful motivator and selfishness its wayward child. It is now dog eat dog. The sooner you accept that, the easier our relationship will be.'

The president lifted his head angrily. 'How dare you talk to me in such a way, madam! We *have* no relationship. It appears

120

hubris has made you forget whom you are addressing. I am the President of the United States of America, having sworn an oath of office to uphold the constitution of this country. What you are proposing strikes at the very heart of everything that constitution stands for. I was democratically elected to serve the will of the people, not the whims of a group of glorified market traders. Tell your precious *collective* that I will not be intimidated or bullied into action because of a temporary shift in circumstances... not least by a mafia of unprincipled, grasping leeches, no matter how cleverly you think you may have organised yourselves.'

'Firstly... I am perfectly aware of your position,' said Miss Eris unmoved. 'As in authority *and* predicament. Secondly... democracy has nothing to do with this matter. Rest assured, *Mister President*... I am looking forward to having this very same conversation with your counterpart in China... and all the other leaders of countries – democratic or otherwise – who find themselves struggling to feed their citizens. I am not interested in politics.'

Her last assertion raised an eyebrow.

'Did I just hear you say... *I?*' He looked at her warily. 'And what about the rest of your *collective?*'

'Thirdly...' she ignored him, 'you would do well to trust me when I say the circumstances you face are *far* from temporary. The world is changing. It will soon become even *more* challenging to govern. You will eventually be grateful for our assistance and thankful we operate beyond global divisions. I am offering stability... albeit at a price. But it is one only a fool would refuse to pay. It is not just the issue of food that should concern you. My colleagues and I now control the supply of every vital resource on this planet... from oil and gas, to the rights to essential technology and the minerals required to ensure it all keeps running. They are ours to apportion as we see fit. Regardless of your personal distaste for such a situation, *that* is why you do not want to make us your enemy.'

119

'The *people* will make you their enemy,' rejoined the president. 'They won't idly sit back and accept this, even if I did. Such an arrangement would result in anything *but* stability.'

'On the contrary. The control we exercise now stretches to thoughts put inside people's heads whenever they log on to their social media accounts or get their news from television or newspapers. I guarantee you will have no trouble selling my appointment to them. The populace will understand... because they will be *made* to understand.'

'Such an admission of manipulation is outrageous!' shouted the president, apoplectic with rage. 'I can have you arrested for sedition!'

'I'm sure you can. But then you'd have to explain to those you misguidedly think you're protecting, why it is they're unable to feed their children... or keep them from freezing when winter comes.'

Having exploded, the president's emotions had nowhere left to go. He stared at her in stunned disbelief. 'Have you absolutely no soul, woman?' he gasped.

She smiled back sweetly. 'Of course I do.'

'Then, where, in God's name, is it?'

'Well... certainly not registered in *his,*' she laughed. 'After all... I doubt *he'd* have been willing to pay the price I demanded for it!'

*　　*　　*

'I'm sorry it's taken me so long.' Chad handed Norman the bag he was holding. 'I've had one helluva walk. We're not exactly close to amenities here. The laptop's second-hand, but fully charged. The portable internet connection's brand new. So you should be able to start work immediately.'

Norman gave them a cursory examination. 'They'll both do nicely,' he said, nodding his gratitude.

'And while I've been out getting those, Brandon's been hard at work implementing Xanthia's instructions for reconnecting this place to the grid. Assuming he doesn't end up frying himself, it shouldn't be long 'til you have as much juice as you need.'

'Good... because that last bit's essential,' said Norman. 'By the time we're done, this entire building will be crammed with power-hungry equipment.'

'How are the logistics for that looking?'

Norman held up the bag. 'We're ready to go as soon as I've used these to put our finances in place. Xanthia's drawn up a list of every store within a 50 mile radius of here that sells computers. She's also devised the most efficient routes to take in order to acquire their stocks as quickly as possible. She reckons we could have *Ark Two* fully operational within a week, if we work around the clock.'

'I'll need a large truck, of course.'

'You'll need two. That calculation's based on you and Brandon working independently.'

Chad whistled his appreciation of the task ahead.

'As our fugitive status prevents us drawing cash or obtaining any form of bank card, everything will be paid for in advance by direct payment,' said Norman. 'It'll also speed up the collection process.'

'Sounds good to me,' nodded Chad. 'The least time Brandon and I are seen in public, the better.'

'Talking of which... I'm just praying someone doesn't stumble across us here while we're assembling it all. That would be disastrous. There's no *way* we'll be able to hide the amount of equipment I intend putting in here.'

'Don't worry... we'll deal with that should the problem arise. Brandon's got his CIA badge to flash if people need scaring away. Failing that, we'll just have to incarcerate 'em in Donald's turbine! The best thing we can do to lessen the risk is work as quickly as possible.'

Norman raised the bag again. 'In that case, I'll get started.'

*   *   *

'I owe you an enormous debt of gratitude, John.' The president's vice-like handshake conveyed his level of appreciation. 'Without your insistence on a swift intervention, who *knows* what that girl Xanthia would have done to me.'

'I'm just glad I was able to do my duty and repay your government's trust in me, sir.'

'Well... I'm about to cement that trust even more. Having fully justified your recent elevation within the CIA, I believe a man of your skills and integrity should be given a chance to excel at an even *higher* level. I'm making you my new Secretary of Homeland Security. Congratulations, John. As of this moment, you're now an integral and valued member of my cabinet, in sole charge of its third largest department.' The president winked. 'By the way... it also makes you eighteenth in line for succession to the presidency... so I hope you won't take that as an incentive to relax on the job when it comes to protecting me!' He laughed at his own humour. 'Joking aside... I know the security of our country couldn't be in safer hands. I'm delighted to have you on board.'

John... AKA Mister Prometheus... struggled to find the right words. *Irony* should probably have been at the top of the list, but he thought it best not to go anywhere *near* that. 'I don't know what to say, sir,' he stuttered, his mind a whirl of contradictory thoughts.

The president's expression changed to one of concern. 'Your insights and expertise have never been more needed than they are right now, John. We're facing a threat to our democracy from a direction I never thought I'd see. It appears a cabal involving some of this nation's very own industrialists and entrepreneurs are seeking to exploit our current tribulations by making an unconstitutional grab for power. They're attempting to use their market dominance to secure themselves a prime position in my government. Can you believe that?'

Yes... he most certainly could.

'But I promise you... it ain't gonna happen... not while there's a breath left in my body. We're going to war, John...

116

and it's *you* who's gonna help me put an end to these unconscionable lowlifes. I'm afraid you're in for a baptism of fire. You won't find this new position of yours easy.'

Of that, AKA Mister Prometheus hadn't the slightest doubt.

'Be it far from me to tell you how to do that job, John… but I suggest the first thing you do is thoroughly investigate the woman who looks to be spearheading this despicable affair. It's essential we know everything about her. Your new department has already made inroads into that… but I want you to apply that special skill set of yours to the matter. I need you to get to know her better than you do your own wife.'

For a few, brief seconds, AKA Mister Prometheus came as close to believing in a benevolent god as he ever had or ever would. Could a divorce court judge be persuaded that the President of the United States had actually *commanded* him to commit adultery… or was that taking things a little too far? The element of doubt jerked him back to a reality far harsher than it had been a few minutes earlier. His position was now even *more* precarious. How on *earth* was he going to square this particular circle? Having already ceded control of his life to a group of ruthless megalomaniacs, it seemed his new job not only entailed hunting down those very same people, but… by association… himself!

That said… not *everyone* would consider it a poisoned chalice. He pictured how proud Mrs AKA Mister Prometheus would be when informing her friends and family that she was only eighteen unfortunate mishaps away from getting to redesign the White House rose garden. She might even be slightly proud of *him*.

But *far* more appealing was to consider what *Miss Eris'* reaction might be. Could there be an upside to his latest promotion *after* all? Power, they said, was an aphrodisiac. Would his elevated status make him more attractive to her? Would she be less likely to look down her nose at him and finally treat him as her equal? He pictured that nose… and everything attached to it.

'Did you hear what I said, John?'

He'd pictured it a little too long.

'Sorry, Mister President. I was assessing the task in hand.'

'She's a cold one, John. I've seen it in her eyes. Take it from me… when she gives you that stare of hers, it'll chill your entire body.'

AKA Mister Prometheus begged to differ. As it happens, it had *warmed* his… or at least a certain part of it. 'I promise to make my investigation as thorough as possible, Mister President,' he avowed. 'As per your instructions, I'll leave no crevice unexplored.' He pictured doing that as well. He was living dangerously enough anyway. He'd take his chances with Mrs AKA Mister Prometheus' lawyers in court.

The president nodded keenly. 'Excellent. I *knew* I'd picked the right man for the job.'

AKA Mister Prometheus inwardly cringed as the absurdity of his situation sunk in. The line now needing to be trod was even finer than before… and that was saying something. On the one side, a charge of treason and the rest of his life in prison… on the other, a charge of betrayal and the rest of his life curtailed. The only thing that could possibly be more awkward now was if the president were to put him on the spot and ask what had happened to Xanthia.

'So, John,' said the president, leaning towards him, his brow wrinkled with intrigue. 'On the subject of dangerous women… what exactly has happened to Xanthia?'

* * *

Miss Eris' hands hovered tentatively over the large, leather-bound book that had just been placed in front of her. 'This is definitely it?' she asked in an uncharacteristically reverent tone.

'We found it exactly where the old man at Arwan El Kahab said we would,' replied an individual in black combat fatigues.

'I wasn't talking to you!' she barked, her mood instantly changing. 'Of *course* it was where that old fool said it would be. I just need to be sure we haven't been outwitted by those whose

114

duty it was to keep such a valuable treasure hidden. Can we really trust this to be the genuine article?'

'I absolutely believe it is,' nodded Professor Cottingham, stepping forward. 'I am happy to stake a reputation built over countless years of studying Templar history, that this is the *very* book that precipitated their meteoric ascendancy throughout Europe on their return from the crusades. I confidently vouch… without an iota of doubt… you now have before you… the legendary…' He breathed in slowly through his nostrils to compensate for the lack of a drum roll. '…*Magnum Compendium Secretorum.*'

'It also says so just there,' said the man in combat fatigues, helpfully pointing to worn, embossed lettering on the front.

'Get your idiotic hand away from it!' shouted Miss Eris, thrusting it aside with an angry sweep of her own. She took a moment to resettle herself before placing her hands over the book again. 'I can't believe I have so sublime an object… considered by many to be a construct of myth… within my touch.' She closed her eyes… much like she had with Reverend Humbold in that very room… and sensually savoured the fact.

'*Ahem*… transcribed from the original ancient parchments, it is the greatest collection of secrets ever assembled,' concurred Professor Cottingham, pretending not to notice her facial expressions. 'In their original format, they would have been pored over and studied by King Solomon himself!'

Miss Eris made the sort of noise Professor Cottingham had once heard his wife make… though curiously not because of him.

'My own reward,' he continued, after politely clearing his throat, 'is that I have finally justified a lifetime's work by assisting in proving its existence, thereby advancing and enriching our understanding of history.'

'That and the huge amount of money I've paid to enrich *you*,' she muttered, though just loud enough for him to hear.

He put his fingertips together and gave an obsequious nod of gratitude.

'I actually believe I can feel its vibrations,' she purred, basking in the sensation.

'With respect, ma'am... are you sure that's not the maid vacuuming the room above?' enquired the man in fatigues, looking to redeem himself.

'Get out, you imbecile!' she screamed.

'Yes, ma'am.'

The imbecile departed.

'You will help me translate and make sense of its contents, Professor,' she instructed. 'I assume that is within your capabilities?'

'I would be humbled to assist you in such a task,' he bowed. 'I cannot express what an honour it will be to gaze upon the contents of this wondrous tome. I have... as per your instructions... only permitted myself the briefest glimpse in order to verify the item's authenticity. It will be an indescribable pleasure to gaze upon its wondrous secrets in more detail.'

'But therein lies a problem for me, Professor,' said Miss Eris, looking directly at him. '*You* will then know those secrets too.'

He smiled weakly, trying to ascertain whether the steely gaze she was giving him was part of a test. 'I *would*,' he drew out slowly.

'So... how do we get around that?'

'I'm sure we can find a way,' he replied, his mind racing to work out how.

'I'll leave that little conundrum with you.' She looked away to a corner of the room. 'It reminds me of the one faced by Tsar Ivan the Fourth when he commissioned the building of St. Basil's Cathedral in Moscow's Red Square. As I'm sure you know... it was a structure of such magnificent beauty, it is said he didn't want whoever designed it replicating their work for anyone else. So, once it was completed... living up to his epithet of *The Terrible*... he had their eyes gouged out.'

'Yes... I *am* aware of the legend,' the professor winced.

'And... as you say... it is just a legend, of course. Who knows if he *actually* did such a cruel thing?' She looked at him again

112

with the sweetest of smiles. 'But, I can tell you this… if it had been *me*… I most definitely *would* have.'

* * *

Davy Fury bounded in front of the cameras and greeted his Saturday night audience with the energy of a man half his age and a left nostril hiding the tell-tale remnants of a little bit of assistance.

'Thank you. Thank you. Wow… what a crowd we've got in!'

He waited for the excitement to subside.

'And we've certainly got a show for you, ladies and gentlemen. Because, boy… do we need some cheering up at the moment.' He feigned a pained look at camera three. 'It's getting pretty grim out there, ain't it folks?'

Folks up and down the country agreed.

'If I'd told you six months ago that I nearly didn't make it here this evening because a group of the biggest rats you've ever seen in your life laid siege to my house and did their best to prevent me getting to my car, you'd be waiting for the punchline… wouldn't you?'

Ordinarily, they would. But these weren't ordinary times… as Davy confirmed.

'But, there isn't one. It's absolutely true! A mischief of rats… yes, you learn something every day… decided to live up to their name and stop me reaching this studio. I'm sure my critics will wish they'd succeeded. But, the weirdest thing is… I'm not alone in experiencing such an encounter. Apparently, another mischief of renegade rodents gnawed their way into 10 Downing Street the other day and interrupted an emergency COBRA meeting that had been called to discuss the current state of affairs. I think that's the first case of rats *joining* a sinking ship! But I kid you not… they were everywhere I turned. Thank god I'm handy with a number five iron.' He enthusiastically mimed the perfect tee shot. 'It was carnage!'

The action induced nervous laughter.

'It sure as hell confused the neighbours sunbathing in their gardens. Looking up, they couldn't work out why the little critters weren't wearing parachutes.' He shook his head, not waiting for a reaction. 'I mean… seriously… what *is* happening out there, ladies and gentlemen?'

The ladies and gentlemen were wondering the same thing, too. It was all part of a depressingly familiar narrative. Animals of every type were going rogue. Reports of dive-bombing crows, sparrow hawks, red kites, and even the odd, pumped-up robin keeping people prisoner in their own homes were becoming commonplace. As were cases of old age pensioners having to be rescued from their own pets. God help you if you'd ever upset your hamster.

'Before we take our minds off it all with some lighter stuff… and in keeping with this show's reputation for blending the fun with the facts… we thought we ought to at least *try* and get to the bottom of what's going on. So, coming up… I'll be talking to Miriam Prudenberry, Chair of CRAPOLA, the Clairvoyants, Readers and Psychics of London Association… they really need to do something about that acronym… who says it's down to angry spirits having got tired of being dead and trying to possess whatever low form of life they can…' He glanced at camera three again. 'Boy… is my *agent* in trouble!'

The audience liked that one… his agent, *not* so much.

'And I'll be speaking to world-renowned scientist and atheist, Kurt Schitter… who says it's all a fuss about nothing and down to the media prioritising negative stories… thereby distorting our perception of what's going on. All I can say, Kurt, is… those rats were real… ask my neighbours!' He mimed another tee shot.

The show's director cued a close-up on his face.

'But perhaps the award for the most bizarre set of occurrences this week has to go to the arrest, incarceration and subsequent escape of this country's greatest, living playwright and eccentric… Donald Tucker-Jenkins… who the Americans have accused of fomenting global unrest, terrorism and market rigging.' He gave camera three another of his asides. 'Why wasn't *Shakespeare* that interesting when I was at school?'

It produced further laughter.

'What's more… if *that* isn't off-the-scale weird enough… he's said to have been aided and abetted in these shenanigans by the current partner of model and would-be messiah, Zany Xanthia… who sat here on my couch in total silence three weeks ago, as her boyfriend was inadvertently exposed as being the mastermind behind the recent Stonehenge controversy. Wow… what a car crash of an interview *that* turned out to be!'

The audience agreed.

'And on the subject of crashes… that wasn't the *only* wreck we had on the show that day. Colourful rock legend and wearer of unfeasibly tight trousers… the unique and incorrigible Stump… proved to us all that sitting in a chair isn't as easy as you might have thought.'

A cheer went up as memories were jogged.

'I'm just relieved the identity of Stonehenge's mystery benefactor was the *only* thing *Trouzerbulge's* wacky frontman exposed that night! The good news is… we've mopped up after him and… much against the advice of the doctor treating my producer's high blood pressure… I've decided to accede to Stump's surprise request for a return appearance and allow him back on tonight's show to explain himself.'

An even louder cheer sounded… which is precisely why Davy had overruled the objectors. He wasn't daft. He knew where the ratings lay.

'The *bad* news is… I'll probably never work again if it all goes horribly wrong!'

Those in the production gallery put their heads in their hands and prayed that *wouldn't* be the case.

'I guess there's only one way to find out, isn't there? So, ladies and gentlemen… without further ado… please welcome… that well-known tsunami of excess… along with a worryingly volatile amount of hairspray… the hopefully-sober-for-my-sake… and not smoking… STUMP!'

The audience whooped their delight as the man himself strutted onto the set, his fist raised in recognition of his notoriety.

'Bit rude,' he mumbled, dropping down into his seat and ruffling his hair to prove it was still capable of moving.

'So is passing out midway through a conversation and decorating the studio floor with your lunch,' sparred Davy. 'I hope you're not looking to give us a repeat performance.'

'Yeah... about that,' Stump drawled. 'I think I owe the viewers an apology... especially any little kids who were watching. It was an appalling example of how to behave in such a situation.'

Davy gave a nod of respect.

'I absolutely did the wrong thing,' Stump grimaced. 'I should've remained *compos mentis* and smacked you in the mouth when you tried to make a fool out of Xanthia.'

Buttocks instantly clenched in the gallery.

'I didn't have to *try,*' Davy parried, his *own* suddenly not occupying as much of his chair as he'd like. 'But let's not go over old ground. You said you wanted to come on here tonight to deliver an important message... which I understand is connected to all this craziness I was talking about earlier.'

'That's right,' said Stump, trying to remember how sitting upright went. 'Primarily about Xanthia... but also that boyfriend of hers, Norman, and his alleged partner in crime, Donald.'

'What about them?'

Stump shook his head. 'That professor you had on here last time... the one with the over-enthusiastic socks.'

'Wotaspanner.'

'Yeah... you're right... he *totally* was. Well... he tried to make out the whole Stonehenge thing was nothing more than a case of mass hysteria. So... I'm here tonight to state... categorically... he was wrong. That ball of light was a gift from a higher power, and as real as you and me sitting here.'

Davy leant forward, though keeping just enough distance between him and his guest to avoid being thumped. 'Forgive me for asking the question... but have you been drinking... as in... more than usual?'

The audience sniggered.

Stump gave Davy a look suggesting the chat show host might've miscalculated the length of his arm. 'As a matter of fact, I'll have you know not a *single* drop has passed these lips since I sat here last.'

'*Multiple* drops, perhaps?' chanced Davy.

Stump gave a saintly shake of his head.

Davy returned another appreciative nod. 'I'm impressed. That can't have been easy for a man like you.'

'It's wasn't,' admitted Stump, 'although the copious amounts of drugs have helped.'

Davy felt the seat of his chair become even more a stranger to him. He quickly changed the subject. 'Okay... so why this sudden change of heart? What spurred the need for a public display of support for your ex-girlfriend?'

'Cos I believe she's in serious trouble and needs my help.'

'And what makes you say that?'

Stump reached into his pocket and pulled out a piece of paper. 'This.' He held it up to the camera. 'It's a note she wrote before agreeing to a meeting with no less than the President of the United States. She wrote it because she knew there was a chance she would never be seen alive again if she went. It gives a graphic account of her treatment at the hands of the CIA a few days earlier, which included being waterboarded.'

The astonishing claim drew a loud gasp from the audience.

'That's why she suddenly disappeared from an idiot evangelist's show over there. The CIA kidnapped her. They knocked her out with some kinda drug and spirited her away to be interrogated.'

Davy stared at his guest incredulously. This wasn't quite the fun entertainment he'd intended for the opening part of his show.

'They resorted to torture because she refused to allow her newly-acquired gift to be used for national or commercial

107

gain... believing it to be for the benefit of *all* mankind... which includes you and everyone watching this.'

The studio fell silent.

'What's more... she sent it to me because I was the only person she thought she could trust... despite letting her down on your show by being more concerned about my image, and what the public would think, than backing up her claims... which I knew to be true. And the reason I *do* know is because I was involved with her and Penkridge in a plan to stop the Universe from being annihilated.' He stuck a hand up, anticipating Davy's reaction. 'Now... you can have your ten minutes of fun at my expense if you like, but I'm telling you the God's honest truth. I'm willing to risk losing my hard-earned, bad boy reputation and suffer every single bit of ridicule that *she* has, to tell you this... that girl is one hundred percent *genuine* in her claims, and has more guts than anybody I've ever met... and I've met some mean motherfu_'

Beeep.

'...in my time.'

Thanks to the lightning reactions of someone in the gallery... their sweating finger having been hovering expectantly over a button... the audience at home were spared some of the less family-friendly details... though, ironically, they concerned being a little *too* family friendly.

Davy put his hand to his earpiece. 'My apologies for that, folks. And, yes... I've been told to remind you, Stump, we're still pre-watershed. There are youngsters watching this show who may have caught your colourful language.'

'Given what you've just told 'em about your mischief of rats... that should be the *least* of their fucking worries!' he exclaimed.

Someone in the gallery winced and mouthed the word *bollocks.*

'Even if you think she and I are completely nuts, we're talking about a girl who could be undergoing more horrendous torture as we speak. Forget paranormal nightmares... *this* one's manmade!' Stump searched for the right camera to look into.

106

'And by the way… if anyone out there is stone-hearted enough to think she should've kept her mouth shut in the first place, I'd like to point out that… having escaped her captors first time around… she bravely walked back into the lion's den, knowing full well she might never come out again. She didn't *need* to go back, but she did… because she was trying to save us all… despite the ridicule she'd already received for it.'

You could have heard a pin drop.

'Can I see that?' asked Davy, reaching for the note.

'Sure. I've had copies sent to every media outlet in the country. And not because I thought I might get cold feet and change my mind before I got here… but because we need to act fast.'

Davy's brow wrinkled. 'And do what, exactly?'

'Find out where she is, of course, and rescue her!'

'And her boyfriend?'

'Yeah, him as well… and Donald. They're both as innocent as she is.'

'But how can you be so sure?'

Stump drew himself nearer to Davy. 'Let me tell you something about Norman Penkridge. That man doesn't have a bad bone in his body.'

'He stole your girlfriend,' Davy pointed out… *carefully*.

'He didn't steal her,' returned Stump coolly. 'She simply came to her senses and realised he was a far better person than I could *ever* be. Despite how the media like to portray her, that girl was *never* stupid… even before Stonehenge.'

Davy threw up his hands in mock surrender. 'Okay. So, given all that… how, exactly, do you intend going about this rescue?'

Stump raised himself in his chair. 'Well… for starters… I'm demanding the American president comes clean and tells us where Xanthia is. She's a guest in his country, so all he needs to do is produce her and let her come home. As for the other two… he needs to allow the evidence he *claims* to have on 'em to be examined by an independent panel.'

'You're referring to two suitcases of incriminating notes taken from their hotel.'

'Yeah… and if he does all that, I'll cease my campaign.'

'*Campaign?*'

'Yeah… Free the Friggin' Three.'

'That's quite an interesting slogan you've gone for,' Davy choked. 'Is the second F word *really* necessary?'

'Take it from the writer of one of the greatest rock anthems in history… you need a standout hook to get people to sit up and listen. Waggy, my bass player, even suggested I try and crowbar *sex* in there somehow. But… as I'm sure you'll agree… not only would that mess up the alliteration… it'd be just as inappropriate a word to use as motherfu_'

Beeeeep.

'But we're not talking about the lyrics to a song,' Davy frowned.

'Actually… we *are.* I'm putting them to *Sex Wench* and releasing it as a single. That'll guarantee it gets played around the world and embarrasses the yanks into getting off their fat ar…'

Beeep.

'…nd doing something.'

'Are the rest of *Trouzerbulge* with you on this?'

'Yeah… in fact, it's the first time we've agreed on anything in years. I mean… how could you not? We go into the studio tomorrow. Luckily, Waggy's currently out on bail. We'll use the power of the chorus to ram the message home… with different words, of course.' Standing and making a fist, he began punching the air. 'Free them! Free them! Free them!'

As he passionately sung the iconic two note refrain, people up and down the country felt an overwhelming urge to join in.

'Well, there you have it,' said Davy, turning to the camera. 'A *Trouzerbulge* world exclusive. I just hope we're not going to have to pay royalties for that impromptu performance!'

Stump immediately stopped what he was doing and glared at Davy. 'This is hardly a time for joking, you daft cu_'

Beeeeeeeeeeeeeeeeeeeeeeeeeeeeeeeeeeeeep.

Reaching inside his jacket, the president removed a slim, leather wallet containing a handful of credit cards and a single, one dollar bill. Taking out the dollar bill, he carefully unfolded it and placed it face up on his desk.

'Time for one of our special chats, George,' he addressed the portrait at its centre.

'It's been a while since our last one, but I'm hoping you'll be able to give me some much-needed inspiration… or at least a sign that things are gonna be alright. God knows I need that right now! I've tried asking *Him,* of course, but he doesn't seem to be listening.'

He grimaced.

'For one glorious moment I thought he was and had sent me the answer… but she turned out to be the devil in disguise.'

He nodded at a large pile of folders on the side of the desk.

'As you can see… I've got my work cut out for me. I'm being presented with an endless stream of national emergencies faster than I can read the damn reports. If it's not floods, it's droughts… and if not an extremely vexed population intent on taking umbrage with every single issue under the sun, it's plagues of things unholy infesting this glorious land of ours and creating a climate of fear and panic. And, as for the *actual* climate… let's not go there on *that* one! I doubt *any* of the presidents that have filled the gap between you and me have ever faced such a dire situation.'

He looked beyond the window.

'Abe might wish to disagree on that, of course… and I'm sure Woodrow, Franklin and Harry would tell me to stop feeling sorry for myself and do whatever a president is supposed to do in these circumstances. But what exactly *is* that, George? I mean… where's the enemy?'

George Washington maintained his offset look of inscrutability and said nothing.

'Where do I look for *my* Trenton or Yorktown? What on earth am I supposed to do?'

He anxiously drummed his fingers on the desk. 'And if being under attack from every direction imaginable wasn't bad enough… I've now got a group of self-serving capitalists taking advantage of the situation and demanding a seat alongside me at my table in return for their favour. How would you have dealt with *that* one, George?'

He stoically raised his head.

'I'll fight 'em, of course. As I'm sure you'll concur… there's no way the holder of our office could ever agree to such a price. Perhaps I should be grateful. At least they've given me a definite line in the sand to draw. I need a victory to hold up to the public and get them on my side again. But where exactly do I strike? The only appropriate weapon at my disposal would be totally counterproductive, seeing as I can hardly sanction companies whose goods I desperately need. And as for whose heads I should sever in order to put a stop to this particular problem… having thought I'd successfully done just that, yet another… far more callous and calculating… has sprung up to take their place. It seems my only chance of victory is to slay the actual *body* of this infernal hydra. The problem is… I'm not sure where or what that is anymore.'

He sank back in his chair and gazed up at the presidential seal on the ceiling.

'*E pluribus unum.* I fear those words are starting to mock me, now. So much for us being one nation, eh, George? I doubt we've ever experienced a time when it's been more fractured and divisive… Abe's tenure included. The irony is… that means we've only got *ourselves* to blame.'

He picked up the dollar bill.

'Forgive me a second.'

He turned it over.

'If we're to get ourselves outta this mess, those words need pride of place on these notes… just like you… not relegated to an awkward squint somewhere away to the right. We need to *shout* them and remind the populace of what you and your fellow compatriots managed to achieve… and the benefits that were gained by everyone standing together.'

He snorted his irony.

'Besides... *In God We Trust* is starting to look a *little* optimistic right now.'

As his eyes idly scanned the rest of the bill, they suddenly froze.

His jaw dropped as he stared in stupefaction at the Eye of Providence looking back at him from atop a thirteen-tiered pyramid.

It wasn't the all-seeing icon itself that had induced his reaction. He'd long known that claims its use was part of a dark conspiracy, involving those who shared its symbolism, conveniently ignored the fact the government had adopted the image first. It was *who* shared that symbolism that caused his blood to chill.

'Oh... thank you, George,' he mumbled through his shock. 'I *knew* you wouldn't let me down.'

His finger shot towards the intercom on his desk.

'Jenny... get Gus in here... PRONTO!'

He didn't have long to wait before his breathless Chief of Staff was quizzing him with a look of concern.

'I've discovered the Hydra's body, Gus! I know who's behind the corporeal side of this endless torment we've been suffering. Tucker-Jenkins, Penkridge, Xanthia and that other she-devil you had me meet... they're just mere *pawns* in this whole affair. I know who's been moving the pieces and where we must strike to put an end to at least the manmade misery that's been plaguing us.'

His Chief of Staff looked at him warily. 'And where would that be, sir?'

The president returned a grin so wide it nearly dislocated his jaw. 'The Templars!'

'I beg your pardon?'

'They control the vast network of Masonic organisations that stretch around this planet and exert their influence at every level of society and... more appropriately... *business*.' He shook his head. 'I can't believe I didn't pick up on it earlier. Donald mentioned them in passing when he told me they'd financed the work his partner had been doing. I didn't think anything of it at the time. I was more concerned about all the *other* stuff he was telling me.'

'He actually said they'd *financed* Penkridge?'

'His very words!'

'But they're a force for good... *aren't* they?'

'They're an extremely secretive one, Gus... I know that much. So... you tell me.'

'It's just that...'

'Wait a minute...' The president eyed him suspiciously. 'I take it *you've* never rolled up a trouser leg?'

'Never while wearing an apron, sir.'

The president nodded. 'Glad to hear it.'

'But some of our founding fathers were freemasons, Mister President.'

The president stuck up a finger. 'You're right.' He looked at his Chief of Staff with alarm. 'My god, Gus... this plot's been around longer than I thought!'

'Including *George Washington*,' his Chief of Staff added delicately, realising he wasn't quite getting his message across.

'George?' The president turned over the dollar bill he was still holding. 'How *could* you?' he groaned. 'I thought you were my friend!'

His Chief of Staff pretended he hadn't heard that.

'We need to come down hard and fast on every part of this Masonic conspiracy!' the president declared, the revelation merely strengthening his determination.

'But, Mister President... are you *seriously* suggesting they're responsible for all this turmoil?'

'All I know is the admission of their involvement with Penkridge came from Donald's own mouth... and we've just designated him joint public enemy number one. Think about it, Gus... freemasons are likely to be sitting on the boards of every single one of those corporations that are now holding us to ransom!'

His Chief of Staff shifted uncomfortably. 'That may be so... but we'd have to proceed with *incredible* caution if we were to launch an investigation against so august a body. Such an action would be political dynamite... if not outright suicide. And who's to say those undertaking the investigation wouldn't be freemasons themselves?'

'You're right... this whole situation is as difficult as it gets. But so is the one we've been enduring these past months and for which they're *clearly* responsible. We can't stand idly by. We *have* to do something... and quickly.'

'What exactly are you proposing?'

'We don't have time for caution... or an investigation. We need to act decisively. As of today, I'm designating them a terrorist organisation and offering an amnesty to all those who hand in their aprons. Now... I'm not naive enough to expect a massive uptake on that offer... but at least they'll have had their wings clipped. Then we'll hit them where it *really* hurts. I'm gonna issue an immediate presidential decree and embargo to freeze their funds and assets around the world... those within our jurisdiction, of course. But I'm pretty confidant other governments will follow suit, once they realise what these Templars have *really* been up to.'

'But sir... what if they *are* innocent and working for the good, as claimed?'

The president waved the thought down. 'Then, they'll understand our predicament and appreciate that desperate times require desperate measures. Better safe than sorry, eh, Gus?'

His Chief of Staff wondered which end of their predicament that adage should be applied to. 'With respect, sir... are you absolutely *sure* about this?'

'Never more so,' asserted the president. 'The tide has definitely turned in our favour. I mean... consider our position. Tucker-Jenkins and Penkridge are dead men walking... the Templars are about to be neutered... and, for the icing on the cake... we now have the best Secretary of Homeland Security we could ever wish for. I tell you this, Gus... we couldn't have played a better hand.'

His Chief of Staff bowed awkwardly. 'As you wish, Mister President, I'll go ahead and make the necessary arrangements.'

The president stuck out a hand to stop him leaving. 'And talking of aprons... there's *another* group of fifth columnists we need to eliminate. Having been bold enough to openly fraternise with Tucker-Jenkins and his cohorts in public, we must assume their meetings to be *riddled* with dodgy handshakes. Given they don't have the same political clout as the Templars, we can safely have them all rounded up and incarcerated immediately.'

'And who might these home-grown terrorists be, sir?'

The president looked at his Chief of Staff with the air of man at the top of his game. 'The Association of American Saucepan Manufacturers.'

*　　*　　*

'What d'ya mean *the money's not there?*' Chad exclaimed. 'Your friend *must've* received that cheque we sent him by now and made the transfer.'

Norman removed his hands from the laptop and raised them in bewilderment. 'You're absolutely right. We should be staring at an extremely healthy balance. But this new account's still showing a big fat zero.'

'Do you think he's kept the money for himself?' asked Brandon. 'With the amount involved, I think even *I'd* have been tempted.'

A furious bout of typing and some expert hacking confirmed he hadn't.

'Is it possible the chequebook's been deactivated for a second time?' Xanthia offered, from over Norman's shoulder. 'D'ya think Kevin's involved in this somehow?'

'I thought you said you'd put an extra layer of security around it to prevent that ever happening again.'

'I did. As far as I'm concerned, it's impenetrable... even for the likes of him. But he's nothing if not resourceful. Maybe he found another route. Here… let me have a look.' Nudging him out of the way, she set about attacking the keyboard herself.

After a short while her manic clattering stopped.

'That's strange,' she scowled, pulling back from the screen. 'Whatever I do, I'm getting the same *denial of access* message for the main Templar account.'

'Not *that* unusual, given what you're attempting,' Norman shrugged. 'Keep trying. There's always a way around them.'

'No… I mean exactly the same *style* of message I encountered when trying to access another website earlier today… and I wasn't hacking that.'

'What site?'

'*That's* the strange part. I was simply looking to buy stuff for our new stove when we get it.'

'Come again?'

'We need a decent set of saucepans.'

'I recognise this notice,' said Brandon, tapping his temple knowingly. 'It's designed to look perfunctory, but is there courtesy of the darker side of our security agencies. This isn't any *ordinary* block. It might be outside their jurisdiction, but someone at the top clearly doesn't want anyone having access to this Templar account.'

'Or saucepans… apparently,' boomed Donald from the open service hatch of his turbine.

Chad scratched his head. 'What's all *that* about?'

'Dunno,' said Brandon, shaking his. 'Perhaps we oughta check the news. Something might be going on out there we're not aware of.'

What that *something* was became obvious as soon as Xanthia followed his advice and alighted upon a headline decrying the president's decision to outlaw two seemingly benign organisations and freeze their assets.

'Has he gone mad?' cried Norman, as she read the article aloud. 'The Masons and the Association of American Saucepan Manufacturers? What the *hell* are we gonna do now?'

'Buy a microwave instead,' came the voice from the hatch.

'I meant about the money! If we don't have the finances in place, we won't be able to build my new Ark!'

'On top of which, we're soon gonna find ourselves getting hungry,' added Chad. 'Brandon and I exhausted the last of our funds getting you online. Last time I looked, we only had a single packet of biscuits left.'

'Sooner than you think,' Donald munched from inside his retreat.

Norman grabbed his head. 'We're done for!'

'Well... while not wishing to put too fine a point on it... we were *anyway*,' Xanthia softly reminded him.

'You have to do something,' insisted Chad, looking at her imploringly. 'You're our last hope. If you can't find a solution to this mess... like Norman said... we're doomed!'

The hatch door slammed shut with mute resignation.

* * *

Miss Eris excitedly ran her hands over the folder in front of her. 'This is it?'

'As comprehensive a translation of the opening sections of the *Magnum Compendium Secretorum* as it's possible to produce in so short a time,' answered Professor Cottingham. 'There is much more work to do, of course... but you said you were keen to see the results of my efforts so far.'

'And our little dilemma, Professor? How has that learned mind of yours fared in working out a way to undertake your task and not be privy to the secrets it reveals?' She stared at him dispassionately while awaiting an answer.

The professor ran his tongue along the front of his teeth to unstick them from his lips. 'As I'm sure you can appreciate, such a thing would be impossible.'

This wasn't strictly true. He'd considered enlisting the help of some of his brightest students and assigning them individual, numbered lines of text to translate, which could then be sequentially presented to her without anyone knowing the full picture... including him. But given her fearsome reputation, he figured she would merely assume they might all get together at some point and assemble the work for themselves... in which case, he might find himself lecturing to a considerably reduced class.

'But I believe I've found a solution that will satisfy you,' he added hastily. His eyes flickered nervously as he scanned her face for the merest hint of a favourable reaction.

'Go on.'

'Hypnosis,' he announced with as much positivity as he could muster. 'I have already ensured that, as I complete each section of work, all knowledge of it is erased from my mind, courtesy of a dear friend of mine who happens to be one of this country's most eminent clinical hypnotherapists. They've guaranteed I'll have permanent amnesia when it comes to the work I've undertaken and the knowledge uncovered. You can rest assured that you, and you alone, will hold the secrets of the *Compendium*.'

Guaranteed was a bit of an exaggeration. Neither of them knew if this approach would work in the long run, given the professor's deep-rooted interest and level of passion in the once-fabled manuscript. But that wasn't the point. He just needed Miss Eris to believe it would.

She held her gaze as she considered the solution.

'Very well,' she finally nodded. 'It's probably a lot less messy than a full-frontal lobotomy.'

The professor's lips attached themselves to his teeth again. 'You're right... it thertainly would be,' he lisped.

'So... you must now double your efforts. I need you to finish translating the rest of the *Compendium* as quickly as possible. I have no desire to wait any longer than is necessary.'

'I will do my bethed.'

'You most certainly will,' she glared. She picked up the file and sensuously caressed its edges, 'I, in the meantime, will avail myself of what has been achieved so far. I trust I will find the contents here within exceedingly enlightening?'

'I have no idea,' he replied, looking at her blankly.

That, *also*, wasn't strictly true. Something in the back of his mind vaguely hinted at a method of obtaining immense power from crystals, and… bizarrely… something to do with yawning. But he quite liked the layout of his forehead as it was.

*   *   *

Norman struggled to believe his stunning *volte-face* in fortune as Chad reversed a brand new truck through the large, shuttered opening at the far end of the building. Where once it had witnessed the daily passage of supplies essential for the operation and maintenance of the power station, it now provided the portal for goods way beyond the comprehension of its builders.

'I know you don't want to tell me how you managed this, Xan,' he exclaimed, 'but, in all honesty… I don't care! Twenty-four hours ago I thought it was all over for us.'

'I'm not sure if Gabriel would approve of my method or not,' she smiled. 'But at least you can get on with building your *Ark Two.*'

'This lot should keep you busy for a while,' shouted Chad, jumping from the cab and enthusiastically slapping the side of his truck. 'This thing's packed to the roof. Everything went like clockwork, just as Xanthia planned.' Walking briskly over to a large set of rusty chains, he began pulling on them, so as to lower an enormous metal shutter and keep their exploits hidden. 'As soon as everything's unloaded, I'm off for a second run.'

'It shouldn't be long before Brandon's here with *his* delivery,' said Xanthia, checking her watch. 'We need to get you out again as quickly as possible.'

Chad glanced around the loading bay. 'In that case… where's Donald?'

'He told me he doesn't do manual work,' answered Norman, 'so I've put him in charge of catering… which may not have been the best idea I've ever had. He's still trying to work out how the oven works. He says he's only ever used gas... and, even then, failed miserably to kill himself with it.'

The shutter reunited with the floor, Chad switched his attention to the one on the back of his truck. Enthusiastically sending it rattling skyward in a single motion, he exposed his packed cargo of boxes, the smell of fresh cardboard invigorating Norman's nostrils. 'So... where do you want this lot?'

Norman pointed at the ground. 'Here will do. To speed up the turnaround, I'll sort everything once you've gone.'

Chad grabbed a handful of boxes. 'I've never seen so many empty shelves... or euphoric store managers. I think they all thought Christmas had come early.'

'It has,' Norman beamed, taking them from him. 'Xan and I managed to access the NSA's server this morning far more easily than I ever supposed. You'd think they, of *all* people, would know to take more care!'

'And did you find what you were looking for?'

'We certainly did. They have it all... every piece of data I'd uploaded for my original Ark.'

'All we need now are those art supplies I requested,' she added. 'Once I get those, I can start work on recreating the Turner. Norman should then have all the data he needs to produce his vibrations.'

Chad passed him another set of boxes. 'Just one question... how are you gonna trigger them all?'

'I'll leave that to an old friend of mine from back in the day,' Norman smiled. 'It'll be nice to see him again. It's been a while.'

Chad flashed a look of concern. 'The *Provider?*'

'No... I'm talking about Spikey. He's a little metal aardvark who's particularly good at bouncing.'

'I'll pretend I understand,' said Chad, handing him another load.

It took fifteen minutes for the truck to be emptied and sent on its way again. Soon after, Brandon arrived with *his* delivery and the process was repeated.

Norman spent the next few hours transporting the boxes to the centre of the building where Xanthia had been tasked with unpacking them.

By the time Chad returned with his second and final load of the day, Norman had already begun placing the assorted collection of computers in a series of concentric circles around the most central of the turbines, their screens all facing inwards.

'It's got a quasi-religious vibe to it... like electronic monks in silent prayer,' observed Chad, admiring his work. 'I reckon it's gonna look pretty spectacular when done.'

'At least I don't have to worry about the load-bearing capabilities of my landlord's floorboards this time,' Norman laughed.

'Just as well,' said Chad. 'I've another heavy truckload. How are those muscles of yours feeling?'

'Much like the rest of me... completely exhausted... and we're only on day one. Xanthia reckons we've at least another six more ahead of us before we're ready to switch this thing on. I just hope my body lasts that long!'

'It better,' said Chad grimly. 'And it won't be a moment too soon when we do. Things are kicking off big time out there. Basic manners – or *any* semblance of courtesy – have gone the same way as commonsense. Stop lights are now arbitrary... sidewalks are for losers... and the middle finger appears to be the new greeting. Everyone's angry. I've seen several road rage incidents turn into serious, physical blows. It's scary how things can deteriorate so fast. I reckon I misinterpreted the store managers' smiles this morning when taking their stock off their hands. It wasn't joy... it was *relief.* They probably figured it was only a question of time before the stuff was looted. At least they've now got their money in the bank. A handful of shops I passed this evening weren't so lucky.'

'It's only going to get worse,' warned Xanthia, joining them. 'Bank deposits will soon be worthless, anyway. We're witnessing the start of a death spiral. As negativity feeds on itself, selfishness and violence will increase exponentially until...' She grimaced. 'You know what.'

'Not if I can help it,' insisted Norman. 'It just needs a serious amount of positivity thrown into the mix.'

'*Amen* to that,' said Chad. 'But you'll have your work cut out preaching to *that* lot. A couple of times I felt the need to check my sidearm, just in case someone took an interest in my cargo.'

'I rest my case,' Xanthia sighed.

Norman straightened his back and nodded. 'Let's do this, then.'

Making their way over to the truck, they'd just reached the rear of it when Chad froze.

'When are you expecting Brandon back?' he asked apprehensively.

'Not for a couple of hours,' replied Xanthia. 'I had to send him further afield for his second run.'

Chad shot a look of alarm towards the loading bay shutters. 'There's someone outside!' he whispered frantically.

* * *

'This is the *last* thing I needed,' groaned the president, reading the report he'd just been handed. 'As if I haven't got *enough* on my plate at the moment.'

'It appears to be gaining a huge amount of momentum, sir,' observed his Chief of Staff. 'That's why I thought you needed to see it. I don't think we can simply ignore this matter.'

The president shook his head incredulously. 'You're right, Gus. But, I ask you... *Free the Friggin' Three...?* And from a country that produced such sublime wordsmiths as Shakespeare, Milton, Dickens, and Tucker-Jenkins.' He winced at the irony of the last name.

'We're still fending off universal indignation at us having detained the latter and labelled him a terrorist,' said his Chief of Staff. 'There's even been widespread support for his escape. That outrage appears to have been combined with everyone's fascination for Xanthia and used to fuel this campaign, via an annoyingly catchy jingle that's grabbing everyone's attention. It's got the public questioning whether all three of our detainees are the criminals we say they are. This thing needs addressing head on, sir. If not, there's a danger of it turning those three into folk heroes.'

'And making *me* out to be the bad guy,' the president scowled. 'Don't people realise how precarious the situation already is? I'm fighting fires from every conceivable angle on their behalf. When will they realise I'm on their side?'

'The problem is you represent everything they're rebelling against. People now see individual freedom as more important than collective responsibility. They're looking for a target to attack... and you're the one on top of the hill.'

'Not for long if certain people get their way,' the president scoffed.

'And... with respect, sir...' His Chief of Staff looked at him awkwardly. 'Those two recent embargos you imposed haven't helped. The press are having a field day with them.'

'I did what needed to be done, Gus. Strong leadership requires strong decisions. Besides... you'd think people would have more to worry about right now than the fate of the Masons.'

'They do, sir. Our polling suggests they're more worried about the fate of their saucepans.'

'They won't have anything to put in 'em if I fail to turn things around,' the president retorted. 'Talking of which... have we managed to persuade those countries we talked about this morning to drop their threats of an export ban on foodstuffs?'

'It's not looking promising, sir. Like everyone else, they're concerned about not being able to feed their own people.'

'Then we'll implement a reciprocal blanket ban on all our goods, if they go ahead. Tell 'em that!' The president turned to the report again. 'This is ridiculous. The implication here is that I've had this Xanthia done away with!'

'That could be to our advantage, sir. If we parade her in front of the world's press and prove it to be false, it should undermine the rest of the campaign and remove the wind from its sails.'

The president pursed his lips. 'I know he's some kinda rock icon… but what more do we know about this Stump fella who's behind it all?'

'I'm told he's from England, sir.'

The president sighed and raised a hand. 'Enough said.'

'He also happens to be Xanthia's ex-boyfriend.'

'God help me! No *wonder* the press are jumping on this. It's got everything… larger than life characters… a perceived sense of injustice… and now a celebrity love triangle!'

'Not to mention an extremely unpopular government.'

The president glared at his Chief of Staff.

'I'm merely reporting the polls… sir.'

Having considered the situation, the president drew a defiant breath. 'Here's what we're gonna do… I want you to set up that meeting with the press. I'll personally get hold of John at Homeland and have him arrange for Xanthia to attend. She's obviously being cooperative, because the last time we spoke, he assured me I no longer need concern myself about her. I've no intention of releasing her, of course… but we'll show she's alive… remind the public of the threat she poses and put this nonsense to bed.'

'Shall I inform her ex about it?'

The president raised a finger. 'Better still… invite him to the meeting. It'll make the perfect optic, having his claim disproved and being forced to eat his words in public. As you know, the vice-president's been in Rome discussing the current crisis with the Vatican. Get him to divert Air Force Two to London on his way home and offer this troublemaker a courtesy ride. That'll guarantee he's here tomorrow.'

'You'll have to issue him a Presidential Pardon first, sir. I understand he's been banned from entering this country because of his drug misuse.'

The president blinked in shock. 'That's ridiculous! I thought it was only the odd snort of cocaine.'

'Hardly, sir. My understanding is, at any time of the day, he's a walking pharmacy!'

The president's eyes narrowed. 'We *are* talking about the vice-president?'

* * *

Chad carefully approached the loading bay door with his gun drawn. Stealthily drawing back its rusty bolt, he squeezed it open just enough to see what was occurring outside.

'Brandon!' he shouted, kicking it fully open. 'What the hell are you doing here?'

'Jesus!' Brandon yelped, grabbing his chest. 'You nearly gave me a heart attack! What's with the gun?'

Chad checked his watch. 'We weren't expecting you for at *least* another couple of hours. Has something gone wrong?'

'Yeah... I reckon the whole of society!' Brandon shook his adrenalin out. 'There's no *way* I'm driving this thing outside of daylight. I figured it better to return with *half* a load than no load at all. It's getting heavy duty out there. What I need is someone riding shotgun... but I'm not sure about the wisdom of putting Donald anywhere *near* live ammunition!'

Chad holstered his weapon and anxiously surveyed the waste ground around them. 'We'd better get you in.'

* * *

AKA Mister Prometheus slowly put the phone down, his face ashen-white.

'Is everything alright, dear?' asked Mrs AKA Mister Prometheus from over the top of her magazine. 'Only... you look like you're about to be sick. And if you are, would you kindly do so somewhere else. I've only recently had this carpet cleaned.'

'Thank you for your concern,' he mumbled in a daze.

'Was that the president?'

'Yes... it was. That's why I kept saying... "yes, Mister President".'

'I hope that's not sarcasm, John! You know it's not allowed in this house.'

'I'd never be sarcastic to the president,' he replied.

She narrowed her eyes, wondering whether that counted. 'I hope not! Having just been promoted, you don't want to be doing anything silly.'

It was a bit late for that, he thought.

'John... you're really not looking well... and if I see so much as a single speck of vomit on my carp_'

'How do you fancy living somewhere hot?' he interrupted her.

She put down her magazine. 'I beg your pardon?'

'Don't you think it would be nice to live someplace where we never had to put the heating on to keep warm?'

She considered the question. 'What... do you mean like Florida?'

'I was thinking more of... Djibouti... or... Vanuatu.'

'Where on earth are *they?*'

'Somewhere non-extraditable,' he muttered to himself.

She tutted and shook her head. 'I'm perfectly happy where I am, thank you. Besides... I'd miss my circle of friends.'

He studied her as she went back to her reading and wondered what she'd do when the truth came out. Short of Xanthia turning up of her own volition at the president's planned press briefing in a little less than twenty-four hours, he figured divorce would be a pretty good bet.

'What if I said that's what *I* wanted?'

The magazine lowered dangerously.

'Have you been drinking?' she glared.

'No... but I think I'll start. Will you care to join me?'

She huffed... which was never a good sign. 'What's got into you, John? You've been acting incredibly strangely these last few days. You haven't been your normal self... and *that's* trying enough at times. Is it something to do with work?'

'You could say that,' he groaned. 'I think I might need to get away for a while.'

She laid the magazine on her lap. 'Fair enough. Now you mention it, I could do with a break myself. A change of scenery might not be a bad thing. When were you thinking of going?'

He glanced at his watch. 'That depends.'

'On what?'

He stood up. 'How long it takes to pack our suitcases.'

*　　*　　*

As the press corps took their seats, cameras were focused on the solitary lectern and microphones dutifully checked.

'Ladies and gentlemen... the President of the United States.'

A smattering of applause greeted his entrance.

'Thank you,' he said, taking his place behind the lectern and waving down the few who had bothered to stand. He surveyed the rest of the room for friendly faces and wished he could find one. 'Well... good afternoon everyone and thanks for attending this hastily scheduled briefing.' He placed his hands on either side of the lectern for support. 'As some of you may be aware, I've called it in order to dispel an egregious rumour that's been gaining traction over the last forty-eight hours and threatening the integrity of this government. It concerns the fate of a recent British visitor to these shores... someone who has already been making sensational headlines... Xanthia.'

Her name brought a buzz to the room.

'Now... despite there being a plethora of far worthier stories for you to concentrate on at this difficult time... it seems you guys have chosen to focus on one consisting of nothing more than untruths and supposition. It's *that* story I'm here to address this afternoon.'

The room instantly sat up.

'Speculation about Xanthia's fate... and the inference she's come to harm... has been fuelled by a campaign set up by a close friend of hers... a gentleman I believe you all know as *Stump*. By using a popular earworm of his to get people's attention, he's stoked their imaginations and given his campaign a momentum beyond its merit. Now, don't get me wrong... I admire and applaud *anyone* who shows such loyalty to those they love. But I've invited him here today so that he can confirm for himself she's not only alive and well, but being treated in accordance with the law while in detention. A detention, I should point out, that's necessary so that an investigation into her actions and intentions, while in our country, can be properly carried out.' He looked to a small group of people standing at the side of the room. 'So... Stump... if you'd care to join me, please.'

The request produced an even greater buzz of excitement.

Stump stepped forward and acknowledged the interest in him with a defiant victory sign.

The president extended his arm warmly. 'Firstly... welcome to our country. I'm pleased you were able to find time to accept my invitation.'

'I wouldn't have missed this for the world,' returned Stump, wondering whether protocol required he stop chewing his gum. Deciding it probably did, he removed it and stuck it on the side of the president's lectern. 'And I appreciate your intervention to make it possible. I'm not sure if a presidential pardon gives me the freedom to do what I like from now on in your country... but if it does, I'll try my best not to abuse it.'

'It's for *past* misdemeanours,' the president clarified with a polite smile.

'Not that I'd be alone in any mischief making,' Stump grinned. 'That ride from the airport was pretty interesting! Things have certainly changed since I was last here. I reckon it's just as well you lot are allowed to carry guns!'

The president found these last comments less amusing. 'The mischief you're referring to is the reason those individuals you're campaigning for are currently being incarcerated,' he said firmly. 'What's more... I think you'll find we're not alone in suffering from a populace that has temporarily abandoned its sense of community and allowed itself to be led down a path of self-destruction by those who would do us harm.' He flashed a quick look at his Chief of Staff, who returned a private thumbs-up.

'You're not wrong there,' Stump nodded earnestly. 'It's why I find it so strange you've chosen to incarcerate the one person who's done nothing other than preach peace, love and understanding in order to try and turn it all around.'

Those in the press seats exchanged barely concealed smirks. Briefings weren't usually this entertaining.

The president played with the sides of his lectern. 'That is what she *says* she stands for,' he said carefully. 'We are merely trying to ascertain if it matches her actions... along with those of her two associates.'

'A playwright and a philanthropic art collector,' Stump pointed out.

'Words are powerful things in the wrong hands,' countered the president. 'And images can warp our sense of perspective. One should not judge a man solely by what he's best known for.'

'In my case, you should,' Stump avowed. 'I intend to be as big a pain in the arse as my reputation says I am, until this matter is satisfactorily resolved!'

Suddenly finding himself on the back foot in an unexpected sparring match, the president sought out his Chief of Staff's thumb, only to see it quickly being retracted. 'In that case, I'll immediately address the first of your concerns,' he said over the laughter, cueing up what he assumed would be a knockout sucker punch. 'You've alluded to the fact we may have caused your ex-girlfriend harm. Under any other circumstances, such an absurd accusation would be rightfully ignored. But seeing as you've chosen to hitch your campaign to the current atmosphere of distrust in governments... and successfully ridden its coattails, using a song I assume is earning you a considerable amount of royalties... I've decided to accept your challenge and demonstrate to you and all conspiracy theorists out there that Xanthia is not only alive and healthy, but being treated fairly.' He issued a nod to his Chief of Staff, instructing she be brought into the room as prearranged.

To his bewilderment, his Chief of Staff appeared to be engaged in a fraught conversation with those around him.

He licked his lips and gripped the lectern.

The room waited.

'Well?' said Stump.

When the president finally realised that staring into space wasn't going to cut it, he called out in a less assured tone. 'Gus... do we have a problem?'

The returned look of consternation suggested they most certainly did.

Immediately registered by the rest of the room, a scrum of voices lobbed questions at the lectern.

'What's going on?' Stump demanded. 'Where is she?'

'One minute,' said the president, silencing him with an outstretched palm.

'You've already had it,' Stump retorted, striding purposefully towards the door he'd been expecting Xanthia to be brought through.

The ensuing commotion suggested he wasn't the only one to have made that assumption.

'There's obviously been a slight hiccup, ladies and gentlemen,' the president announced nervously above it.

His security detail swiftly stepped in to prevent his guest from progressing any further... though not in time to stop a boot from lashing out at the door and kicking it open to reveal...

'What the hell just happened!' shouted the president, striding furiously along the corridor, a trailing retinue of staff attempting to keep pace with him. 'Why wasn't she there? We couldn't have looked guiltier if we'd tried! What a complete and utter clusterfuck! The new Secretary of Homeland Security gave me his word that girl would be standing behind that door when I made my announcement! So, where the hell *was* she?'

'We're trying to find out, Mister President,' squirmed one of those in pursuit, frantically fiddling with their phone. 'We were told she'd be here well before the briefing started.'

'So was I,' he barked. 'I put a call in to John at his home last night to make sure. But didn't anyone think to check?'

According to the silence… apparently not.

'I want that man in my office… on his knees, if he has any sense. And he *better* have that girl in tow. See if you can keep the press in that room. Pay them, if you have to. We need to rescue this situation before it gets dangerously out of control!'

He stopped abruptly and tested the air with a finger. 'Wait a minute… what's that?'

Troubled faces scanned one another.

'I think it's singing, sir,' ventured one.

'Catchy tune,' opined a second, giving an appreciative nod.

The president frowned. 'It sounds like it's coming from outside.'

'It is, sir.'

'In that case, that's one helluva crowd to be making *that* amount of noise.'

'They've been assembling in front of the building since early this morning, Mister President.'

'They have? What do they want?'

The aide cocked an ear. 'To *free them*… sir.'

'Oh… for cryin' out lou_' Not bothering to finish his utterance, the president spun and faced the way he'd just come, his expression one of incredulity. 'Am I going mad… or is it *also* coming from the briefing room?'

Another of his aide's winced awkwardly. 'It appears so, sir.'

Scattering his entourage like a ten-pin bowling ball, the president stomped back towards the room in question.

The sight that greeted him when he stormed through its doors caused his jaw to drop. Pinned to the wall… loudly humming his iconic two-note melody through a struggling hand placed over his mouth… Stump was doing his best to carry on conducting an enthusiastic press pack with a piece of the broken lectern… the middle finger of his other hand defiantly instructing them to sing louder.

As the president stood in stunned silence, one of his entourage aimlessly put their lips together and attempted to pitch a note.

He turned on them, eyes ablaze. 'Don't you *FUCKING* dare!'

*   *   *

Miss Eris triumphantly inhaled the evening air and smiled. She could just make out the faint smell of burning tyres. The sun was beginning to set and turn the sky a fiery red, a chill wind inducing a feeling of foreboding rather than romance.

From the sprawling grounds of her hilltop mansion, she watched as sporadic plumes of black smoke interrupted the onset of a twinkling panorama below... the distant wailing of sirens confirming they were a sign of people's anger. Like frustrated children breaking their toys, they were hurting and wanting to show their pain. God, the planet, and politics had failed them. The world they'd always known was slipping from their grasp and nothing was certain anymore. Not life... security... possessions or pleasures. *Everything* seemed to have become a target. Even ancient edifices... once revered symbols of defiance against the relentless march of death and decay... were now succumbing to those inevitabilities... albeit with a helping hand from some of those lighting the bonfires. Daily news bulletins reminding people of the fragility and futility of life only confirmed what had been known all along... it was a rigged game. No matter how stoically you endured it, you could never win. The end result would always be the same. Oblivion.

Miss Eris had never doubted it. Ever since a child, she'd questioned why she should forgo actual pleasures now for the promise of a greater one in an unproven place called Heaven. It seemed far too great a risk to take.

It was not dissimilar to an absurd contractual agreement her parents insisted on telling her about at bedtime. Jack swapping his perfectly good cow... for what a complete stranger had promised him were magical beans... was beyond all comprehension. How was *that* supposed to make her sleep? She agreed with the boy's mother... her son was a complete and utter idiot.

Not that mothers always did the right thing themselves. Her *own* had told her she'd screamed like a child possessed when the priest had been allowed to dip his finger in holy water and draw the sign of a cross on her forehead. She'd replied that it was clearly an objection to being entered into a contract in which she'd had no say. In any other circumstances such a thing would be deemed child slavery. She'd vowed that if she *was* going to swear allegiance to an unseen power residing somewhere in the ether, it would be to one that didn't require she squander her future dancing around the sensibilities of others in the hope of the equivalent of a magical beanstalk at the end of it.

From that moment on, she'd never looked back.

A cold gust of wind caused her to shiver.

Preparing to return to the warmth of the house, a movement in the bushes caught her attention.

'Who's there?' she demanded. 'Make yourself known!' Assuming it to be one of the gardeners, she was curious as to why they were working so late.

The branches of a mapleleaf viburnum parted to reveal a stooped body.

'I was just about to,' said the bushes occupant.

'Mister Prometheus?' she started. 'What are *you* doing here? What's the meaning of this?'

'I needed to see you,' he explained, extracting himself from the foliage.

'We have a designated place for that!' she returned angrily. 'This is my home! How *dare* you visit me here? How would you feel if *I* ignored protocol and turned up unannounced at yours?'

Mister Prometheus would've liked that very much... Mrs AKA Mister Prometheus maybe less so. It certainly wasn't the greeting he'd fantasised about. He'd at least expected a small kiss on the cheek.

'We have a problem,' he announced, brushing down his trousers.

'No we don't,' she said tersely. 'You mean… *you* have a problem.'

His eyes pointed towards the house. 'Can we go inside?'

'No. Absolutely not! You're not supposed to be here.'

'I'm freezing.' He rubbed his arms. 'I couldn't risk being seen knocking on your door, so I've been hiding for hours, waiting for a chance to grab your attention.'

'Well… now you've got it, I'll get the maid to bring some coffee to warm you up… and then you can go.'

'I think I could do with something stronger,' he grimaced.

'Yes, you could.' She gave him a look the president had warned him about. 'A *backbone,*' she spat.

He looked at her, befuddled.

'You found yourself in a difficult position and bolted like a coward.'

His face folded. 'You've heard, then?'

'I should think the whole world has. It's just witnessed a textbook example of how *not* to prove you're a competent leader who's fully in control.' Her sneer abated. 'Which bodes extremely well for me. People are crying out for someone strong enough to rescue them from this mess. They'll see me as a saviour, not a conqueror, when I eventually seize power.'

'That's precisely why I'm here,' he said, trying not to make his desperation too obvious… despite a confused snail scouting out its options on top of his head. 'You need to make your move as soon as possible. It's my only way out. Having promised I'd deliver Xanthia to the White House, I'm now in an impossible position.'

'You should've been honest and reported what really happened to the girl.'

He looked at her askance. 'Are you *serious?* I could hardly tell the President of the United States I had a handcuffed, female prisoner shot in the head and buried in an unmarked hole in the ground!'

'I meant to me,' she said icily.

79

Mister Prometheus' blood froze. His mind went into overdrive as it attempted to work out if she could *really* know Xanthia's true fate. 'What do you mean?' he stalled.

She stared at him in silence, making him squirm on the hook he'd baited for himself.

'I don't understand this sudden hostility,' he blustered. 'I gave you information about a secret Templar location you said could be the catalyst to seizing power. I'm simply asking you to do so as quickly as possible.'

'Was it a deep hole, John?'

His core temperature plummeted. He assumed she was talking about the one prepared for Xanthia and not any he might've encountered in her garden. 'Deep enough,' he assured her.

'You mean... like the one you're digging for yourself now?'

His breathing slowed to almost non-existent. *How could she possibly know what had occurred in the forest? Was she simply getting pleasure from playing mind games?* 'I thought we had a special connection,' he said, desperate to change the subject. 'An *understanding*.'

'We did. And because of it, I now have an even greater one... thanks to me gaining access to a wisdom that transcends time.'

'You found what you were looking for, then,' he exclaimed, moving towards her enthusiastically.

She put a hand out to stop him. 'I did... but I also lost something in the process.'

His furrowed brow enquired as to what that might be.

'My trust in you,' she answered it. 'We both know Xanthia isn't *really* nourishing the worms, don't we?'

'She's been in touch?' he gasped.

'Assuming you don't mean via a clairvoyant... I'll take that as a *yes*.'

'I can explain,' he grovelled. 'She had help. There was little I could do. I had a gun to my head... literally... and was offered a way out that would suit us all. She promised she'd disappear from public view and never be heard of again... which meant you'd be rid of her... the president none the wiser... and my brains remained where they should be. How was I to know the public would suddenly swap their hostility towards that girl for concern?'

'You flatter yourself if you thought your brains worth keeping,' she hissed.

'I told you... I had no choice. There was a gun being pointed at my head!'

'There still is... metaphorically speaking. You've now become a liability, so of no use to me anymore. Outside of experiencing the delights of my garden, your journey here was a complete waste of time.'

He held up his hands in despair. 'What was I *supposed* to do?'

She stared at him contemptuously. 'Not the one thing you did... *panic*. When you were asked to produce that girl, you should've thought of an excuse. You could've said you'd discovered she *had* been mistreated while in detention and needed time to recover before being paraded in front of the press. You could've blamed a subordinate and then concocted a convenient escape for her. But as I told you... that's *your* problem now.' As the sound of a nearby siren caught her ear, a thought suddenly crossed her mind. 'I trust you haven't forgotten your tradecraft and allowed yourself to be followed here?' She looked about the grounds anxiously.

'I've been hiding in a bush for the last three hours! How much *tradecraft* were you expecting me to employ? Besides... I doubt I would've made it this far if they'd already unleashed the dogs.'

'It'll only be a question of time,' she shrugged. 'You still have an opportunity to make your escape.' She turned to leave.

'But what about the *other* part of that connection we've made?'

Spinning around, her eyes narrowed. '*What* other part?'

He looked at her longingly. '*Us?*'

Her head tilted. 'I *beg* your pardon?'

'Us,' he repeated with a little more fervour. 'When I gave you the information about Arwan El Kahab, you said we made

77

a great team. I was hoping we might be able to take it a little... *further* than that.'

Her lips gently puckered as they mirrored her incredulity. 'Are you saying what I *think* you're saying?'

His heart pounding with the audacity of his last remark... and an excitement he'd not felt since a teenager... he waited for her to run towards him and throw herself into his arms.

She gave a laugh that had little to do with humour. 'You deluded imbecile! Let's get something straight... I told you we made a great team *before* you gave me the information about Arwan El Kahab precisely in order that you *would*.'

A sickening pain gripped him. He stared at her, dumbfounded, the muscles holding his jaw no longer caring to be useful. 'It was a honey trap,' he blurted.

She gave another one of her laughs... though this one tinged with irony. 'Oh, most *definitely* not. There's nothing *sweet* about me.'

As Mister Prometheus floundered in his foolishness, he thought about Mrs AKA Mister Prometheus and the look she'd given him when he'd told her to enjoy the rest of her life. He thought about his annoying neighbour and the key line now etched into their prized Bugatti... not to mention the fact he'd artistically added his own initials, just in case the smug jerk didn't get the point. He thought about his previously distinguished career and the president who'd placed so much trust in him, he might've gone on to even greater things. And then he stared at the multitude of fires burning in the distance.

'A visual metaphor for your predicament, wouldn't you say?' said Miss Eris, reading his mind.

*   *   *

As the loading bay shutters were hastily reunited with the floor, it marked the end to yet another frantic day of collections. With only one further trip required, there was relief the project would soon be safe from deteriorating conditions outside.

'You might wanna see this,' hollered Brandon, jumping from his cab and waving a newspaper at Xanthia.

'Is that Stump?' she squinted, trying to make out the picture on the front page.

He nodded.

'What's the crazy fool done now?' she laughed, running over and snatching it from him.

'According to that... defending someone's honour.'

Her brow crinkled. 'Whose?'

'Yours.'

'Mine?' She peered closer. 'But he's waving a piece of wood!'

'He's making sure you haven't been forgotten by keeping you in the headlines.'

'That could prove awkward for some,' Chad winked, coming to see what the fuss was about.

She unexpectedly stifled a small sob and looked up at the roof to hide a tear in her eye.

Chad gently removed the paper from her hands, 'That's quite something,' he said, reading the article himself. 'He obviously still cares a great deal for you.'

'I never doubted it,' she struggled, the words catching in her throat. 'I just never realised *how* much.'

'You mean... you were never tempted to take a closer peek like you did with Norman?'

She shook her head. 'I didn't *dare.'*

He placed a hand on her shoulder and gave it a sympathetic squeeze. 'Well... at least now you know.'

'Maybe he's atoning for Lake Como,' she sniffed.

He was about to ask her what she meant when Norman joined them.

'What's happening? Did someone mention my name?' He gave an inquisitive smile. 'Is everything all right?'

'It appears Stump's been riding to your rescue yet again,' Chad answered. 'I reckon he's competing with Donald on that score.' He handed Norman the newspaper. 'He's doing it by using the same two-note melody that was so important on those previous occasions. All I can say is... it must represent one *helluva* vibration.'

'It says here... he's demanding the case against me and Donald be reviewed by independent judges... and that Xanthia be allowed to go home,' read Norman.

Her head still turned, she wiped her eyes. 'It won't do any good, of course.'

'You never know,' he said brightly, oblivious to her emotional state. 'With this amount of goodwill towards us, people might start listening to what it is we have to say!'

She saw no point in openly disagreeing with him. She'd said enough to make sure everyone knew her views on that particular subject. His enthusiasm was part of a new Norman she'd witnessed in recent days. She'd never seen such determination and commitment in him. Exuding a confidence and energy that shocked her, he'd even insisted on using a head torch to work through the night... Chad deeming any greater illumination a flag to the curious. Toiling alone under its limited beam, he'd only permitted himself the odd pocket of sleep when his brain became so gridlocked through concentrating, it needed time to free itself.

Ark Two was already an impressive sight to behold. Standing out in stark contrast to its background of dereliction and decay, the smartly ordered, concentric circles of pristine computers – surreally radiating out from the centremost turbine – almost touched the nearest walls. But despite only requiring one more truckload to finalise its boundaries, the fact a spider's web of wires and sockets criss-crossed only a mere fraction of it showed the extent of the task still ahead.

Something no one had taken into consideration was the state of the building's roof. It was only when Brandon brought it to their attention, did a panicked examination of the local weather forecast ensue... which didn't bode well. If his and Chad's tales of increasing mayhem in the streets weren't incentive enough to work as quickly as possible, the imminent threat of rain most certainly was.

Xanthia had been busy recreating the Turner. She, too, was finding it exhausting... having to concentrate for hours on channelling the exact muscle movements and thought process the great artist had undergone when producing his masterpiece. Despite Norman suggesting it needn't be an *identical* replica... providing the same vibrations were suitably encoded... she saw no point in taking any risks.

Donald had observed her brushstrokes from a safe distance... refusing to get close while she held anything pointy in her hands... mesmerised into a rare state of silence as the canvas slowly revealed the thoughts of a genius.

Frustrated at being unable to take time to witness them himself... and being the person most desperate to... Norman had asked if she'd recreate one of his favourite paintings for him as a reward, when everything was over and he'd saved the Universe.

She'd readily agreed, of course... while reminding everyone within earshot that that was never going to happen.

'So... you still reckon we'll have this thing operational by the weekend?' Chad asked, surveying their progress so far.

Norman returned a thumbs-up. 'If your final collection run goes without a hitch tomorrow... and I can survive another four nights without sleep... I reckon that's achievable.'

'It has to be,' winced Brandon, pointing at the roof. *'Remember?'*

* * *

Alien One looked up at Alien Two and wondered why their noses were touching. He'd been wondering it for quite some time.

Lying on top of Alien One, Alien Two wondered what he was supposed to do next.

Alien One asked if Alien Two had perhaps revamped his comedy routine and was having another go.

Alien Three interjected and said... if he *had*... it was certainly more entertaining than the first time.

73

Alien One made a slight gurgling noise... which Alien Two recognised as laughter.

Alien Two found himself *cringing* at the *irony*. If only he'd done this instead of sky and surface of the planet jokes, he might've gone on to greater things. It certainly wasn't the reaction he'd anticipated. He asked Alien One what was so funny.

Alien One replied he wasn't laughing because the logical thought process had momentarily been subverted... though having Alien Two lying on top of him wasn't *quite* what he'd expected... he was laughing because having another body so close to his was giving him a warm feeling which made him happy.

Being the *last* thing he'd intended, Alien Two wrapped his hands around Alien One so as to increase the pressure.

Alien One gurgled even louder.

Alien Two squeezed as hard as he could.

To his consternation, Alien One reciprocated.

Alien Three confessed he was starting to feel a little uncomfortable.

Alien Two said that's what Alien *One* was supposed to be feeling.

Alien Three asked why.

Alien Two said that, having annoyed him so much... and God... he'd vowed to spend the rest of his existence punishing Alien One.

Alien One said that didn't just seem a waste of Alien Two's existence, it seemed a sad waste of his *potential*.

Potential?

Yes... it was an idea he'd come up with that allowed Alien Two to put his *experience* of *disappointment* behind him and look forward to a future that could be firmly grasped with both hands.

Much like he'd done to Alien One?

Not *really*. He'd explain how it worked later.

Alien Three said he liked Alien One's way of thinking... that ideas could improve their life. Alien Two seemed set on doing the opposite... so why punish himself in such a ridiculous way?

Alien Two said Alien Three was missing the point. He was punishing Alien One.

Alien One shrugged as best he could and said he *wasn't*. Had he forgotten about *perspective?*

Alien Two said he was still trying to get his head around *claptrap.*

Alien One said Alien Two should concentrate on developing his creative side... with perhaps the exception of anything that involved comedy. Considering the pleasure his latest idea was inducing, he obviously had a gift for it. He suggested they call it *hugging.* Such was his enthusiasm for the concept, he invited Alien Three to try it for himself,

Alien Two said something had clearly gone wrong. The purpose of his action had been to cause discomfort

Alien One said, in that case, *hugging* perfectly demonstrated his latest theory. One Alien's hug was another Alien's hurting. It just depended on the *perspective* of the person doing the squeezing.

And the person being squeezed, Alien Three pointed out.

Alien One suddenly felt an excruciating pain... though couldn't work out why. Unable to see beyond Alien Two's splayed nose, he asked if *he* knew the reason.

Alien Two said it felt like Alien Three had taken Alien One's advice and was now lying on top of them... but, as he was facing Alien One, he couldn't be sure.

Alien One told Alien Three he'd changed his mind. Could he please get off as it was hurting him.

Alien Three said surely that was a matter of *perspective.*

Via a diminishing wheeze, Alien One said he'd now introduced a caveat to his *perspective* theory. It was fine to have your own... just so long as it didn't directly interfere with anybody else's.

*   *   *

71

'Sit down, John. I think you've got some explaining to do.'

AKA Mister Prometheus followed the line of the president's hand and took the chair in front of the historic Resolute desk as instructed. He wondered if anyone had ever sat in front of it in such a precarious position as his.

The president leant across it ominously. 'To be frank, John... despite your brief call this morning and the promise of a fuller explanation as to why Xanthia wasn't at the press conference yesterday, I'm disappointed you failed to alert my office to the *real* situation in time to save me from an embarrassment that's *vastly* exacerbated my current predicament.'

AKA Mister Prometheus nodded earnestly. 'I totally understand your frustration, sir. I can't tell you how truly sorry I am that operational measures required you to go through what you did. But... given the extremely serious nature of my investigation... it was *essential* there was a wall of total secrecy around it... as is still the case. We simply don't know how far this conspiracy goes.'

The president lowered his voice. 'Are you saying there could be *other* fifth columnists in our ranks?'

'It's certainly something I'm not ruling out at this stage. It's possible it could even be someone you interact with on a regular basis.'

'Thank god it's not you, John!' exclaimed the president, leaning back and shaking his head in disbelief. 'I've never felt more like the walls are closing in on me than I do now.'

'That's why this matter has to be kept between us and these four here, sir. Until I'm certain who can be trusted, it must go no further than this room.'

'I understand. You have my word on that.'

AKA Mister Prometheus breathed an inner sigh of relief. The president's compliance meant his lies could now go unchallenged. 'As mentioned in my call... several suspects were being monitored as you announced Xanthia's appearance. Knowing only an insider could've facilitated her escape... and that they'd be thrown into a state of confusion by the news... I was looking to gauge each individual's reaction and flush out the offender. That required *everyone* being unaware of the truth... including you... no matter the cost to my professional and personal reputation when the deception was exposed.'

The president looked at AKA Mister Prometheus with admiration. 'You're a brave man and true patriot, John. Such a selfless sacrifice won't be forgotten.' His gratitude morphed into a less comfortable expression. 'Unfortunately for you, many of my team are now clamouring for your head. Without me being able to divulge the reason behind your actions, that sentiment is going to persist until you have this matter concluded.'

'I'm fine with that, sir... just as long as I have *your* trust.'

'You have more than that, John. This is the second time in a little over a week that you've excelled yourself and ridden to my rescue. I think overseeing Homeland is *way* below your abilities. I see far greater potential in you. Who knows... maybe even running for *this* esteemed office one day. We need to look at lifting you higher than eighteenth-in-line to it. Secretary of Defence would position you at number six. I need to know good people like you have my back and that of every citizen in this country. It's a conversation for another day, of course... but one we'll definitely be having.'

'I'm extremely honoured you feel that way, sir. I'm just happy to serve this nation in any way I can.'

The president studied the briefing notes his *soon-to-be-promoted-again* Secretary of Homeland Security had provided. 'While mightily relieved your ruse worked, I notice you don't yet have this turncoat in custody.'

'It's merely a matter of time, sir. We just need to ascertain where he is.'

'And you're absolutely certain he's the one responsible for the girl's escape?'

'Without question, sir. Under the misapprehension she'd been recaptured and would be forced to reveal the name of her accomplice, he blew his cover in ways I'd rather not go into, given certain surveillance sensitivities.'

'I understand, John,' said the president, tapping the side of his nose.

'Being given responsibility for her detention and interrogation, it appears he decided to change sides, for reasons yet to be ascertained.'

'He'll get a chance to explain himself when he's finally standing in court for this unforgivable act of treason.' The president shook his head. 'I can tell you this... I wouldn't want to be in *his* shoes. This country still reserves the death penalty for the worst cases of that offence.'

AKA Mister Prometheus didn't intend letting it get that far. Having his scapegoat testify in public was the *last* thing he wanted. The poor unfortunate would opt for *suicide-by-cop* rather than capture... even if they didn't yet know it themselves.

The president continued reading the brief. 'This name I'm seeing here...' He ran his finger under it. 'I assume this is the individual in question.'

'It is, sir... and regrettably someone I personally once put great trust in... a serving CIA agent by the name of Robert Papadopoulos.'

* * *

Chad threw up the shutters of his truck to expose its final cargo and exhaled his relief. 'Well, this is it... we're done.' He wiped a crumpled sleeve across his forehead. 'Jeez... that was the toughest run of 'em all. I know this place is on the outskirts of a deprived neighbourhood, but it feels like I've driven through the suburbs of Hell to get back here. You won't *believe* what's going on outside.'

Norman readied himself for his first armful of boxes. 'Even worse than yesterday?'

'Like you can't imagine. Things are deteriorating by the hour. If law enforcement hasn't given up entirely in some places, it's so stretched as to be almost non-existent. Communities have resorted to setting up armed roadblocks to protect their own areas. Not that the hordes of scavenging cats, dogs and everything else that's gone feral are paying much attention to them. The streets are littered with the result of their territorial disputes. At one point I was forced to swerve to avoid a pack of dogs feasting on the carcass of a horse! People have abandoned their disruptive pets to save their own skins. I reckon it won't be long before they start doing the same with each other. We're encircled by a growing ring of chaos and it's only a matter of time before the more affluent districts go the same way. This *Ark Two* of yours had better work, Norman, or there'll be no point in us getting outta here.'

'Xan said we'd see an exponential curve of self-destruction,' he grimaced.

Chad returned an equally troubled look. 'Then let's hope she's not right about the *other* thing.'

'That what we're doing here is a complete waste of time?'

Chad handed him the first set of boxes. 'Exactly.' He scanned the hall. 'Where is she, by the way?'

'Finishing off the Turner. She reckons she'll have it done by this evening. I've instructed Brandon to carry on with the wiring.'

'How's that going?'

'Progressing nicely, thanks. It's made a massive difference having him here to help me. And now *you're* available, the two of you can work together on that side of things while I start inputting the all-important data. We're nearly there, Chad.' He gave a cheeky wink. 'Just think... in a little under seventy-two hours, I'll know everything about you... including what makes you tick.'

'God forbid,' Chad laughed. 'I'm not sure I do myself!'

'There's one thing I know already... I'll encounter a good soul.'

Chad returned the wink. 'You'll certainly find it's been on one helluva journey recently... and I'm not referring to the time spent in my truck!'

'Ditto,' Norman smiled.

'Talking of penetrating someone else's skin...' Chad momentarily stopped what he was doing. 'Have you ever thought what it would be like to spend a few moments in Donald's?'

Norman gave a small shudder. 'I'll probably give that one a miss. But, now you mention it... it'd be interesting to spend a few moments in Whitebait's!'

'*Very*... seeing as he doesn't have any,' said Chad, handing over another set of boxes. 'So... what have *those* two been up to while the rest of us have been hard at work?'

Norman shook his head. 'As far as I can tell... arguing about this evening's meal. From what I gather, Whitebait's been advising Donald he'd be better off sticking to salads.'

'He may well have a point,' nodded Chad. 'He's not so much cooking the food as cremating it.'

On cue, a loud *clang* emanated from the direction of their makeshift kitchen.

'Sounds like it's getting physical.'

'You know what they say about too many cooks.'

'For crying out loud!' called out Xanthia, making her way towards them. 'Normy... you really must have a word with Donald. He's affecting my concentration. It's getting ridiculous! You'd think he actually had someone in there with him right now.'

Another *clang* cemented her point.

'Not only is he delaying completion of the Turner... if he carries on like this, we're not going to have any saucepans left... and it's difficult enough getting hold of those as it is.'

Norman dropped his head and sighed. 'Okay... leave it to me.' Raising his hands in exasperation, he set off towards the source of the commotion.

'And tell him you're not supposed to fry lettuce!'

Carefully navigating the detritus in the corridor, he followed the sound of Donald's irate voice until he came to the room they'd designated a kitchen. As he entered, he was shocked to see a man holding his head with one hand while keeping the other outstretched towards Donald.

'Who the hell are you?' Norman gasped.

'He's an American,' Donald answered matter-of-factly.

'I *assumed* that much, given where we are,' Norman exclaimed.

'And a thoroughly unpleasant one at that.'

'I got that bit from the fact he's pointing a gun at you.'

'Only because I ran out of saucepans to throw and he seized the initiative.'

'Is that why he's bleeding?'

'No... that was a frying pan.'

'You could've killed me!' the man shouted angrily.

'I did my best,' said Donald.

Waving his firearm, the man signalled for them both to move towards the turbine hall.

'Better do as he says,' advised Norman, carefully retracing his steps. 'I would've come sooner, but I thought you were arguing with Whitebait.'

'*That* coward disappeared as soon as I was reduced to using my spatula,' tutted Donald.

'Brave of you... if a little optimistic,' acknowledged Norman.

'Oh, I'm not frightened of *this* idiot!' Donald scoffed. 'After all... it's not the first time we've had a physical disagreement.'

Norman almost fell over a discarded kerosene can. '*What?*'

'He's moved the threat level up a notch with the gun, though. It *usually* involves us wrestling.'

'You *know* him?'

Before Donald could answer, they found themselves backed into the turbine hall.

Glancing over and seeing their predicament, Brandon immediately jumped up from his wiring task.

'So this is what you've been up to,' shouted their armed visitor, marvelling at the hall full of computers.

Chad shot a startled look from the truck. 'Bob?'

*   *   *

Miss Eris voraciously scanned the pages of notes and diagrams in front of her, her eyes greedily darting to and fro with excitement. 'Is this everything?'

Professor Cottingham made a point of theatrically shielding his gaze from them. 'I believe so.'

'The *Magnum Compendium Secretorum* in all its glory,' she cooed.

'Not... *quite,*' he winced.

Her eyes froze as they locked onto his. 'You have something to tell me?'

He made a weird shape with his mouth, but nothing came out.

She tilted her head ominously. 'I trust you remember me telling you I needed a *complete* translation of everything in the original *Compendium*?' she reminded him coldly.

'Indeed,' he nodded, his face contorted with awkwardness.

'And you're aware that things could get pretty nasty for you if it transpires you're unable to deliver on that request?'

'Y...... u...... p,' he wheezed, glancing anywhere but directly at her.

'In that case... your explanation as to why I don't appear to have what I paid you for better be an extremely good one!' she growled.

'I've come across a bit of a problem,' he began nervously, 'and I don't know how to get around it.'

Her scowl hardened. 'You're the world's leading authority on this period of history. That's why I hired you! Are you telling me its transcription is beyond even *your* capabilities?'

He whimpered quietly to himself. 'While I'm extremely embarrassed to admit so... it seems the final part of the *Compendium* has been written in a language I neither understand nor even...' he struggled with the next word, '*recognise.*' He looked at her uncomfortably. 'And because I've ensured, through hypnosis, that I retain no memory of any work previously undertaken on this project, I'm unable to figure out why.'

She held her stare for longer than he would've liked. 'Then perhaps I might be able to enlighten you, Professor.' She turned to the very last page of notes he'd written and read the final sentence aloud. '*Let they who seek ultimate dominion over all creation know it shall only be granted by the grace of fate.*'

'Did I write that?' he asked, forgetting himself for a moment and trying to steal a glimpse.

'More accurately, you translated it,' she corrected him, shielding the paper from his gaze. 'And this better be your handwriting in front of me,' she glared, 'because if it's that of any other individual, I guarantee your life ends right here in this room.'

'I think we can safely assume it is,' he gulped... adding hastily, '*mine*... I mean!'

She reflected on his panicked assurance then leant back imperiously. 'In that case... what do you think it means?'

His breathing quickened as he wrestled for an immediate answer. 'Well... if we take the word *dominion* as our starting point... understanding that to mean control or the exercise of such... one would think obtaining such a thing would be sufficient enough, given it pertains, in this context, to *all creation*. But the fact the writer deemed it necessary to add the qualifier *ultimate*, suggests the granting of a power... *beyond*...' he stopped and looked at her incredulously, '*...God*,' he muttered in shock.

She nodded in agreement, as if somehow having known that all along.

He stared at her, dumbfounded.

'Now you can appreciate why the final part of the *Compendium* was cloaked in something preventing it from being easily read,' she said. 'It provides the key to a power that could never be gifted to the casual observer.'

'*It shall only be granted by the grace of fate*,' he mumbled.

'Exactly.'

'They employed some kind of cipher,' he said to himself, still in a daze. '*That's* why I was unable to transcribe what I saw.'

'Which puts you in an extremely awkward position, wouldn't you say, Professor?'

Knowing the position she was talking about was as "extremely awkward" as it could possibly get... and that there was nothing left to lose... he grabbed whatever breath he could for courage. 'I believe that makes *two* of us,' he wheezed stoically.

* * *

'Can someone please tell me what's going on?' implored Norman, looking at Donald and Chad.

'This is my ex-partner in crime,' Chad obliged.

'Crime?'

'Well... if you consider some of the things we got up to back then. But, unlike Brandon and myself, he's still actively working for the CIA.'

Norman shot a look of consternation at Xanthia.

'Now you know why I threw the saucepans,' Donald huffed.

'But how did he know we were here?'

'I was given that information by a member of your inner circle,' answered Bob.

Donald stared at Xanthia and rolled his eyes in disgust.

'Who?' demanded Norman.

Brandon dropped the cable he was holding and stepped forward. 'Me.'

* * *

'You're right, Professor.' Miss Eris stared at him without emotion. 'Your inability to give me what I need could indeed prove difficult for us both. But, perversely... so would've your *ability.*'

The professor looked at her nonplussed.

'You see... it's one thing me having you transcribe the bulk of the *Compendium* and trusting you really *had* erased all memory of it from your consciousness. But to take such a risk with its most important part would've been foolish in the extreme. After all… who could resist availing themselves of a power greater than God and turning the tables on those who'd given them that opportunity?'

'I gave you my word I was only interested in proving the *Compendium* was genuine and not a fanciful myth. Knowing I have finally achieved that is reward enough.'

'Indeed you did… and you have. But I needed to be sure you could be trusted one hundred percent.'

'As an academic, I've only ever sought the truth,' he affirmed.

'As have I, Professor… ever since I took issue with others indoctrinating me with their particular versions of it. That's why I'm delighted you passed my test.'

The lines on his forehead knitted together in confusion. 'What on earth do you mean… *test?*'

She smiled. 'Knowing the fate that awaited you, should you not deliver what I demanded, you were prepared to stand by that truth and admit your transcription was incomplete. A less honest individual would've taken advantage of the fact I'd be none the wiser and kept their mouth shut.'

The professor raised an enquiring finger. 'With the greatest of respect… to have tested my integrity in such a way would've meant you knowing in *advance* that the *Magnum Compendium Secretorum* could not be translated in its entirety… which is impossible.'

She savoured his confusion. 'Well… *that* depends on who told me about it in the first place.'

*   *   *

'Bob… I think you can put the gun down now,' advised Chad. 'Unless he's concealing a scouring pad, we can all see Donald's out of ammunition.'

'That man's a lunatic,' Bob snarled, pointing to the blood coming from his head. 'I've said so from day one.'

61

'His actions are understandable,' said Brandon. 'Your presence here is a shock... even to me.'

'I assume the fact you *are* means we've got a serious problem,' Chad frowned.

'Would someone *please* tell me what's going on,' pleaded Norman.

'And me,' seconded Xanthia. 'The last time we had dealings with Mister Papadopoulos, here, it involved a worrying amount of gun pointing and testosterone.'

'Some things never change,' tutted Donald.

'You can all relax. Bob's one of us,' Chad assured them. 'He's on *our* side... which means I guess it's now confession time.' He shifted uncomfortably. 'I'm sorry for all you went through back in the forest, Xanthia... but that whole thing between Bob, Brandon and me was a well-choreographed charade... or at least it was until that idiot preacher turned up and almost threw a spanner in the works.'

'*What?*'

Chad put a hand out to temper her indignation. 'Oh... the order to have you killed was genuine enough... and we knew the man giving it had arranged to be there to ensure it was carried out. Knowing how close Bob and I had always been, it was vital our standoff with each other looked as *real* as possible to him... including your own reactions to it. Seeing as his entire life has involved uncovering deception, we couldn't risk you inadvertently giving him any reason for suspicion.'

She stared at him in disbelief.

He raised his hand further. 'I *know*... and trust me... putting you through such a trauma didn't sit easy with us. But it was *essential* he believed Bob would've obeyed orders and pulled the trigger on you... and *us,* if given the chance.'

'At one point, I really believed you were going to pull yours on me,' whistled Bob. 'There was a moment when I saw the veins in your arm flex and thought you'd forgotten the script.'

'I have to admit... things got a little tense when I feared Xanthia was about to spill the beans on what I *really* thought about you,' Chad admitted. 'I wasn't sure how you'd react.'

Bob gave him the evil eye. 'Yeah... we'll talk about *that* bit later.'

'We knew the boss would intervene... so I hung back ready for when he did,' Brandon explained. 'We just didn't expect *extra* company.'

'You never thought to tell me all this afterwards?' she gasped.

'We couldn't risk compromising Bob's position. Tough as it sounds, there was always the possibility of you being recaptured and interrogated. The less you knew, the better. It's crucial Bob remains on the inside to keep an eye on things. It's highly likely his boss will need stopping again.'

'I guess Xanthia's told you he's in the pay of others,' said Bob.

'Operating under the pseudonym *Prometheus*, apparently,' Chad confirmed.

Bob logged the fact. 'I was keeping him under surveillance so as to gather enough evidence to put a case to his superiors. But that just got *way* harder. Not only am I back on desk duties, following a little disagreement we had in the forest... *he's* been upgraded to Secretary of Homeland Security!'

'You're *kiddin'* me?'

'Wish I was. He now poses an even *greater* threat. But that ain't why I'm here.'

'I figured as much,' Chad nodded. 'As alarming as that news is, I reckon it's gotta be something *way* more serious to risk blowing our cover... and yours.'

'Those Templar contacts that old man at Arwan El Kahab gave you... they've been in touch with me.'

'You've had a wasted journey,' Brandon interrupted him. 'We already know they've been designated a terrorist organisation.'

'I ain't surprised, given the headlines it's made around the world,' said Bob. 'As a crusty old professor, Chad and I met in London, would tell us... it's Friday the thirteenth of October 1307 all over again. Their organisation is in meltdown.' He looked at them all apprehensively. 'But that's the *least* of their problems.'

Chad returned the look.

'That book of theirs you told me about,' Bob continued, 'the one you thought could help us.'

'The *Magnum Compendium Secretorum*.'

'Yeah... well, it's been seized from them by force.'

'By the *government?*'

'From what my sources tell me... by a woman who's trying to *become* it. She's offered the president an ultimatum that involves her gaining a powerful seat at his top table. Further intel suggests she intends using that position to replace his entire cabinet with four of her co-conspirators and relegate him and the vice-president to nothing more than constitutional figureheads.'

Donald let out a piercing shriek. 'AND I SAW A WOMAN SITTING ON A SCARLET BEAST THAT WAS FULL OF BLASPHEMOUS NAMES... AND IT HAD *SEVEN* HEADS AND *TEN* HORNS!'

'More to the point,' said Bob, immune to his outbursts, 'I believe it's the same woman our *Prometheus* met with last night.'

'She wasn't *arrayed in purple and scarlet* by any chance, was she?' Donald whimpered.

The remark finally got Bob's attention. 'As a matter of fact, she *was*.' He recalled the image of her through his binoculars and wondered how Donald could've possibly known.

'AND ON HER FOREHEAD WAS WRITTEN A NAME OF MYSTERY: "BABYLON THE GREAT, MOTHER OF PROSTITUTES AND OF EARTH'S ABOMINATIONS".'

'Actually... it looked more like an angry scowl... albeit from a distance.'

'ERIS!' wailed Donald, sinking to his knees and throwing his hands in the air. 'Now it all makes sense! *Now* I understand!' He slapped his forehead repeatedly. 'How could I have been so foolish?'

Bob was about to utter the phrase *"you need to ask?"* when Donald lunged at Xanthia's legs.

Wrapping his arms tightly around them he looked up at her in anguish. 'I'm so sorry. I was *convinced* it was you.'

'*Now* what's he talking about?' frowned Bob.

Norman shook his head. 'It doesn't matter. What *does* is that this incredibly important book is in someone else's hands. How serious *is* that, Xan?'

'Surely it doesn't make any difference if it wasn't of use to us,' ventured Chad. 'Am I right?'

She remained silent… staring straight ahead, her mouth agape.

'According to you, it would only be calamitous if whoever had it also possessed the *Detromunkos*,' he reminded her.

She suddenly let out a blood-curdling scream.

Bob flinched and covered his ears. 'What the friggin'…'

'Chad used the *D* word,' Brandon explained, covering his.

'But it's true,' maintained Chad. 'So, what's the problem? You said it no longer existed.'

'Because I couldn't see it!' she shrieked, pulling her hair in anguish.

'Then… that's okay… *isn't it?*' suggested Brandon delicately.

She stared at him, her eyes ablaze with fear. 'You don't understand. I couldn't see the password Kevin used on Norman's bank account, either!'

'What?'

'Oh… dear God,' groaned Donald, releasing his grip and sliding down her legs.

'That boy was in the Devil's presence when he used it,' she howled.

'The evil one's vibration is so negative it exists as a form of anti-energy,' Donald addressed the concrete.

'Which puts him beyond the scope of the sphere of knowledge. Everything he's ever done is hidden from me.' She gave a haunting wail and looked at them, her face ashen. 'Including anything he's kept in his possession!'

*   *   *

Miss Eris removed a silver chain from around her neck and dangled the object on the end of it in front of the professor's nose.

'It's a key,' he confirmed through crossed eyes... though more for his benefit than hers, given he assumed she knew that already.

'The key to the cipher,' she nodded.

The professor scratched his head... though more for her benefit than his.

Walking over to a magnificently ornate cabinet, exquisitely inlaid with silver stars and gold crescent moons, she inserted it into its lock and reverently opened its doors.

The professor watched transfixed as she carefully removed a large, carved, marble casket and placed it on the table in front of him.

'That looks *extremely* old,' he offered, eagerly studying the iconography on it.

'It has had many keepers through time,' she replied, caressing one of four winged serpents standing sentinel on the corners of its lid. 'Many will be familiar names to you... though not all its intended owners. Heinrich Himmler... the last of those... secretly kept it for himself at Wewelsburg Castle, though it was *clearly* destined for someone with higher authority.'

The professor resisted the temptation to reach out and touch it himself. 'How did *you* come by it?'

'It was a gift... from an admirer. A *father* figure, if you like. Someone who's been mentoring me since I was a child.'

'And how did *they* acquire it?'

She looked at him as if the answer was obvious. 'It has *always* been theirs. The others were merely custodians.'

'But surely that's impossible,' he scoffed. 'Judging from its considerable age, this friend of yours would have to be *thousands* of years old!'

'It's not the casket itself that is of importance, of course,' she said, ignoring him. 'It's what it *contains* that has enthralled its previous keepers.'

'Then... am I permitted to see inside?' he asked breathlessly.

'I'm told it's essential that you do.'

She slowly lifted its lid.

As the contents of the casket were revealed, the professor gasped in astonishment.

'The Templars called it the *Detromunkos*,' she said. 'It's the final piece of the jigsaw. You will now be able to complete your work. As I'm sure you've already realised... you have before you the *original* parchment, not a later copy or transcription. I cannot stress enough how *extremely* privileged you are to be gazing upon it, Professor. Those who were allowed to do so before earned that honour through levels of infamy that have guaranteed them immortality.'

'I *am* truly grateful,' he wheezed, the significance of what he was looking at beginning to sink in. 'Considering its great antiquity, it's in the most *astonishing* condition! I've never seen anything quite like it!'

'Of course it is. Given its owner... woe betide those who cause it harm.'

'I will take the greatest care... I assure you of that,' he grovelled.

'You most certainly will. What's more... you'll stay here and work every hour there is until you've unlocked the final part of the *Magnum Compendium Secretorum* and revealed its greatest secrets. You have until Sunday morning to do so.'

'But that's less than three days from now!' he exclaimed.

'Then you'd better start straight away. I have a date with destiny and it will not be kept waiting.'

*   *   *

'If you're suggesting the Devil possesses the key to deciphering the most dangerous part of the *Magnum Compendium Secretorum*, we're in unimaginable trouble,' said Chad with alarm. 'It's inconceivable he won't make contact with its new owner.'

Trembling, Donald looked pleadingly at Xanthia. 'This *Eris*... surely you know who she is? Can't you pop yourself inside her skin for a few moments and work out what her next move is likely to be? We might be able to figure out a way to stop her.'

She shook her head despondently. 'The fact I *don't* know who this woman is means she could only have recently adopted that name. Without her *real* one... or some other connection... it'd be like looking for a needle in a haystack. She could be *anybody*.'

'Hardly,' said Bob. 'I know where she lives.'

Chad clicked his fingers. 'Tell her, Bob!'

'Well... let's say I have a fair idea of what her garden looks like and the neighbourhood it's in,' he winced awkwardly.

'*Anything*,' she implored.

He gave as detailed a description as his memory allowed.

'A house on top of the hill, you say?'

'One of a number.'

'Whose owner has a penchant for wearing purple and scarlet, don't forget,' added Donald.

Xanthia's eyes flicked back and forth. 'Sharp facial features?'

'Cuttingly so.'

She suddenly reeled backwards. 'Oh... dear God!'

'You got her?'

She nodded wildly and tried to steady her breathing. She grabbed out for someone's hand.

'I take it she's a badun?' said Brandon, offering his.

'I'm so cold!' she cried. 'This is the darkest heart I've ever encountered!'

'SHE HAS BECOME A DWELLING PLACE FOR DEMONS, A HAUNT FOR EVERY UNCLEAN SPIRIT,' shouted Donald.

'Revelations?' enquired Norman.

'Eighteen,' he groaned.

54

'What's she up to?' Chad pressed her. 'What's in it for this *Eris*? How does she *possibly* hope to benefit from such an apocalyptic future?'

'She doesn't realise what will happen,' Xanthia howled. 'She's been fooled into thinking she'll be in control. She has no idea what she's about to unleash!'

'Classic evil,' wailed Donald, rolling his eyes. 'They never do.'

'How do we stop her?'

'We're fugitives. We're not in a position to.' She grabbed hold of Norman. 'You know what this means, don't you? There's no hope left. Everything we've done here has been a complete waste of time.'

'But you've *always* thought that,' pointed out Brandon.

'No... I've *said* it. That's not the same thing. Norman and I had a secret plan.'

Norman put a finger to his lips to silence her.

'It doesn't matter anymore, Normy. They might as well know. The other side won't care *what* happens here, now.' She pointed at the array of computers. 'This really *has* all been for nothing.'

Chad raised a hand. 'Hang on a second... *what* secret plan?'

Xanthia opened her mouth to speak.

'Don't, Xan!' Norman pleaded.

She stared at him, tears welling in her eyes.

'If you love me, you won't say anything,' he begged.

She held his stare for a brief moment... then turned to Chad. 'You're not the only one who felt it necessary to keep things hidden for a good reason.'

A heavy gust of wind caused a section of the roof to shake violently.

'That's the start of it,' Norman warned her. 'You know they're listening. Why give them an advantage? At least let me have a chance to try what we discussed.'

'*Discussed?*' struggled Chad. 'You might've pulled the wool over *our* eyes with whatever it is you were planning... but how could you keep it hidden from *them?*'

'Donald gave us the idea,' she replied.

'He's in on it, too?' Chad exclaimed.

'Am I?' Donald gasped.

'He helped… by discovering he could spend time away from Whitebait and all those in the spirit world who wanted access to his head.'

'In his turbine,' nodded Brandon, with as close to a smile as the situation allowed.

'Precisely… so we picked one of our own. Every time we needed to discuss something we didn't want them to know about, we'd climb inside and close the hatch. We figured they'd assume we were up to something else.'

'Well I never,' declared Donald.

'Don't say any more, Xan,' implored Norman. 'You might've already given too much away!'

She splayed her arms. 'So where are they…. these legions of worried entities… suddenly alarmed at the prospect of having been fooled into thinking all this is an irrelevance? You'd think they'd be descending on this place in droves right now in sheer panic, wouldn't you?'

'She's right,' said Donald, tapping his head. 'I have to say… it's unusually quiet in here.'

She dropped her arms. 'That's because they know they have an unbeatable hand. Whatever you and I were *really* up to here doesn't matter to them in the slightest.'

'It's only unbeatable if they have a chance to play that hand,' insisted Norman.

'And do we know how this *Eris* intends doing that?' Chad pressed her.

She shrugged. 'I don't. At the time of receiving my gift, she hadn't managed to work it out.'

'Work what out?'

'How to have a spell resonate with enough vibrational energy to cause irreparable damage to the Universe.'

'Spell?' scoffed Bob.

'That was my initial reaction,' said Brandon. 'But believe me… we don't want it to happen.'

52

He acknowledged the warning with a nod of his head. 'Well, if that's the case...' He looked at them all pointedly. 'Given the level of distress my news appears to have caused... let's hope she *still* hasn't figured it out!'

*　　*　　*

Reverend Humbold straightened the lapels of his spotlessly white suit and waited for the secretary to announce him.

'Your ten thirty appointment is here, ma'am.'

'Send him in.'

The reverend wasn't interested in second-hand instructions. 'Good to see you again,' he offered, barging past her.

Miss Eris signalled for him to sit. 'Coffee?'

'With a biscuit, if you have one.'

The secretary nodded and left.

'Unlike my last visit here, I'm pleased to report a more courteous reception from your staff on *this* occasion,' he drawled.

'That's because I've told them how important you are to me,' said Miss Eris.

'I take it that's on account of this high profile job you said you had for me last time we met.'

'As my spokesperson.'

The reverend coughed politely. 'I'd be happier if we used the term *advocate*.'

'As you wish.'

'When do I start?'

'The day after tomorrow.'

He looked at her askance. 'But that's *Sunday*.'

'Yes... meaning you'll reach your biggest audience.'

'But that slot's reserved for God,' he frowned.

'Will he be paying you as much as I will?' she asked casually.

The reverend licked his lips. 'I'm sure we can fit you in somewhere.'

'You'll do better than that. I want the whole of your sermon.'

'But I've already written tomorrow's message,' he objected. 'I've put a heck load of research into it. I'm preaching about the iniquities of commercial phone sex. Not only is it offensive in the eyes of the Lord... you've no way of guaranteeing how attractive the person is on the other end of the line.'

'That can wait. You're going to deliver *my* sermon,' she instructed him. 'It includes a prayer.'

He looked surprised. 'Is it one I know?'

She gave a small snort. 'I most certainly *hope* not!'

'Can I see it?'

'The sermon, yes. The prayer... you'll have to wait. It's still being formulated.'

'Formulated?' he scoffed. 'You make it sound like a mighty fancy procedure.'

'It's *a mighty fancy* prayer,' she mimicked him coldly. She handed him his script.

Studying the first part, his eyebrows rose approvingly. 'I'm pleased to see this ain't gonna be as difficult to incorporate into my service as I thought.'

'And what *did* you think?'

'I believed at best I'd be selling some kinda political message pertaining to your previously expressed desire to dominate this planet.'

'And at worst?'

'*Toothpaste...* or any of those other products you're invested in.'

'You think God would be offended by your congregation having clean teeth?' she laughed.

'Certainly not when they're facing heavenward and requesting of him. I'm sure it would come as a welcome relief. But there's only so much cash in their pockets... and I'd rather they were doing so on my new prayer cushions... bad breath or not.' He read further. 'This person I'm supposed to instruct them to pray for *en masse*... is it you?'

'I don't need their prayers,' she dismissed him haughtily.

'But according to this… you need 'em all to speak *your* one at precisely the same moment in order that…' he peered at the paper a little closer, '*it resonates throughout the Universe.*'

'That last bit's *essential*… do you understand?'

'I understand alright. I'm just wondering *why?* I mean… God ain't exactly deaf.'

'Some might disagree,' she returned acerbically.

'He created ears,' the reverend pointed out. 'I reckon that means he'd make sure he had a pretty fine set of his own.'

'I want him to *feel* it,' she said malevolently.

The reverend shrugged. 'If you say so. I'll have it projected on the screens behind me and the congregation can join in like they do the hymns.'

'They may not find it easy at first,' she warned. 'But it's crucial you insist they persevere.'

'You do my followers a great disservice if you doubt their intelligence, ma'am,' he responded indignantly. 'I'll have you know a large percentage of them can read.'

'They'll be doing so phonetically,' she explained.

He looked at her blankly.

'That's saying the words *exactly* as they see them.'

'Ain't that normal reading?'

'Not necessarily sew.'

The reverend scratched his head. 'However you want it done… if this *fanatically* read prayer ain't for you… who's it for?'

She smiled mischievously. 'You're going to tell them it's for Xanthia.'

His own face looked like it was about to explode. '*WHAT?*' he bellowed.

'Because if you've been anywhere near the news in the past forty-eight hours, you'll know the current zeitgeist is to see her as a victim.'

'That's exactly what she wants!' he exclaimed. 'She's trying to outdo our Lord and Saviour Jesus Christ on that score. That's part of her deception.' He shook his head furiously. 'I know you don't *actually* believe she's dangerous, but there's no point in

49

giving that lascivious charlatan any more publicity than she's already had.'

'She'll be giving it to you,' Miss Eris corrected him, putting a finger on her intercom. 'Carla... get Roland from PR in here *immediately.*'

The request was quickly actioned.

'Roland,' she barked, as a young man entered the room. 'Tell the reverend here what the number one trending phrase on social media is at this precise moment.'

'Free the Friggin' Three,' he replied without hesitation.

'And the highest trending person?'

'Xanthia.'

'Now tell him what we have planned for his sermon the day after tomorrow.'

'Alongside it being shown on an extensive worldwide network of cable, satellite and terrestrial TV channels, it'll be live streamed to every major outlet on the internet. With a publicity budget for prime-time adverts for the next two nights set at over ten times that of your recent debate... and the new wave of interest in her created by her ex-boyfriend and his song... we're expecting a record breaking global audience of over two and half billion people to tune in and hear what you have to say on the matter.'

'Did you get that number, Galveston? Two and half *billion* sets of eyes and ears focused on just *you.* That's roughly a *third* of this entire planet.' Miss Eris paused for that fact to sink in. 'What's more... they're going to see you at your best as you *magnanimously* do the Christian thing and offer her your forgiveness. Then... you'll tap into that universal wave of sympathy she's suddenly gained and have everyone recite that *mighty fancy* prayer we talked about on behalf of that wretch's poor, mistreated soul. You'll tell them you thought it fitting to use one written in a language historians believe was spoken by your all-time, personal hero.'

The reverend's brow creased. 'John Wayne?'

'Jesus. It'll be in ancient Aramaic... hence the phonetics. You'll have that red, rubber ball of yours bounce over each syllable to ensure it's recited in perfect unison.'

He returned a look of unease. 'But what if not everyone joins in?'

She shrugged away the concern. 'With a projected audience of over two and half billion people, I only need a *fraction* of them to do so.'

He looked at her, puzzled. *'Need?'*

'For God to feel its effect,' she hissed, 'Perfect hearing or not.'

* * *

'Norman... wake up.'

'What?'

'It's time.'

He struggled to open his eyes.

'Did you manage to get everything finished?'

A vague recollection of the last thing he'd done wafted across his consciousness. 'Almost,' he mumbled, relaxing them again.

'No... we don't have time for that,' said Chad, shaking him. 'I know you're exhausted... but we need to get this thing operational as soon as possible. Brandon says the weather's closing in. We don't have long. You *have* to get up.'

Norman rolled on his side, happier to turn his back on memories from the last forty-eight hours that were slowly emerging from the fog of sleep.

He particularly wanted to forget the fierce arguments he'd had with Xanthia in the privacy of their turbine. While she'd finally conceded that the chances of incantations being recited with enough force to shatter the boundary between the physical and spiritual realms were incredibly slim... she'd vociferously pointed out that... with the possibility of doing so now in the hands of their enemy... it was only a question of time before they figured out a way.

47

He groaned as Chad grabbed his shoulders and rolled him back.

'Come on!'

'Where's Xanthia?' he yawned.

'Waiting like the rest of us. Donald says he usually has a lie-in on a Sunday, but he's prepared to make an exception in this instance.'

'That's very good of him,' said Norman, raising himself on one arm. 'There's just one final thing I have to do.' Fumbling in his pocket, he pulled out a USB stick. 'I need to load the code for Xanthia's painting into the last computer. I was too tired last night.'

'That antiquated, handheld scanner I picked up for you worked, then?' Chad grinned.

'I'm amazed the old boy kept hold of it,' Norman nodded. 'It's nigh on a museum exhibit.'

'You wouldn't be if you'd seen the state of his garage. I reckon he'd never thrown a thing away in his life. The best bit was the shock on his face when I knocked on his door and offered him a brand new laptop in exchange for it... though more through wondering how I knew he had it in the first place. That gift of Xanthia's truly is remarkable.'

Norman glanced at the roof. 'How long does Brandon reckon we've got?'

'The storm's supposed to be hitting later tonight... which is fine if everything works first time. But, with so much equipment involved, I can't believe we won't encounter the odd glitch or two. We need to get a move on.'

'Everything will work exactly as planned,' said Norman confidently. 'Trust me... when it comes to computers, I don't make mistakes.'

'Should Brandon and I start firing everything up?'

Norman got to his feet and ran a hand through his dishevelled hair. 'Yeah... let's do this!'

*   *   *

46

'Steven,' barked the reverend, waving his briefcase at him. 'I hope you're not expecting *me* to carry this?'

His assistant took it from his hands.

'You're acting kinda vacant this morning, boy. This is most *definitely* not the time for being distracted. You know I've got an exceptionally important day ahead of me.'

'Of course, sir... I've seen the commercials.'

The mention of them lightened the reverend's demeanour. 'Weren't they fantastic? I particularly liked that one where they depicted me in cartoon form with the physique of a superhero.' He patted his stomach. 'Maybe I should start working out a little more.'

'They were all very clever, sir... designed, I guess, to appeal to every possible demographic.'

'Which country are demographs inhabitants of? Are they particularly into that sort of thing?'

'I'm referring to age... sex... class...' Steven looked at the reverend pensively. '*Intellect.*'

'You bet they were,' he beamed. 'There's an awful lotta smart thinking gone into those beauties... not to mention money. They reckon a third of this planet will be tuning in today to watch me as a result. Just imagine... some of those must be on the other side the world where the sun never gets to shine. I doubt they'll even know who God *is*.' He glanced at his watch. 'But they will do by the time I've finished speaking. We should get going.'

'I'll call the car, sir.' Steven started towards the door, then stopped. 'Just one thing, Reverend Humbold... Is it true what you said last night... that you're gonna give Xanthia your forgiveness?'

'It's the Christian thing to do,' he nodded.

Steven's brow suggested a struggle between its youthful collagen and the brain in charge of it. 'But I thought you said she was an acolyte of the Devil.'

'I did... I did,' the reverend confirmed quickly.

'And that she was a wolf in sheep's clothing that had been sent to tempt us.'

'That is *also* true,' he said, though with slightly less patience.

'And that she had evil oozing out of every pore of her body.'

'YES... YES... I SAID THAT AS WELL!' he shouted irascibly.

'Then, with respect, sir...' Steven looked at his employer, nonplussed. 'What's changed?'

The reverend placed his hands on his hips. 'Hell's teeth, Steven! What's got into you this morning? What's with all the questions?'

Steven struggled with his next utterance. 'I know the Lord expects us to forgive... but I'm not sure I *can*. I mean... it's not as if she's repented of her sins.'

The reverend strode towards him and planted his face as close to his assistant's as his masculinity allowed. 'Oh... so you want me to stand there in a few hours' time and tell the watching world I disagree with nearly every single one of 'em... and that the poster girl for its latest indignation against those in authority deserves every single bit of punishment she gets? Perhaps you want me to lambast them as moronic imbeciles for thinking she's the next *Mother Teresa* purely on account of one foul-mouthed song sung by a long-haired hippy who's previously fornicated with her?'

'I simply think you should speak the truth,' said Steven. 'After all... isn't that what Jesus would've done?'

'And look what happened to him!' exclaimed the reverend, throwing up his hands. 'Besides... *he* didn't have to worry about private jet hire fees and rising staff costs. Not only did he travel by donkey, *his* disciples worked for free.'

'Have you actually spoken to God about this, sir?'

The reverend's lips pinched awkwardly. 'As a matter of fact... I *have*.'

'And was he in agreement?'

'Well... I'm not saying he was entirely *happy* about the whole situation... but he eventually came round to my way of thinking.'

'Did he say anything else to you?'

'About what?' the reverend scowled irritably.

His assistant looked at him awkwardly. '*Anything.*'

'What the *HELL'S* wrong with you, boy?'

'I'm just trying to make sense of the thoughts in my head.'

The reverend shook *his* in exasperation. 'Well... may I suggest you do so in your *own* time. Mine is *extremely* precious... not to mention *valuable.*'

Steven nodded. 'I'll get the car.'

* * *

His heart pounding, Norman carefully positioned a small laptop inside the service hatch of the turbine at the centre of his creation.

'Everything done?' shouted Chad over the competing chatter of computers.

Norman stood back. 'Yeah... this is it! We're ready to go!'

'Why in there?'

'The Sphere should form around this final vibration. If anything goes wrong, the hatch can be closed and the remaining computers protected so that we can try again.'

'I guess you oughta move a little closer,' Chad advised Xanthia from their viewing position at the edge of the outer ring. 'You don't wanna miss out on this *phase cancellation* idea of his.'

She returned a thin smile. 'There's no such thing, I'm afraid. He only came up with the idea in order to persuade me to assist him. I agreed to keep the pretence going so as to provide a credible excuse for me helping, despite outwardly insisting it was all a waste of time.'

'That's a shame,' said Brandon, standing beside them. 'I was really hoping that might work for you.'

Chad looked at her warily. 'So... all that *other* stuff you told me about Norman *needing* to do this... and it being the main reason for your involvement... that was all part of the deception, too?'

'Oh, no... that bit's *very* real. You and I had that conversation *before* he lured me into his turbine and explained his true intentions. But even if he hadn't persuaded me to change my mind, I'd still have done everything he asked of me.'

'Stand by your beds!' yelled Norman. 'Spikey's about to be unleashed!'

'That's his metal aardvark friend,' she explained.

'Yeah... he told me,' Chad nodded. 'He said his dream had always been to make the little guy famous for saving the Universe in a computer game... and that now he'd get to do it for real, having failed the first time.'

'Well... let's hope history doesn't repeat itself.'

As she spoke, Donald let out a huge yelp from the other side of the hall.

'You okay, buddy?' shouted Brandon.

'BE SOBER MINDED... BE WATCHFUL,' he wailed. 'YOUR ADVERSARY THE DEVIL PROWLS AROUND LIKE A ROARING LION, SEEKING SOMEONE TO DEVOUR.'

Norman flashed a look over at Xanthia. 'I knew he'd come!'

As the steady drone from the computers momentarily dropped in pitch, the roof above them shook violently, sending a cascade of once-optimistic plant life plummeting to the floor. Simultaneously, a disturbance in the air in front of Norman heralded the appearance of a small, greenish cloud that expanded rapidly... until it became so dense it was in danger of engulfing him.

'Come on, then!' Norman yelled into it. 'Let's get this over with!'

'He's baiting him?' exclaimed Chad.

'Believe me... he'd *love* his old adversary to put in an appearance,' she answered. 'It'll mean what he's doing here matters.'

As the cloud began to churn violently, the stench emanating from it caused Norman to retch. Before he had time to recover, a grotesque, horned figure strutted imperiously from its noxious vapours and casually surveyed its surroundings.

'Chad... are you seeing this too?' cried Bob from across the hall. 'That thing's covered in friggin' scales!'

Chad had already drawn his gun and was trying to steady his hands as he took aim.

'I think you'll find that's not going to be much use,' Xanthia advised him.

'I can't believe what I'm seeing!' he gasped.

'Ironic really... given it's exactly what you think you should.'

'Come again?'

'It's a sensory projection of your expectations, formed from a culturally inspired image ingrained over time in the collective consciousness. Or... in laymen's terms... a complete waste of bullets.'

'You mean... that thing ain't really there?'

'The source of evil that's causing it is.'

'It's the friggin' Devil!' shrieked Bob. 'He's even got a goddam tail!'

Norman already knew all that. He straightened himself up. 'I bet you didn't ever think you'd see *me* again,' he taunted his mephitic visitor.

Ignoring him, the Devil slowly turned his attention to Xanthia, his reptilian eyes studying her intently. 'Who'd have thought they'd pick *you*,' he croaked contemptuously... the deep, discordant frequencies of his voice vibrating the air. 'I had you marked down as one of my own.'

'So did everyone else,' she replied.

He acknowledged her comment with a snort of irony. 'Then... you should hang your head in shame at wanting to preserve the old order. You have a privileged understanding of the mess your current master has made of Its own creation... unlike these naive, misguided disciples of yours who could be forgiven for thinking the way they do.' It turned its attention back to their ringleader. 'And you... you tiresome runt... believing you could reverse the tide of everything I... Lucifer, Lord of the Underworld... have patiently worked for over countless millennia. I have stood at the ear of every individual who's ever drawn breath and whispered my advice as history's

41

pendulum has swung… influencing every *tick* and *tock* of its inexorable journey. I have counselled men and women with minds so great they dwarf yours like the planets dwarf the dust from which they're made.' He drew back his shoulders and raised his head in anger. 'SO… WHO IN THE NAME OF MY ABODE DO YOU THINK YOU ARE?' The question was delivered with such force, Brandon feared it would bring entire sections of the roof crashing down.

Braving the venomous blast, Norman stepped forward defiantly. 'Haven't you worked that out yet?' he said through heavily gritted teeth. 'I'd have thought that was obvious. Don't you recognise me?' He opened his arms and grinned. 'I'm *you*.'

The Devil seemed momentarily unsettled by the answer.

Unsurprisingly… it didn't sit well with the others in the hall, either.

*   *   *

And dark is his path on the wings of the storm.

Reverend Humbold prepared for his entrance as a troupe of adolescent girls dressed in leotards put the finishing touches to an energetic, tassel-laden performance.

'Are you sure everything's in place, Steven?' he asked, running a handkerchief across his glistening brow. 'You know I can't afford there to be any mistakes today… especially with that prayer I want everyone to join in with. I take it our AV boys have everything they need?'

'It's all in hand, sir. They'll play the media file I've given them on the screens behind you as soon as you make your announcement. It'll also be incorporated directly into the live feed and seen by the millions watching at home.'

'Make that *billions,* son. But I reckon folk ain't gonna find it easy reading those strange homophobics… or whatever they're called… so you'd better have that red ball above 'em bouncing higher than both of mine do when lowering myself into a hot bath.'

'They'll see it all clearly, sir.'

40

'And tell our sales team to expect a flood of donations once I'm done speaking. That phone room's gonna sound like tinnitus at a bell ringers' convention.'

'Stand by, Reverend. The opening hymn medley's about to finish,' interrupted the stage manager. 'As soon as we've cleared up any dropped tambourines, you're on.'

A last minute adjustment was made to his hair.

The Lord God made them all.

The reverend took a deep breath. 'I'm about to go down in evangelical history, young man. What you're witnessing is the culmination of a lifetime's hard work.'

'For whatsoever a man soweth, that shall he also reap,' Steven nodded.

'Apposite scripture, boy. The Lord has indeed seen fit to reward me... even *before* I get to heaven.'

'The stage is yours, Reverend Humbold,' announced the stage manager. 'We have clearance.'

* * *

'What foolishness spews from that mouth of yours *this* time?' the Devil roared.

Xanthia was fairly curious herself.

'I think the lack of sleep's finally got to him,' Chad whispered sideways.

Norman drew as close to his opponent's face as his gag reflex allowed. 'I once learnt a very important lesson. You know because you were there in the room with me at the time... although, for a brief while, I found myself *everywhere* at the same time. You tricked me into demanding I be allowed to comprehend the workings of Heaven... remember?'

'Just another whisper in another ear,' the Devil shrugged.

'Well... that *whisper* allowed me to appreciate some fundamental truths. I got to see that everything is connected to everything else... and cause and effect are partners in a meaningful dance beyond the constraints of time and space, which are merely constructs of a limited imagination. In other words… there's no such thing as *separateness*. Everything that exists, exists because of everything.'

'Spare me the metaphysical lesson,' hissed the Devil.

'Logically… that makes me a manifestation of *you*.' Norman stepped back so his adversary could get a proper look at him. 'Think about it… you have in front of you the result of every fork you've ever taken… every act of evil you've influenced… every one of those *ticks* and *tocks* of which you so proudly boast. If just *one* had missed its beat, history would read differently and the interconnected paths laid out for my ancestors would've been altered. I'll spare you the details… but mathematics alone guarantees I wouldn't be standing here.' He stared the Devil in the eye. 'So… congratulations, you twisted piece of shit… you've successfully created your own downfall!'

The Devil glared at him in silence.

'I believe he's just summed up the interconnectivity of souls and the causative nature of being,' marvelled Xanthia. 'Though, it could've done without the expletive at the end.'

'And probably a tad long for a fridge magnet,' added Chad.

As Norman considered treating himself to a self-congratulatory grin, the Devil threw back his head and emitted a thunderous roar of laughter.

'The boy still thinks he can win,' he howled derisively. 'Maybe he's right… Maybe he *is* a chip off the old block.'

Norman stood his ground. 'You're here, aren't you? I figure that means you're desperate to stop me.'

'You irksome cretin,' the Devil jeered. 'You obviously didn't learn *enough* in that room that day. Your foolish assumption couldn't be further from the truth. If I'd wanted to put an end to whatever pathetic games you're playing here, I'd have sent an army of sewer rats to gnaw on your precious wires. Why do you think I've allowed your work here to continue unencumbered? Didn't you ever stop to wonder why there wasn't even a single *fly* buzzing around this place to bother you?' The corners of his mouth bent mischievously. 'No… my presence here is for a different purpose. It's purely for *pleasure*.' He said the word as if enjoying it a little too much for Norman's liking. 'I'm here to feast on your torment and savour that delicious pain when you realise everything you've placed your faith in has let you down.' He drew in so close his horns almost touched Norman's forehead. 'And to tell you face to face that I will ensure your suffering under the new order will be beyond that of *all* other souls combined. Your contumacy has made this personal.' His chest expanded rapidly as his eyes filled with venom. 'HOW *DARE* YOU HAVE RAISED YOUR CHIN AGAINST ME, YOU INSIGNIFICANT NONENTITY! HOW *DARE* YOU HAVE CHALLENGED MY SUPREME AUTHORITY!' The force of his anger caused the ground to shake. 'I'M HERE TO TASTE *REVENGE*... TO PARTAKE OF A WINE I'VE PATIENTLY WATCHED AGEING IN THE BARREL AND LONGED TO POUR. NOW IT'S TIME TO DRINK MY FILL.'

'AND THEY WILL BE TORMENTED DAY AND NIGHT... FOREVER AND EVER,' came a competing outburst from across the hall.

'Shut up, Donald!' shouted Norman.

'It's from Revelations,' he explained.

'There's a surprise! What *shouldn't* be, is that it's not exactly what I wanted to hear right now!'

'I don't know why,' Donald persevered. 'I was trying to offer some encouragement. It refers to that crowing abomination in front of you and his cohorts being thrown into a lake of fire and sulphur after they lose the fight.'

'Under the old order, maybe,' spat the Devil. 'But in a few minutes from now, the rules underpinning creation will be turned on their head. Those prophecies will become meaningless. The force about to be unleashed is unstoppable. *Nothing* you do here will matter.' He stabbed a talon at Xanthia. '*She* knows that. She always *has*. She's felt the destructive potential of the *Detromunkos* and understands its power. It's only her misguided faith in you that's blinded her to the inevitable. Unlike those deluded dreams with which you clouded her thinking... the two of you *don't* get to live happily ever after.'

'Whitebait says... for what it's worth... he thinks he may be right,' called out Donald.

The Devil rolled his neck. 'The barrier that's selfishly kept the pleasures of this physical plane an exclusive preserve of the living is about to be ripped apart. Every soul that's embraced my doctrine and yearned to express its individuality again will be able to do so for *eternity*.'

'You're bluffing!' Norman challenged him. 'That would be *extremely* difficult to achieve... even *with* the advantage of the *Detromunkos*.'

'Oh... *phenomenally* so,' the Devil nodded heavily. 'You're right... we're talking about the very fabric that separates dimensions.' A glint appeared in his eye. 'But I note you didn't say *impossible*.' He switched his attention to Donald. 'Still wondering what the majority of those purple strings represented, old man?'

Donald stuffed a knuckle in his mouth.

'Every ceiling dripping with clues and you *still* couldn't work it out,' the Devil mocked. 'Warnings of what I was up to hanging before your very eyes and you failed to read the room... literally.'

'We know about the *red* strings,' said Norman defiantly. 'Eris. We know she's doing your bidding.'

'The final piece of the jigsaw,' the Devil gloated. 'But I'm talking about the purple ones you chose to damn Xanthia with.'

'The coordinates!' cried Donald.

'Of *course* they meant nothing to her,' the Devil grinned. 'Their importance had yet to unfold.'

'Then, what *were* they?' Norman demanded.

The Devil's grin widened. '*Perforations*.'

Donald's eyes shot upwards. 'YES... YOU *DID* HEAR CORRECTLY. LIKE YOU GET IN TEABAGS. I ASSUME HE'S REFERRING TO SEEPAGE.'

'Not quite,' the Devil sneered. 'Though... as the world is witnessing... that precious barrier is now leaking like a sieve! I'm talking about perforations that, when lined up strategically, make it easier to separate something that needs to be removed.'

'OKAY… FORGET ABOUT TEABAGS,' shouted Donald. 'THINK STAMPS.'

'Better still… think each set of coordinates representing the point at which a story I'd patiently invested time in would reach its explosive denouement,' the Devil smirked. 'A moment where my whispering finally became a scream and darkness triumphed over light. Those you were warned about were just a few of *countless* that have punched points of weakness in that barrier you believe to be so resilient. There's just one final perforation to be inflicted… and then all that's required is to give it all a good shake.'

Xanthia moved towards him. 'Then, why did I feel such pain when viewing the grave of Alice Mumpstead and not the others? She *couldn't* be a part of those stories… she'd already been dead for a year.'

'Ah… dear Alice,' the Devil smiled. 'Hers were the most important coordinates of all. Not a perforation, though… but a warning to you of an imminent *exhumation*. And the answer as to *why* lies in the very fact you couldn't see what was to be exhumed. And you know what *that* means.'

She stared at him in disbelief.

'Well… I had to hide the *Detromunkos* somewhere safe until it was needed,' he sneered. 'They were going to build a shopping centre over its previous resting place. Thankfully, her husband proved most accommodating. That's the wonderful thing about my devoted followers… they come in all shapes and sizes. If his local bowl's team knew what he gets up to in his spare time, they'd never have made him captain. It was all done under cover of darkness, of course. Not that there was much left of poor Alice when what she was keeping safe was finally recovered from the ground.'

'How sick can you get?' gasped Norman. 'Are there no depths to which you won't stoop?'

The Devil looked at him and grinned. 'As you're about to find out for eternity… NO!' He placed a finger in the air. 'And here's another perforation I had *particular* pleasure working on.'

He threw Xanthia a set of coordinates and waited for her reaction.

'It's the hotel lobby where Normy and I had our argument,' she said, surprised.

'The sweetest victory of them all,' he roared. 'The one where... thanks to two simple words that tumbled out of the mouth of the person she loved and trusted the most... a poor girl finally gave up on the fate of mankind. *Sorry, Xan*,' he mimicked, grinning triumphantly. 'And the boy thinks *I'm* the sick one!'

'We've sorted that,' Norman hit back. 'I've made my apologies.'

'Well... as I believe Gabriel once warned you... thoughts produce ripples in the ether that have consequences. You can't reverse those on a lake by simply retrieving the stone you threw in the first place.'

'I forgave him,' said Xanthia, coming to his rescue. 'And it was *me* who was wrong to have such doubts about mankind.'

'There's that misplaced loyalty again,' the Devil bellowed. 'I'm just curious how this scrawny waste of *ticks* and *tocks* in front of me managed to persuade you otherwise, when you know *everything*.'

'Everything about what's happened in the past,' she retaliated. 'But, as he pointed out with that infallible logic of his... that doesn't mean we need to keep repeating the same mistakes. He reminded me the future is a blank canvas... and said an artist who's painted nothing but landscapes all their life can just as easily wake up and choose to paint portraits... or anything else they please. That means the possibilities for what lies ahead are limitless.'

The Devil looked at her incredulously. 'And you *seriously* still believe that matters after everything I've just told you?'

'Actually... no, I don't,' she said quietly. 'But I learned a long time ago not to doubt he can pull off the impossible.'

'Not this time,' the Devil said, calmly shaking his head.

Norman quickly moved towards the service hatch. 'We'll see about that!'

His adversary made no attempt to stop him. 'Be my guest. All but one of my perforations have been actioned. That's *more* than enough for what I need. The only thing now is to give that barrier protecting this world from the next the biggest shock it's ever had.'

* * *

Hands came together in rapturous appreciation as a solitary spotlight focused on a familiar white suit and accompanied it to the podium.

Taking his place at the lectern, Galveston Humbold III waited for the excitement to subside.

'Good people of America... and lands not so blessed,' he started. 'A short while ago I stood on this *very* spot and warned y'all about Satan's diabolical attempt to corrupt our minds by hijacking a misguided deviant called Xanthia.'

Heads were nodded in gratitude.

'As if that wanton girl's past hadn't damned her enough, the evil one infiltrated that poor wretch's body... like many men before him... but in a not so carnal way. Using her like some kinda fancy dress costume, he brazenly strutted amongst us, attempting to lull those of a weak mind into believing his filthy and despicable lies. But, as y'all witnessed for yourselves... despite extreme personal danger, I stood firm in the face of iniquity and confronted that vile puppet master face to face... except it wasn't his... and forced him to vacate her body, leaving his victim dazed and confused.'

Shouts of *'Amen'* rang around the auditorium.

'However, before I could use my powers to heal her broken soul, she was immediately spirited away from my presence... against my will, I should point out... by those in authority.'

The mood instantly changed as a ripple of disapproval swept around the auditorium.

'I know,' he rode it. 'I was as enraged as you. But I was forced to remain silent through a combination of threats to my well-being... a sense of patriotism... and the expectation my lawyer

33

would end up submitting a hefty legal bill if I ignored his advice to keep my mouth shut.'

He leant forward on the lectern.

'But now her whereabouts is the subject of public debate, I wish to add my voice to those expressing their concern.'

Rocking back, he raised both hands, as if to fend off an imaginary wave of outrage.

'You're right… you're thinking how can a man who's had to battle so hard to defend his much-deserved title, *Saviour of Mankind*, be that charitable to the very individual who tried to steal if from him? Well… the answer lies in my exceptional humility.'

He piously lowered his hands.

'Despite my global-wide fame, I remain a servant of God… duty bound to walk my way to the very special place in Heaven he's reserved for me in a virtuous and magnanimous manner.' A side thought momentarily distracted him. 'In fact… such is that virtue, I'm told I've earned a reputation in my neighbourhood for collecting young girls from the street… those who've fallen on hard times… and offering them a temporary seat at my dinner table and a bed for the night.'

He wiped his brow.

'Naysayers often question why I don't do the same for young boys… but it's obvious they eat more, are prone to stealing your things, and don't clean the bath properly after using it. But I digress… I'm here today to ask y'all to pray with me for that poor girl's soul… wherever it may have ended up. And don't be thinking it's a request too far. If Galveston Humbold the Third can forgive her, so can you lesser folk.'

Vocal pledges of support peppered the auditorium.

'We're gonna pray to Jesus and ask him to forgive her transgressions… even the full-colour ones with staples down the middle. And to guarantee he hears us correctly… cos I reckon he's gonna be a tad surprised, given some of those I've looked at… we're gonna do it in an ancient language I'm informed he spoke when he was at home. While we know from the bible that English was his preferred method of communication... I'm sure he'll appreciate the gesture.'

He pointed at the giant screens behind him.

'In a minute, you'll see the words up there, written in a way that makes it simple to read... even for the academically challenged among you. All you have to do is say what you see. Don't worry. As long as you're making the effort, I'm sure he'll get the picture.'

The congregation readied itself for the task ahead.

'And I want the millions of you watching around the world to join in, too. Remember... God gave us voices for a reason. So... let's make sure the *whole* of Heaven hears us!'

*　　*　　*

Luca squeezed his fiancée's hand excitedly, encouraging her to follow him. 'Come on... you're being silly. It'll be such a romantic thing to do!'

'I don't want to,' she shrugged awkwardly, leaning back against his gentle pull.

Her resistance surprised him... and hurt a little. 'But I don't understand... we've been planning this for a long time.'

'I know. But now I'm here I'm not so sure.'

He looked around. 'Is it all the people who'll be watching? If it is... we can come back after dark when there's nobody about.'

She gripped his hand tightly. 'No! I definitely don't want that. There'd be no one to help if something went wrong.'

'What could go wrong, Caterina?' he laughed. 'People have been doing this for years. You can *see* how many have expressed their eternal love for one another.'

'That's the problem... I didn't think there would be so many. Besides... there are signs asking you not to do it anymore.'

'That's for the tourists.'

'We *are* tourists.'

'*Foreign* tourists. We live here.

'Not in Venice.'

'Look… we'll only be on the bridge for a few minutes… I promise.' He held up a heart-shaped padlock inscribed with their names. 'We'll choose a spot and quickly attach it. As soon as that's done, we'll make our wish and throw the key into the water. Think about it… there'll forever be a sign of our commitment to each other at the most romantic spot in one of the most beautiful cities in the world. We might even come back one day and show it to our grandchildren.'

'I've read the weight of them is bad for the bridges. They caused an old lamppost to collapse on a famous one in Paris.'

'This isn't Paris. Besides… who's going to know? One more won't make any difference.'

She shrugged her reluctance. 'It *might*. There's got to be a point when it proves too much.'

He smiled. 'If it's the *weight* you're worried about, we'll hang around until there are no fat people crossing the bridge!'

She didn't appreciate his humour. 'But what if it *were* to collapse? You can't swim.'

'Then, I'll just have to be rescued by a gondolier,' he laughed. 'We can tell that to the grandchildren, too.'

'There aren't going to *be* any grandchildren if it falls on top of us. We'll be trapped under falling masonry and drown.'

He let go of her hand. 'Okay… here's what we'll do. I'll go on my own and fix it in place. That way, there'll be less weight on the bridge for you to worry about… and you can stay here and watch me. I'll return with the key and we'll make our wish safely by the side of the water.' He motioned to leave.

'NO! I *really* don't want you to!' she said, anxiously grabbing hold of him and pulling him back.

He smiled reassuringly. 'Trust me… nothing will go wrong. It's an expression of *love*… a *positive* thing. We'll have the angels on our side.'

She shook her head. 'I've just got a very bad feeling. I can't explain it.'

He gently removed her hand and pouted comically. 'So… now you don't love me?'

'Don't say that,' she giggled, playfully slapping his arm. 'You *know* I do... more than *anything* in the world. That's why I couldn't bear it if something happened to you.'

'Nothing's going to happen,' he grinned. 'I'll run there and run back.' He threw the padlock in the air and smartly caught it again. 'I won't be long.'

*   *   *

'Remember, folks... just say what you see.' Galveston Humbold III turned around and lifted his hands towards the giant screens above him. 'Okay... let's hear those voices nice and loud!'

A picture of a discounted prayer cushion bearing his face was replaced by a clock counting down the seconds... a red ball to its left patiently waiting to bounce.

As the countdown reached its conclusion, what followed took everyone by surprise... not least the reverend.

What appeared to be shaky, handheld phone footage of two men standing in a forest clearing turned out... after an unprofessional zoom... to be even shakier, handheld phone footage of the legs of two men standing in a forest clearing... while a *third*... kneeling subserviently on the ground... clung tightly to one set of them.

An awkward murmur swept through the auditorium.

In case no one caught the barely audible words being uttered, Steven had helpfully included subtitles where needed.

The assembled congregation... joined by those watching around the world... did as they'd been instructed.

I'LL PAY YOU... I'LL DO ANYTHING YOU WANT... JUST TELL ME WHAT WOULD PLEASE YOU MOST, a sizeable proportion of the planet's population recited in unison, as the bouncing red ball neatly cued each word.

The reverend shot a panicked look to where, moments earlier, Steven had placed a hand on his back and encouraged his entrance.

The voice of the person doing the filming could be clearly heard telling the assembled group that he was nearing the end of his shift.

Steven was nowhere to be seen.

The reverend looked back in horror at the screen.

As the kneeling individual released his grip and turned towards the camera, there were gasps of incredulity as his face was revealed, his expression one of sudden ecstasy.

OH, DEAR GOD... I'M COMING NOW, they recited.

In case people missed it the first time, Steven had put the footage on a permanent loop.

'STEVEN!' the reverend screamed.

I'LL PAY YOU... I'LL DO ANYTHING YOU WANT... JUST TELL ME WHAT WOULD PLEASE YOU MOST, the audience repeated.

Spinning back to face his congregation, the reverend flapped his arms frantically. 'Trust me... this ain't what it looks like, ladies and gentlemen!'

Unfortunately for him, he was no longer visible to those participating at home.

OH, DEAR GOD... I'M COMING NOW, a good proportion of his two and half billion viewers repeated mantra-like.

They would do so for an additional fifty-seven seconds... until someone in a stunned production gallery finally recovered enough from the shock to put an end to the reverend's tortured cries of anguish.

* * *

'WAIT!' the Devil shouted, as Norman's hand hovered over the laptop in the service hatch.

'I told you he was bluffing,' Norman grinned.

The Devil seemed momentarily distracted... pacing around as if trying to make sense of something.

'Do it now,' yelled Xanthia.

Norman smartly brought his finger down on a single key, triggering an image of Spikey to appear on the screen. '*Now* we'll see who's going to win.'

Never one for standing still, the little, metal aardvark began bouncing up and down in accordance with his creator's instructions.

'You fool,' the Devil bellowed. 'You're wasting your time. Do you honestly think the baying mobs are going to listen to a wimp like you?'

An irregular rhythm of *boings* came from the turbine.

'I've filled people's heads with enough negativity to ensure anything to the contrary will be smothered and suffocated.'

Norman stared intently at the laptop.

'You've *already* lost,' taunted the Devil.

The other computers suddenly increased their chatter.

'Something's happening!' called out Norman excitedly, as the edges of the laptop began to phosphoresce.

A thin halo of blue light materialised above it.

'It's working!' he cried.

'You're too late,' the Devil jeered. 'I've set the world on a path no individual can steer it away from.'

'That's why I'm not even going to bother trying,' Norman laughed.

His opponent's expression changed. '*What?*'

'You're absolutely right. I mean… who would ever listen to a nobody like me?'

The Devil shot looks of disbelief at the four remaining candidates. 'One of *these?*' he gasped. 'You can't be serious?'

Bob stared at Chad in astonishment. '*You?*'

His old partner raised his hands in denial. 'I think he'd have probably asked me first.'

'Same thing applies here,' said Brandon, shaking his head.

All three stared at Donald.

'I *already* have the ear of the world,' he pointed out. 'And a fat lot of good *that's* done us!'

The halo rapidly increased in size.

Norman smiled. 'Not true, Donald. You made it sit up and listen for a while. Your words enable people to look at things in a different light. That's what all great art does.'

'What I put on paper, maybe… but that hasn't stopped me being branded a terrorist. Besides… I don't think I'm the best candidate for the job.'

'What makes you say that?' asked Norman.

'My huge dislike of people in general,' Donald replied.

'You're probably right,' Norman winked.

The inside of the turbine was now glowing brightly.

Donald's eyes suddenly widened. 'SURELY TO GOD HE'S NOT CONSIDERING GIVING IT TO *YOU!*' he gasped, his eyes shooting skywards. 'IF HE THINKS I'M GOING TO ACT AS A CONDUIT FOR WHATEVER WORDS OF WISDOM COME OUT OF *YOUR* IRKSOME MOUTH… AND THAT'LL BE A FIRST… HE'S GOT ANOTHER THING COMING!'

Unexpectedly darting out from the service hatch, small fingers of lightning began anointing the encircling computers, causing a series of shimmering lights to shoot in both directions around each ring.

Chad and Bob gazed in awe at their pulsating source, as incandescent streaks of purple and blue entwined with vibrant yellow and orange ones to produce a mesmerizing display that fuelled memories from the past. But unlike their experiences at Armageddon Terrace and Stonehenge, the heart of the sphere was being constrained by the turbine's thick ironwork.

Though a mere sideshow by comparison, the scintillating rings of computers increased in luminosity.

Recoiling from the myriad of lights, the Devil squealed as he found himself trapped between them.

'Surely you don't intend giving it to *that* odious thing!' Donald exclaimed, as a far more alarming option crossed his mind.

'Perhaps that's the idea,' enthused Bob. 'Maybe Norman intends blasting that friggin' freak into oblivion!'

'He's lured him here!' exclaimed Chad. 'He's set a trap.'

As the dancing lights inside interacted with greater intensity, the outer surface of the turbine sparkled with specks of dancing rust.

'I reckon it could blow any minute,' Brandon warned, stepping back.

Unperturbed, Norman stood his ground as a ball of iridescent light began squeezing its way out of the service hatch towards him. 'Here we go!' he shouted excitedly.

'Stand by! Any second now,' cried Xanthia.

Just as the others were expecting him to be engulfed by the expanding light, the *boings* from the turbine abruptly ceased.

Unseen within the unfolding turmoil, Spikey had frozen mid-jump.

The nascent sphere began to pulsate erratically.

As angry static discharges shot past him in all directions, Norman grabbed hold of the service hatch door.

'CLOSE IT!' Xanthia yelled.

He'd just managed to swing it shut before the troubled ball of light exploded.

Instead of a single, perfect sphere being transferred to one of those in attendance, multiple chunks blasted through the turbine's pipework and violently expelled themselves into the atmosphere via one of the power station's giant chimneys. Without their beating heart to sustain them, the concentric rings of shimmering light flickered awkwardly and dissipated.

'What just happened?' gasped Chad, lifting his hands in despair.

Released from his entrapment, the Devil raised his own and embraced the lifeless hall. 'You lost,' he thundered triumphantly.

*　　*　　*

Norman pulled back the door of the service hatch and examined the remains of the laptop. The machine on which Spikey had bounced with such enthusiastic intent just moments earlier was now a smouldering mass of warped metal and plastic.

'What an ironic way for your little aardvark friend to go,' the Devil gloated. 'Despatched by a careless mistake from the very person who created him. It seems all those years of self-indulgent art watching have blunted your coding abilities, Norman Penkridge.'

Norman slowly turned to face him. 'There's a reason Heaven chose a *little runt* like me to help it,' he said calmly. 'It's not just because I'm obstinate… for which you should also read *resilient* and *determined*.'

Xanthia smiled.

'I also believe having a forensically logical mind played a large part in that decision… though I can't *personally* take credit for that, of course. It's simply down to the order in which my brain cells decided to hold hands.' He looked the Devil straight in the eye. 'I'd say the *main* reason Gabriel chose 66c Armageddon Terrace in which to materialise that fateful day was because he knew its occupant had one *unique* quality that would be essential when it came to stopping you.' He held the Devil's stare. 'When it comes to anything involving computers, he doesn't make mistakes… *EVER*.'

As the last word left Norman's lips, the Devil spotted a playful twitch in them.

'Xanthia,' Norman called out brightly. 'Can you bring me another one of those spare laptops we purchased, please?'

'I assume it doesn't matter which one?' she responded casually.

'Any one you like. They've all been programmed *identically*.'

'What is this?' the Devil snarled, flicking his head between the two of them 'What are you up to?'

'Would you boys mind helping me?' she begged the others sweetly. 'There are an awful lot of them and we might as well bring the entire pile over now to save time. Norman's got an extremely busy day ahead of him.'

The Devil looked about uncomfortably. 'What foolishness are you planning now?'

'You don't have to stay and watch if you don't want to,' Norman advised him. 'I noticed you found the last attempt rather distressing... so I doubt you're going to fare any better with all the others.'

'*Others*,' he hissed. 'What could you *possibly* hope to gain by repeating the same mistake?'

Norman wagged a finger in admonishment. 'There's that word again.'

Xanthia handed him a fresh laptop.

Removing the remains of the old one, he positioned its replacement in the exact same spot. 'Okay... let's do it all again.'

'For what purpose?' demanded the Devil uneasily.

'There's another benefit to being obstinate,' replied Norman, waiting for the laptop to boot. 'You appreciate *just* how difficult it is for anyone to change your mind about something.'

The screen burst into life.

'And... if that's true of me, it's also true of others.'

Opening a file, he carefully positioned the laptop's cursor.

'Which is why Xanthia's mission was always doomed to fail.' He looked at her and winked. 'She was right and I was wrong. It didn't matter *how* she dressed. Because, when she explained just *how* dark some people's thinking can be, I realised it wouldn't even matter what she *said*. To change a mind that's become so detached from those around it that it's no longer capable of empathy, such change can only come from within. Believe me... I know!'

He readied a finger over the *enter* key.

'And *that's* when I knew how you could be beaten.'

Striking the key, he brought Spikey to the screen... who immediately got to work, filling the turbine with *boings*.

'You see... *my* change came from experiencing something I never had before.'

A faint light appeared around the laptop.

He smiled.

'Something I doubt you're capable of.'

A halo quickly followed.

His smile broadened.

23

'Wonder.'

Xanthia giggled with delight.

'That's what all those great artists who encoded the original sphere of knowledge were trying to do... pass on their sense of it to others. From everything I've learnt since meeting Gabriel, I reckon it's the most powerful and positive vibration we can send out into the Universe... to show we appreciate the miracle of everything around us and understand how privileged we are to be able to experience it. To connect with whatever power you believe lies behind it all in such a way that... for a brief moment... we are truly part of it and it a part of us. To know we're as important in the scheme of things as the observer, as that which is being observed. To know we are one. To *feel* that moment when there is no such thing as separateness. To finally connect with our origins.' He looked at the Devil with pity. 'I feel sorry for you that you will *never* get to experience such a magnificent thing.'

The Devil flinched as the inside of the turbine began to glow.

'A few years ago, I inadvertently distracted this world from your negativity, when fragments from my failed sphere inspired artists of all kinds to express that wonder and pass it on. People temporarily stood up and listened. What I'm doing here is making sure they never want to sit back down again.'

A finger of brilliant light shot from the service hatch and struck the nearest ring of computers. Others quickly followed as a now familiar effect took over. The rapidly dispersing illuminations caused the Devil to wail in agony.

'In a few moments, Spikey will come to a sudden stop again and this sphere that's being created will explode. But not before I shut the service hatch door and send its constituent parts into the ether... just like I did the first time. As I think you've realised by now... I'll be doing so until I run out of computers or the storm finally hits. Either way... by the time that happens, I'll have generated enough inspiration to trigger a renaissance in creativity, the likes of which this planet has never seen... and *then* let's see what happens to that all-important negative positive balance!'

The Devil emitted a scream of such excruciating intensity it gave solace to the victims of every perforation he'd ever instigated. And in the dimensions where they now resided, where time is irrelevant, it would be enjoyed for eternity.

'I think that's the last time you'll be heard,' smiled Norman. 'You're voice will now become inaudible.'

'NOW!' shouted Xanthia.

Norman slammed the service hatch door shut and sent a second blast of inspiration hurtling through the turbine's pipework and out of its giant chimney.

As the Devil wailed and slowly evaporated, Norman politely waved him goodbye.

*   *   *

'I think this was a *far* better idea,' Caterina smiled, as the key she and Luca had thrown over their shoulders, after making their vow, slowly sank into the water to join the padlock below. 'Besides… no one can come along and cut it free, so it'll remain here as a symbol of our love for ever and ever.'

Gazing at her adoringly, he squeezed her hand. 'I've only ever wanted to make you happy. And when I heard this beautiful music coming from the balcony as I ran towards the bridge, I realised it would be the ideal place to express our commitment to each other… *together*… as we'd always planned.'

'I think it's Vivaldi,' she said, closing her eyes and listening to the violinist practising above. 'It never ceases to amaze me how someone can write a piece of music so beautiful it touches the heart of all those who hear it.'

'Maybe I'll write a piece like that for you one day,' he proposed.

'You'll have to learn to play first!' she laughed.

He cocked his head as a thought instantly struck him. 'Do you know what… I suddenly feel inspired to do just that.'

'STEVEN! WHERE ARE YOU?' The corridors of his house reverberated with expletive-laden screaming as Reverend Galveston Humbold III stormed his way through them. 'DO YOU HAVE ANY IDEA WHAT YOU'VE JUST DONE TO ME? I'M RUINED!'

Had Steven not already packed his bags and actually been there to answer him, he would've pointed out that any outrage being hurled at his now-former employer was of his own making. Had he preached love, inclusively and compassion during his sermons... instead of hate, intolerance and damnation... a video clip of him seemingly enjoying himself in the company of two other individuals in a beautiful forest, might not have garnered the negative reaction it had in some bigoted quarters. And while he'd loyally turned a blind eye to some of the reverend's more questionable antics and utterances over the duration of his employment, his increasingly troubled and conflicted conscience had deemed it best to let the *public* decide if the video he'd been sent by an irate taxi driver... angry at the stitching on his cheaply made prayer cushion coming apart... was worthy of deeper scrutiny.

'I BARELY MADE IT TO MY FRONT GATE. I'VE HAD EVERY GAWPING JACKASS WITH A CAMERA CHASING AFTER ME. YOU'VE TURNED ME INTO A COMPLETE LAUGHING STOCK IN FRONT OF A *THIRD* OF THIS ENTIRE PLANET... AND I'M PRETTY DARN SURE THE *OTHER* FOUR THIRDS WILL BE JOINING IN THE MOCKERY BEFORE LONG. I'LL NEVER BE ABLE TO SHOW MY FACE IN PUBLIC AGAIN!'

Bursting into his office, he snatched up the phone that had been ringing non-stop.

'NOT NOW, ASSHOLE... FUCK OFF,' he bellowed into its receiver, abruptly ending the call. Furiously stabbing at the keypad, he waited impatiently for his own to be answered.

It didn't take long.

'Marty... thank god! I take it you saw the whole thing?'

His forehead wrinkled.

'What…? Well, I'm *real* sorry to have interrupted your back nine,' he said with forced restraint. 'But I think you'll find what I'm about to tell ya is a little more important than getting a POINTLESS GODDAM BALL INTO A LITTLE PISSY HOLE…

I *AM* CALM!' he yelled.

'What d'ya mean, you already *know* what it's about? You just said you hadn't watched it…

The company's CEO called you on a *Sunday?* What moron calls someone about business on the Lord's Sabbath…?

I *know* I'm calling you on the Sabbath…

Yeah… well, their CEO *might* be upset… but I ain't ecstatically delirious about what's just happened *myself*. Any plans I had for my future are now as pointless as an orphan's Christmas wish list to Santa…

Why should I care about their money? There ain't gonna *be* any shows for his company to sponsor. I'm finished!'

The reverend paused his indignation.

'About *me* paying *them?* What on earth are ya talkin' 'bout, Marty?'

He cocked his head.

'Yeah… of course I remember the clause. It was called *reputational damage by association*, if my memory serves me correctly…

Sure… it meant they could claim against me if anything occurred on the show that caused them further embarrassment.'

He nodded irritably.

'I *know* you warned me it was highly irregular and potentially problematic.'

He listened impatiently.

'Yeah, yeah, yeah… and advised against allowing it in the contract. But I was desperate to keep them and their dollars onboard. It seemed a good way of convincing 'em the whole Xanthia debacle was a one-off and they wouldn't be *reputationally damaged by association* again…

19

OKAY... SO WHO KNEW HISTORY WOULD BE REPEATING ITSELF SO SOON...!

Yeah... I'm aware of how heavily their brand was featured throughout the transmission... That's the point of sponsorship...

Too goddam right it's serious! They're suing a man of God who no longer has an income.'

His eyes widened in horror.

'*How* much?'

He leant against the desk as his knees buckled beneath him.

'You're kiddin' me. You *know* I don't have that kinda money... not without sellin' everything I own and emptying my *entire* bank account...

What d'ya mean... *talking of which...*?

My *accountant...*? What the hell's *he* doing calling you today...?

I *know* he has a different Sabbath. If there's a problem, he should be calling *me*.'

He grimaced.

'Ah... in that case... I may have just called him an asshole and told him to fuck off.'

The reverend listened intently, then shook his head vehemently.

'That's bullshit, Marty! I may like to spend my money as quickly as the Lord sees fit to provide it... but I've always made sure there's more than enough in that account to deal with any unforeseen predicaments. And, from what you've just told me... I'll be needin' every single *cent* of it to rescue me from this one...

No... I *haven't* checked it recently.'

His expression turned to one of incredulity.

'HOW many...?

What in hell's name would I be doin' buyin' *THAT* amount of computers? I ain't goddam NASA! Besides... those things ain't cheap...

No... I haven't taken up painting recently...

Saucepans and an oven?'

The colour slowly drained from his face.

'*TRUCK?*'

He fumbled for his office chair and collapsed into it.

'I *know* how expensive they are, Marty... especially a shiny, brand new, top-of-the-range model like you've just described. Some of those things can cost up to quarter of a million bucks! Sweet Lord Jesus and his eleven disciples... I must've been hacked!'

He removed an already sodden handkerchief from his breast pocket and furiously dabbed it against his brow.

'Could this day *possibly* get any worse?'

He stopped abruptly.

'I *am* sittin' down.'

The handkerchief fell from his hand.

'*TWO* BRAND NEW, TOP-OF-THE-RANGE TRUCKS?'

He made a whimpering noise like a mortally wounded animal and squeezed his eyes shut in anticipation.

'Okay, Marty... just how "eye-wateringly horrendous" an overdraft *are* we talkin'?'

* * *

Given its isolation, it was early evening before enough rats had descended upon the power station to make attempts at beating them off futile. But it didn't matter. The rain had finally come.

Norman turned his face to the broken roof and refreshed himself with its first droplets. 'I'd like to squeeze one more sphere out before this water does its worst,' he said exhaustedly.

Xanthia scanned the mass of electronics anxiously. 'Are you sure?'

'I most certainly am,' he grinned wearily, picking a final laptop up from the few that remained and carefully fixing it in place. Setting Spikey in motion for the last time, he stood back and waited for the magic to happen.

The rain increased.

The others watched nervously as the shimmering display began to dance around the faltering computers.

As he'd done so many times that day, Norman placed his hand on the service hatch door and waited as the very last sphere of vibrations pushed its way out towards him.

'Now,' said Xanthia, giving him her well-honed warning.

Three-quarter-closing the service hatch door, he removed his hand.

'Norman,' she shouted. 'It's not fully shut.'

Staring at the door, he gave a short nod of acknowledgement. 'I believe you're right,' he smiled, his hand staying where it was.

'I don't understand. What are you doing?'

'I guess you'd better all stand back,' he advised. 'This one's going to be *slightly* different.'

'It most definitely *will* be!' she cried. 'You'll be struck by a part of it!'

'I certainly hope so,' he beamed. 'I'm going to live my dream. I'm about to become a great artist! After years of envying the abilities of others, I'll finally be able to express my *own* innermost feelings and no longer be invisible.' Triumphantly lifting his head, he stretched out his arms majestically. 'This one's for *me!*' he said, as the sphere exploded.

* * *

Alien One, Alien Two, and Alien Three stared out over the sterile landscape and at the coal-black sky rising above a numbingly flat horizon.

Alien One said that agreeing to respect each other's *perspective*... so long as it didn't directly interfere with anybody else's... had not only made their lives more pleasant, but considerably more interesting. Being able to express themselves freely in unlimited ways had produced some exciting, new concepts... like his most recent one, *philosophy*.

Alien Two said he found *philosophy* an even greater affront to God than *perspective*... seeing as it intellectualised heresy.

16

Which he was perfectly entitled to think, Alien One and Alien Three acknowledged graciously.

Alien Three said he liked the fact he could now comfortably talk about his own belief... that there might be a planet out there with other aliens on it... without fearing ridicule.

And that they'd all be punished in hideous ways if they displeased God... just like Alien One had done, concurred Alien Two.

Unless those other aliens had a god with a *hugging-not-hurting* mindset, Alien Three pointed out.

Or no gods at all, added Alien One.

Alien Three gurgled a little and said he found Alien One's last comment rather *ironic,* given it was *him* who'd come up with the concept of God in the first place.

Alien One said... if Alien Three took a moment to step out of his own perspective and into a neutral one... he'd recall God was a name he'd chosen to give all those things that caused him wonder. He'd simply allowed himself to become railroaded by Alien Two and Alien Three into thinking it needed to involve a superior being. Having done much staring into space since then, he didn't see why that had to be the case.

Putting a finger in the air, Alien Three asked what *railroaded* meant.

Alien One said it involved being coerced or rushed into a decision... pertaining, as it did, to the tracks of a railroad. But if he preferred a different word, they could call it *indoctrination.*

Putting *his* finger in the air, Alien Two asked him what *the tracks of a railroad* were.

Alien One replied he was yet to work that one out. But with enough staring into space, he was sure he'd eventually come up with the answer. Suffice to say... it was a bad thing.

From *his* perspective, Alien Two pointed out smugly.

No... it was a bad thing.

Alien Three said *perspective* was clearly a *good* thing, because... taking his *other Aliens* theory to its logical conclusion... there could be a planet out there with *hundreds* of aliens on it... not just three.

Thousands, even, Alien One agreed.

Millions maybe, nodded Alien Three.

Billions possibly, suggested Alien Two, getting the hang of the game.

Alien One and Alien Three told him not to be so cretinously ridiculous.

And if there *were* so many... it would only be possible for them to coexist successfully if they respected each other's *perspective* and didn't try to *railroad* people into only believing their own.

Alien One gave what he would later call a *shudder* and asked them to imagine what that planet would be like if they *didn't.*

It would be *hell,* proposed Alien Two.

What?

Alien Two explained *hell* was an idea he'd come up with... following Alien One's advice to be more creative... to explain the punishment awaiting anyone who displeased God. The brilliant thing about it was that its perceived horrors were in direct proportion to the level of *guilt* felt by the displeaser.

The perfect punishment, acknowledged Alien Three... *even* if it didn't exist.

Alien One said he was sad Alien Two still chose to adopt such a negative *perspective.* Surely it was better to have one where everything was positive and pleasant... like *hugging?*

Alien Two said he didn't make the rules.

Alien One said that was precisely the point of *perspective.* He *could.* All he had to do was realise he was his own God. As much as *hell* was a construct in his head, so was everything else... like *disappointment, excitement, guilt* and *fear*... even a vindictive superior being who had nothing better to do with his time than demand revenge.

In that case... said Alien Two, looking at Alien One and Alien Three superciliously... whose idea were *they?*

Alien One said he was pleased Alien Two had finally decided to embrace *philosophy.* While he'd yet to come up with an answer, he was happy just to marvel at the fact he'd been given the ability to ponder the question in the first place. Perhaps the feeling of wonder he got from appreciating *that* would be the closest he would ever get to understanding the power behind what made it all possible. If so, it would do for him.

Alien Three said he liked Alien One's *perspective*.

Alien Two said he'd settle for *understanding* it.

Alien One looked up into the coal-black sky and expressed regret there wasn't a way for him to communicate his incredible sense of wonder more succinctly to Alien Two. Words alone seemed inadequate. Perhaps, one day, he'd devise a way of displaying it in a form that allowed Alien Two to visualise what he was feeling and directly experience it too... or express the thoughts and emotions in his head in such a radically different manner, they would be instantly conveyed to whoever encountered them using a sound that surpassed talking.

Alien Three said... seeing as words were all they currently had... why didn't he do the best he could?

Alien One put his arms around Alien Two and Alien Three and smiled. He said the sense of wonder he got felt like receiving the biggest hug of all. And as long as all Aliens... wherever or however many there might be... got to feel it too, then whatever coal-black sky they found themselves staring into wouldn't seem so coal-black after all.

*   *   *

It's a little known fact that inspiration likes to come at you sideways. It figures if you see it coming, it won't have quite the same impact. That's why it waits until you least expect it before taking advantage of a gap in your thoughts. As it can often be the one between deciding to wash your hair and reaching for the shampoo, one wonders if bald people are heavily disadvantaged.

It's a *better* known fact that... regardless of the state of your hair follicles... its effect is instant.

The shattered fragments of inspiration Norman dispersed into the ether got to work with immediate effect. Whereas the

13

remains of the sphere at Armageddon Terrace had produced only a temporary period of global reflection and wonderment, the sheer volume of those blasted from the turbine's chimney caused a permanent feeling of euphoria to engulf the planet. People stopped mid-fisticuffs to question the point of what they were doing... while those about to set fire to barricades of stacked furniture wondered if their components wouldn't be better put to use being recycled in an original and aesthetically pleasing manner.

The eyes of the world turned from selfishly gazing inwards to enthusiastically exploring outwards in a blink of them, leaving its inhabitants to marvel with a fresh perspective at what they'd been missing.

That *volte-face* in thinking extended to the very top... a fact acknowledged by the President of the United States as he placed the Presidential Medal of Honour around the neck of each of its six recipients. His deepest apology was reserved for Donald... albeit one made in private. But his public admission that they had all been right, when he had been so badly wrong, left the world in no doubt as to the debt of gratitude owed to its new superheroes.

There should have been a seventh recipient, of course. But Stump graciously declined the honour on the grounds it would have made him look respectable... and that would never do.

Ironically, the president's new perspective... resulting in their immediate pardoning... had been triggered by events *prior* to the release of the shattered spheres... though not simply as a knee-jerk reaction to their newfound status as folk heroes, thanks to Stump's campaign. As was quickly brought to his attention... the legs to which Galveston Humbold was clinging, in the now-infamous video, belonged to no less than his current Secretary of Homeland Security. But what was of even greater interest to him was the owner of the *other* set of legs... CIA operative Robert Papadopoulos... the very man he'd been assured was a traitor.

Unable to come up with an explanation that sounded *remotely* plausible, AKA Mister Prometheus realised he'd been hoisted by his own petard and finally stuck his hands in the air. In an attempt to come close to being able to look himself in the mirror again… should he be allowed one in prison… he provided the authorities with as thorough a dossier of what he'd been up to as a man of his profession could compile. Augmented by information later supplied by Xanthia, the gods of Olympus were issued with an ultimatum… either donate the vast stocks they'd hoarded and help the planet get back on its feet… or face the wrath of all those who governed it and the laws over which they prevailed.

Many should've found themselves dining with AKA Mister Prometheus in the prison canteen, of course. But some things never change. Money will always retain its ability to conveniently warp some people's perspective, regardless of the truth. Besides… *someone* would have to supply the planet with all the things it needed. So, better the devil…

As for Miss Eris… her RISE corporation suffered a catastrophic fall following the public outcry at its owner being the ringleader of an attempt to subvert democracy. Narrowly escaping a raid on her home by the authorities… she was last seen boarding a private plane clutching the only thing she'd been able to grab before fleeing… an ornate, marble casket.

With their reputation restored and profuse apologies bestowed upon them, the Templars ensured the *Magnum Compendium Secretorum* and its unauthorised translation were handed over to them, and any mention of their existence expunged from official records. Both are now kept safely hidden in what is probably the *last* place on Earth anyone would think of looking for them… which is precisely the point. If you knew *where,* it would certainly raise a smile. It's rumoured that, should an Antichrist ever appear and attempt to use the translation's darkest secrets to threaten the planet again, it's likely to be an expert in the field of ancient history going by the name of Professor Cottingham… provided he can get his memory back.

Most importantly of all… the supply of saucepans returned to normal.

Well...

...there *was* something *slightly* more important than that.

Stump's campaign ensured Xanthia's words were listened to with fresh and eager ears. Though, such was the universal outpouring of creativity and positivity generated by the shattered spheres, she preferred to encourage people to embrace their newfound sense of wonder and discover the truth for themselves. She said the fact they felt the desire to look for it in the first place meant they were closer to it than they might have thought.

Asked to clarify her controversial comment that there was no such place as Hell, she explained that there was no such place as Heaven, either... just a state of eternal being where one's actions in the physical realm would be self-judged with a naked honesty devoid of any biased perspective for all eternity.

You might want to think about that for a bit.

She also said the following:

'There exists a force greater than imagination. The name you choose to give it, or way you attempt to envisage it, is irrelevant. Present in every particle... and dimensions beyond our comprehension... it does not recognise hierarchy. Therefore, you cannot claim to speak for it, nor assume favoured access to it. There is no part so small, it cannot make a difference... including that part within you. It is love in its purest form... creativity in its physical expression... and everything good in its manifestation. Being omnipotent, it has no boundaries. We are it and it is us. There is no such thing as separateness. If you know and understand that, you will know and understand everything.'

*   *   *

A heavy mist hung above the sodden grass, completely obliterating the landscape.

Worker Two and Worker Three were reminiscing about the old days. It all seemed so long ago... a time when there were so many different gods to choose from you didn't know where to proselytise next. Things were slightly easier now, thanks to the man with antlers on his house though formerly on his head's successor... if you ignored their old colleague's brief and troubled tenure, that is. Their current high priest... the man with an awful lot of pointless greenery on his head... had stripped things back to basics and adopted a more organic approach. Granted, you now had to pay a lot more respect to a tree before chopping it down, but at least everyone knew where the boundaries lay.

Just as Worker Two was recounting stories from a time when he used to have fingers, a figure eerily emerged from the veil of mist.

Worker Two and Worker Three watched with intrigue as it slowly approached.

Worker Three called out and asked the figure if they were lost.

With a voice sounding vaguely familiar, it replied that it had never been more certain of where it was... thanks to leaving where it was in the first place.

Worker Three stood up excitedly... though it took a little longer than it used to.

Worker One?

The figure smiled in acknowledgement.

Worker Two tutted and raised his eyebrows. After all these years, he *still* insisted on talking in bloody riddles!

Greeting him more enthusiastically, Worker Three requested he join them.

Worker One said he could only do so for a moment, as it was essential he made his visit as short as possible.

Worker Two said that was fine by him.

Worker Three said it was wonderful to see him after all these years. He asked if he'd managed to find the great monuments he'd gone in search of and the people who'd built them.

Worker One replied that he had... and that they'd opened his eyes in ways he'd never imagined.

9

Did that mean he now had the answers he'd been looking for... those *ramps* that lay behind everything mysterious?

Worker One said not only had he discovered great truths, he'd persuaded those who held that wisdom to collate it in a form that could be passed on to others for the betterment of mankind. The best bit was... it could be done in a way that didn't require placing a ridiculous antler on your head.

Or an awful lot of pointless greenery?

Of course not. The clue was in the use of the word *pointless.*

In which case... how *was* it done?

Worker One said it had been written down.

It had what?

It had been written down.

Again... *pardon?*

Worker One explained there was a way you could transcribe what was in your head so that it could be left for others to understand, even if they hadn't yet been born.

Worker Two laughed dismissively and stated such a thing was clearly impossible.

Worker One said it wasn't. You simply made a series of marks that corresponded to various different bits of your thoughts, which could then be interpreted by others, no matter how far apart in time or place they were.

Worker Three asked if that meant he could show them how to pass on to their grandchildren's children's grandchildren the reason they'd attempted to build their own monument... just in case they ever wondered?

Attempted?

Worker Two gave Worker Three a surreptitious kick.

Did that mean he could show them how to pass on to their grandchildren's children's grandchildren the reason they'd *toiled so ridiculously hard* to build their own monument?

In theory, yes... if they actually knew the reason themselves.

Worker Three said, as the man with antlers on his house though formerly on his head was now dead, it was a shame he hadn't realised he could have written it down.

Worker Two asked… if everything was so *wonderful* where Worker One had been all these years… why had he bothered to come back?

Worker One said he'd returned in order to carry out an extremely important task.

Worker Three asked him what it was.

Worker One explained there was a part of that knowledge he'd been talking about which needed to be kept separate from the rest. Having acquired the wisdom he had, he'd come to realise the ring of lintels they'd been instructed to build… combined with the location of the henge itself… provided a remarkably powerful barrier against negative vibrations and what they might manifest. He'd therefore decided to bury that knowledge in the centre of the henge, so as to keep it safe from those who might seek to abuse it. The thick mist blanketing the area would ensure his actions went undetected. It was just a shame the clandestine nature of his visit meant he couldn't hang around long enough for it to clear and see the completed ring of lintels in all their glory. Praising Worker Two and Worker Three for persevering with such a difficult construction task, he said they must have been exceptionally proud when it was finally finished.

Worker Three looked at the ground and sheepishly twisted his foot in the dirt.

Worker Two quickly changed the subject. He asked Worker One if they could see what he'd come to bury.

Placing his knapsack on the ground, Worker One carefully removed an ornately carved, marble casket.

Worker Two and Worker Three gazed upon it in awe… especially the four winged creatures guarding its lid.

Worker One said, while building the henge had obviously taken its toll on backs over all those gruelling years… *and* fingers… it was a good thing they'd gone to the extra effort of constructing it out of something as durable as stone. For, so long as the completed ring of lintels remained perfectly intact, the casket and its contents would be forever safe… which was absolutely essential for the future of every living being... not to mention their grandchildren's children's grandchildren.

Worker Three glanced at Worker Two with widening eyes.

Purposely ignoring him, Worker Two said, if that was the case, Worker One shouldn't waste any more time. It was very nice seeing him again... and he hoped he enjoyed the rest of his life... which no doubt included being with his clever friends and writing things down.

Thanking them for their understanding, and bidding Worker Two and Worker Three farewell, Worker One gathered up his belongings and disappeared into the mist.

Worker Three opened his mouth to call out.

'Best not,' said Worker Two, gently grabbing his arm. 'It's not as if he'll ever know... and besides...it sounds like a completely implausible story to me.'

* * *

Shepherd One gazed down on the parched and barren valley below and expressed surprise that, despite hearing what sounded like thunder from the direction of Arwan El Kahab some months ago, they *still* hadn't seen or felt any rain.

Shepherd Two admonished him for his impatience and suggested he should've waited a little longer before making such a rash statement.

Shepherd Three said it had been so long since it had last rained he'd forgotten what it looked like.

Shepherd One and Shepherd Two nodded in agreement.

Shepherd Two suggested it was possible, therefore, it *had* rained and they just hadn't noticed.

Shepherd Three suddenly shot out an arm. 'Tumbleweed!'

Shepherd One shook his head and said he wasn't falling for that again.

'No... it really is!' Shepherd Three insisted.

'It'll be a bush,' said Shepherd One... adding, 'Fool me once, shame on you. Fool me for the *twenty-seventh* time, and I'll seriously consider punching you in the face.'

'No... I think he may be right this time,' said Shepherd Two excitedly. 'It's moving!'

Shepherd One sprang to his feet and gazed at where Shepherd Three was pointing.

It wasn't tumbleweed, of course. Shepherd One immediately recognised that. Tumbleweed didn't use crutches... or limp.

They watched in stunned silence at what they finally agreed was an old man hobbling his way along the road leading from the abandoned temple, an expression of determination etched into his face.

As for the old man... there was no way he wasn't going to reach his destination... not having survived against such overwhelming odds.

The stone plinths had helped.

In order to shield himself from the blast a cruel wink had warned him was about to occur, he'd managed to crawl behind the nearest of them. Taking the brunt of the first falling lintel, the cavity it created afforded him protection from the devastation that ensued.

The road ahead would be long and arduous... but at least he'd finally get to experience the pleasure of greenery again... and a wind that *wasn't* sapped of its power on his face.

*   *   *

'Oh, Normy,' Xanthia beamed, 'Everybody loved it! I've lost count of the number of people who've come up to me and said how brilliant you are. I'm so proud of you.'

He hugged her tightly. 'Do you know... after all these years, I *still* find it weird. I can't get used to the fact people appreciate my work so much.'

'Well, of *course* they do. You make them connect to something beyond the normal. That's what all great artists do.'

'And the girls... are they alright?'

'They've had a fabulous time. They get so excited seeing their daddy being the centre of so much attention.'

5

'I guess it makes a change from it being focused on their mum.' He looked around. 'Where are they now?'

'Being entertained by Uncle Stump. He's reduced all three to helpless fits of giggles by getting Sharky to do his impersonation of a constipated chicken laying an egg. I told him to make sure it was the clean version.'

'Do you think they'll be okay if we stay a little longer? They've kept the bar open for us VIPs and it would be nice to wind down and relax a little before heading back.'

She rubbed the side of his arm affectionately. 'You stay. You deserve it. But I fink I need to get them to bed. You know what they're like the next morning if they stay up too late.'

His eyes narrowed. 'Xan?'

She looked at him awkwardly. 'Have I done it again?'

He nodded.

'Sorry... *think*,' she said, enunciating the word correctly.

'It doesn't bother me,' he smiled, 'but it might raise a few eyebrows if it happened during one of your annual global addresses.'

'Who'd have thought it?' she laughed. 'Phase cancellation... it really *was* a *fing!*'

'Well, at least just enough to be able to enjoy a little bit more of the real you.'

She gave a contented sigh. 'I can't tell you what a difference it's made. And every year that passes, life gets that little bit easier. I can now meet people and *not* know what they've been up to in their recent past... or *thinking*.' She giggled. 'I guess it's a lot less unsettling for them, too!'

'If you're sure it's okay, I *will* stay for that drink. Stump said he wants to have a quick chat about us collaborating on a project... though goodness knows what he's got in mind. Apparently, he's been planning something for a while. If we thought phase cancellation was an unexpected surprise, who'd have thought *that* would ever happen?'

She looked at him knowingly. 'Although you'd never admit it to yourself, you've been sending those wishful vibrations out into the Universe from the day you first met him.'

He grinned and gave her a kiss. 'Tell the girls I'll be out to say goodbye to them in a minute. I just need to pack up my things.'

She gave him a friendly nudge. 'Just don't let Stump lead you astray. You know what he's like.'

Most of the lights in the auditorium had been turned off by the time Norman crossed its floor to get to the bar. Where only a short while earlier it had been filled with rapturous applause, only the sound of cleaning staff cursing a malfunctioning floor buffer now broke the silence... with the exception of one other voice.

'Mister Penkridge?'

Norman stopped and looked away to his side. Someone had managed to avoid the clearing of the hall and was furtively making his way towards him.

'I'm not really supposed to be here,' the interloper confessed. 'But I couldn't resist sneaking a chance to meet with you for a few seconds and tell you how I truly feel.'

'*Okay,*' said Norman cautiously, glancing around and noting a worrying absence of security.

The man offered a friendly grin. 'Oh, don't worry... you've nothing to fear. To the contrary. I just wanted to let you to know I've been an admirer of everything you've done for many years now.'

'That's very kind of you,' said Norman politely. 'And thanks for going to this amount of trouble to say so.'

'No... it's I who should be thanking you,' his admirer replied. 'After all... you've brought so much pleasure to so many people, and I wanted you to know how much it's appreciated. That's quite a gift you've been blessed with, and one I think you've used to perfection... not least tonight.'

'We've *all* been blessed with a gift,' returned Norman with a smile. 'Even if it's just the opportunity to experience those of others. But I'm very pleased you think what I do has such a positive effect.'

3

The man nodded earnestly. 'It most certainly does. People feel inspired when they hear you play... and your music gives them a common bond. You've managed to turn the keys on your piano into a connecting bridge between this world and another... a world where everything is possible. I think I speak on behalf of the entire planet when I say what a great example you've set it... not least because of the bravery and resilience you and your wife demonstrated *before* it got to hear your wonderful music.' To Norman's surprise... and a little embarrassment... the man gave a long and heartfelt bow. 'I am so *very* grateful for all you've done for us.' Straightening up, he looked at Norman and winked. 'There you are... I just wanted you to know all that... and now you do.'

'Wow,' said Norman, taken aback. 'I believe that's one of the nicest compliments anyone's ever paid me.' He placed a hand to his heart. 'I'm extremely touched you feel that way about my work. The funny thing is... I never intended to be a musician. Would you believe I wanted to be a painter?'

'I had heard,' the man nodded.

'But... as I've discovered over the years... the Universe possesses a sense of humour and doesn't always function the way you think it will.'

'That comes as no surprise to me,' said the man. He stared at Norman as if drinking in the moment. 'Well... Norman Penkridge... it was a pleasure making your acquaintance, and I can tell you it's something I'll *definitely* never forget.'

Norman smiled inwardly. Admirers of his work came in many shapes and sizes, but none had ever expressed themselves so sincerely.

As the man turned to leave, Norman thought it would be nice to return the kindness. 'Look... I tell you what... why don't you join me for a drink?'

'That's very kind of you, but I don't,' said the man, heading off towards an unilluminated part of the building.

'A non-alcoholic one, maybe?'

'As I said, I shouldn't really be here at all.'

'That's alright. I'll say you're with me,' Norman called out. 'I'll tell them you're my guest.'

The man raised his hand by way of thanks and a polite refusal.

Fearing the offer of alcohol might have caused offence, Norman considered suggesting he could get the bar staff to make his admirer a coffee.

'Nice try,' came the man's voice surprisingly clearly, as he melted into the shadows. 'But, as you should know by now... I wouldn't be able to hold the cup.'

THE END

THE END

If you've enjoyed reading this book and think others might too, please could you take a few seconds of your time to leave a rating or review online... or even a mention on social media, as all authors need as much help as they can get.

This would be *greatly* appreciated.
Thank you!

Interested in finding out more about what goes on in Andy's head?

For various "things"... including subscribing to his mailing list, so that you can be the first to know what he's up to, visit:

www.andydanenye.com

Pssst…

www.aaandsomething.com